ACKNOWLEDGMENTS

I am grateful to the community of Lebh Shomea for the quiet refuge its members have offered me from time to time. Sister Maria, Sister Marie, and Father Kelly: my thanks. Your commitment and joyful sacrifice allow me a glimpse into the soul of the spiritual life and show me that God is larger than I thought. To Jean Springer, my deepest gratitude. Your gentle guidance and your insights into contemplative life have taken me further along my own path. Thanks, too, for your generous and helpful reading of this book. To Bob Goodfellow, thanks for the comments that helped fill out the basic plot idea, and thanks to Natalee Rosenstein, Berkley Prime Crime editor, for your thoughtful suggestions. And to my husband and fellow author, Bill, thanks and hugs for all you do, always.

"A unique series." —*Seattle Post-Intelligencer*

Nominated for both an Agatha and an Anthony Award, Susan Wittig Albert's novels featuring lawyer-turned-herbalist China Bayles have won acclaim for their rich characterizations and witty, suspenseful stories of crime and passion in small-town Texas.

In search of respite, China takes off to St. Theresa's Monastery with her friend Maggie, a former nun. The goal is a brief, tranquil retreat—but there's a conflict at the convent. The mother superior has recently died, and a battle over the future of St. Theresa's suggests that her sudden demise might not have been accidental. Now, China's quest for a replenished spirit takes second place to a more earthbound pursuit: catching a killer . . .

"Intelligent . . . quiet humor . . . and soul to spare . . . A page-turner." —*Publishers Weekly*

"A well-plotted mystery with strong characters and a wonderfully realized setting." —*Booklist*

"Albert's characters are as real and as quirky as your next-door neighbor."
—*The Raleigh News & Observer*

"Albert artfully [brings] the down-home town of Pecan Springs alive." —*The Dallas Morning News*

Herbalist-sleuth
CHINA BAYLES

is

"in a class with lady sleuths V. I. Warshawski and Stephanie Plum."

—*Publishers Weekly* (starred review)

Laurie Stover

China Bayles Mysteries by Susan Wittig Albert

THYME OF DEATH
WITCHES' BANE
HANGMAN'S ROOT
ROSEMARY REMEMBERED
RUEFUL DEATH
LOVE LIES BLEEDING
CHILE DEATH
LAVENDER LIES

CHINA BAYLES' BOOK OF DAYS

MISTLETOE MAN
BLOODROOT
INDIGO DYING
AN UNTHYMELY DEATH
A DILLY OF A DEATH
DEAD MAN'S BONES
BLEEDING HEARTS
SPANISH DAGGER

With her husband, Bill Albert, writing as Robin Paige

DEATH AT BISHOP'S KEEP
DEATH AT GALLOWS GREEN
DEATH AT DAISY'S FOLLY
DEATH AT DEVIL'S BRIDGE
DEATH AT ROTTINGDEAN
DEATH AT WHITECHAPEL

DEATH AT EPSOM DOWNS
DEATH AT DARTMOOR
DEATH AT GLAMIS CASTLE
DEATH IN HYDE PARK
DEATH AT BLENHEIM PALACE
DEATH ON THE LIZARD

Beatrix Potter Mysteries by Susan Wittig Albert

THE TALE OF HILL TOP FARM
THE TALE OF HOLLY HOW
THE TALE OF CUCKOO BROW WOOD

Nonfiction books by Susan Wittig Albert

WRITING FROM LIFE
WORK OF HER OWN

RUEFUL DEATH

A CHINA BAYLES MYSTERY

Susan Wittig Albert

BERKLEY PRIME CRIME, NEW YORK

THE BERKLEY PUBLISHING GROUP
Published by the Penguin Group
Penguin Group (USA) Inc.
375 Hudson Street, New York, New York 10014, USA
Penguin Group (Canada), 90 Eglinton Avenue East, Suite 700, Toronto, Ontario M4P 2Y3, Canada
(a division of Pearson Penguin Canada Inc.)
Penguin Books Ltd., 80 Strand, London WC2R 0RL, England
Penguin Group Ireland, 25 St. Stephen's Green, Dublin 2, Ireland (a division of Penguin Books Ltd.)
Penguin Group (Australia), 250 Camberwell Road, Camberwell, Victoria 3124, Australia
(a division of Pearson Australia Group Pty. Ltd.)
Penguin Books India Pvt. Ltd., 11 Community Centre, Panchsheel Park, New Delhi—110 017, India
Penguin Group (NZ), Cnr. Airborne and Rosedale Roads, Albany, Auckland 1310, New Zealand
(a division of Pearson New Zealand Ltd.)
Penguin Books (South Africa) (Pty.) Ltd., 24 Sturdee Avenue, Rosebank, Johannesburg 2196,
South Africa

Penguin Books Ltd., Registered Offices: 80 Strand, London WC2R 0RL, England

This is a work of fiction. Names, characters, places, and incidents either are the product of the author's imagination or are used fictitiously, and any resemblance to actual persons, living or dead, business establishments, events, or locales is entirely coincidental. The publisher does not have any control over and does not assume any responsibility for author or third-party websites or their content.

RUEFUL DEATH

A Berkley Prime Crime Book / published by arrangement with the author

PRINTING HISTORY
Berkley Prime Crime hardcover edition / November 1996
Berkley Prime Crime mass-market edition / August 1997

Copyright © 1996 by Susan Wittig Albert.
Excerpt from *Death at Daisy's Folly* copyright © 1997 by Susan Wittig Albert and William J. Albert.

All rights reserved.
No part of this book may be reproduced, scanned, or distributed in any printed or electronic form without permission. Please do not participate in or encourage piracy of copyrighted materials in violation of the author's rights. Purchase only authorized editions.
For information, address: The Berkley Publishing Group,
a division of Penguin Group (USA) Inc.,
375 Hudson Street, New York, New York 10014.

ISBN: 0-425-15941-8

BERKLEY ® PRIME CRIME
PRIME CRIME Books are published by The Berkley Publishing Group,
a division of Penguin Group (USA) Inc.,
375 Hudson Street, New York, New York 10014.
The name BERKLEY PRIME CRIME and the BERKLEY PRIME CRIME design
are trademarks belonging to Penguin Group (USA) Inc.

PRINTED IN THE UNITED STATES OF AMERICA

21 20 19 18 17 16 15 14 13

If you purchased this book without a cover, you should be aware that this book is stolen property. It was reported as "unsold and destroyed" to the publisher, and neither the author nor the publisher has received any payment for this "stripped book."

AUTHOR'S NOTE

The fictional landscape of *Rueful Death* closely resembles that of the Texas Hill Country, and some of its characters eat, drink, and carry on like the people who live there. However, the town and county of Carr are wholly imaginary, St. Theresa's is a monastery of the mind, and the Sisters of the Holy Heart are a fictional creation. Don't let the bits of real life that the author slips in from time to time fool you into thinking that the characters, settings, and events of this book are anything but figments of an insubordinate imagination.

Here in this place
I'll set a bank of rue, sour herb of grace;
Rue, even for ruth, shall shortly here be seen . . .

Shakespeare, *Richard III*

Rueful
Death

CHAPTER ONE

When Satan stepped out of Paradise after the Fall,
it is rumored that garlic sprang up from the spot
where he planted his foot.

Muslim saying

Afterward, when I thought about what happened at St.
Theresa's, I felt embarrassed and a bit rueful. If I'd been a
police officer and drawn those wrong conclusions, my ser-
geant would have bawled me out for my errors in judgment.
If I'd been a private investigator, I might have been fired.
But I'm neither, thank God. I'm just an ordinary person
who was asked to do something a little unusual, and I made
a mistake here and there.

But everybody makes mistakes. And every so often, our
mistakes are criminal. If we get caught, we have to pay the
prescribed penalty—when the system works right, which it
doesn't, most of the time. But even when justice fails,
there's the universe to be reckoned with, or God, or whatever you call it. One way or another, you pay for what you
do. And sometimes, what you think was a mistake, or even
a crime, turns out to be something else altogether.

It's all very mysterious.

But I wasn't thinking about any of that when I was getting ready to leave that first Saturday in January. I was
listening to McQuaid, who didn't want me to go away. Or,
more precisely, he didn't want me to go away without him.

"If what you want is a vacation," he said, "how about
Cozumel? We can rent a condo and a dune buggy, go fish-

ing, scuba diving, dancing. We can take the ferry across to the Yucatan and see the ruins at Tulum." He spoke alluringly, his slate blue eyes warm. "Let's do it, China. It'll be a belated Christmas present for both of us. We don't get to spend enough time together anymore."

My name is China Bayles, and Mike McQuaid is the guy I live with. This discussion was occurring in our bedroom. I was packing for my trip and McQuaid was still trying to talk me out of it.

I stuck a second pair of jeans into my suitcase and counted my rolled-up socks. Seven pairs, all I could find. I would be gone fourteen days, which meant that I'd have to wear dirty socks or do some laundry. I dropped to my knees and fished a pair of sneakers out from under the bed. The toes were scuffed and the laces frayed, but where I was headed, poverty was a virtue. I stuck the shoes in the suitcase, moved Khat (my seventeen-pound Siamese) to the pillow, and sat down on the bed next to McQuaid.

"Look," I said wearily. "I don't want to go fishing or diving or bounce around in a dune buggy. I want to *rest*." I didn't want to tell him the whole reason I was going away without him. I settled for half. "Christmas was a killer."

"You mean you've finally OD'd on Christmas?" McQuaid was gently teasing. "I thought you loved the holidays—all those herbal wreaths and candles and stuff. You certainly looked like you loved it, and you had lots of business. Thyme and Seasons is a great success."

"I'm *supposed* to look like I love it," I said, scratching Khat's back. "If I looked like Scrooge, my customers would go someplace else." Thyme and Seasons is my herb shop. Lately, I've been spending most of my waking hours there. Maybe that's the trouble. I sighed. "To be honest, a person can only stand to make so many bushels of potpourri in one lifetime. I'm beginning to wonder if I'm cut out to be a successful herb shop owner."

McQuaid was startled. "Seriously?"

"Seriously."

He narrowed his eyes. "How seriously?"

"Enough to think twice about Wanda Rathbottom's offer to buy me out."

"I thought you didn't like Wanda."

"I don't. But I might be persuaded to like her money—if there's enough of it." Wanda owns the nursery outside of town. She's coveted Thyme and Seasons from the day I opened. Tired as I was right now, I'd almost have given it to her.

Six years ago, I left my busy Houston criminal-law practice and moved to Pecan Springs, Texas. I wanted to have more time for myself, for friends, for doing things I enjoyed. Until the past six months, I'd been pretty successful in balancing my work and my life. But lately, I'd been at the shop from eight in the morning to six or seven in the evening. After business hours and on weekends, there was the newsletter and the bookkeeping and the ordering and the tax forms, not to mention the time I'd spent developing a plan to open a tea shop at the back of the store. I hadn't been in the garden for weeks, and I certainly wasn't doing what I started out to do. Enjoy myself. Have a life.

"It's probably just burnout," McQuaid said sympathetically. "You need to get away."

Just burnout? "Isn't that what I've been telling you?" I asked.

"Look, China," McQuaid said patiently, "nobody made you work fourteen hours a day for the entire Christmas season. You could have taken off whenever you felt like it." McQuaid teaches in the criminal justice department of the local university. On a long day, he's in the classroom for maybe three hours. He's on sabbatical leave this semester, which means he'll put in mornings on his research project and call it a day. From where I sit, calling it a day at eleven sounds pretty darn good.

"When you're in business for yourself," I said tackily, "you don't get a sabbatical."

He shrugged. "You could have given Laurel more hours.

Or made a deal with Ruby." Laurel Wiley helps out in the shop. Ruby Wilcox runs the Crystal Cave, next door. We take turns minding each other's shops. "And what's going to happen when you open the tearoom? You'll be even busier than you are now."

"Laurel was away for the holidays," I said defensively, "and Ruby had her hands full at the Cave. Anyway, it wasn't just the shop, it was the *season*. I had the house to decorate and the presents to wrap and the cooking. I don't think our Christmas guests would have appreciated it if we'd sent out for tacos."

"Nobody made you cook all that stuff, either," McQuaid went on, in the even, logical tone that he uses when he's lecturing his classes. "Mom and Dad would have been perfectly content with sage stuffing—we didn't need oyster and corn bread stuffing, too. We've got enough fruitcake to last until next Christmas. And how many hours did you spend on the gingerbread house? And the tree decorations? You must have put in two days on those angels."

I wanted to slug McQuaid for not appreciating my efforts to make Christmas special, but I had to agree with him. This was the first holiday he and Brian and I had lived together, and I'd wanted to give us something to remember. The best Christmas of our lives. What I'd given myself was one huge Christmas hangover.

"You're absolutely right," I said. "I've been doing too much. I need to slow down. I need to think. I need some time alone."

McQuaid and I had lived together for six months, and I have to admit that it's been pretty good—better than I expected, actually. He's a patient man, and fair, a former cop who plays by the rules even when he doesn't particularly like them. For the most part, he's respected my need for independence, and he's been willing to let our relationship develop without asking for more commitment than I can give. And on my side, I've been learning to care for—*love* is a word I'm still not sure about—McQuaid and Brian.

But living together creates its own pressures, and lately, I'd begun to feel that somebody else was organizing my life. The house that seemed big enough for a circus when we leased it last May now felt like a crowded elevator stuck between floors. When I came home at night, someone was always there, expecting me to act more or less sociable. There were also wet towels to pick up, dirty socks to wash, the cooking and the shopping and the errands to do. McQuaid and I shared these chores, of course, but I was expected to make my contribution.

There were other expectations, too, some of them uncomfortable. McQuaid's parents were obviously hoping we'd make it legal before long, my mother let me know at least once a week that she was eager to arrange a wedding, and our friends acted as if we were already married. On top of all this, the shop was like a runaway horse, taking me someplace I wasn't sure I wanted to go. My life wasn't my own anymore. I needed a break.

Business is slow the first week of January, and half of Pecan Springs closes down for a midwinter vacation. Ruby and I usually take a week to catch up on our bookkeeping and do our spring ordering, and Ruby often goes away for a few extra days. Nobody would be surprised if Thyme and Seasons was closed too.

McQuaid was frowning. "If it's space you're after," he said, "you won't get it where you're going. Won't you and Maggie be staying in the same cottage? And isn't Ruby going too?"

"Ruby's driving us, but she's going on to Albuquerque to see some friends. She's only staying overnight. And Maggie and I will each have our own cottage."

Maggie is Maggie Garrett, who runs the Magnolia Kitchen, the restaurant across the street from my shop. A few weeks before, seeing how frazzled I had become, Maggie had suggested that a winter retreat might give me a different slant on things, and arranged for the two of us to stay for two weeks at a place she knew, where we could relax and be quiet. It sounded heavenly. Fourteen days with nothing to do but breathe the fresh scent of Texas red cedar, watch the morning mist rise off the Yucca River, and see the white-tailed deer picking their way across the meadow at sunset. Ah, paradise.

The bedroom door opened and Brian came in, trailed by Howard Cosell, McQuaid's overweight basset hound. Brian's tee shirt was flapping around his knees like a ragged kilt, his untied Reeboks were the size of ski boots, and he was wearing a large green iguana on his shoulder. The iguana is named Einstein. He lives in Brian's closet, along with a tarantula called Ivan the Hairible (I am not making this up) and a varying assortment of lizards, snakes, and frogs.

"Some woman named Maggie is here," Brian said. "She wants to know if you're ready." Howard Cosell gave a mournful cough and flopped full-length in the middle of the doorway.

Khat growled deep in his throat, tensed, and leapt from the bed to the dresser, where he sat, staring malevolently at the dog. Howard Cosell bared his teeth. I glanced with distaste from one to the other. Was I ready, or was I *ready*? "Tell her I'm on my way," I said. I glanced in the mirror, picked up a brush, and ran it through my short brown hair. The gray streak at the left temple is getting wider and Ruby tells me I should color it, but I don't want to be bothered. "All I have to do is find a couple good books," I added, stowing my camera and a flashlight in my bag. "There'll be plenty of time to read."

Read? When was the last time I'd read anything but *The Business of Herbs*? How long was it since I'd given myself a manicure or soaked my weary self in a leisurely bath? Most mornings, I was lucky to duck under the shower for three minutes, and my nails would make an armadillo blush.

"I wouldn't be surprised to see you back in a day or two," McQuaid remarked astutely. "You weren't cut out to be a nun. Poverty might be tolerable. You might even manage celibacy. Lord knows, though, you're anything but obedient.''

Brian turned, startled. ''You're going to be a *nun*? I thought you were taking a vacation.''

''I am going on retreat,'' I said with dignity. ''To St. Theresa's monastery. For two weeks.'' I didn't look at McQuaid. ''Fourteen entire days. Not an hour less.''

''A monastery?'' Brian blinked. ''You mean, where they like pray all the time and stuff?''

''I doubt that they do it all the time,'' I said. I went to the bookshelf. ''But I expect they do pray a good bit. That's what they're there for.''

''Will they make you pray?''

''They won't make me,'' I said. ''But maybe I'll want to. Maybe I'll start by saying thanks.'' Thanks for no customers, no Howard Cosell, no Einstein, no twelve-year-old kid, nobody with expectations. Thanks for peace and harmony and an ordered, spacious quiet among women who cherish the inner life.

St. Theresa's monastery—which is known among herb people for its great garlic—is only a couple of hours' drive to the west of Pecan Springs, in the beautiful, rugged Yucca River country near Carr, Texas. I would have my own private cottage, eat somebody else's cooking, and walk in a garden that I didn't have to weed. I'm not especially religious, but I was looking forward to a spiritually uplifting experience. The only hitch, apparently, was getting approval for my retreat from the abbess, Mother Winifred. But that wasn't likely to be a problem, Maggie assured me. And Maggie—formerly Sister Margaret Mary—should know. She'd been in charge of St. Theresa's kitchen until just a few years ago, when she'd left to open the restaurant.

Now that I think about it, maybe I should have been suspicious of the way everything all came together, as if it had been preordained. At the time, I was just relieved that there weren't any hassles about rates or dates or vacancies.

Maggie phoned in our request for two cottages for the first two weeks in January, plus a third cottage for Ruby for one night, and the next day Mother Winifred called me to say that she would be delighted to have us come for a visit. Maggie had obviously told her about my interest in herbs, because Mother Winifred added that she hoped I would enjoy seeing the monastery's garlic farm. She didn't sound like the kind of person who would twist my arm about prayer. She did say she'd like me to help her solve a problem, though.

"A minor mystery," she said lightly. From her voice, I guessed that she was an older woman, in her sixties, maybe. "I hope you can share some of your expertise."

My herbal expertise, I figured she meant. Was there a problem with the garlic? If so, there are plenty of people who know a lot more about it than I do. The few garlic varieties I grow hardly qualify me to be a consultant. "If it's the garlic you need help with, Mother," I said, "I don't think I'm the best person. You might get in touch with—"

She cut me off firmly. "I won't bother you with the details now. I hear the voice of God in this, my child. Your cottage will be ready for you."

Brian shifted Einstein from one shoulder to the other. "I guess prayer is like having a direct line to God," he said. "He probably hears nuns better than ordinary people. Because they're so holy, I mean. And they get a lot of practice praying."

"That's the theory, I suppose."

"I guess I won't ever be holy enough to ask God for a favor," Brian said regretfully. "Do you suppose you could ask the nuns to put in a good word for the Cowboys? If they hurry, it's not too late to do something about tomorrow's game. Tell them it's, like, well, crucial."

"I'll inquire," I said, and dropped several mysteries and a romance into my bag. No herb books this trip. I would feed my fantasies while I relaxed.

McQuaid picked up my suitcase. "Want me to carry this?"

"Thanks," I said. "I just need to get a jacket."

Brian was still looking at me, his brow furrowed. "You *will* be back, won't you, China?"

I nodded as I took a denim jacket out of the closet and pulled it on over the tee shirt Ruby had given me for Christmas. On the front was the declaration I Am a Woman, printed in big, bold letters. Beneath, smaller but still firm, was the statement I am invincible. Beneath that was a small, shaky scrawl: I am tired. It was entirely appropriate, I thought.

Brian's question came again, anxious. "You're *sure* you're coming back?"

"I'm sure." I knelt and gave him a hug. I could understand his anxiety. After all, his real mother—who, just last summer, had threatened to jump out of a hotel room window right in front of him—had moved away. He hadn't heard from her for months. For all he knew, I was about to do the same thing. I was touched. I might feel burdened by the responsibility of being a stand-in mom to a twelve-year-old boy, but it felt nice to be wanted.

"Of course she'll be back," McQuaid said complacently. "Where else would she go?"

I started to protest at the idea of being taken for granted, but Brian cut in.

"Boy, am I *glad*," he said, relieved. "I need a costume for the Valentine's Day play. I found out about it before Christmas, but I forgot to mention it. I'm going to be the King of Hearts." He looked at me. "Mrs. Howard's got this pattern you're supposed to sew it by, China. I'm supposed to have a crown too. Gold, with emeralds and rubies. She's got a picture you can look at so you'll get it right."

A costume for the King of Hearts. A gold crown with emeralds and rubies.

Maybe I wouldn't come back.

CHAPTER TWO

The best place to find God is in a garden. You can dig for Him there.

George Bernard Shaw

"You look like you're glad to get away," Maggie said.

We were headed into Pecan Springs, several miles away, to leave Maggie's van behind the restaurant and meet Ruby, who would drive us to St. Theresa's. The sky was a chilly gray and drops of rain were splattering on the windshield. In central Texas, winter is never what you expect, and usually not what you want. Before Christmas, when I'd been stuck in the shop, the sky was clear, the sun was bright, and the temperature was a balmy seventy. Now that I was free, the next two weeks would be cold and blustery. But what did it matter? I had books to read, a place to stay warm, and time to be quiet. A blizzard could blow down from the Panhandle, and I'd still be content.

"Glad? You bet." I stretched my legs in the roomy front seat. "I've got a lot to think about while we're gone."

"St. T's is the place for thinking," Maggie said. She grinned wryly. "There isn't much else to do out there but cultivate the inner life."

Maggie is in her mid-forties and stockily built, with sturdy arms and hands made for work. Her graying hair is razored flat in a no-nonsense boy-cut, and in the two years she's run the restaurant, I've never seen her wear lipstick. Her beauty is in the smile that softens her square face. And in her eyes—blue, intelligent, caring. She's been out of the monastery for a while, but she still has the look of a nun. It's a quiet, inward-turning look, as if she were engrossed in a reality that the rest of us don't see.

Nuns are a mystery to me. They seem different, other-worldly, untouchable, self-contained. But there's a deeper mystery about them, a contradiction I've never quite understood. They're independent enough to reject things that women in our culture are supposed to want—a career, a house, a husband, children. But at the same time, they're dependent on God and the Church and obedient to their superiors, including the male hierarchy that has such power over them. Then there's commitment. How can somebody commit herself for an entire lifetime, for God's sake? It's hard enough for me to commit myself to an eighteen-month lease on a house.

"Yes, St. T's is very restful, very quiet," Maggie remarked. She paused. "Or at least it was. Now . . ."

I glanced at her. "Now what?"

"It's complicated," Maggie said. "There are a lot of uncertainties. A lot of unrest."

"In a monastery?" I asked, surprised. From the outside, monastic life looked settled and certain, a cocoon of perpetual calm.

Maggie was looking straight ahead. She didn't answer.

"Tell me about the place," I said. "I don't know much except that it's famous for its garlic."

There is garlic and there is garlic.

The garlic you buy in the grocery store in spring and early summer (eight or nine months after it was dug out of the ground) has probably already expired. The living, breathing bulb was sprayed with sprout inhibitors and asphyxiated in a tightly wrapped plastic coffin. By the time it arrives in your kitchen, it's DOA, a victim of the packing and shipping industries. It can be moldy on the outside and empty inside. You'll probably throw half of it out.

But even if it's fresh, garlic fanciers say, supermarket garlic still isn't the most flavorful garlic. Commercially grown garlic is called "soft-necked" or "nonbolting" garlic. The bulbs are small and tight and white, easy to harvest, easy to store and ship. But if you want sweet, sharp, smooth-tasting garlic, you want rocambole, which is not easy to find.

If rocambole (the word rhymes with soul) tastes so much better, why don't more producers grow it? The answer lies in the odd growth habit of this plant, which is sometimes called "top-setting" or "serpent" garlic. Cheered on by spring rains and bright sun, rocambole sends up an enthusiastic flower stalk, two or three feet high, coiled like a snake. At the top of this curlicue stalk is a pod of a hundred or so bulbils, each one keen on sprouting into a new garlic plant when the top-heavy flower stalk falls over. This curious arrangement is garlic's way of ensuring that another generation will be around to carry on the delightful business of being garlic.

Rocambole's fervent insistence on providing for the future, however, makes it a commercial disaster. The snaky stalks snarl harvesting equipment. The bulbils fall between the rows, where they sprout, come spring. To make matters worse, the cloves are only loosely attached at the root base. They fall apart and bury themselves in the soil, happily intent on growing into adult rocambole. These untidy procreative habits result in a whole slew of eager volunteers sprouting greenly between the rows in April and May, where they must be pulled by hand or rousted out by a cultivator. Finally, and perhaps most damning of all, the cloves aren't paper white (which is the politically correct color if you happen to be garlic). Sometimes they're brown skinned. Sometimes they're red. Sometimes they're purple.

The garlic that is grown by the sisters of St. Theresa's is a hard-necked, top-setting rocambole with flavorful, colorful cloves that practically pop out of their richly purpled skins. It is arguably the best garlic grown in the state of Texas—or anywhere else, for that matter. In the past few years, St. Theresa's rocambole has become increasingly popular among cooks who are fussy about garlic.

I turned toward Maggie. "You'd have to sell quite a bit of garlic to make ends meet. Do the sisters really manage to support themselves growing rocambole?"

"Pretty much," Maggie said. "But there's always maintenance and equipment and emergency expenditures. They'll be glad of the trust fund."

"What trust fund?"

But the answer to that question would have to wait. Maggie was parking in the lot behind her restaurant, where she planned to leave the van for her employees to use. We got out and carried our bags across the street to the Crystal Cave. I steadfastly averted my eyes from the wreath-decked front door of Thyme and Seasons, which I had recently painted an inviting forest green.

I'd locked the store the night before, and I didn't need to check to see how things were. I know the place by heart—stone walls, scarred wooden floor, beamed ceiling hung with braids of garlic and *ristras*—strings of dried red peppers. Wooden shelves that hold glass jars and stone crocks full of dried herbs, as well as vinegars, teas, herbal soaps, potpourri. Baskets of strawflowers, nigella, globe amaranth, celosia, blue salvia, and poppy pods. Wreaths of artemisia and dried sweet Annie. Red clay pots of lavender, thyme, rosemary, scented geraniums.

Thyme and Seasons is the shop I had dreamed of, filled with useful, delightful plants. But the dream had swallowed my life. I thought of Wanda Rathbottom owning the store instead of me—a thought that six months before would have turned my stomach. Today, it almost seemed inviting. Maybe I could sell the shop to Wanda with the provision that I stay on as gardener. That way, I could spend spring in the garden, rather than behind the cash register. Maybe I could—I pushed the thought away. There was time later to think of options. For the next fourteen days, I planned not to think at *all*.

Before we actually reached the Crystal Cave, the door

opened and Ruby came down the walk, carrying a large suitcase. I did a double take. Ruby is six feet tall, with fiery red hair that she wears in a wild frizz. She was dressed in an ankle-length brown caftan belted with a length of rope. The hood of the caftan was pulled up, hiding her hair.

"I've never been to a monastery before," Ruby said, seeing my inquiring glance. "I didn't know what to wear." She looked nervously at my jeans and Maggie's dark slacks. "Am I okay? Should I change into something more appropriate?"

"What could be more appropriate?" I asked. "You look like you're auditioning for *Sister Act III*."

"I didn't wear perfume," Ruby said, as if that explained something. She unlocked the trunk of her red Honda, which was parked at the curb. "Or nail polish. Or my tinted contacts."

"You must feel practically naked," Maggie replied with a grin, putting her bag into the trunk.

Ruby nodded, taking her seriously. "I didn't think nuns were into that sort of thing. I thought I should be just plain Ruby."

"Whatever you do, you'll never be just plain Ruby," I said affectionately, adding my bag. "It's a contradiction in terms." Ruby's suitcase went in last, with difficulty, and we climbed into the little car, Maggie in the back. As we drove off, I said to Maggie over my shoulder, "Now, tell me about that trust fund."

"Trust fund?" Ruby asked, making a left turn in front of a telephone company truck. "Did somebody inherit something?"

"The monastery inherited some money," I said, fastening my seat belt. Riding with Ruby can be thrilling. "Maggie was just starting to tell me about it."

"Actually, it was quite a lot of money," Maggie said. "But the story goes back a few years, and it's complicated. Maybe I'd better start at the beginning."

So while Ruby drove westward under an increasingly

threatening sky, Maggie told us the tale of St. Theresa's legacy. It began in a Catholic high school in San Antonio, where an English teacher named Sister Hilaria befriended Helen Henderson, a young student teacher. The two maintained their friendship through frequent letters even after Helen married her college sweetheart, Bert Laney, and moved to his two-thousand-acre ranch near Carr, ninety miles northwest of San Antonio. A few years later, he died in an automobile accident, leaving Helen Laney a wealthy, childless widow. The next year, Helen was diagnosed with amyotrophic lateral sclerosis—ALS, or Lou Gehrig's disease. It would ultimately kill her.

Meanwhile, back in San Antonio, Sister Hilaria's energetic work had brought her increased visibility within her order, the Sisters of the Holy Heart. She was active in every community project and served on a dozen local and national boards. But over the next few years, Sister Hilaria began to think wistfully about living a quieter, more prayerful life. After consulting God and receiving His approval on the project, she went to her superior and requested permission to establish a contemplative house where sisters might step out of their active lives of service to engage in prayer and reflection.

Sister Hilaria's superior was not exactly overjoyed at the idea of retiring one of her most outstanding achievers, but she dutifully bumped the request up the chain of command. After a great deal of hemming and hawing, the order's Reverend Mother General finally said yes—*if* Hilaria could find an acceptable site for her contemplative community *and* raise the operating expenses to keep it going. Obviously, Sister Hilaria had gotten permission to do what she wanted because nobody in the order believed she could actually do it. Real estate in Texas was booming, land prices had shot up like Roman candles, and people who had been accustomed to investing in God were looking for better returns from Mammon and Company. In that economic climate, why should anybody sink a nickel into a new religious community that would never turn a dime?

But Sister Hilaria was praying, and when Sister Hilaria prayed, God listened. She was also writing letters. One of the letters went to her old friend Helen Laney, who invited her to visit the Laney Ranch and look around. By now, Helen was quite ill, she was living alone in a large house, and she had no children to inherit her property when she died—no relatives at all, in fact, except for her husband's nephew and his wife, the Townsends. The ranch, Helen thought, might satisfy Sister Hilaria's needs.

When Sister Hilaria arrived at the Laney Ranch, she saw that God had answered her prayers with a resounding "Yes, ma'am." Remote but accessible, the property was situated along the wild Yucca River a couple of hours south and west of Austin. The rambling stone-and-cedar ranch headquarters could serve as office, chapel, and refectory. The large bunkhouse could easily be converted into a dozen eight- by ten-foot cells, and several small cottages along the river could serve as guest quarters. There were the usual outbuildings—barns, vehicle storage sheds, a repair shop—and plenty of room to build more. With her practical eye, Sister Hilaria observed the tillable acreage along the Yucca River and the river itself, which could be partially diverted for irrigation. While she had enormous faith in the long-term productivity of prayer, she also believed in the short-term rewards of work. If the nuns wanted to eat, they could get their hands dirty.

Following visits from the Reverend Mother General, correspondence with Rome, and enough red tape to stretch from here to the Pearly Gates, the final arrangements were blessed by the order's lawyers. After the initial fuss, however, nobody paid a lot of attention to the details of the transaction. The Laney land wasn't oil or coastal property, and it had no real value except to Sister Hilaria and her new community. Helen Laney deeded the ranch house and eight hundred acres to the Sisters of the Holy Heart, and constructed several necessary facilities—a small chapel, a dormitorylike building with individual cells for sisters, and additional residential cottages. In return, the nuns cared for Mrs. Laney until she died, five years later. In her will, she created a foundation to be managed by Sister Hilaria—now Mother Hilaria. She endowed it to the tune of some seven million dollars.

"Seven million dollars!" Ruby exclaimed.

I gave a long, low whistle. "That's a lot of garlic. The nuns obviously don't have to work for a living. Why didn't they give up their garlic farm long ago?"

"Because in monastic life, work is a kind of prayer," Maggie said. "You do it for love, not for money." Her voice thinned. "And because Bert Laney's nephew—Carl Townsend—challenged the will in court."

"Did Mrs. Laney leave him anything?" I asked. Relatives who aren't mentioned in a will often feel neglected. Sometimes they decide to take the matter to court. To forestall such a challenge, most lawyers suggest that you leave a dollar to any relative you're not fond of.

"She gave the Townsends twelve hundred acres when she split the property. And she left them a hundred thousand dollars in her will."

"Only a hundred thousand?" Ruby clucked her tongue against her teeth. "Some people are never satisfied."

Maggie shifted her position, as if talking about the Townsends made her itchy. "The trouble is that they didn't get access to the river. They apparently expected to get the bulk of the estate, too. They were Bert Laney's only relatives and the money came from his side of the family in the first place."

We were miles out of town by now, still heading west. Outside the window, a pale sun flirted with the dark clouds. The gray light gleamed on an arid landscape of scraggly cedar and bare mesquite, the rocky hillsides studded with patches of gray-green prickly pear. The annual rainfall in this area is only twenty inches a year, and surface water is at a premium. If I were a rancher in Carr County, I'd want access to that river. It didn't surprise me that the Townsends had challenged Mrs. Laney's will.

"Has the dispute been settled yet?" I asked. Estate claims are often appealed from one court to another, dragging on for ten or twenty years.

"Last April, finally. The money's coming in now." Maggie's face grew somber. "Unfortunately, Mother Hilaria didn't live to see it. She died in September. She was . . . electrocuted."

Ruby gave a startled cry.

I shuddered. "How did it happen?"

"She was making coffee on the hot plate in her cottage. She spilled milk on the floor and apparently stepped in it when she switched off the hot plate. Even so, the jolt wouldn't have been enough to kill her if it hadn't been for her bad heart."

"Mother Winifred—the woman I spoke with on the phone—is the new abbess, then," I said.

"Yes. By the way, she's the one who's responsible for the monastery's herb garden. Not the garlic farm—that's somebody else. Mother Winifred grows all kinds of herbs. She's looking forward to showing you the garden."

"I'm surprised that an abbess has time for gardening," Ruby remarked. She pulled out to pass a tractor pulling a wagon loaded with baled hay. A dog was perched on top of the bales, surveying the road ahead.

"I'm surprised too," I said. "Especially an abbess with seven million dollars to manage—plus whatever the legacy has earned since it was invested. The principle must have doubled since then." Fourteen or fifteen million dollars, maybe more, depending on the savvy of the monastery's financial advisers.

"I don't think Mother Winifred has much to do with finances," Maggie said. "The bank manages the trust. Anyway, she's only acting. Last spring, you see, there was another complication. A surprise, actually, and not altogether pleasant.'' Her voice darkened. ''The Sisters of the Holy Heart has eight or ten communities, scattered around the country. The day after the court decision was announced, the Reverend Mother General closed the community in Houston, St. Agatha's. Three months later, she sent a bus and some trucks and moved the St. Agatha sisters to St. T's.''

''Closed the community?'' I turned to look at Maggie. ''Why?''

Maggie looked out of the window. ''It's the way things are these days, I'm afraid. The Holy Heart Sisters have been losing vocations, like a lot of other orders. When I came to St. T's ten years ago, there were thirty-five sisters. Now they're down to twenty. But the situation at St. Agatha's was worse—down from sixty-something to twenty. The St. Agatha property was valuable because it was close to the airport. So Reverend Mother General sold it and packed the nuns off to St. T's.''

The sun had given up and let the clouds take over, and the windows were beginning to steam up, a sure sign that the temperature outside was dropping. I pulled my denim jacket tighter around me and wondered whether I should have brought mittens and a scarf. ''How do the St. Agatha nuns feel about garlic?''

Maggie's laugh was wry. ''I haven't visited the monastery since they moved in, but Dominica—one of my friends at St. T's—tells me that they're definitely not happy campers. St. Agatha's was a conference center. The nuns were used to seeing important people and being on the fringes of important decisions.''

''And St. T's is on the fringe of nowhere,'' I said. It must have been quite a comedown, from serving church bigshots in a conference center to digging in a garlic patch. The sisters must be terribly hurt and resentful about having been moved.

Maggie was going on, her tone reflective. ''The groups have different spiritual practices, too. When I lived at St.

T's, Mother Hilaria encouraged us to design our own Rule, write our own liturgy, choose our own dress. St. Agatha's was the most conservative house in the order. The sisters still wear a modified habit and a veil, and they held Chapter of Faults until they moved to St. T's.'' She shook her head. "This was not a marriage made in heaven."

Ruby glanced curiously at Maggie in the rearview mirror. "What's a Chapter of Faults?"

"A meeting where the nuns accuse themselves and one another of their sins. Envy, covetousness, anger—stuff like that." Maggie looked uncomfortable. "Then they make a penance—a certain number of strokes with a leather whip."

"A *whip*?" Ruby's red eyebrows shot up under her curls.

"Self-flagellation was common practice for centuries," Maggie said. "But Mother Hilaria wouldn't have it at St. T's. She said it was barbaric."

"My kind of woman," I remarked.

"She was pretty special," Maggie said, lifting her chin. "She was fascinated by Buddhism, so she encouraged us to learn meditation and yoga and read the Eastern mystics."

"Yoga!" Ruby exclaimed. "In a Catholic monastery?"

"Sure," Maggie said. "A lot of Catholics are interested in Eastern spirituality. Not the St. Agatha nuns, unfortunately. They think it's pagan nonsense, or worse." She hesitated. "The two groups are exactly the same size, you see. Mother Winifred can't get a consensus on anything."

"She said something on the phone about a 'minor mystery,' " I said reflectively. "I thought she was talking about the garlic, but maybe not. Do you know?"

The rain had begun in earnest, and Ruby turned on both the wipers and the defroster. "A mystery?" She wriggled in her seat. "I *love* mysteries! When I was a little girl, I wanted to grow up and be Nancy Drew." After that, it was Kinsey Millhone, then V. I. Warshawski, and finally Kay Scarpetta. More recently, though, she's given up on hard-boiled women detectives. "Raymond Chandler in drag," she says sadly. "Lotta guts, no soul."

Maggie looked out the window, not answering, and I sensed an apprehension in her that both surprised and disturbed me. Of all my friends, Maggie is the most serene, the most balanced. She can always be counted on to keep her head during the crises that happen regularly in the restaurant business. But now, her outer calm was less opaque, and through it I glimpsed an inner worry, a fear, even. Something was wrong at St. T's, and Maggie knew what it was.

When she finally answered my question, though, her voice was controlled. "Yes, I think I know what Mother Winifred has in mind. But she should tell you first. Then I'll be glad to share what I know."

That was fair enough. "You said Mother Winifred is acting abbess," I said. "Who will take over when she steps down?"

"The nuns will elect an abbess," Maggie said. She paused. "If they can."

"What do you mean?"

"There are two candidates. Sister Gabriella is from St. T's. She's managed the garlic farm for five or six years. Sister Olivia was named abbess of St. Agatha's the week before it closed. She ran the conference center."

"Uh-oh," Ruby said. "Sounds like trouble."

Ruby was right. You didn't have to be a Vatican diplomat to understand the implications of the choice. The new abbess would have control over fourteen million dollars, give or take a million or two. Sister Gabriella would no doubt want to use the money to raise more rocambole. Sister Olivia would presumably transform St. T's into a conference center.

"When will the election be held?" I asked.

"They've already had one vote," Maggie said. "But the two groups are evenly matched, twenty on each side."

"So, they're deadlocked, huh," Ruby said.

Maggie nodded. "The order's charter says the abbess has to be elected by a majority—in this case, twenty-one votes. Of course, Reverend Mother General would like the new abbess to have more support than that. She won't schedule another election until it looks like one of the candidates can get a majority."

"Meanwhile," I said, "Mother Winifred is still acting."

"I'm sure she'd rather be working in the herb garden," Maggie said, "but she's stuck with the job for a while. Until one of the sisters changes her mind, or leaves, or . . ."

"Or dies," Ruby said, with a laugh to show that she was only joking.

Maggie didn't laugh.

CHAPTER THREE

The heat of garlick is very vehement, and all vehement hot things send up but ill-favoured vapours to the brain. In choleric men it will add fuel to the fire.

Nicholas Culpeper
The Complete Herbal & English Physician

Carr, Texas, is not a bustling metropolis. You might drive through it before you could say, "Where are the Golden Arches?" But it's a very pretty town, with pecans and live oaks arching over narrow, brick-paved streets, lined by frame cottages trimmed with turn-of-the-century gingerbread and set in neat gardens. It looked like Pecan Springs a couple of decades ago, before tourism brought the developers into town. I wondered fleetingly what it would be like to live here, maybe even move my shop here. Life would certainly be more peaceful. But it was too far for McQuaid to commute, except on weekends. Which might not be a bad idea, I thought. It would give us a little breathing space.

"We'll get to St. T's too late for lunch," Maggie said. "Make a left turn at that light, Ruby. We'll stop at Bernice's and get something to eat."

We were on the square. The hardware store was on one corner, its window full of saws, coiled rope, water heaters, and a gleaming white commode. The Carr State Bank was on another, fronted by a concrete planter containing a leafless tree still draped with Christmas lights and a sign that said, Be Good, for Goodness' Sake. A Carnegie library was on the third corner, next to a five-and-dime. Our Lady of Sorrows Catholic Church, with a letterboard announcing that Father Steven Shaw celebrated Mass at eleven on Sundays, stood on the fourth. A stone courthouse commanded the center. It might not have qualified as Most Picturesque Town Square in Texas, but the church was painted, the bank looked prosperous, and the hardware store had three or four pickups parked out front. Next to the bank was Bernice's Cafe.

"St. T's is mostly vegetarian and low-fat, so this is your last chance for chicken-fried steak," Maggie said as Ruby swung diagonally into the curb. "And you haven't had fried onion rings until you've eaten Bernice's."

I blinked. "Chicken-fried and onion rings? I thought you were into gourmet cooking."

Maggie grinned and slipped into a West Texas drawl. "Yes, ma'am, honey. Out here, Bernice's chicken-fried *is* gourmet cookin'. But don't believe everything she says," Maggie added in her usual voice. "She's the switchboard operator on the local grapevine. If you encourage her, you'll get an earful of gossip."

Inside the cafe, we were greeted by a weathered, gritty-voiced woman in jeans and a plaid Western shirt, standing behind a green Formica-covered counter. "Well, Margaret Mary," she said, grinning at Maggie. "I'll be durned. Been a couple years, ain't it? How are you?" The woman, whose apricot-colored hair turned up in an Andrews Sisters puff, wiped her hands on a white apron and lowered the volume on a pink plastic radio that was playing an old Johnny Cash ballad called "Ring of Fire." Over the radio hung a fly-specked cheesecake poster girl with a Budweiser in her hand. We had just stepped into a time warp.

"Hello, Bernice," Maggie said. "It's nice to see you." She pulled out a scarred wooden chair and sat down at a table covered with a red-and-white-checked oilcloth. Ruby and I joined her.

Bernice took in Ruby's hooded caftan and came to the obvious conclusion. "Don't tell me, let me guess. Y'all are headin' out to St. T's." She didn't wait for confirmation. " 'F that's the case, you'll need somethin' fillin'." She went behind the counter and pushed mugs under the old-fashioned coffee urn. "From what I hear, the cookin' out there has went straight to hell since you left, Margaret Mary. And that's not the only thing that's went to hell, either," she added, carrying the mugs to our table. She glanced at Ruby. "Pardon my French, Sister."

Ruby looked taken aback, then inclined her head gently as she took the coffee.

Maggie ignored Bernice's invitation to gossip. "I'll have the chicken-fried," she said, "French fries and an order of onion rings."

"I will too," Ruby said. She looked up with a beneficent, nunlike smile. Bernice's mistake was giving her a new view of herself.

"Make that three," I said, but unlike Maggie, I'm not above tweaking the town grapevine. "Is something going on at St. T's?"

Bernice wiped her hands on her apron. I could have sworn she was wearing Midnight in Paris. Maybe she was. The five-and-dime across the street might still have a few of those little blue forty-nine-cent bottles stashed under the counter.

"Some folks say it's just coinkidinks. Other folks think it's bad luck." She raised both plucked eyebrows. "Ya ask me, somebody's tryin' to fix their wagon."

Ruby was looking divinely unconcerned. Maggie was trying not to listen. "Whose wagon?" I asked.

"Why, them nuns, of course." Bernice bent over my shoulder and lowered her grainy voice. "You go out there, you watch yourself, y'hear? Keep a bucket o' water by your bed."

There was a moment of silence. Then Maggie sighed the sigh of someone who's been trapped into a knock-knock joke. "Okay, Bernice, we give up. Why should we keep a bucket of water by the bed?"

Bernice feigned surprise. "What? Oh, sorry, Margaret Mary. I thought you wadn't interested."

"Has there been a fire?" I asked.

"Christmas Eve, in the chapel." Bernice's voice signified disaster. "Wadn't the first, neither. Thanksgivin', it was a grease fire in the kitchen. Couple weeks 'fore that, the barn."

"Grease?" Maggie was incredulous. "Why would there be grease in the kitchen? They don't cook fried foods."

"Did any of the fires do much damage?" I asked.

"Not a whole lot." Bernice waved her hand. "You remember Dwight Baldwin, Margaret Mary? The maintenance man? Well, Dwight was out in the yard when the kitchen got afire, an' he run in an' grabbed a pot lid. He got to the barn fire, too, 'fore it could spread, and he and Father Steven put out the chapel fire. None of 'em had much of a chance to git goin'. But it all adds up, don'cha see?"

"Adds up to what?" I asked.

She gave me a withering look. "To one coinkidink too many, that's what. You mark my words—somebody's got it in for them nuns." She turned to Ruby and modulated her tone. "You oughta try a piece of Betty Ann's peach pie, Sister. She brung it in this morning. Fredericksburg peaches, fresh outta her freezer."

Ruby couldn't resist. "Bless you, my daughter," she murmured. Beatrice smiled and walked briskly toward the kitchen.

"Bernice must be exaggerating," Maggie said. "If the fires were serious, Dominica would have written to me." She frowned. "But I haven't heard from her since before Christmas. I wonder . . ."

We stirred our coffee. A mechanical cuckoo popped out of a red-plastic cuckoo clock and whistled the first bars of "The Eyes of Texas." Johnny Cash had finished "Ring of

Fire'' and Buddy Holly was starting on ''Peggy Sue.'' After a moment, Ruby poured cream into her coffee and leaned toward Maggie.

''I've known you for over two years and I've never heard how you got to be a nun, Maggie.''

Maggie's mouth was wry. ''Why did I do such a crazy thing, you mean?''

Still captured by the image of herself as a monastic, Ruby frowned. ''Maybe it wasn't crazy,'' she said.

''My mother thought I'd lost my mind,'' Maggie said reflectively. ''I'd just finished my degree in social work, and I was volunteering with the Sisters of the Holy Heart in Chicago. One morning I woke up, put on my clothes, walked into the Vocations Office at the convent, and said, 'I want to be a nun.' ''

Ruby blinked. ''That was it?''

''That was it,'' Maggie said matter-of-factly. ''No finger of God, no choir of angels, no heavenly light. It was just something I had to do. It didn't even feel like I had a choice.''

''How did you get from Chicago to Texas?'' I asked.

''I ran into Mother Hilaria at a conference. She was looking for sisters to help get St. T's up and running. I told her I wasn't interested, but she wrote to me and sent me some pictures and . . .'' She was tracing a wet design on the table with the tip of her spoon. ''God wanted me here, I guess. So I came. If it hasn't happened to you, it's kind of hard to explain. We say we've been called. We've been given a vocation.''

Ruby cleared her throat. ''If God wanted you here, why did you leave?'' The question might have been tactless, but it was on my mind, too.

Maggie picked up her coffee mug. I could sense a softening in her, a sadness. ''I thought I'd be at St. T's for the rest of my life. I loved the quiet. I loved my work in the kitchen. I even loved the garlic field.'' She paused and took a sip of coffee. When she spoke again, her voice was low.

"It wasn't easy, believe me. Leaving was like tearing out a piece of my soul."

I was startled. I'd expected to hear that she felt stifled by the discipline or fell in love with a priest. This was something quite different.

Ruby stared at her. "Then why did you do it?"

For a minute, I thought she wasn't going to answer. "Vocations are fragile," she said finally, without inflection. "Sometimes they last a lifetime, sometimes they don't. I was angry. I was fed up with the Church's attitude toward women. We're okay for cheap labor, but they'll never allow us to be full participants. They can't afford to. They know we'd change things."

Bernice came with our food, and the next few minutes were filled with moving plates around and making sure we had what we needed. While we got started eating, I was thinking. Anger against the hierarchy must drive a lot of women out of the Church these days. But something made me wonder if there hadn't been another reason for Maggie's leaving. When she'd spoken about living at St. T's, her voice had been soft and shaken, deeply truthful. When she'd told us why she left, she might have been reading from a newspaper. I could feel her longing for the life she had abandoned. But I couldn't feel her outrage.

Ruby was blunt. "But if you really liked your life at St. T's, why didn't you fight for it?" She pushed her sleeves back and picked up her fork. "The Vatican is seven time zones away, for cryin' out loud. They wouldn't know if you got together with a few nuns and celebrated Communion. Or you could have joined a group and tried to change things."

"I'm sure you're right." Maggie looked down at her plate. "But about that time my father died and left me some money. It was as if God had handed me an invitation to do something else with my life." A smile ghosted across her mouth.

I was about to observe that the money might have been

a test of her desire to stay just as easily as it could have been an invitation to leave, but Ruby spoke first. "You've been happy doing your restaurant thing, haven't you? You always *seem* happy."

Well, maybe. I wasn't sure that it was happiness I'd sensed in Maggie as much as acceptance. She takes life as it comes, without trying to do much about it. It's a state of mind—of soul, maybe—that I have to admire. It's totally different from the aggressive I'm-going-to-get-what-I-want-come-hell-or-high-water attitude of the people I knew when I was practicing law. But acceptance can be a problem too. If I had chosen to live at St. T's, you can darn well bet I wouldn't have let myself be driven out by the backward ideas of a few old men.

Maggie nibbled on an onion ring, musing over Ruby's question. "Am I happy? Mostly, I guess. The restaurant has given me self-confidence—I needed that. And I've loved having friends, especially you two. But I still miss the community. Mother Hilaria, the other nuns. It's . . ." She swallowed. "It's as if I've been in exile for the last two years."

"Well, if you miss it so much," Ruby said practically, "why don't you—?"

The rest of her question was lost in a sudden *whoosh* of chill air from the open door. A fair-haired man in a dark Stetson, jeans, and boots strode in, shrugged out of his sheepskin jacket, and hung it on a peg by the door. He turned in our direction and stopped.

There was a long moment, freeze-frame, while our eyes met and held. My heart lunged to the top of my windpipe and stayed there while I struggled to breathe past it.

"China?" the man asked. "China Bayles?" He was lean and narrow-hipped, almost thin. His face was more tanned and weather-beaten than I remembered, but then it had been eight years since I'd seen him. He covered the distance in three strides, not taking his eyes off me.

"China? What the hell are you doing *here*?"

"I'm eating lunch," I said incoherently. Ruby gave a delicate cough. "With friends," I added, and waved my hand to cover my confusion. "Ruby, this is an old friend of mine, Tom Rowan. Tom, Ruby Wilcox."

"Hi, Tom," Ruby said, lifting a graceful hand. She caught my eye. "An old friend, huh?" she asked meaningfully, with a Why-haven't-you-mentioned-him-before? look.

I ignored her. "And this is Maggie Garrett."

Tom glanced at Maggie, and his brown eyes lightened. "Maggie Garrett," he exclaimed, taking her hand. "Haven't seen you since you left St. T's. What are you up to these days?"

"I run a restaurant in Pecan Springs." Maggie squeezed his hand and let it go. "So you and China know one another?"

"You bet." Tom took the fourth chair at the table, next to me. "Last time I saw China, she was defending some big-time crook." His eyes went to my left hand for a fraction of an instant, then came back to my face. "You got the bastard acquitted—Douglas, wasn't that his name?" He glanced at Ruby. "Excuse me, Sister."

Ruby colored. "Oh, I'm not . . . I mean—" She looked down at her robe, couldn't think of any logical explanation for her monkish garb, and blurted out the next thing that came into her mind. "Has anyone ever mentioned that you look *exactly* like Robert Redford?"

I didn't have to listen to his flip response—I'd heard it a dozen times before. I was thinking of the Douglas trial, the most demanding of my fifteen-year career. Interminable days in the courtroom, long nights and weekends at the office. Somewhere during that period, my relationship with Tom Rowan had come to an abrupt and catastrophic end.

At the time, I was so totally focused on the case that I put Tom's departure aside to deal with later—something unpleasant that had to be faced, like getting the brakes fixed on the car or replacing the crown I lost halfway through the trial. I didn't feel the pain until the jury came in with a not-guilty verdict and I woke up and realized that where Tom had been, there was now a large and gnawing emptiness. We'd been intimate for less than a year, but he was the first man I ever really loved, and I hadn't thought it could end. I hadn't known, you see, that love dies when you don't pay attention to it—especially when there isn't much beside physical attraction to build on. Later, still feeling the loss, I handed in my resignation, moved to Pecan Springs, opened the shop—and McQuaid came along to fill the emptiness.

I pulled my eyes away. "The Douglas trial," I murmured. "It was a long time ago."

Tom brushed his blond hair out of his eyes with the boyish gesture that had always made me want to smile. "Eight years is a long time. Are you in Carr on a case?"

"I'm not in practice anymore."

He tilted his head curiously, but didn't say anything, just glanced around the table, taking in Maggie and Ruby in her brown monk's robe. "The three of you are on vacation, then?"

"Sort of," I said. "We're staying at St. T's for a couple of weeks."

"Not all of us," Ruby said. "I'm just here for one night. I'm leaving for Albuquerque tomorrow morning." She gave Tom a charming smile, anxious to redeem herself. "What a small world it is. And what a coincidence—you and China running into one another like this. You must be *totally* surprised." She hesitated, debating, then stepped into it. "How well did you know one another?"

Tom's tanned face crinkled in the familiar smile that had once made my heart turn over. "Not very well, actually. We only thought we did."

Ruby's eyes flew to me and her eyebrows became giant question marks.

"You'll enjoy St. T's," he added. "It's quiet and peaceful—well, mostly anyway. And the Yucca River country is as wild as it gets in this part of Texas." He looked up as Bernice came through the kitchen door. "Hey, Bernie, how ya doin'?"

Bernice's eyes lit up. "Well, hi there, handsome! Thought mebbe you'd given up eatin'."

Tom laughed. "Not on your life, beautiful. Took Dad to Dallas for chemo. Miss me?"

"Did I miss you?" She rolled her eyes expressively. "Nobody calls me 'beautiful' when you ain't around, Tommy."

"That's *their* problem. Say, you got any of that world-famous chili back there, darlin'? If you do, I'll take a bowl."

"Sure thing," Bernice said. She chuckled as she poured his coffee, then refilled our cups.

I looked at Tom. "*Mostly* peaceful?"

"Except for a little excitement from time to time," he replied casually. He turned his chair sideways and crossed his long legs. "A couple of small fires, but no damage." He glanced from me to Maggie. "What would you two say to going riding one day next week? We can get horses from Sadie Marsh—she lives out that way."

"You know this area, then?" I asked.

Come to think of it, what was Tom Rowan doing in this little one-horse town? When I knew him, he was a fair-haired, pinstriped superstar at one of Houston's biggest banks. He was talented, confident, and not above using his substantial charm to get what he wanted. Why had he left? How had he ended up here?

"Does he know this area?" Bernice mimicked sca-thingly. She put her hand on Tom's shoulder. "Listen, lady, this guy went through all eight grades and high school right here in Carr. He may have had his big-city fling, but he's home now."

"Tom's president of the local bank, China," Maggie put in.

"And a member of every community group around,"

Bernice said proudly, as if she were giving him a recommendation. "Lions, K of C, Community Chest. The town couldn't do without him."

"He's also chairman of the Laney Foundation Board," Maggie added. At my blank look, she added, "The board that manages St. T's trust fund."

As Bernice went back to the kitchen to get the chili, Tom had the grace to look embarrassed. "The bank is one of those small, family-owned banks you hardly ever hear about anymore," he said. "My grandfather established it and turned it over to Dad when he retired. Now it's my turn—or will be, when the old man can't handle it anymore. Sick or not, though, he's still the bank's big cheese. I tell him I'm just filling in until he's able to get back to work."

I was skeptical. The Tom I remembered hated it when somebody else threatened to become a bigger cheese than he was.

Maggie's face was sober. "How is your father, Tom? Dominica told me he has cancer."

"Hanging in there. The doc says he's got six months, more or less. He'll be back at the bank for a few more weeks. After that . . ." He shrugged.

"I'm sorry," I said, and meant it. I'd met his father a time or two and had enjoyed him.

"That's the breaks." He smiled crookedly. "Tell you what. The foundation board is meeting at St. T's on Tuesday morning. Sadie is one of the board members, so she'll be there. After the meeting, we'll go to her place, pick up some horses, and take off into the backcountry for a few hours." His eyes were on mine, searching. "What do you say, China?"

I hesitated. Did I really want to go riding with Tom? Our relationship hadn't so much ended as been broken off, and I'd hungered for him a long time afterward. If I said yes, what would I be letting myself in for?

But Maggie couldn't know about my reservations. "Why

don't you go," she said. "You'll see some country you won't otherwise see."

"I think you should, too, China," Ruby put in unexpectedly. "You might not have another chance."

Tom grinned. "Good," he said. "Tuesday afternoon, then." He looked up with satisfaction as Bernice came in with a bowl of chili. She put it down and turned to Ruby.

"Well now, Sister," she said, "are you ready for some of that pie?"

Outside, a brisk northern breeze was ripping the clouds apart, leaving ragged patches of blue. We had said good-bye to Tom and were about to get into Ruby's car when a man wearing a deputy's badge, a dark blue jacket, and a holstered .357 hurried down the courthouse steps and across the street. He greeted Maggie familiarly, then turned to me. He was a long-nosed man with sagging satchels of skin under bulging brown eyes.

"Stu Walters," he said, thrusting out his hand. "Miz Bayles?"

I nodded.

"Mother Winifred told me you was comin' today. I figgered it was you when I saw Sister Margaret Mary here." He looked down his nose at Maggie. "Haven't seen you around lately, Sister."

Maggie shook her head. "I left the order two years ago, Stu."

The deputy frowned. "You kin do that? Jes' up an' leave, I mean?"

"Yes," Maggie said, smiling slightly. "We're not joined at the hip."

The deputy's puzzlement deepened, as if he were trying to cope with the idea that a nun might not be a nun forever. He gave it up and turned to me. "I was gonna call St. T's in the mornin' an' ask you to come in, Miz Bayles. Guess we kin talk now an' save us both the trouble."

I turned sideways against the wind. The sun was momentarily bright but there was no warmth in it. "What do you want to talk to me about?"

"You don't know?"

"What am I supposed to know?" I said testily. "I've been in your county just long enough to put down an order of chicken-fried steak and onion rings and two cups of Bernice's coffee. If I've broken a law, you'll have to tell me what it is."

He shifted from one foot to the other. "I guess Mother Winifred ain't told you, then."

"Told me what?"

"'Bout one o' her nuns bein' a firebug."

"You think one of the *sisters* is setting those fires?" Maggie exclaimed. "But that's crazy, Stu!"

"'Xactly what I told Mother Winifred," the deputy said. "Trouble is, that kind of crazy is well-nigh impossible to catch unless you jes' happen to be standin' next to her when she flicks her Bic."

Ruby pushed her hands into her sleeves. "Then how do you know it's one of the nuns?"

The deputy gave her a long, squinting look. "Excuse me for sayin' so, Sister, but you ain't in full possession of the facts."

Ruby sighed. "I'm not a sister either."

The deputy had had enough. "Then what's that thing yer wearin'? Yer bathrobe?"

"You're absolutely right," I said hastily. "We're not in possession of the facts, full or otherwise. All we've heard so far are rumors."

He swiveled to look at me. "You ain't talked to Mother Winifred?"

"Not about arson."

"She ain't asked you to look into the fires?"

I shook my head, but the situation was coming clearer. It became crystal clear when the deputy said firmly, "Well, she will."

Great. I had thought I was going on retreat. Instead,

Mother Winifred and God had decided to call me to do an arson investigation. I sighed. "You were the investigating officer at these fires?"

"Yep. Sheriff Donovan's been laid up since he got broadsided by a drunk a couple months ago." He pushed his mouth in and out. "Gotta tell you, though, Miz Bayles. It's real tough to get a fix on what's goin' on out there. Nobody sees nothin', nobody knows nothin', ever'body covers for ever'body else." He looked from Maggie to Ruby. "They don't call you 'sisters' for nothin'."

Ruby opened her mouth and Maggie was about to say something, but I spoke first. "In your mind, Deputy Walters, where exactly do I come into this?"

He scratched his jaw. "Well, Mother Winifred—"

"No," I said, "what do *you* think?"

He puffed his cheeks, debating with himself. Finally he said, "Well, usin' an undercover civilian, 'speshly a woman, ain't somethin' the sheriff's office would norm'ly agree to. But seein's how all the suspects are sisters, an'—"

"Undercover!" Ruby exclaimed excitedly.

Maggie pulled at my sleeve. "I swear, China," she said in a low voice, "I didn't know Mother Winifred was going to ask you to do something like *this*. I thought she meant to ask you to look into the letters."

"What letters?" I asked.

The deputy raised his voice and plowed on. "Seein's how the suspects are all women, I says, yeah, sure, go ahead, find yerself an investigator. Just lemme know so's I can clue her in. Couple days later, she gives me yer name." He hitched up his pants. "I figure what the hell, might as well be you wastin' yer time as me. Them fires was pretty dinky anyway."

I was beginning to get the drift. Baffled and frustrated, Walters had more or less given up on the investigation. And he was trivializing the fires, which was a bad mistake. They might have been minor so far, but fire can be deadly. Dwight might not be around to put out the next one.

I gave Walters a measuring look. "Just what makes you think I can find the arsonist when you've already struck out?"

"'Cause Mother Winifred says you're an experienced investigator." He looked uneasy. "That's right, ain't it? I wasn't expectin' no private license, but you do know what you're doin', don't you?"

"Of course she knows what she's doing," Ruby said. "China is *very* smart."

I turned to Maggie. "What did you tell Mother Winifred about me?"

"I didn't have to tell her anything," Maggie said, half-defensively. "When I mentioned your name and said you wanted to come for a retreat, she knew who you were. She said she'd heard about Rosemary Robbin's murder, and the way you identified the killer." She bit her lip. "But I had no idea she was going to ask you to investigate arson."

"Well, if you've had investigative experience, this little job oughta be a cinch," the deputy said briskly, forgetting that "this little job" had already frustrated him all to hell. "I'll give you a copy of the report an' my notes. All you gotta do is ID the torch an' I'll make the arrest." He frowned. "This don't mean yer offish'ly on the team, though," he added, in case I thought he was inviting me to become one of the Carr County good old boys. "Sheriff says no way kin I dep'tize you, untrained an' a woman an' a ex-lawyer an' all that. You get hurt, you might sue." He narrowed his eyes. "You ain't armed, are you?"

"Not unless you count my cuticle scissors," I said.

"That's good," he said. "Anyhow, you won't need no gun. Firebugs don't go in fer rough stuff. Especially a sister." He waved at a silver Trailways bus pulling up to the corner, belching foul-smelling black smoke. "You won't have no trouble."

"I knew about the letters," Maggie muttered, "but I can't believe a nun would deliberately set a fire."

"*What* letters?" I asked again.

"Letters?" The deputy pulled his eyebrows together. "Somethin' I shoulda bin told about?"

The driver got out of the Trailways bus and began pulling things out of the baggage compartment. An old man draped in an ankle-length brown army overcoat and a short, plump blond woman in jeans and a green parka climbed out and stood, waiting for their luggage.

Ignoring the questions, Maggie turned to me, her mouth set. "The arsonist *has* to be an outsider. I don't want to accuse anybody, but the Townsends certainly have a grudge against—"

"Lemme give you the straight of it, Sister," the deputy broke in, speaking with authority. "The Christmas Eve fire was in the sacristy, behind the altar. There was mebbe twenty people in the chapel besides the nuns an' Father Steven. None of the congregation could git into that sacristy without bein' seen. Nope, the torch is a sister. You kin bet yer boots on it."

Maggie's voice held an edge. "Have you questioned the Townsends? You know how much they hate St. T's. For ten years, they've threatened to—"

"The Thanksgivin' fire was in the kitchen," the deputy said, raising his voice. "Nobody was on the scene but nuns, the good father, an' the maintenance man. Mr. and Miz Townsend was over at their boy's house all day." He smiled toothily at Maggie. "You 'member their boy, I reckon—*Judge* Townsend?"

"What about the maintenance man?" I interrupted. "Did you check him out?"

He shook his head. "Didn't need to. Hadn't of been for Dwight, the whole place mighta burned down. He's not an employee with a grudge, 'f that's what you're thinkin'."

Maggie was about to say something else, but she was

interrupted. The plump woman in the green parka suddenly ran up, flung her arms around Maggie's neck, and cried, ''Oh, Margaret Mary, my prayers have been answered! You've come back!''

And Maggie, calm, serene Maggie, burst into tears.

CHAPTER FOUR

There is a northern legend that bad fairies gave
the blossoms of foxgloves to the fox that he
might put them on his toes to soften his tread
when he prowled among the roosts.

Mrs. M. Grieve
A Modern Herbal

The woman in the green parka was Dominica, the friend
Maggie had mentioned. We were introduced when I came
back from Deputy Walters's office with a copy of the arson
report, and I learned that she'd been in Austin at a two-day
computer school. She had arrived in Carr expecting to call
Dwight to pick her up. But that wasn't necessary now. We
shoved her duffel bag into the trunk of Ruby's Honda and
squeezed her into the backseat, beside Maggie.

"Computer school?" Maggie asked when we'd shut the
doors. She had regained her equilibrium, but her eyes were
still teary.

Dominica's round, pleasant face was flushed and she was
holding on to Maggie's hand. She might have been thirty-
five, but it was hard to tell—she had the kind of youthful
face that doesn't betray age. "It was Reverend Mother General's idea. She put Sister Olivia in charge of the bookkeeping, and Olivia put me in charge of the computer."
She pulled off her green wool cap and shook out her hair.
It was long and a gray ash-blond that added years to her
age—and startled me. I thought nuns had to wear their hair
short. Obviously, I wasn't up to date on monastic hairstyles.

"A *computer*?" Maggie asked wonderingly, as Ruby put the Honda in reverse and backed away from the curb. "Poor Mother Hilaria must be turning over in her grave. She hated the things."

"Oh, the computer's no problem," Dominica said. She ran her fingers through her hair. "It's what we're supposed to do with it that's the problem. Olivia wants us to keep track of everything, down to the number of biscuits we eat every morning." Dominica talked fast, without taking a breath. "She ordered Sister Ruth—she's the new house-keeper—to count all the sheets and towels and bottles of Lysol and scrub brushes and things like that, and I'm sup-posed to enter everything and figure out what it's worth so we'll know how much we've got in assets." She cast her eyes heavenward. "Assets, would you believe? Olivia even told Gabriella to put the garlic into the computer. So we'll know the bottom line, she says."

Ruby pulled onto the highway and headed west. "The bottom line?" I asked. I didn't know that monasteries cared about bottom lines.

Dominica made a face. "Olivia says we can't tell how much money we're losing on the garlic because we've never kept track of what we spend. Which of course makes Sister Gabriella look like she doesn't have a brain in her head."

"Sister Gabriella?" If I was going to keep track of all the sisters, I might need a scorecard.

"Gabriella runs the garlic farm," Maggie reminded me, and I remembered that she was one of the two candidates. Sister Olivia was the other one. Maggie half-frowned. "She knows everything about garlic, and she's always seen to it that the farm pays for itself. I'm sure Olivia doesn't really think—"

"Are you kidding?" Dominica asked sarcastically. "Oli-via *hates* our garlic. And she'd do anything to make Ga-briella look bad in front of Reverend Mother General." Maggie started to say something else but Dominica shook her head firmly. "Don't you lecture me about Christian charity, Margaret Mary. Charity is a virtue that eludes Olivia." She leaned toward Maggie and her voice softened. "I just couldn't believe my eyes when I looked up and saw you standing there, Margaret Mary. It's been two years! Why didn't you tell me you were coming?"

Maggie hesitated. "Because I wasn't sure I would actually do it," she said in a low voice.

I glanced at Maggie. Her eyes flickered away from mine and I sensed, once again, that she had a private purpose for coming. What was it?

"I can't wait to tell you *everything*." Dominica squeezed Maggie's hand and let it go. "I know I should have written," she added repentantly, "but since Olivia assigned me to that wretched computer, I've had precious little time to myself. Would you like to stay in Sister Perpetua's room, next door to me? How long will you be here? At least a month, I hope. It'll take that long for us to catch up." The questions tumbled out in a breathless rush. If Dominica kept on talking so fast, it wouldn't take them a month to catch up—more like a couple of days.

"I don't know where I'm staying. We haven't checked in yet." Maggie tilted her head. "Where's Perpetua?"

"In the infirmary." A shadow crossed Dominica's face. "It's her heart. Doctor Townsend wants to take her to San Antonio for tests."

Ruby executed a right turn onto a two-lane paved road. "Doctor Townsend?" I asked. "Is he any relation to the Townsends who challenged Mrs. Laney's will?"

"Doctor Townsend is Carl and Rena's son," Maggie said. "Their other son—the one Stu Walters mentioned—is a judge. We'll be driving past the Townsends' place. I'll point it out." She looked at Dominica. "When is Perpetua going to San Antonio?"

"She's not. She's seventy-nine, you know. Mother's afraid the trip will do her in." Her mouth twisted down. "If she dies, of course, we're in trouble."

Ruby glanced in the rearview mirror. "In trouble? Why?"

Dominica was grim. "Because Sister Olivia is absolutely, positively determined to be St. T's next abbess. And she will, too, if Sister Perpetua dies."

"I already explained the situation to them," Maggie said.

"It sounds very complicated," Ruby said. "Terribly political."

"It's political, all right," Dominica said. "But there's nothing complicated about it." She sat forward. "As long as there are twenty of us and twenty of them, there's no point in bothering with an election. The St. T sisters will vote for Gabriella, and the St. Agatha sisters will vote for Olivia. If Sister Perpetua dies, though, we'll be down to nineteen. Sister Olivia will be on the phone and Reverend Mother General will have us voting before matins."

"So the Reverend Mother What's-it has a favorite, then?" Ruby asked, shifting down into third for a long uphill climb.

Dominica made a grim face. "You bet she's got a favorite. As far as she's concerned, God has ordained St. T's as the next vacation paradise for Church higher-ups. It's the bottom line again. There's more money in conferences than in garlic, and Sister Olivia is the world's champion conference manager." Her voice became bitter. "Everybody knows that Reverend Mother General brought the St. Agatha sisters here so Olivia could turn St. T's into a moneymaking operation."

"It doesn't sound like St. T's is the peaceful place I imagined," I said. "Back in town, Deputy Walters was telling us about his investigation of the fires."

"Investigation?" Dominica snorted. "That's a joke! Stu Walters wasn't on the scene five minutes before he decided that half of us were suffering from PMS and the rest from postmenopausal nuttiness—and that one of us is a firebug." She shrugged. "What else can I say? We've got a problem. We're all praying about it." She turned back to Maggie.

"I'm more interested in talking about *you,* Margaret Mary. Have you been dating anybody interesting? How's the restaurant?"

I was a little surprised at Dominica's dismissal of the fires. If I lived at St. T's, I'd do more than pray. At the least, I'd be looking over my shoulder, wondering where the arsonist might strike next and making plans to be somewhere else when it happened.

While Maggie and Dominica talked, I sat back and looked at the rugged countryside, its limestone rock carved by dry streams into rocky cliffs and flat meadows, its vegetation sparse. This part of Texas is wild and almost completely undomesticated—not surprising, since it was settled only a century ago. Before the white man arrived with his cattle and plows, the Comanches were in charge of it. But they were nomads, following the migrating buffalo, and their seasonal comings and goings did little to tame the raw land. We haven't made much of an impression on it, either.

In fact, as far as humans are concerned, this part of Texas isn't good for much. There's not enough water, no oil, and despite the rumors of gold that lured Coronado into a long wild-goose chase, limestone is the only resource with any commercial value. Goats do well because they browse the abundant cedar and mesquite, and in the thirties and forties Carr County was the Angora Capital of the World. But there's not much market for angora hair these days, and goats are notoriously footloose. Fence that will hold them costs anywhere from ten to twenty-five thousand dollars a mile—which substantially raises the sticker price on your average sweater.

I grinned to myself. Back to the bottom line. But while this country might not be economically productive, it certainly is *empty*—which makes it perfect for a monastery. And for me, too, at this point in my life. Looking up at a hawk wheeling in the vast spaciousness of sky, I realized how cramped I'd been feeling lately. The shop was too small, the house was confining, my relationship with

McQuaid and Brian seemed always to demand something from me. Out here in this wild, undomesticated land, there was room to roam, room to be free. Out here, it didn't matter what anybody thought, what anybody expected. You could do what you liked. I stretched out in the seat and clasped my hands behind my head. Maybe that was what had brought Tom back.

Tom. Handsome, charming, wheeler-dealer Tom, who had abandoned a promising career to come back to a town the size of a shopping mall. It was an odd thing to do, now that I thought about it. If he'd planned all along to come back and take over the family bank, as he'd claimed at lunch, he'd never mentioned it to me. Maybe there was someone else involved. A woman, maybe.

Ruby must have been reading my mind. She gave me a sidelong glance. "That guy we met at lunch, that Robert Redford look-alike—an old flame, huh?"

"I suppose you might call him that," I said. "It was a long time ago."

"Some flames stay lit. He couldn't stop looking at you."

Ruby is an incurable romantic. If I didn't stop her, she'd go on like this for hours. "Don't be silly," I said. "Tom Rowan and I called it quits eight years ago. Nobody carries a torch for eight years."

She didn't answer right away. A pickup truck passed us, a guy and a girl sitting close, country style. "Did you love him?" she asked finally.

"I suppose so," I said. "Neither of us knew much about loving. We were more worried about getting promoted." I looked out the window. "It's all in the past, Ruby. There's no point in talking about it."

"It doesn't look like he's worried about getting promoted now," she said, as if she hadn't heard the last part. "Does that change anything?"

"Change what?" I asked crossly. "McQuaid and I are living together, for Pete's sake. I haven't thought of Tom for years."

Ruby looked unconvinced. "Well, maybe. But . . ."

"But what?"

"Oh, I don't know," she said vaguely. "I guess I'm just partial to men who look like Robert Redford and sound like Paul Newman. If he was my old flame, I'd be tempted to fan the fire."

I was trying to think of a witty comeback when Maggie tapped me on the shoulder. "That's the Townsends' place," she said, pointing out the right-hand window.

"Hey, that's some house," Ruby said admiringly, and slowed so we could have a good look.

The stately white house—ostentatiously Old South, with a wraparound veranda and neo-plantation columns—was set on several acres of clipped lawn. An ornate iron fence across the front was interrupted by a massive iron gate between brick pillars. The sign beside the gate read "Carl & Rena Townsend, Registered Brahmas." Beneath the words was a drawing of a massive, long-eared bull with a shoulder hump like a 747.

I grinned. "It looks like they're rich enough to eat their laying hens, as McQuaid's mother says."

"They're not only rich, they're powerful," Dominica said. "Carl Townsend has been elected to the County Commissioners Court so many times that nobody bothers to run against him. His wife, Rena, manages the county political organization. Their older son, Royce, is a doctor—and a justice of the peace. The younger son is a lawyer. He was elected county judge last fall."

I was beginning to understand. In Texas, the county commissioners have control over the sheriff's office budget. When the deputy testifies in county court on criminal cases, Judge Townsend is sitting on the bench. And a good relationship with the local JP is essential to making traffic citations and other minor charges stick. The Townsends held every important office in the county. No wonder the deputy wasn't eager to question the Townsends in connection with the fires.

"They're rich, powerful, and *nasty*," Maggie said. "But I have to admit to being biased. They caused Mother Hilaria so much pain."

"You're not biased, you're *right,* Margaret Mary." Dominica was indignant. "Mother would probably still be alive if they hadn't made life so miserable for her. It wasn't the hot plate that killed her—it was *frustration.*" She laughed shortly. "And if she'd known that Royce Townsend was going to pronounce her dead, she'd have told St. Peter to hold off until she got somebody to drive her to the next precinct."

"Royce Townsend?" Ruby asked. "Which one is he?"

"The doctor," Dominica said. "If there was another to be had, we'd have him. Or her."

"He's also a justice of the peace," I said. In Texas, the JP, an elected official, has the job of pronouncing somebody dead. In a rural district, it's convenient to have JP and doctor rolled into one, although some folks might argue that there is an occasional conflict of interest.

We had come to an intersection and Ruby, following Dominica's instructions, turned onto a narrow gravel road. Ahead was a locked gate. Maggie got out, lifted a rock, and found the key. We drove through. On the other side, the gravel road twisted and turned through a rugged landscape colored in somber but beautiful grays and greens and browns. Patches of Indian grass, buffalo grass, and silver bluestem—remnants of the short-grass prairie that once covered these hills—were interspersed with clumps of shinnery oak, mesquite, and cedar. After ten minutes of driving, we came to another gate, this one standing open. Beside it was a simple wooden cross, six feet high. On it was a sign. St. Theresa's Monastery.

I glanced over my shoulder at Maggie. She was taking in the landscape hungrily, as if she were starved for the sight of it. She let her breath escape in a long sigh.

"I feel like Eve being let back into the Garden," she

said as Ruby drove through the gate. "I knew I missed it. I just didn't know how much."

Dominica touched her hand. "Why don't you come back?"

"Maybe I will," Maggie said.

"No kidding?" Ruby asked, startled. I was surprised, too, but not as much as I might have been yesterday. All during the drive, I had sensed some sort of purpose in her. Perhaps this was it.

"I've considered it," Maggie said. Her voice was low. She was looking out the window. "More than once."

Ruby glanced up at her in the rearview mirror. "If you did, you'd swing the election."

"That's right," Dominica said excitedly. "It would be twenty-one to twenty. Do it, Maggie! We could elect Gabriella and raise garlic for the rest of our lives and I could stop putting all those stupid biscuits into the computer."

Maggie frowned. "Hey, come on, now! We're talking about a vocation, not an election."

Dominica shook her head. "Believe me, honey, if this election doesn't come out right, there'll be a lot fewer voca—Look out!"

Ruby locked the brakes and jerked the wheel hard to the right, fighting for control. The Honda's rear end skidded on the wet gravel, slamming my head, hard, into the passenger-side window. The little car rocked onto two wheels and nose-dived down a steep embankment, coming to a stop inches away from a twenty-foot drop-off above white-water rapids.

"Sweet Mother of God!" Dominica breathed.

"Is everybody all right?" Ruby cried anxiously.

"Don't move," I said, looking out the window. "We're hung up on a tree. If we come loose, we'll end up in the river." From below, we could hear the deep-throated noise of water tumbling over the boulders.

"What happened?" Maggie asked in a half-whisper.

White-faced, Ruby was clinging to the steering wheel.

"There were big logs in the road," she said. "I was trying to keep from running into them." She looked at me. "What are we going to do?"

"Pray," Dominica replied promptly. She closed her eyes, clasped her hands under her chin, and began to mutter in a half-audible voice. I sat back, trying to get a fix on our situation. To my right, barely within reach, was a small tree. If I eased the door open, slid out, and grabbed for the tree—

"Hey, down there!" came a rough voice. "Y'all right?"

Dominica's eyes flew open. "There, you see?" she cried triumphantly. "It works every time!"

The answer to Dominica's prayer turned out to be Dwight, St. T's handyman, who had just driven up. He clambered down the hill to survey our predicament, climbed back up, then came down again with a heavy chain. He fastened one end to the Honda and the other to his truck and snaked the car up the hill, the four of us still inside. I don't know about the others, but I felt very nervous while this operation was going on. I could imagine the weight of Ruby's Honda pulling the truck over the edge and landing us on the rocks, with the truck on top of us.

It didn't. When we reached the top and climbed out, I saw why Ruby had swerved. A dozen large logs were scattered at the entry to a narrow bridge, completely blocking the road.

Dwight was a dark, burly man with dirty brown hair, a scar on his stubbled jaw, and a crumpled pack of Camels poking out of the pocket of his plaid shirt. His GMC pickup had a rifle slung in the back window—a modified combat weapon, from the look of it, as macho as he was.

"Sure am sorry about them cedar posts layin' in the middle o' the road," he muttered. He dropped his cigarette and ground it out under his heel. "I was haulin' 'em out to where I'm buildin' some new fence. When I got there, the load was half-gone. Figgered I musta dropped 'em off the truck an' come back to see."

"That's okay," Dominica said. "We're just glad that

God brought you along when we needed you.''

"Yeah. It was real lucky." Dwight's shrewd grin showed two broken, tobacco-stained front teeth. "You goin' to tell Mother Winifred 'bout how I drug y'all up that drop-off?''

She nodded, and Maggie said, "Of course. We're very grateful to you, Dwight.''

"We sure are," Ruby said earnestly. "I hate to think how long we might have hung there on that cliff—*if* we'd hung there." She glanced down at the river and shuddered.

"Good," he said, and unhooked the tow chain. "Don't hurt none fer a man to be rekkanized fer helpin' folks out."

I frowned. Dwight had been there to help when the fires broke out, too. While we gave Dwight a hand with the fence posts, I wondered if there was any connection.

When the road was clear, we got back in the Honda. "How far is it?" Ruby asked nervously.

"We're almost there," Maggie said. We drove down the road a hundred yards, through an oak grove, and saw the ranch house ahead of us.

"That's Sophia," Dominica said. The house was a single-story, multiwinged building, large and sprawling. It was constructed of native limestone and cedar, with porches on three sides and a metal roof painted barn red. "It's the main building," she added. "The refectory and the kitchen are there, and Mother's office and the library and a couple of guest rooms.''

"Sophia?" I asked, puzzled.

"You'll get used to it," Maggie said with a smile. "In most monasteries, everything has names—the buildings and the rooms, the paths, the gardens, even the trees. It's true here, too. That barn, for instance. It's called Jacob.''

The picturesque red barn stood to the left of the ranch house. To the right was another long, low, stone-and-cedar building, with an addition built at right angles to it—Rebecca, according to Dominica, where the St. T sisters lived. She also pointed out Hannah, a dormlike brick residence hall behind a clump of oaks, where the St. Agatha sisters lived.

"You're still living separately?" Maggie asked, surprised. "I thought you were all going to move into Hannah."

"Maybe that's part of the problem," Ruby said, following the long, curving drive around Sophia. "If you and the St. Agatha sisters lived together, you might get along better."

"That's what Mother Hilaria said," Dominica said. "Just before she died, she reassigned us. But afterward, Olivia convinced Reverend Mother General that we ought to wait until her successor took over."

"That's unfortunate," Maggie said. "The longer the two groups are separated, the easier it is to stay that way, if only because there's less tension."

"Less tension?" Dominica shook her head. "Don't count on it. Even separated, we're at one another's throats. Figuratively speaking, of course. Although sometimes I wonder." Abruptly, she leaned forward and changed the subject. "Margaret Mary tells me you're an herbalist, China. What do you know about foxglove? I understand it's poisonous."

"You bet," I said emphatically. "It used to be called Dead Men's bells." The name was a reference to foxglove's bell-shaped blossom, as well as to the knell that was rung for the dearly departed. "Why do you ask?"

"Because I heard someplace that it can be confused with other plants. It affects the heart, doesn't it? Like digitalis?"

"It *is* digitalis," I said. Foxglove is a cardiac herb. It contains four glycosides, the most powerful of which is digitoxin, a stimulant that increases cardiac activity, causing the heart and arteries to contract and raising the blood pressure. Why was Dominica asking about it? "Foxglove is a lovely ornamental," I added, "but it shouldn't be used as a medicinal. There's too much danger of making a fatal mistake."

Ruby pulled into a parking lot and stopped the car. "We're here," she said, and opened the door.

I got out, intending to ask Dominica why she was so interested in foxglove. But I was distracted by two women who seemed to be having an argument a short distance away. One wore a navy coat with a gold cross in her lapel, a starched wimple, and a short veil. Her arms were full of file folders. The other wore jeans, a Cowboys sweatshirt, and knee-high rubber boots. She was pushing a wheelbarrow full of empty terra-cotta pots. Both had angry faces and set mouths. They were scowling at one another.

"Uh-oh," Dominica whispered as Ruby opened the trunk. "They're at one another again."

"Who are they?" I asked.

"That's Sister Gabriella with the wheelbarrow. The one with the file folders probably started it—she's Sister Olivia. Our next abbess, if Reverend Mother General has her way." Dominica sighed. "And she will, unless somebody does something to prevent it." She squeezed her eyes shut. "Please, God," she whispered urgently. "*Do* something!"

Given Dominica's track record, I wouldn't have been surprised to see Olivia struck down by a bolt of lightning. Dominica opened her eyes. "Sometimes it takes a while," she said.

"My grandmother had an old saying," Ruby remarked sagely. "God helps those who help themselves."

Dominica considered this. "My grandmother had another. With the fox, play the fox." She narrowed her eyes. "There *must* be a way to get rid of her."

I get the jitters when people talk that way.

CHAPTER FIVE

> Rue lends second sight. If you carry a bundle of
> it, mixed with broom, maidenhair, agrimony, and
> ground-ivy, you will be able to see a person's
> heart and know whether she is a witch.
>
> Medieval folk saying

The argument ended, obviously without a resolution. Sister
Gabriella turned on her heel and strode angrily away, pushing her wheelbarrow as if she were powered by the wrath
of God.

Sister Olivia raised her head and saw us. The flush spread
over her cheeks and her eyes became steely behind her
gold-rimmed glasses. She marched in our direction, shoulders back, spine erect, with a look that reminded me of
General Patton. But under her stiffness, I saw a deep hurt.
Whatever she and Sister Gabriella had been arguing about,
it had pained her. I wondered how much emotional effort
it took to maintain the stern exterior that hid her feelings.

To Dominica, she said crisply, "Put your bag in your
room and come to the office, Sister. We've fallen behind
while you've been away." To the rest of us, she gave a
thin smile. "Welcome to St. Theresa's. You'll need to
check in with Mother Winifred. Her cottage is down that
path." She turned on her heel and marched off.

Ruby raised her eyebrows. "Somewhat abrupt, wouldn't
you say?"

"She's a witch," Dominica said feelingly, taking her bag
out of the trunk. She looked at Maggie. "Ask Mother for

Perpetua's room, won't you? It would be wonderful to be close together. We've got so much to talk about. There are things going on here that you wouldn't—'' She broke off with a glance at me. ''We just really need to talk,'' she finished lamely.

When Dominica had gone off, Ruby and I followed Maggie down a gravel path that led past a statue of St. Francis, through a small oak grove, and across a grassy meadow bordered with weeping willows and cottonwoods. At the foot of the meadow I could see the Yucca River, a broad band of rippling silver glinting in the pale afternoon sun, and on the other side, the high south bank, a spectacular cliff festooned with ferns and rimmed with cedar trees. It was as lovely as a garden.

''The Townsend Ranch boundary runs along up there,'' Maggie said, pointing to the top of the cliff. She pulled her jacket closer around her and pointed in the other direction. ''And that's the garlic field.''

The expanse of rich brown soil, perhaps five or six acres, was sliced lengthwise by furrows of blue-green spikes, already a foot high. St. Theresa's famous rocambole, preparing to fling itself into another growing season.

It might be the last, if Dominica was right about the order's plans. St. T's had the beauty of a remote paradise, but it could be reached from either coast in a matter of hours. It also had a treasure chest fat enough to finance whatever the Reverend Mother General wanted in the way of a plush retreat center—if the Laney Foundation Board could be coerced into going along with the scheme. Not to mention an abbess-in-waiting who was eager to get started. Give Sister Olivia the go-ahead and three years to construct a small but luxurious residence and visitor center, a spa, golf course, and tennis courts, and every American bishop would be packing his golf clubs for a leisurely visit. Give her five years, a decent golf pro, and plenty of rain on the greens, and the entire Vatican would be here.

But all that development would cost something—and not

just money, either. I could imagine what this lovely place would look like in ten years. The garlic field would be gone, the flat, rich earth paved over for tennis courts and parking. The picturesque red barn would be replaced by an auditorium, chapel, and conference rooms, and the visitor residence would fill the meadow we were crossing. And the sisters could forget about their contemplative life. They'd be so busy tending prelates they wouldn't have time to pray.

I was considering this sad scenario when we turned a corner and were nearly run down by a wheelbarrow loaded with filled seed trays. Behind it was Sister Gabriella, moving with a fierce energy that suggested she hadn't quite forgiven Sister Olivia for whatever had sparked their argument.

"Whoops, sorry!" She dropped the wheelbarrow with a thud and pushed her windblown dark hair out of her eyes. "I should have been looking where I was—" Her tanned face broke into a smile. "Margaret Mary, bless you!" she exclaimed. "It's good to see you!"

Gabriella enveloped Maggie in a warm embrace, then turned to Ruby and me. As Maggie introduced us, she held out a dirty, garden-worn hand, her nails every bit as unspeakable as mine. I saw that her dark hair was liberally streaked with gray, and revised my estimate of her age. She was probably closer to sixty than fifty.

"When you get a little time," she said to me, "drop by my office in Jacob and let me give you a tour of our garlic operation." She paused, eyeing me. "Unless of course you're here to get away from herbs, in which case you probably don't want—"

"No," I said hastily. "It's the pressure I'm trying to get away from, Sister, not the plants."

Her grin was infectious. "Lord knows, we all need to go over the wall every so often."

"You're questioning your vocation?" Maggie asked teasingly.

Gabriella's weathered face grew serious. "Only a fool doesn't question her vocation—minute by minute. And God's got plenty of fools. She doesn't need another one." She picked up the wheelbarrow handles, nodded a cheerful good-bye, and started up the path. As she went around the corner, she began whistling, "We're Off to See the Wizard."

We went in the other direction. As we walked, Ruby said, "Why in heaven's name don't the St. Agatha sisters vote for *her*?"

"It's the vow of obedience," Maggie said. "Until a few years ago, novices were taught to obey their superiors whether they agreed with them or not. When you're trained to obey, questioning authority feels like you're questioning God. The St. Agatha sisters, especially the older ones, wouldn't even consider voting for anybody but Olivia." She paused. "And they're all older, come to think of it. When I was there a few years ago, I don't think I saw anybody younger than fifty."

We had reached a small cottage. Maggie was raising her hand to knock at the door when it was flung open wide by a tiny, stooped woman in a white blouse and trim navy slacks, less than five feet tall. Her darting eyes were an electric blue, and she had flyaway white hair and an elvish face. She welcomed Maggie like a long-lost daughter, and greeted Ruby and me with enthusiasm.

"Please, come in and sit down, all of you," she said, ushering us into the warm, cozy room. "Did you have an uneventful trip?"

"Actually, it was full of events," Maggie said wryly, and told her about our accident.

"We were lucky," Ruby said. "If the car had gone over, we might have been pretty badly hurt. Believe me, I was awfully glad to see your handyman."

"It was providential that Dwight came along when he did," Mother replied. She went to a hot plate and took off a steaming kettle. "You need a nice cup of peppermint tea to settle your nerves."

In a moment, Mother Winifred had poured our tea and settled us at a table in front of an uncurtained casement window which looked out over a square expanse of stone-walled garden. In the middle was a large circular bed, centered with a stone statue of Mary and divided into pie-shaped wedges by red bricks. Gardens are subdued in winter, but this one was still lovely. I could see the layered mounds of santolina, the silvery velvet of lamb's ears, and the stiff gray-green of lavender bushes, striking against the ferny green of tansy and yarrow and the feathery leaves of southernwood. And there was blue-green rue, a lively companion to a large potted rosemary that had been expertly trained into a neat, conical topiary. Nearby were several other untrimmed rosemaries, exuberantly green against the stone wall. In this part of Texas, they'd likely make it through the winter outdoors. Much farther north or west, it was another story.

"A pity the wind is so chilly today," Mother Winifred remarked. "Perhaps tomorrow it will be comfortable enough to walk in the garden." She looked out the window. "It looks a bit bleak now, but in the summer, it is really quite beautiful."

"Even in the winter," I said. "The design is classic."

The walled square contained five gardens, one in each corner and one in the middle. The corner to the right was the kitchen garden, bordered by mounds of thyme, with clumps of marjoram and parsley and sage in the center and a handsome rosemary at the back. One of the back corners was a fragrance garden, with old roses climbing against the stone wall. The other was a dyers' garden, with teasel— not a dye plant, actually, but used by weavers to tease fibers—and madder and woad, a sprawling, noxious weed that has to be carefully contained.

"The apothecary garden interests me most." Mother Winifred pointed to the fourth corner. "We have quite a few medicinals. Peppermint for an upset stomach, catnip and chamomile for a sound sleep. As well as sage, foxglove, rue, comfrey, pennyroyal, feverfew—"

"Mother also has a stillroom," Maggie said. "That's where the sisters make salves and lotions."

"A growing number are interested in herbal medicines," Mother Winifred said. "I try to keep up on current research, and several of the sisters enjoy trying out old recipes. We have quite an extensive shelf of reference books, if you'd care to see them."

"I would, thank you," I said. "I'd like to see your stillroom, too." It was pleasant to sit here in the warmth, sipping tea and talking about gardens. But there was something else to be done, and we might as well get to it. I pushed my cup away. "We ran into Deputy Walters in town," I said. "He told us about the fires. He also said you wanted me to look into them. Is that right?"

A look of consternation crossed Mother Winifred's face. "Oh, dear," she said. "I wanted to be the first to tell you."

So it was true. I sighed. "The fires are the 'minor mystery' you mentioned on the phone?"

Mother Winifred fixed her bright, birdlike eyes on me. "I hope you'll forgive me, China. I've been duplicitous."

"If you don't mind my saying so, Mother," I said, "arson isn't a minor matter. Especially in a place like this, with so many people living so close together."

"You're right, of course." She gestured at a telephone on the wall. "The difficulty is that we have only two phones here—this one and the one in the main office in Sophia. They're on the same line. I needed to let you know that I had a special reason for wanting you to come, but I was afraid our conversation might be overheard."

"You thought someone might be listening? Who?"

Mother Winifred shifted uncomfortably. "Something troublesome and dangerous is going on here. I understand that you have been helpful to the police on several different occasions, and that you have a background in criminal law.

And since you wanted to make a retreat here, I felt you were the right person to help us.''

Ruby leaned forward. ''China is *very* good at solving mysteries. And I'm always glad to help.'' She made a face. ''It's really too bad that I can't stay. If I hadn't already made plans—''

I shook my head. ''What Mother Winifred needs is a trained arson investigator, Ruby. Someone who—''

''But it's not just the fires, China,'' Maggie broke in. She folded her arms on the table. ''Tell her about the letters, Mother.''

Mother Winifred shifted nervously. ''Yes. Well, the letters are really quite distressing. They have the potential to make a difficult situation much worse.''

I took a deep breath. The matter was obviously quite complicated, but we had to start somewhere. ''Let's begin with the fires, shall we?'' I said. ''I know something about them already.''

''Of course. The fire in the craft room in the barn—that was in October—started with an electrical short. Dwight said he thought it was accidental, so after he repaired the short, I wasn't especially concerned. Sister Gabriella wondered whether there might be something more to it, but I'm afraid I rather brushed her suspicions aside.''

''The second fire was at Thanksgiving?'' Ruby asked.

''Yes. It had to have been deliberately set. A large pan of cooking oil was placed on the stove and the burner turned on high—something our kitchen staff would never *think* of doing. No one was ever in danger, fortunately. Our meal was over and the kitchen crew had finished. There was nobody in the building.''

''Except Dwight,'' I remarked. I frowned. ''And Father Steven. Is that right?''

She nodded. ''Father Steven had been here for dinner. They were both outside, talking. Dwight smelled smoke and ran in and put a lid on the pot. There was no actual fire damage, but we had to repaint the kitchen. The fire was obviously deliberate. I thought we'd better have Deputy Walters take a look.'' She made a face. ''For all the good it did us.''

''Was Father Steven here when the fire started in the barn?''

Mother Winifred looked at me, shocked. ''You're not suggesting—''

''I'm just asking.''

She hesitated. ''Actually, I'm not sure whether he was here that day or not. Perhaps you should ask Gabriella. She might remember.''

''But he was here the night of the chapel fire.''

''Yes. It was Christmas Eve, and he was preparing to say Mass. That fire was also deliberate, I'm afraid. A candle was placed close to a curtain in the sacristy.'' Her face was distressed. ''We *must* identify the person who is doing this. She is mentally unbalanced. She needs help.''

Maggie frowned. ''Why does the arsonist have to be one of the sisters, Mother? How about Carl Townsend? I was in Mother Hilaria's office one morning when he stormed in, mad enough to throttle her. Now he's lost the battle over Mrs. Laney's will, and Mother Hilaria is beyond his reach. Setting a fire is the sort of thing he would do.''

Mother Winifred was dubious. ''I don't know—I mean, I really don't think...'' She clasped her hands with a heavy sigh. ''But I suppose anything is possible. Carl and Rena Townsend *were* here on Christmas Eve. Rather unexpectedly, too, I might add. Not at the other times, though. At least not to my knowledge.''

''But there are two other Townsends.'' Maggie leaned forward. ''How about Royce?''

''Doctor Townsend?'' Mother frowned. ''Since Perpetua fell ill, he's been here quite often. Whether he was here when the fires broke out—You must ask Sister Rowena. She's our infirmarian. I'm sure she keeps track of his visits.'' She shook her head. ''Really, Margaret Mary, I can't see a *doctor* setting fire to our chapel. Can you?''

"Can you see a nun doing it, Mother?" Maggie asked bleakly.

Mother Winifred's hand went to her mouth. "Oh, dear," she whispered.

It was time to ask another question—one that had been at the back of my mind for several hours. "Mother Hilaria's death—you're absolutely sure it was an accident?"

Mother took a deep breath. "Oh, there's no doubt about that," she said. "The hot plate was quite old, and it's no surprise that it malfunctioned. Doctor Townsend said the shock probably wouldn't have been fatal if she hadn't been standing in some spilled milk. And of course she had a bad heart, and high blood pressure too. She was trying to untangle the financial business you see. She was under a great deal of stress."

"Could I have a.look at the hot plate?"

"I'm sure it's in Sister Ruth's storeroom." Mother Winifred smiled wryly. "It takes God's signature on a piece of paper to get our housekeeper to throw anything away. I'll ask her to show it to you."

I came back to the arson. "So you agree with Deputy Walters that the fires are an inside job?"

She glanced reluctantly at Maggie. "Yes, I'm afraid so. I understand your arguments, Margaret Mary, and the Lord knows that Carl Townsend isn't one of my favorite people. I just don't believe that someone from the outside could have set the fires without being seen." Her voice became firm. "And of course Deputy Walters isn't at all the right sort of person for an investigation like this—an inside job, as you say. You have to be *shrewd*. You have to listen and detect things cunningly, the way Brother Cadfael does. You've read the books about him, I'm sure—the medieval monk who grows herbs and solves mysteries." She looked at me brightly. "I'm confident that you'll do a much better job than Deputy Walters."

"I'm not Brother Cadfael."

Her smile was winsome. "But you're the detective God

saw fit to send us. The handmaid of the Lord.''

I had never pictured myself the handmaid of the Lord. If the Deity had picked me out of a lineup of potential detectives, He—or She, if you were of Sister Gabriella's persuasion—must need glasses. But it was probably futile to resist. I thought of what happened to Jonah, who refused a first-class ticket to Nineveh and wound up going steerage in the belly of a whale.

"Do you have any suspects, Mother?" I asked. "Perhaps a sister who is behaving erratically?"

Mother looked weary. "Lately, we've all been behaving erratically. It's the strain of merging two very different communities and trying to create some sort of shared future.'' She pursed her lips. "But no. I have no suspects.''

"Or to put it another way," Ruby said sagely, "everybody is a suspect.''

Mother's eyes were sad. "I am afraid you're right, my child.''

"You've alerted the sisters to watch for suspicious behavior?" I asked.

"Yes, although my warning may have made things worse. People are already apprehensive and suspicious.'' She paused. "And please remember that we are monastics. We spend a great deal of time alone. It would be easy for one of us to set a fire.''

Maggie's fingers tightened on her cup. Her voice was tense. "Or push a letter under a door.''

I glanced at her, then back to Mother. "Tell me about the letters.''

"In July," Mother said, "Sister Perpetua went to see Mother Hilaria. Perpetua was terribly distressed. She had received a letter accusing her of stealing a book of psalms from the library in Sophia. She had apparently forgotten to check it out.''

"Forgetting isn't a sin!" Ruby exclaimed, indignant. "She didn't intend to steal it, did she?''

"Of course not. That's what Mother Hilaria told her. But

Perpetua felt that the letter-writer was accusing her for the good of her soul, as we used to do in the Chapter of Faults." She glanced up. "Do you know about that practice?"

"Maggie told us," Ruby said. "It sounds pretty barbaric."

"Not if it's done in the spirit of Christian love," Mother Winifred said. "Chapter of Faults was a way of airing minor problems before they became major. Although I have to admit——" She stopped and shook herself. "But that's beside the point. The letter was written in the somewhat archaic language of the Chapter of Faults. 'I accuse you of the theft of a book of psalms from the library.' It instructed Perpetua to confess and make a public penance—to stand at the door of the refectory every mealtime for a week, holding the book. Given her age and physical condition, it was a rather stiff penance."

"Where is the letter?"

"Mother destroyed it. She kept the next one, however. Two others were brought to me several weeks ago."

"May I see them?" I asked.

Mother Winifred produced a key and unlocked a desk drawer. Each of the three envelopes she placed on the table contained a sheet of plain white paper. The messages, brief and explicit and accusatory, were printed in black ink in block letters. The first was dated August 15 and addressed to Sister Anne.

> *I accuse you of lewd behavior, of baring your nakedness when you were bathing in the river yesterday. You must make confession, and in penance, resume your full habit.*

My eyebrows went up. "Sister Anne was swimming nude?"

"Hardly." Mother coughed delicately. "Her suit was rather revealing. One makes allowances for modern customs, however, and our swimming spot *is* private. The penance was quite out of the question for Anne, who gave up

the habit some years ago. In any event the letter-writer had
no authority to demand a penance. Mother told Sister Anne
to disregard the letter. But a week later, somebody stole her
swimsuit out of her room.'' Her tone filled with distaste.
''It was found hanging from the cross in the chapel,
smeared at certain strategic places with what looked like
. . . blood. It turned out to be ketchup.''

Ruby made a face. ''How obscene!''

Obscene, but not particularly threatening. Still, in a
closed community where the atmosphere had already been
poisoned . . .

''There was quite a furor among the older nuns,'' Mother
Winifred went on. ''It was several days before things got
back to normal.''

Maggie pushed the other letters at me. ''There's more,''
she said tersely.

The second and third letters, one addressed to Sister
Dominica and the other to Sister Miriam, were dated December 2 and printed in the same block letters. They were
identical. I read one aloud.

> *I charge you with indulging in a particular*
> *friendship. Your lewd and lascivious behavior*
> *must be punished by public exposure and removal*
> *to separate houses elsewhere in the order.*

''That's crazy,'' Ruby said, bewildered. ''What's so
lewd and lascivious about friendship?''

Maggie opened her mouth to answer, but Mother Winifred silenced her with a look. ''When we live in community, Ruby, it is important for us to care equally about
everyone. A 'particular friendship' is the term we give to
a relationship that becomes so intense that the two friends
forget their obligation to others.''

Maggie's lips had tightened. ''It's a lesbian relationship,'' she said quietly.

There were two bright spots of color on Mother's weathered cheeks. ''Margaret Mary, must you always be so de-
finitive? Not all particular friendships involve . . . sex.''

"Lesbian relationships don't always involve sex, either," Maggie said bluntly. "But they do involve passionate feeling. And human passion, whether it's heterosexual or otherwise, makes the Church very uncomfortable. People who are devoted to God are supposed to be passionate only about God."

"What happens if people get passionate about one another?" Ruby asked.

"What happens to priests who want to marry?" Maggie asked with a shrug.

"In the past," Mother said quietly, "nuns have been expelled from the order for being particular friends."

Maggie gave me a straight, clear look. "Or they have voluntarily abandoned their vocations."

"I see," I said. Suddenly I saw a lot of things.

Maggie cleared her throat. "There's no point being oblique about this," she said. "Dominica and I were once very close. I wanted us to be even closer, but Dominica felt—" She stopped. "It wasn't what she wanted. I didn't know how to handle it, and things got pretty uncomfortable between us." She took a deep breath. "I began to think of finding another house somewhere else in the order. Then my father died and left me the money. As I said, it seemed like a sign that it was time to go back to the world."

"But you and Dominica have kept in touch," Ruby said sympathetically.

Maggie nodded. "We write to one another a couple of times a month. She wrote the day after she and Miriam received the anonymous letters. She was quite upset, as you can imagine. She says that the accusation isn't true, but of course it's impossible for her and Miriam to defend themselves. If their accuser wants to make trouble, she can—especially if Olivia becomes abbess." She closed her eyes briefly, opened them again. "She's known to be very strict about particular friends. If it was Olivia's decision, they'd be transferred immediately."

"Just like that?" Ruby asked in surprise. "But what if they don't want to go?"

"We have made a vow of obedience, my child," Mother Winifred said mildly. "If our superiors feel we would be of greater usefulness elsewhere in the order . . ."

Ruby's eyes flashed. "But that's not fair! St. Theresa is their home!"

"Nobody asked the St. Agatha sisters if they wanted to move," I said.

"Dominica was one of the first sisters to come to St. T's," Maggie said. "Leaving would be very difficult for her."

"I pray it doesn't come to that," Mother said.

Maggie's face was grim. "We might have to do more than pray, Mother."

I looked down at the letters spread on the table in front of us. "How were these delivered?"

"They were slipped under the doors sometime during the night," Mother Winifred said. She shook a leaf from one of the envelopes. "Each one also contained a pressed leaf."

I picked up the leaf and turned it in my fingers. "Rue," I said.

"The herb of grace, Shakespeare called it," Mother said bleakly. "There's no grace in this matter, I fear."

In the early church, rue was dipped in holy water and shaken in front of the doors and in the aisles to repel demons and evil. It was also believed to be an antidote to poison, and in medieval Europe, was thought to be capable of revealing who among your friends was a witch. By the sixteenth century, the plant had come to be associated with the idea of ruefulness and repentance, with sorrow for one's wrongdoing. Perhaps that was why the poison-pen writer had put it into the envelopes. Rue, regret, repentance, grace. It was a powerful symbol.

I glanced out the window. Rue was growing in the apothecary garden, its leaves glowing blue-green against the wintry foliage. "Is the plant grown anywhere else on the grounds?"

"No." Mother Winifred anticipated my next question. "I'll give you the names of the sisters who work in the garden. But many use it for prayer, and the gate is never locked. Anyone might have picked a few leaves."

I looked down at the letters. "The three recipients accused—are they St. Agatha or St. T sisters, or both?"

"They're all St. T sisters," Mother Winifred said sadly. "I'm afraid that's not a coincidence." Her voice trembled. "You can see the difficulty we're in. We are a deeply divided community, both sides resentful of the changes imposed on us by our merger. The fires have made us suspicious and fearful. And these letters—" She gave me a pleading look. "We *must* discover who is responsible, China. You will help us, won't you?"

I sighed, thinking again of Jonah. "I'm not sure what I can do," I said. "But I'll try."

Mother's face relaxed into a smile. She looked as if I had just turned water into wine. "God's blessing on you, my child."

"There's a condition," I said. "I want you to tell the sisters who I am and what you've asked me to do, and that I'll be talking with several of them. In particular, I need to talk to those who have received the letters."

"Sister Perpetua is very ill, but I could take you to her this evening."

"Thank you. And please ask everyone to bring me any information they may have about either the fires or the letters."

"I thought you were going to be undercover," Ruby said.

Mother frowned. "That's right. Won't an announcement give you away? Won't it alert whoever's behind this?"

"Yes," I said. "But it may also rattle them. People who are rattled are more likely to make mistakes."

Maggie looked at me. "So you think there are two separate crimes here? Arson and . . ." She paused, frowning. "Is it a crime to write a poison-pen letter?"

I shook my head. "None of these letters threaten actual violence. They're not criminal, at least according to the Texas Penal Code."

"Criminal or not," Mother said firmly, "the letters *are* violent. They disrupt the recipients' peace of mind and threaten the stability of the community. And the writer is placing her soul in jeopardy. We must find out who she is. I'll speak to the community tonight at supper, China, and tell them that you're here to help us." She paused. "There's something else I should mention. Mother Hilaria's diary."

"Her diary?"

"Yes. A spiral-bound notebook, black, as I recall. Every evening, she was in the habit of jotting down the events of the day, the weather, her meetings with individuals, her plans. After Reverend Mother General appointed me, I went to Mother Hilaria's office to get it. I thought I should see whether there were any ongoing projects I should know about. The diary was gone. I've searched everywhere, but it hasn't turned up."

"Can you think who might have taken it?" I asked.

"No, nor why. Mother Hilaria was a very open person. She didn't have any secrets."

If she did, they'd stay that way. Mother Hilaria was dead.

CHAPTER SIX

If gun-flints are wiped with rue and vervain, the
shot must surely reach the intended victim, regardless of the shooter's aim.

C. M. Skinner
*Myths and Legends of Flowers,
Trees, Fruits, and Plants*

I asked for a roster of room assignments and a map of the
monastery's grounds. Mother also gave us an information
sheet and keys to our cottages. Maggie was staying in Ezra.
Ruby, who was here just for the night, was in Ezekiel. I'd
been assigned to Jeremiah.

As we were leaving, I thought of one more thing. "I
promised a certain young Cowboys' fan that I'd put in a
prayer request for tomorrow's game," I said. "Maybe it
sounds a little strange, but would you mind—"

"Not at all," Mother Winifred said with a smile. "In
fact, I believe that Sister Gabriella has already been praying
for them. But God moves in mysterious ways, you know,"
she added. "Tell your young friend that we can triumph
even in defeat."

I didn't think Brian would buy that idea, but I only
smiled and nodded.

Ezra, Jeremiah, and Ezekiel were a mile from the main
complex by road, although the hand-drawn map revealed a
shorter trail through the meadow. We drove, then parked
the car and grabbed our bags, agreeing to meet again just
before six. "You'll hear the bell outside Sophia," Maggie

told us. "It's rung for every meal." Then we split up to go to our separate cottages, which were about fifty yards apart along the river.

Jeremiah was a wood-shingled cottage with a screened porch. Its two small rooms—a bedroom-sitting room and a bathroom-dressing room—were clean and simply furnished, with a bed, an upholstered chair, and a wooden desk and chair. There were brown plaid drapes at the windows and a crucifix on the wall. In the bathroom was a Texas-sized cast-iron bathtub with old-fashioned claw feet, almost big enough to swim in. On the bathroom shelf, I saw a hot plate, a coffeepot, and a cache of tea and coffee supplies. The cottage was surrounded on three sides by a dense growth of cedar. The porch looked out over the river only ten yards away, at the foot of a gravel path. I imagined myself sitting there in the evening, listening to the water and watching the sun set behind the high cliff.

I spent a luxurious half hour hanging up my clothes, organizing the books and other belongings I'd brought, and making up my narrow bed with the sheets I found folded on the pillow. Then I sank into the chair and gazed around the room, letting its clean spareness sink into me, its healing silence wash over me. It had been so long since I'd been alone, truly *alone*—no other people, no telephone, no television, no radio. I could picture myself sitting here in quiet meditation for days on end, writing in my journal, reading a little, sleeping a lot.

But I sat for only a few minutes. The conversation with Mother Winifred weighed heavily on my mind. The accusing letters seemed to be the most pressing problem from her point of view. But while poison-pen letters are spiteful and traumatic, arson can be fatal. The fires had to be stopped before somebody burned to death.

I got up and found the handwritten report I'd gotten from the sheriff's deputy, which turned out to be very sketchy and nearly illegible. Walters hadn't been called to the October fire, because Mother Winifred had decided it was accidental. He'd been called after the other two fires, however.

I read the report and made a list of the people Walters had talked to, noting the names of the three people who had shown up at both scenes. Dwight was one, which wasn't surprising, since it was his job to be available for emergencies. Father Steven was another. Sister John Roberta, whose name I hadn't previously heard, was the third. I looked her up in the roster and decided she must be a St. Agatha nun, since she lived in Hannah.

I put the report aside and stood up and stretched. Three fires had been set in a community where forty nuns lived within arm's length of one another. Somebody was bound to know *something*. I was hoping that tonight's announcement would jar loose some essential piece of information. I wanted to get to the bottom of this thing and spend the rest of my time doing what I had come to do: nothing. I smiled wistfully. Two whole weeks with absolutely nothing to do. Except, of course, for going riding with Tom Rowan.

The thought made me restless. I pulled on my jacket and walked down the gravel path to the river's edge, where I stood for a few minutes, hands in pockets, breathing in the spicy fragrance of cedar, the crisp, clean smell of windswept meadow.

How well had I known Tom Rowan? At the time, of course, I'd thought we were intimate. We certainly talked enough over the restaurant meals we shared after work, and during the late-night hours when we lay in one another's arms. But now, with the clarity of hindsight, I had to admit that we hadn't been intimate at all—that we hadn't known the first thing about intimacy. Mostly, we'd talked about our careers, about work—who had won that day's battles, who had lost, how we had somehow managed to come out on top. And beneath the talk there was always a hard, brittle edge of competitiveness. Tom was poised to top my story about the day's achievements; I was ready to do him one better. We'd been lovers, yes, but our relationship probably had more to do with sex and power than with love.

Now, thanks to McQuaid, I knew a little more about intimacy—enough to realize that what Tom and I had back then was the kind of shallow, casual relationship that career people often substitute for genuine caring. To give us credit, of course, neither of us had much choice in the matter. When you're on your way to the top, the climb occupies most of your waking hours and a big hunk of your dream time. It's practically impossible to have both a rising career and a deeply engaged relationship. It was for me, anyway.

I made a wry face. When I left my career and found McQuaid, I'd gotten what I wanted: a warm and nurturing connection that grounded me and held me close. The irony was, though, that being held close also made it hard to find space for myself, and being grounded made it tough to fly free. It was a dilemma a lot of women might welcome, but not me.

I thought back on the lunchtime meeting. Leaving the city and coming back to rural Texas must have been hard for Tom, after all those glittering successes in Houston. What had brought him here? What kept him here?

I looked around and saw part of my answer. This part of Texas has to be one of the most beautiful spots on earth. The Yucca River rippling at my feet was a broad, shallow stream, bordered with mesquite and cedar. Across the stream rose the rugged limestone cliff I had seen earlier, fringed with willows and hung with maidenhair fern. It was a Garden of Eden, a paradise of peace and profound tranquillity, punctuated only by the inquisitive whistle of a mockingbird and the soft, sweet whisper of—

Ka-boom!

I ducked for cover behind the nearest boulder as the high-pitched ricochet whined over my head. Somebody was shooting at me!

I poked my head cautiously over the rock, which was barely big enough to hide me. "Hey!" I yelled, indignant. "What the hell do you think you're—"

A second report, followed by the flat, hard slap of a bullet hitting the water ten yards to my left.

I ducked down. The shooter was on the cliff on the other side of the river. The Townsend side. Was it one of the Townsends up there, carelessly enjoying some Saturday afternoon target practice? "Hey, lay off, you idiot!" I yelled. "You're going to kill somebody!"

When the third shot came and the bullet thwacked into the trunk of the cottonwood six feet to my right, I didn't wait around. I scrambled over the rocks to a thick clump of willows, where I flopped on my stomach and caught my breath.

Paradise, huh? I thought darkly. Garden of Eden? Well, where there are gardens, there are snakes. And one of them was holed up on the cliff across the river, taking potshots at me.

By five-fifteen, twilight was falling and I had calmed down. The third shot had been the last. I'd hunkered down behind the willows for ten minutes, then made a dash for the safety of Jeremiah. I'd had a short nap and a long bath, and I had put things in perspective. Given the spread of the shots—off the rocks and over my head, into the river to my left, and into the cottonwood tree to my right—it wasn't likely that anybody was shooting *at* me. It was probably some dude with a new deer rifle, not firing at anything in particular, not even bothering to look where his bullets might end up. Chances were, he hadn't heard me yelling, or he knew that he'd come that close to wiping me out.

I was pulling a flannel shirt over my jeans when the bell began to toll. I looked at my watch. Not yet five-thirty. Dinner was at six, I thought, but maybe my watch was slow.

It wasn't. The bell had just stopped tolling when Maggie knocked at the door. I started to tell her about my adventure with Hawkeye and his Christmas rifle when I saw her face.

"What's wrong?"

"Sister Perpetua died this afternoon," Maggie said soberly. "I went back to Mother's cottage for a talk. While I was there, Sister Rowena came with the news. That was the bell just now, tolling for her."

"That's too bad," I said. I was genuinely sorry that Perpetua had died, and almost as sorry that I hadn't gotten to talk to her. "Her heart?"

Maggie's mouth tightened. "Royce Townsend has other ideas. He was there when she died. He's ordered an autopsy."

An autopsy? In the routine death of an elderly woman with a history of heart trouble? "Why?"

"Who knows? Maybe he suspects something."

I looked at Maggie, startled. "Suspects what?"

"God only knows," Maggie said. "Maybe he thinks he can embarrass St. T's by implying that there's something suspicious about the way Perpetua died, the same way he did with Mother Hilaria." She shook her head bleakly. "Perpetua would be so humiliated at the idea of an autopsy. She was tired and sick and ready to die. That's all there is to it."

"You're sure?"

"Of course I'm sure," she said. "Who would want to kill poor old Sister Perpetua?"

I stuck my flashlight in my coat pocket and Maggie and I walked over to Ezekiel to get Ruby, who had changed from her monk's robe into slacks, a sweater, and jacket. The three of us set off on the path through the meadow to Sophia. On the way, Maggie repeated the story of Perpetua's death and I told them about the shooting.

Ruby stopped in her tracks and stared at me. "Somebody tried to kill you!" she exclaimed.

Maggie frowned. "If the shots came from the cliff, it had to be one of the Townsends. That's their land."

"Wait a minute," I said. "Whoever it was, he wasn't aiming to kill me. The shots went all over the place."

"It could have been a warning," Maggie said.

"It wasn't a warning," I said. "It was an accident. Some idiot was up there with a new gun, not paying any attention to—"

"If it was a warning, the guy had to know who China is and why she's here," Ruby said.

"Stu Walters knows," Maggie said. "He could have told Carl Townsend."

"Hey, you guys," I protested. "Haven't you been listening? It was an *accident*."

But now I wasn't so sure. Even if I allowed for Maggie's anti-Townsend bias, I had to admit she might be right. Given the influence of the county political machine, the sheriff and the deputy might very well be in cahoots with one of the county commissioners. Which meant that Walters could have mentioned to Townsend that the abbess intended to bring in her own arson investigator. And if Townsend had anything to do with the fires—which I had to admit was also possible, even though everybody insisted it wasn't—he might have decided to warn me off.

Ruby was frowning at me. "What are you going to do?"

"Eat supper," I said. "And think about it."

Sophia emerged out of the twilight at the end of the path, like a ghost of the old ranch headquarters. I almost expected to see tooled leather saddles hung over the wooden porch rail and the heads of trophy bucks nailed to the walls. But if they had been there once, they were gone now. Maggie opened a wooden screen door and we stepped into a high ceilinged entryway that smelled of old stonework, overlaid with the scent of the lemon polish that had been used on the large oak cabinets along the walls and the pine oil used on the tile floor. But what struck me most was the utter silence, a calm, weighty presence that was almost as physical as the walls themselves.

"Gosh, it's quiet in here!" Ruby said in an awed whisper. She looked up at a heavy wooden cross encircled by a wreath of rusty barbed wire that was decorated with orange-red pyracanthus berries.

"Of course it's quiet," Maggie said in a low voice. "It's a cloister." She lifted her eyes to the cross.

"Do I have to whisper?" Ruby whispered to me.

Maggie turned, smiling. "No," she said. "People talk at mealtimes."

Ruby and I followed Maggie down the silent hall, past a large laundry room and kitchen on one side and a community room on the other. We turned a corner.

"That's the main office," Maggie said, pointing to a closed door. "Someone is on duty there during business hours. That's where the phone is located, if you need it."

The refectory—already crowded with sisters—was at the end of the hall, a large, square, cheerful room, brightly lit, with undraped floor-to-ceiling windows that looked out onto a small, shady garden. It was furnished with wooden tables and chairs arranged in orderly rows. At one end stood another large table, on which the food—soup, bread, sandwich fillings, salad, and fruit—was laid out on a bright yellow cloth, buffet style. Although the women were older than most students, the scene reminded me of a college dining hall.

But as I glanced around, I saw that there seemed to be an invisible line drawn down the middle of the room. On one side, the tables were filled with women wearing jeans, slacks, and skirts, talking in low voices, laughing and smiling, their heads close together. The women on the other side—most of them older—wore navy skirts, white blouses, and the same short blue veil and white wimple Sister Olivia had worn. They ate with their eyes cast down, observing what Maggie called "modesty of the eyes," and only a few were talking. If I'd needed a visual demonstration of the gulf between St. T's and St. Agatha's, this was it.

We filled our plates, then went in search of Dominica. We found her at a table with Sister Miriam, a thin-faced woman with hair the color of autumn oak leaves and an intense, darting glance. As I sat down, I saw a look pass between Maggie and Dominica. I thought I understood that look now, and the softening at the corners of Maggie's mouth when Dominica returned her smile. Love is love, wherever you find it. The trouble is that some kinds of love are hard to fit into our lives. The glance wasn't missed by Sister Miriam, either, who turned away, her face unreadable.

We were still getting settled when we were joined by Sister Rachel, who was short, plump, and all in a dither. Her nose and eyes were red and she seemed distraught, not so much over Perpetua's death, but over the fact that her body had been taken away.

"We have a very special ritual when a sister dies," she explained to Ruby and me. "Our infirmarian—that's Sister Rowena—washes our dead sister and dresses her. Then we carry her to the chapel and light the paschal candle and take turns reciting the Psalms. It's all very beautiful, very reassuring. To have poor Perpetua hauled off like a dead cow . . ." She shook her head, despairing. "It happened the same way with Mother Hilaria. So horrible! Where will all this end?"

"With a new abbess, unfortunately." The angularity of Miriam's face was matched by her thin voice. "Unless a miracle happens, we'll be voting before compline tomorrow."

"We should have prayed harder for Perpetua," Dominica muttered.

I seconded that. Maybe Perpetua couldn't have told me anything more than I already knew about the letter she'd received. On the other hand . . .

"There won't be an election tomorrow," Maggie said, buttering her roll.

"Oh, really?" Miriam asked dryly. "With Perpetua dead, the score is nineteen to twenty. Just in time, too. Olivia is getting tired of holding her breath."

Who would want to kill poor old Sister Perpetua? Miriam had just given me an answer to Maggie's rhetorical question. But that was ridiculous. Nuns only killed other nuns in murder mysteries.

"I'm afraid Olivia will have to hold her breath a little longer," Maggie said. "There are still twenty votes for Gabriella." Everybody was looking at her, but she didn't seem to notice. "I asked Mother Winifred if I could come back to St. T's, and she said yes. It's up to the Council of Sisters, of course, and Reverend Mother General has to agree, but Mother says there won't be a problem."

Miriam didn't look overjoyed. "Reverend Mother will jump on the idea like a duck on a Junebug," she said, "even if it does put Olivia on hold a while longer. The order needs every vocation it can get."

Ignoring Miriam, Dominica clasped her hands, her round face shining. "Oh, Margaret Mary, I'm *so* glad! I've missed you so much. We've *all* missed you!"

Ruby was gaping. "But what about your restaurant? You've put two years of work into it, Maggie. You can't just turn your back and walk away!"

"Why not?" Maggie's face was sober but her blue eyes were twinkling. "It's just a restaurant. No big deal." She patted Ruby's hand. "This is right for me, Ruby. I belong here."

Ruby subsided, muttering. She enjoys an occasional retreat, but she also loves her fun. She would find life in a monastery unutterably boring.

I searched Maggie's face for a hint to how she was feeling, but all I could see was her normal serene calm. Her announcement wasn't totally unexpected, of course. She'd been telegraphing it all day. I hoped she was coming back for the right reasons, but I had to wonder.

"I don't suppose you're doing this to keep Olivia from being elected," Miriam remarked. She was watching Maggie obliquely, and I wondered how much she knew about the relationship between Maggie and Dominica. She herself was linked with Dominica, at least in the poison-pen writer's imagination. I studied her more closely. Was there a hint of jealousy in her look?

I wasn't surprised when Maggie answered Miriam's question with a firm, clear "Of course not." If Maggie had another motive, she probably wouldn't share it—and certainly not in response to such an obvious challenge.

Sister Rachel cast innocent eyes around the table. "Why in the world should anyone want to keep Olivia from being elected? She isn't my choice, but if she's elected, it will be God's will."

"Really, Rachel," Dominica said impatiently. "You know better than that. God doesn't will *everything* that happens. He wasn't responsible for the fire in the chapel, for instance. Some bad person did that."

Rachel was half-frowning. "But the person who set the fires . . . couldn't she—if it is a she, I mean—couldn't that person be carrying out God's will? There *is* a larger purpose in all things, even if we can't always see it." She paused, took a deep breath, and then plunged deeper into the muddy theological waters. "The person who is setting the fires could be an agent of God. Who are we to question? Who are we to *know*?"

Miriam hadn't been paying any attention to Rachel. She leaned across the table toward Maggie. "If you're coming back to keep Olivia from taking over, it won't do a dime's bit of good, Margaret Mary. You may stall her for a while, but sooner or later she and Reverend Mother will get what they want. Unless we do something about it, St. T's is doomed."

The last melodramatic sentence rang into the dead silence that had fallen suddenly over the room. Miriam raised her head and looked around, her cheeks reddening. Mother Winifred was standing at a table near the front of the room. She was so short that I had to move my chair to be able to see her.

"I am sure you have all heard that Sister Perpetua died this afternoon," she said with dignity. "Father Steven will celebrate a Requiem Mass later in the week. In the meantime, following our tradition, we will say prayers in the chapel for Sister Perpetua's soul." She didn't mention the fact that Sister Perpetua's body would be somewhere else.

When she finished, she introduced me and told the sisters that I was there to look into the fires. She paused for a moment, looked around at her silent audience, and added, "I am sorry to tell you that letters of a quite destructive nature have been delivered to several of our sisters." She spoke in measured, emphatic phrases. "This unfortunate business must be brought out into the light. If you have received such a letter or have any information about the writer, I request—no, I direct you to speak to me or to Ms. Bayles immediately."

I watched the sisters as she spoke. Their eyes were on Mother Winifred, their faces expressionless, with that look of calm serenity I was beginning to think of as a convenient camouflage. If one of them had received a letter or had written one, the guilty knowledge was not written on her face.

The night sky was lit by a sliver of low-hanging moon when Maggie, Ruby, and I walked in the direction of the cottages, our flashlight beams glancing along the path in front of us. We were all shivering in the frosty January air. As if by mutual agreement, we said nothing about Maggie's decision to return to St. T's, although Ruby must have been quivering with curiosity and I still wasn't convinced that Maggie didn't have an ulterior motive. I couldn't help noticing, though, that her step was lighter and she was smiling. Whatever burden she'd been carrying she seemed to have left behind.

But there was something else on my mind. I was trying to puzzle out what to do about the shooting that afternoon. Had it been accidental or deliberate? The answer to that question—if there *was* an answer—was on the Townsend side of the river.

I caught up to Maggie. "What's the best way to get to the top of the cliff?"

"You can cross the river at a narrow spot about fifty yards upstream from your cottage," Maggie said. "The path begins on the other side. The climb takes about half an hour, maybe less."

"It's not straight up, is it?" I asked. I eyed the cliff, which seemed to loom over us. I'm not in bad shape, but I'm not a mountain goat, either.

"It isn't very steep, but it's a bit treacherous. Would you like to go up there tomorrow?"

"Actually, I'd rather go tonight," I said. "If I'm going to snoop, I prefer to do it when I'm not going to run into anybody." I wasn't sure there was anything to find, but I wouldn't know unless I climbed up there and looked.

Ruby zipped up her jacket. "Isn't it a bit cold for us to snoop?"

"You don't have to come," I said. "After all, you've got to get up pretty early tomorrow." Ruby was leaving for Albuquerque before breakfast.

Ruby gave me a look. "Of course I don't *have* to come. But did George and Beth desert Nancy in her hour of need? Anyway, two of us up there snooping are less suspicious than one."

"Three of us," Maggie said. "You need me to show you the path. It's not a snap in daylight—it'll be harder at night."

The path was definitely not a snap. Halfway up the cliff, I stopped to catch my breath and take a look at the moon-washed landscape. Above me, rhinestone stars glittered against a matte black sky and the moon, a quarter-round of stamped silver, was surrounded by an iridescent halo. Under my feet, luminescent chips of rock littered the path like moon pebbles. To my right, several yards away, was a five-strand barbwire fence wearing a "Townsend Ranch—Keep Out" sign. To my left were shadows, deep, dangerous, where the cliff plunged to a platinum ribbon of river far below.

Behind me, Ruby stumbled and slid down a few feet, grabbing at a bush and muttering words that would have made Mother Winifred blush. I turned my attention back to the path, concentrating on putting my feet in the right places. When we finally reached the top, we found a rocky ledge, maybe fifteen feet wide, the barbwire fence slicing across it at an angle. I paused, looking out over the rim. The monastery lay silent and mysterious in the moonlight below, the meadow as silver as if it were blanketed with snow. I could see the lights of Sophia and Rebecca and the flat, square roof of Hannah, and the looping road that tied the complex together. Directly below, on the other side of the silvery braid of the Yucca, was Jeremiah, serene and peaceful in the moonlight. I could see the willow clump where I'd taken cover, and the open, rocky river beach where I was standing when the shot was fired. The silence lay like a blessing across the land.

Maggie stood beside me. "God, it's beautiful," she said. She let out a long sigh. "Please, *please* don't let it be changed." It was a prayer.

I turned and flicked my flashlight across the ground.

"What are we looking for?" Ruby asked.

"I wish I knew." I walked along the fence line. "Some indication that somebody was here, I guess." But if the shooting was deliberate, the shooter would have been careful not to leave any traces. If it was accidental—

The torchlight glinted on something metallic in the loose rock. A cartridge case, brass. "By golly," I muttered. I found a twig and stuck it in the open end, in case there were prints, and used the twig to pick it up. I shone the light on the base and studied the identifying marks around it. 303 BRIT. Oh, yeah?

It's funny, the things that stick in your mind. McQuaid and I went to a gun show not long ago, and he showed me a gun that was once the pride of the British infantry. An

Enfield, a 303—the only rifle of that caliber, its hand guard removed and the stock shortened to sporterize it. And now I was holding a 303 cartridge in my hand. I narrowed my eyes. Somewhere, just recently, I'd seen a gun like that. Now where—

"What did you find?" Maggie asked, coming over.

I held it up.

"A bullet?" Ruby asked.

"Part of it."

She looked disappointed. "Too bad. If you had the rest of it—"

"That's okay, Ruby," I said, wrapping the cartridge in a bit of tissue. "This is all I need."

"Oh," she said. "Then I guess you don't want this."

"What is it? What have you found?"

She shone her torch on an empty Camel cigarette pack. Now I knew where I'd seen that gun.

I was at Mother Winifred's door before the bell rang for breakfast.

"Good morning, China," Mother said. She was wearing a rumpled green robe and she looked tired, as if she hadn't rested well. "I've just put the kettle on. Would you like a cup of tea?"

"What I'd like," I said without preamble, "is your permission to search Dwight Baldwin's living quarters." I had already made a circuit of the parking lot behind Sophia and confirmed my suspicions.

She stared at me. "You suspect *Dwight* of setting the fires?"

"I don't know about the fires," I said. "But I think he was the person who took a shot at me yesterday afternoon."

Her pale blue eyes widened. "Shot at you! But why?"

"To warn me off," I said. "I know it's Sunday, Mother. But I'd like you to invent a task that will occupy him for an hour or so this morning, so I can search. And I'd like a key to his quarters, if you have one."

She nodded sadly. "You can conduct your search during Mass. Dwight is one of our little flock." She went to the cupboard and took down a large ring of keys. "I'm sure there's a key here somewhere."

In Texas, the law doesn't permit the landlord to enter rented or leased premises, even with a key. But Mother Winifred probably wasn't current on the law, and I certainly wasn't going to sweat it. Legal or not, opening a door with a key beats breaking and entering.

Breakfast was a repeat of supper, with the refectory once again divided down the middle, neither side talking to the other. Both sides seemed more tense and fidgety than they had last night. I wondered whether they were upset by Sister Perpetua's death or by Mother Winifred's request, or whether they were counting heads. If they hadn't heard that Maggie was returning, they'd be expecting that an election would be held in the next day or two.

When I had finished assembling my breakfast tray, I looked around for Maggie but didn't see her. Ruby wasn't there either, of course. She had already left for Albuquerque.

After we'd climbed down the cliff the night before, we had all walked to my cottage, where we sat down to talk for a little while. "I'd love to stay and help you figure out what's going on here," Ruby had said regretfully. "But my friends have made all sorts of plans. I really can't disappoint them."

"That's okay," I said. "You're still picking us up for the drive home, aren't you?"

"In two weeks." She'd glanced at Maggie. "Are you going back with us, Maggie?" It was the first reference either of us had made, since supper, to Maggie's momentous decision.

"I've got to go back," Maggie said. "I have to get ready to put the restaurant up for sale, make arrangements, that sort of thing. It'll be a while before I can come back to stay. In the meanwhile, though, I'm considered a member of the order.''

I regarded Maggie thoughtfully. ''I suppose I'd understand it better if the restaurant were a flop. But feeling the way you do about the Church, I'm not sure why you want to come back—especially when things here are so unsettled.''

Maggie looked down at her hands resting quietly in her lap. ''It's true—there's a lot of uncertainty here. And I'm not any more comfortable with the Church than I was when I left.''

I shook my head. ''Then why—?''

''Because it's where I'm meant to be,'' Maggie said simply. ''Haven't you ever felt that your place in life is the *right* place?''

I thought about that for a moment. No, I had never been sure that my place was the right place—not when I was practicing law, not after I'd bought the shop, not even after I'd moved in with McQuaid. Where I was now felt pretty good, sometimes more, sometimes less, but I wasn't absolutely sure it was *right*. I wondered fleetingly what it would be like to experience that kind of assurance.

''Excuse me.'' Ruby stirred. ''You don't have to answer this if you don't want to, Maggie. But what about Dominica? Does she have anything to do with this?''

Maggie didn't seem offended. ''Maybe. I've certainly missed her. But I don't expect anything to be different between us. I'm just sort of doing this a step at a time. Taking it on faith. And loving the questions.''

I was surprised into the recollection of a piece of poetry I had read once. ''*Love the questions like locked doors,*'' I said softly. ''*Like books in a very foreign tongue.*'' Rilke was the poet, I thought.

''Love the questions?'' Ruby shook her head. ''Excuse me, but I prefer answers.''

''In the short run, maybe.'' Maggie smiled. ''But questions take us farther and deeper. I was called here to St.

T's to learn something. Whatever it is, I need to come back and get on with the job.''

''But don't you need to know what job it is that you're supposed to get on with?'' Ruby asked doubtfully.

Maggie's laugh was rich and joyful. ''There is such a thing as faith, you know. Come on, you guys. Love the questions!''

The logic of Maggie's decision continued to escape me, but I felt close to her in a new way. And when she and Ruby left, we all hugged one another for a long time, Ruby and I in our doubt, Maggie in her faith.

I found a spot at a table in a corner of the refectory. If one of the sisters had information for me, I was hoping she'd come and sit down. But perhaps it had been too public an invitation, I decided as I finished my breakfast alone. The only person who spoke to me was Sister Gabriella, who had traded her jeans for a tailored skirt and sweater. She stopped as I was putting my plate on the stack of dirty dishes on the pass-through shelf to the kitchen.

''How about dropping by Jacob after Mass?'' she asked. ''I'd like to give you a tour of our garlic operation.'' A nun in a habit paused to scan a nearby bulletin board and Gabriella bent toward me, lowering her voice so the other woman couldn't hear. ''Sadie Marsh, one of the Laney Foundation Board members, will be here this morning. She wants to talk to you.''

''Oh, yes,'' I said, remembering. ''Tom Rowan mentioned her. She raises horses, doesn't she?''

''That's right.'' Gabriella raised one quizzical eyebrow. ''You've met Tom?''

I felt myself coloring. ''We knew one another years ago. He said that the board is meeting here this week.''

''Tuesday morning. But Sadie doesn't want to wait until then.'' She raised her voice again. ''Does eleven sound all right? We can take a tour of the garlic field, if the weather is still cooperating.''

''Fine,'' I said, and turned to go. ''See you then.''

I was halfway down the hall when I was stopped by a slight, anxious nun in a modified habit and veil that hid her hair. She wore plastic-rimmed fifties-style glasses, and she was so tense that I could almost feel her quivering. She looked over her shoulder in both directions before she pulled me into the laundry room.

"I'm Sister John Roberta." The words escaped from her in whispery gasps. "If I tell you what I know, will you help me get away?"

I was startled. "Get away? Why?" What did she know that would make her so fearful?

She clutched at my arm. "I'm afraid I'll *die* here! Please, help me!"

"I'll do my best," I said reassuringly. "What are you afraid of?"

Her mouth trembled. "Sister Olivia says we have to stick together." She broke into a flurry of dry coughing. "And Sister Rowena says if I tell, I'm being disloyal. They might—"

She pressed her fist to her mouth at the sound of muted voices and footsteps in the hall. The group passed, the outer door closed, and there was silence once again. John Roberta stood still, her eyes apprehensive. Her face was almost as white as the starched band of her veil.

"I'm afraid someone will hear," she said. "Or see us together and guess that I'm—" She bit off her sentence.

"I could come to your room to talk," I said. "We'd have more privacy there."

She shook her head violently. "They'd see you. They'd know I was talking to you. They'd—" She broke off, coughing. "You're staying in Jeremiah, aren't you?" she asked, when she could speak again. "I'll come there. Later."

"After lunch?" I asked. I wasn't sure I could trust her to come, but I didn't have any choice in the matter.

"Not right after. One-thirty." Another cough, a frightened glance, and she was gone, a shadow winging down the shadowy hall.

The encounter was promising, but all I was left with were questions. I would have to wait until one-thirty to learn the answers. I looked at my watch. Mass would be starting soon. I'd better get busy.

Earlier in the morning, in the gun rack of Dwight's GMC pickup in the parking lot, I had seen an Enfield 303 and, crumpled on the floor of the cab, an empty Camels pack. But before I accused the man of assault with a deadly weapon, I wanted to see if I could discover something that might explain his attack. Something that would connect him to the Townsends, for instance.

The bell was ringing for Mass when I walked casually to the door of Amos, Dwight's vintage stucco cottage, and knocked. No answer. I knocked again, harder, and called Dwight's name. Still no answer. I put my hand in my pocket and took out the key. But I didn't need it, because the door wasn't locked.

Amos had the same layout as Jeremiah, although it wasn't nearly as clean. Foul-smelling jeans and work shirts were heaped in one corner, there was a saddle and a dirty saddle blanket under the window, and copies of *Playboy*, open to the centerfold, littered the floor by the bed. The room reeked of stale cigarette smoke and cheap whiskey.

I began by checking the dresser drawers, then moved to the single drawer in the wooden desk, the bathroom shelves, and the jackets and shirts hanging in the closet. But apart from a half-empty box of 303 cartridges and a completely empty bottle of Wild Turkey, I found little of interest. Until, that is, I reached in the pocket of a flannel shirt and found a business card with the name, address, and telephone numbers of J. R. Nutall, Carr County Probation Officer.

Probation officer. So Dwight wasn't totally clean, as far

as the law was concerned. What had he done to earn jail time?

I confiscated one of the shells as a souvenir, jotted down the information on Nutall's business card, and went to the nightstand. Most of the canceled checks I discovered in the drawer were made out to Al's Liquor Store for amounts under thirty dollars. The December bank statement, which I discovered on top of the toilet, showed that Dwight had $74.41 in the bank, after depositing four weekly checks, each for the identical amount of $352.70—his salary, most likely. A chipped saucer on top of the dresser held a silver rosary, nail clippers, a beer bottle opener, and a black book that contained phone numbers and first names, most of them women's. I flipped the book open to the Ts. There was no listing for Townsend.

And that was it—until I raised the mattress and found the black spiral notebook.

The sky was clear, the sun was shining, and the temperature was already climbing out of the fifties when I took Mother Hilaria's diary back to Jeremiah. Today might top out at sixty-five, which almost made up for the ferocious heat of last July and August. Almost, but not quite.

I glanced at my watch. It was only nine-thirty. I'd have time to read a few pages before I went over to Jacob to meet Sadie Marsh. And after I had talked to Sister John Roberta, I would let Mother Winifred know what I'd found under Dwight's mattress. He had some tall explaining to do.

Back in Jeremiah, I brewed a cup of tea and sat cross-legged on the bed with Hilaria's journal in front of me. Opening it, I saw that she had been using it as a multiyear diary, a page for every day in the year, with the years arranged in sequence down the page. She had been keeping the diary for almost five years when she died, and although the entries were short, there were far more than I could read in an hour. Where to begin? Should I start with September 3, the last entry, and read backward? Or start earlier?

I thumbed through the pages for a few minutes, then began with the middle of July, when the St. Agatha sisters moved to St. T. It didn't take long to find a reference to the first poison-pen letter. But if I'd been hoping that Hilaria had recognized the identity of the writer and confided it to her diary, I was disappointed. For July 17, all I found were three enigmatic words: *Sr. Perpetua, letter.*

The other entries were just as cryptic. Hilaria was in the habit of jotting down the names of people she talked to and the topics of their conversations, or short phrases describing the day's activities—*Board meeting, nothing accomplished,* for instance, or *Bank, check records. Tom Sr, questions re: interest.* Tom Senior would be Tom Rowan's father. These entries had been made after the court had finally awarded the money to St. T, so he and Mother Hilaria were no doubt straightening out the complications that had arisen during the years the bank held the foundation's money.

Financial queries seemed to have kept Mother Hilaria busy through July and into August. She devoted several days a week to *Bank, questions re: accounts* or *Investment records, review.* I could understand why. If the court had dumped a fourteen- or fifteen-million-dollar inheritance into my lap, I'd be studying deposit accounts and investment records too. I'd be so busy asking questions that I might not waste much time over a nasty letter that accused a forgetful sister of the petty theft of a library book.

But a week after her meeting with Sister Perpetua, Mother Hilaria was indeed thinking about the letter. *Questioned Sr. O about Sr. P's letter,* I read, on July 24. I reached for the roster Mother Winifred had given me. Conveniently, Olivia was the only sister whose name began with O.

I went back to the entry with a frown, wishing that Mother Hilaria had been less cryptic. I had first assumed that she had questioned Olivia because she hoped Olivia might be able to name the culprit. But perhaps that wasn't the right assumption. Perhaps she thought that Olivia herself had written the letter.

I got up, took a bathroom break, and brewed a second cup of tea. I started reading again with July 26: *Dwight, salary increase, approved.* After that, his name appeared with increasing frequency. August 5: *Dwight, no promotion.* August 8: *Dwight, said no again.* And then, August 12, *Dwight, threats. Spoke sternly.* And on August 13, *J. R. Nutall, questions re: Dwight.*

I sipped my tea and reread all five of these entries, trying to piece together the story that lay behind them. Dwight had been given a raise at the end of July. Less than two weeks later, he was back, asking for a promotion. From handyman to what? Farm manager? Whatever he wanted, he didn't get it. When he struck out again, he retaliated with a threat. Mother Hilaria had clearly been concerned, or she wouldn't have contacted his probation officer.

Again, I wondered what crime had sent Dwight to jail. If he'd served time for a violent felony, Texas law prohibited his carrying a gun off the monastery grounds. Caught with that 303 anywhere else, he could be charged with a third-degree felony—which meant that his target practice at the top of the cliff might just earn him more lockup time. I had J. R. Nutall's home phone number. A call would turn up the information I needed. But first, I'd ask Mother Winifred for a look at Dwight's personnel record—assuming there was one, of course. As far as I knew, he was the monastery's only full-time employee. Mother Hilaria might have hired him without any formalities.

I turned the page to August 16 and found something else. *Sr. A, letter. Questioned Sr. R & Sr. O.* Sister A must be Sister Anne, whom the letter-writer had chastised for lewdly baring her nakedness. Sister O—well, I knew who that was. Sister R? She was new to my cast of alphabet characters. I ran my finger down the roster and counted eight Rs: Ramona, Rachel, Rowena, Ruth, Rosabel, Rose,

Rosaline, Regina. Nine, including Sister John Roberta. I sighed. It was too bad that R names were so popular in this order. It was *really* too bad that Mother Hilaria had been so cryptic. If she had only used names instead of initials, I'd know which of the nine Rs she had questioned. But that was information I could get from Sister O, who would surely remember the August sixteenth conversation.

I turned the pages and found more brief notations. *Phoned Rev Moth G, re: problems, but on retreat at Moth Hs*. Which of her problems had Mother Hilaria wanted to discuss? The trust accounts? Dwight? The letters? But Rev Moth G (Reverend Mother General, I assumed) had apparently remained incommunicado at the Moth Hs (the Mother House?) for quite some time. The diary didn't indicate that Mother Hilaria had succeeded in talking to her.

There was nothing more of interest until August 22, the day Sister Anne's swimsuit was found draped on the cross. *Sr. A's suit!!*, the outraged entry read. *Questioned Sr. O & Sr. R again*. The remaining entries in August were focused on financial affairs—*Bank re: statements, Tom Sr re: funds, bank re: note*. September 1 was blank. September 2's entry consisted of just one word, underlined.

letter.

I stared at the single word. Somebody else had gotten a letter, but who? Mother Hilaria? If so, what had happened to it? Had she destroyed it, or was it still among her possessions?

That was the last entry. On September 3, Mother Hilaria had died. Sometime after that, Dwight had stolen her journal.

CHAPTER SEVEN

Several years ago, a newspaper reporter interviewed me for an herb article. After the interview, the reporter arranged to trade some herb plants with me. He wanted to show me some comfrey, which he had tried in salads and found extremely bitter tasting. The next day I went to his office and there, sitting on a file cabinet, was a box of first-year foxglove plants! To the novice, comfrey and foxglove have a similar appearance. Earlier that same year (1979), an elderly couple had eaten what they thought were comfrey leaves. It was foxglove, and both died within twenty-four hours.

Steven Foster
Herbal Renaissance

Sister Gabriella's garlic operation wasn't exactly what you'd expect in a monastery. Neither was she, come to that. She was tall and strong, and she swung her arms energetically as she talked, her gestures punctuating her rich Southern speech.

"When we first came out here, there were only ten of us, and we had just an acre of plants," she said as we walked through the big, airy barn. "When harvest time came, we dug the garlic with forks and shovels."

"Wasn't that hard on everybody's back?" I asked, trying to imagine what it would be like to spade up an entire acre of garlic. And even after it was dug, the job wouldn't have been done. The sisters had to remove the dirt, dry the plants, separate the bulbs from the tops. . . . People who buy garlic in little cellophane packages have no idea what they're missing.

She chuckled. "You bet. But we were new in the business and everybody was willing. A couple of years later, though, we doubled the acreage, and I started to hear grumbling. Mother Hilaria tried to convince the sisters that they'd get a couple of extra days in paradise for every garlic bulb they dug, but they didn't buy it. So when we doubled the acreage again, I went looking for an old-fashioned chisel plow, like the one my grandfather used to have back in Kentucky." She gestured at a piece of equipment in the corner. "Found it in a junkyard over in Johnson City. All that was wrong with it was a quarter-inch of rust and a broken strap. Now, I just set the tractor tires into the irrigation furrows and drop that plow-point between the rows. The plants still have to be pulled, but at least they're loose. No more spadework."

I grinned at the picture of tall, strong Sister Gabriella poking around a Johnson City junkyard looking for a secondhand chisel plow. "What happens after the garlic's pulled?"

"We used to cart it up here in wheelbarrows and dunk it in a tub to wash off the dirt. Then we'd lay it out on that cement over there to dry." She shook her head pityingly. "Lord sakes, that was *work*. Happy garlic grows three feet high, and we harvest the whole thing, not just the bulb. That's a lot of leaf to be totin' around."

I shook my head, imagining the size of the job. "It was a good thing you had conscripts," I said. "You probably couldn't have found enough people willing to work that hard for what you could pay."

Gabriella grinned. "We had a good crop of novices those years. And Sadie, bless her heart, donated a beat-up old Ford pickup, which we traded for a front-end loader for our tractor." She gestured in the direction of a dusty, antique-looking dinosaur of a tractor. "Then we built some garlic flats—chicken wire on board frames, six feet long by three feet wide by two feet deep—that we lay on the loader. Now, after the field's plowed, we pull the garlic and lay it in a rack. When one rack's filled, we stack on another. When they're all filled, I haul the load up here. We restack the garlic into those thirty-foot-long storage racks in that cement block building over there."

"It looks like a great system," I said.

She nodded. "There's still plenty of toting and hauling. From planting to market we handle the garlic eight times. If we braid it, we handle it twice more. In a good year, we'll move over two tons of the stuff."

I whistled. Two tons of St. T's famous rocambole. "It's all gone by spring, I suppose."

"The biggest cloves are back in the ground by October. The market-grade stuff we sell as bulbs, retail and wholesale. The plants with the best tops we braid into *ristras* and wreaths and swags, along with chilies and dried flowers. Buckwheat, statice, strawflowers, cockscomb—the usual stuff. Sister Cecilia is in charge of that part of it. She also grows a few specialities. Chiles, gourds, strawberry popcorn. With the garlic, they make nice wreaths."

I looked around. "You've got lots of storage, plenty of labor, decent equipment. You've got water for irrigation and room for more fields. How big could the operation get?"

She grew thoughtful. "That depends. We could plant another acre or two of garlic and sell it easily. With an expanded marketing effort, we might sell fifty or a hundred percent more. We could grow more flowers and market them with the garlic, and just about double our revenue." She lifted her broad, capable shoulders, let them fall. "We could get big, sure. We could make a lot more money. But why?"

I cocked my head at her. "Why?"

"Well, sure. Work is good for the soul, and we can al-

ways use a little more money. But we need time for prayer
and study more than we need money." A half-grin cracked
her weathered face. "Woman does not live by work alone,
you know."

I thought of the shop back home and the hours I'd poured
into it last fall. Had I been brought all the way to St.
Theresa's just to hear this bit of advice?

She grew sober. "Anyway, you know what's happening
here. The garlic operation isn't likely to expand. In fact,
the crop in the ground may just turn out to be our last."

"That would be a loss," I said. "A lot of people think
St. T's rocambole is better than anything else on the market."

"The garlic won't be too happy about it, either," Gabriella said. We were at the far end of the barn now, and
she opened the door to a large, chilly room furnished with
worktables, shelves of neatly arranged supplies, and racks
filled with dried flowers, chilies, and whole garlic plants,
stalk and all. "This is Sister Rosaline's part of the operation. It's where her crew braids the *ristras* and makes the
wreaths, swags, baskets, things like that. A dozen or so
sisters work here half-days all year round. August to December, Rosaline recruits an extra half-dozen. They take a
rest after the holiday, but they'll be back tomorrow, starting
on our spring orders. It's work they enjoy."

"I'd enjoy it too," I said. Crafting is a lot more fun than
standing behind a counter all day.

"It's creative work," Gabriella said, "and worth it. The
simplest arrangement sells for ten times the value of the
garlic in it." Her voice grew acerbic. "It beats baking bread
or making altar cloths or selling rosaries, which is what
other monasteries do to make a living. And it sure as sin
beats playing host to a bunch of bishops."

I glanced around. "This is the room where the fire occurred last fall?"

"See where those two walls have been replaced, and that
big patch in the ceiling?" She pointed. "We had to repaint

too. There wasn't a lot of damage, but it cost Rosaline a couple of days' work while we cleaned things up.''

"What happened?''

"There was a work light hanging on that wall. It shorted out. At least, that's what Dwight says.''

"You don't agree?''

She shrugged. "The light was new. After the fire, it disappeared. But I don't have any suspects in mind, if that's what you're asking. It happened on a Sunday afternoon when nobody was here. If it hadn't been for Dwight, we'd have lost the barn.'' She glanced at her watch. "Let's go to my office. Sadie will be here in a few minutes.''

Gabriella's office smelled of woodsmoke. It had once been a tack room, and various pieces of riding gear—bits, bridles, curry combs—still hung on the splintery walls. The rustic decor wasn't enhanced by her gray metal desk and filing cabinet, or by the incongruous-looking computer on the shelf behind the desk. But the woodstove in the corner, topped with a steaming kettle, radiated heat. Next to it sat an old rocking chair with a wicker seat. Gabriella opened the stove door, thrust in a stick of cedar from the stack in a wood box, and adjusted the damper.

"When the wind's out of the north, the smoke blows back down the chimney,'' she said. "But it keeps me warm.''

A moment later, Sadie Marsh arrived. She was a wiry, steely-haired woman of nearly sixty with commanding gray eyes, high cheekbones, a jutting nose, a forceful jaw. Deep vertical creases between her eyes suggested prolonged periods of concentration—or a bad temper. A determined person, I guessed, perhaps a difficult one. She wore jeans and scuffed cowboy boots, a blue work shirt with the sleeves rolled to the elbows, and a Navajo vest striped in reds, greens, and blues. Even in Texas, it wasn't the kind of outfit you'd wear to Mass, so I guessed she'd come here straight from home.

Sadie fixed her eyes on me as she lowered herself into

the rocking chair beside the stove. "Winnie—Mother Winifred—has been telling me about you. Lawyer, huh?"

"I used to practice law," I said. "I own an herb shop now."

Gabriella picked up the kettle. "Coffee?" she asked. Sadie and I nodded. I pulled up an old wooden dining chair with a broken spindle in the back and sat down.

"Once a lawyer, always a lawyer," Sadie said. "Still keep up your credentials?" Her West Texas twang had a biting edge. She wasn't making idle conversation.

"I keep current," I said. It's probably silly to pay the Bar Association dues and meeting the annual professional development requirement, especially with Thyme and Seasons doing so well. But I've wanted to have something to fall back on, just in case.

"What do you know about our situation here?"

Our situation? "Are you referring to the litigation over the will or to what's going on here at St. T's?"

She hooked one ankle over the other knee. "Both. Tell me what you know."

I felt as if I were being interviewed for a job. "I know that the court case was settled last spring and that the foundation finally has control over the trust assets," I said cautiously. "I've been told about the merger of St. T's and St. Agatha's, and I'm guessing that it will have a bearing on the foundation's fiduciary activities and investment plans."

"That pretty well covers it, I reckon," Sadie said. She took the chipped mug Gabriella handed her and rocked back and forth for a minute. "I'm a charter member of the Laney board," she said. "Is there anythin' you want to know about the way it operates?"

"As a matter of fact, yes," I said. I thanked Gabriella for my coffee and cradled it in my hands. I prefer tea, but coffee will do. "Who else is on the board? How is it set up?"

"There are five members. Winnie, of course. As actin'

abbess, she took Hilaria's place. And Gabby here.'' At my half-surprised glance at Gabriella, Sadie added, ''Hilaria appointed her last August to replace Perpetua, who wasn't too well. Tom Rowan Junior, who's taking over for his daddy at the bank, is number three. Number four is Cleva Mason, a woman from the local parish who's missed the last couple of meetings—she's about to be replaced. And I make five. I'm the only one who's actually on the board by name, and I'm on it until I die.'' She rubbed her palm along her blue-jeaned thigh.

''If another abbess were to be chosen, would she have the power to appoint new board members?'' Mrs. Laney would probably have set it up that way, to give the abbess a strong hand.

''Yes,'' Gabriella said. She pushed her desk chair over to the stove and sat down. ''If Olivia were elected tomorrow, she would appoint two new members—one to replace Cleva, the other to replace me.''

''So if it came down to a vote on some crucial issue—''

''It would be three to two,'' Sadie said. ''Assumin' Tom Junior voted with me. That isn't an assumption I'd stake my life on. His father and I are old friends, but we've never seen eye to eye. No reason to believe Tom Junior will be any different. It could be four to one.''

Basically, then, Olivia could count on the Laney Foundation providing the capital she needed to fund the retreat center. ''Who's the fiduciary officer?''

''Tom Junior, as of a couple of weeks ago. Carr State Bank manages the investments.'' She eyed me over the rim of her coffee mug. ''Anythin' else?''

There was something. It had occurred to me last night in bed, just before I drifted into a dream where I was riding through a garlic field with Tom Rowan while Olivia walked behind us with a tape measure, staking out a parking garage.

''When Mrs. Laney deeded the eight hundred acres to

St. Theresa's,'' I said, ''did she impose any restrictive covenants on the property?''

Sadie sat very still, watching me. Her eyes were bright. ''What makes you ask that question?''

''Just a hunch.'' Helen Laney and Mother Hilaria had been determined women, and neither of them had trusted the Church. They would have tried to guard against every possible eventuality.

''You got good hunches.'' Sadie grinned.

I grinned back.

Sister Gabriella put down her coffee cup and stood up. ''You two ladies finished your business?'' she asked mildly.

''Just about.'' Sadie looked at her watch. ''What time's lunch?''

''Same time as always,'' Gabriella said.

''Probably same garbage, too,'' Sadie replied tartly. ''Glad to hear Margaret Mary's decided to come back. Make it worthwhile to drive over here for Sunday dinner.'' She put both feet on the floor and glanced at me. ''You want to have a look at that property deed sometime soon?''

''Do you have a copy?''

''Yep. How about this afternoon?''

I thought. I'd agreed to talk to John Roberta at one-thirty, I had to find Olivia, and I needed to put in a call to Dwight's probation officer. ''How about tomorrow morning? Around ten-thirty?''

''That'll do,'' Sadie said. She hoisted herself out of her chair.

I stood too. There was one other question on my mind. ''The Reverend Mother General who heads up the order now—is she the same one who was there when the deed was executed?''

Sadie shook her head.

''Do you know whether she's looked at the deed?''

Sadie's eyes were very bright. ''I doubt it. It's more than twenty years old. Who cares anymore?''

''That's a good question,'' I said.

• • •

Sister John Roberta wasn't in the refectory for lunch while I was there, which I took to be a bad sign. But I didn't see Olivia, either, or Maggie. It was probably just my timing. But I did see Mother Winifred, who ate with Gabriella, Sadie, and me. She seemed subdued, and even more drawn than she had this morning. Sadie seemed to think she was grieving over Perpetua.

"It's too bad about poor old Perpetua," Sadie said. "We'll all miss her." She patted Mother's hand in sympathy. "When is Father Steven saying Mass?"

"When we have a body to say it over," Mother Winifred said. "We haven't heard when the autopsy will be done."

"Autopsy?" Sadie scowled. "What's that damn fool Royce doin' *that* for?"

"He wants to know how she died," Gabriella said. "It's a perfectly natural request for a doctor to make."

"He wants to make trouble, *that's* what he wants," Sadie muttered. "Which is perfectly natural, if you're a Townsend." She gave Mother Winifred a darting look. "How *did* Perpetua die? Heart?"

Mother spoke almost reluctantly. "It does seem to have been her heart. She had been suffering from cardiac arrhythmia. But at the end, she was quite dizzy and nauseous and had a convulsive seizure of some sort. Perpetua was in her late seventies, you know. It's entirely possible that she was having a stroke."

Cardiac arrhythmia, nausea, dizziness, convulsions. A stroke? Maybe. But another explanation came to mind. I curbed the impulse to mention it. I would ask Mother Winifred about it privately. I had to talk to her anyway, about what I had found in Dwight's room.

Lunch was over at twelve-thirty. I still had an hour before I was scheduled to talk with John Roberta, so after we said good-bye to Sadie, I walked with Mother Winifred back to her cottage. We were accompanied by two other sisters on their way to the herb garden, so we couldn't talk.

When we reached her cottage and she said, "Would you like to see the stillroom now?" I was glad of the opportunity.

The stillroom was once a screened porch, now closed in, that enlarged the small square cottage into a rectangle. It had a terra-cotta floor that was warmed by the sun streaming in through two large casement windows. Some of the floor-to-ceiling shelves held large amber-colored jars, crocks, and urns, all labeled. Other shelves held dark glass bottles full of prepared tinctures and jars of oils and other materials used to create salves and lotions. There were rows of vials and jars of empty gelatin capsules arranged beside baskets filled with scoops, glass droppers, atomizers—all the paraphernalia of an old-fashioned stillroom, the household apothecary shop. A workbench stood along another wall, near a small two-burner gas countertop stove for heating herbal preparations. Above the workbench was an extensive shelf of reference books, old and new, and above that framed botanical prints. Bunches of dried herbs hung from the ceiling.

"This is very pleasant," I said, looking around. Perhaps, I could make a room like this for myself—if I had the time. "How many sisters work here?"

"Eight or ten," Mother said. "We have class once a week, and I assign them individual projects. They come here for two hours a week, on their own, to work. It's good experience for them, very educational, and of course they help prepare the salves and ointments and lotions that we use for . . ." Her voice trailed off. She brushed some loose leaves off the worktable and into a basket on the floor.

I regarded her. "You haven't been experimenting with foxglove, have you, Mother Winifred?"

She looked at me, and I noticed once again how pale and drawn she was. Her skin seemed cracked, like old glaze on a piece of pottery. "No, of course not." She straightened a row of lidded canisters, not looking at me. "You don't think . . . You really can't believe . . ."

"The symptoms of Sister Perpetua's illness," I said gently. "They sound like the symptoms of digitalis poisoning. Wouldn't you agree?"

Her mouth trembled. "Yes," she said finally, almost in a whisper. She turned to look out the window, across the sunny garden, where the two nuns who had accompanied us were bent over the culinary bed, cleaning off the frost-bitten foliage. "To tell the truth, that thought did occur to me. In fact, it kept me up late last night."

"Had the doctor prescribed digitalis?"

"Not as far as I know." She turned around. "You can ask Sister Rowena, who manages the medications. But no, I'm sure he hadn't."

It was entirely possible that we were going in the wrong direction. But it wouldn't hurt to pursue it further—especially since a nonprescription source of digitalis was growing right in front of our eyes. "How many foxglove plants do you have in your apothecary garden?"

"Two," she said faintly.

"So it's possible that someone—perhaps one of the sisters who works here in the stillroom—could have harvested the leaves and prepared a tincture from them?" I glanced up at the row of jars. "Or filled some of those gel caps with the powdered leaf?"

"I suppose," she said slowly. "But you don't think that one of our sisters deliberately . . ."

"It might have been an accident," I said. "The leaves look something like comfrey. The two have often been confused."

"The comfrey is on the other side of our apothecary plot, well away from the foxglove. Both plants are clearly labeled. I don't see how anyone could have . . ." She gave a heavy sigh. "I suppose I should tell you. A few weeks ago, Sister Dominica was weeding the apothecary garden. She brought me a foxglove leaf and asked me about it."

"What did she want to know?"

"She asked whether the toxin was in the leaves or the

root, and whether the plant could be confused with spinach.''

''With spinach?'' I asked. ''I don't know of any spinach varieties that have hairy leaves. What did you tell her?''

''Someone came along at that moment and interrupted us. I don't believe I gave her an answer.''

Dominica had also asked me about foxglove, just a few hours before Perpetua died. But her question to me came long after the digitalis—if that's what had killed Perpetua—had already been prepared and administered. I was sure Dominica hadn't had anything to do with the old nun's death. Still, her curiosity about foxglove had to have been prompted by *something*. What was it?

I went on to a different question. ''Did Doctor Townsend give you any reason to believe that he suspected digitalis poisoning?''

''No, but he barely spoke to me.'' She sat down on a wood bench in front of the window. ''I suppose Margaret Mary has told you about our difficulties with the Townsend family.'' At my nod, she added, ''I'm afraid Doctor Townsend is more interested in causing trouble than in finding out the truth. We wouldn't ask him to attend our sisters if there were another doctor in this area.''

''But Townsend is also the JP,'' I reminded her. ''If he wants to investigate a death, you can't keep him out of it.''

''I know,'' she said. ''I just wish . . .'' She laced her fingers together and looked down at them.

''Well, if it's any comfort,'' I said, ''he probably won't be doing the autopsy. I'm sure Carr County doesn't have the facilities to test for serum digoxin levels. He's likely sent the body to Bexar County—which means it'll be Wednesday or Thursday before there's any news.'' I stirred. I needed to add Dominica to my list of people to talk to, and Sister Rowena, the infirmarian. But first I had to deal with Sister John Roberta and Dwight.

''I have to make a phone call later this afternoon,'' I said. ''May I use the telephone in Sophia?''

"Of course," Mother said. She stood up. "Or the one in my cottage, as you prefer."

"The office phone will be better," I said. "I don't want to be overheard." I paused. "I need to talk to Dwight's probation officer."

"Probation officer?" Mother was startled. "You mean, Dwight has been in *prison*?"

"You didn't know?"

She shook her head. "Hilaria must have known, but she didn't mention it. I suppose she thought the idea might make the sisters . . . nervous." She pressed her pale lips together. "What kind of crime did he commit?"

"I don't know. I wonder—does Dwight have a personnel file?"

"Yes. After you told me you wanted to search his cottage, I found it. There's not much in it, though. What did you discover when you went through his things? Do you think he might be our arsonist?"

"I don't know yet," I said. I thought of the Camels and the rifle I had seen in his truck. "It does look like he's the guy who shot at me yesterday afternoon, though." I paused. "And I found Mother Hilaria's diary under his mattress."

"So that's what happened to it!" she exclaimed. "But why would Dwight have taken a diary?"

"Perhaps because he didn't want anyone to read about his continuing disagreements with Mother Hilaria. She gave him a raise, but he seems to have wanted a promotion."

Mother Winifred stood and began to walk up and down. "He wants to be farm manager," she said. "He's asked me twice, and I turned him down both times. I'd no idea he approached Hilaria as well."

"Mother Hilaria noted that he threatened her. Has he said anything to you that could be construed as a threat?"

"Not exactly. But he has been rather forceful." She shook her head. "Hilaria should have mentioned it, but she kept her own counsel about things like that."

But Mother Hilaria hadn't kept her own counsel where

the letters were concerned. *Questioned Sr. O about Sr. P's letter.* "If Mother Hilaria had needed to discipline one of the St. Agatha sisters," I asked, "how would she have handled it? Would she have spoken to the sister directly, or would she have asked Olivia to intercede?"

Mother Winifred frowned. "Directly, I'd say. I don't think she was very fond of Olivia. Or perhaps it would be more accurate to say that she didn't fully trust her."

"When you went through Mother Hilaria's papers, did you find a poison-pen letter directed to her?"

Mother's pale blue eyes opened wide in astonishment. "To Hilaria? No, of course not! If I had found such a thing, I would have told you." She shook her head. "Her papers are in my desk. You can look for yourself."

"Perhaps later," I said. "Have you had a chance to speak to the housekeeper about the hot plate in Mother Hilaria's cottage?"

"I talked to Sister Ruth this morning after Mass and told her you wanted to locate an item in the storeroom. She said she'd be in her room this afternoon. She lives in Hannah."

"Thanks," I said. "By the way, have you seen Maggie?"

Mother's smile lightened her tired face. "Margaret Mary is spending a day or so on retreat. I believe she plans to come to supper this evening, though." She glanced at me. "She's told you about her decision to return to St. Theresa's?"

"Yes," I said.."I was a little surprised."

"I can't say I was. I've felt all along that God wanted Margaret Mary to be here. I was delighted to learn that she has come to the same conclusion."

"Of course," I remarked, "her coming *will* delay the election that would have taken place after Sister Perpetua's death."

Mother's mouth pursed. "God works in mysterious ways, my child. Perhaps that's why He brought her back just now."

"Perhaps." I glanced at my watch and stood. "Could I see that personnel file?"

"Of course." Mother Winifred went to the door that led to the cottage, then paused. "Oh, I'm forgetting. Tom Rowan called just before lunch. He'll be here this afternoon to discuss some financial business. He asked me to tell you that he'll stop by Jeremiah and say hello, perhaps about four."

Tom?

Mother didn't appear to notice the sudden flush on my cheeks. "He mentioned that you two were friends," she said, and opened the door. "He's a fine man, so attentive to his father. And quite attractive, too, don't you think?"

"I suppose," I said shortly.

Mother gave me a curious glance. "You've been friends for long?"

"We knew each other in Houston."

She walked across the room to an old walnut desk. "His father was glad to see him come back, although I must say that the circumstances of his return were not exactly—" She unlocked a drawer and took out a folder. "But you probably know all about that messy business in Houston."

I didn't. I wondered what it was.

When I'd left that morning for Jacob and my meeting with Gabriella, I had locked my cottage and taken the key. To be doubly secure, I had pulled a tiny feather from my pillow and inserted it between the door and the jamb about four inches from the floor. A bit melodramatic, maybe, but when I now saw that the feather was still there, I knew that nobody had been in my room in my absence—or was there now, waiting for me. And that Mother Hilaria's diary was still safely hidden under the cushion of the chair.

I glanced at my watch. It was almost one-thirty. While I waited for John Roberta, I lay down on the bed and went over Dwight's personnel file. Mother had been right—there wasn't much in it. A partially filled out sheet indicated that

Dwight H. Baldwin had been hired in July, three years before. No prior addresses, no references, no next of kin or emergency phone numbers. If Dwight had had a life before he became St. Theresa's maintenance man, it wasn't documented here. Neither was his prison record. Maybe Mother Hilaria hadn't known about it when she hired him. Or maybe she wanted to give him another chance, and decided to act as if he were clean.

I closed the file and glanced restlessly at the clock. It was one thirty-five and John Roberta hadn't shown up yet. By one-forty, I knew she wasn't coming.

I frowned, remembering the little nun's obvious anxiety. *If I tell you what I know,* she'd said, barely above a whisper, *will you help me get away?* And when I'd asked her what made her think she was in danger, she'd gasped something about Sister Olivia and Sister Rowena. What was it? *Sister Olivia says we have to stick together. And Sister Rowena says if I tell, I'm being disloyal. They might—*

Might what?

Had someone prevented John Roberta from keeping our appointment?

What was it that she was so anxious to tell me?

I stood, filled with determination and a new energy. She wasn't coming. There was no point waiting. I found the roster of sisters and put it in the pocket of my jeans. I had too much to do and too many people to see to waste time hanging around here. I needed to talk to Ruth about the hot plate, Olivia about her conversations with Mother Hilaria last summer, Anne and Dominica about the poison-pen letters they had received—and John Roberta, if I could find her. I also had a phone call to make, and Tom was planning to drop in.

Tom. I ran a hand through my hair and glanced in the mirror to see whether I should add a quick shampoo to my list of things to do. The woman in the mirror was becomingly flushed, her lips were curved in an anticipatory smile, and her gray eyes were sparkling. I leaned closer, startled.

Was this me?

Was Tom responsible?

I straightened up and turned my back on the fluttery-looking woman in the mirror. I had McQuaid and that was enough. Tom Rowan belonged to a past that was over and done with. Over and done with, I reminded myself as I closed the door and headed in the direction of Sophia.

Over and done with.

The monastery office must once have been a study. Three walls were paneled in dark wood and hung with photographs of women in clerical dress, a gilt-framed oil painting of an elegant-looking older woman I took to be Mrs. Laney, and framed certificates of various sorts. Floor-to-ceiling walnut bookshelves filled with heavy, intimidating volumes—the writings of the church fathers, probably—ran the length of the fourth wall. But the wine red carpet was worn, the damask draperies were faded, and the desk was a utilitarian gray metal affair like the one I'd seen in the barn, with a wooden chair. The sisters of St. Theresa took their vow of poverty seriously.

As I looked around, I wondered how Mrs. Laney's fortune, which now belonged to St. Theresa's, would change all this. If Gabriella became the next abbess, things would probably stay the same, judging from the simplicity of her corner of the barn. But what if Olivia took over? Would her office furniture be plain pine or rich mahogany? Would the floor be bare, or wall-to-wall sheared pile?

But those weren't the questions I needed to answer. I closed the door, sat on a corner of the desk, and dialed J. R. Nutall. It was Sunday, and I caught her at home, baking a cake for her son's birthday. She listened to what I had to say, agreed to confirm my story with Deputy Walters, and phoned me back a few minutes later with the information I requested.

I wasn't surprised to learn that Dwight H. Baldwin had spent four years as a guest of the State of Texas Department of Corrections, Huntsville Unit, Walker County.

And under the circumstances, I wasn't too surprised when Ms. Nutall told me why he'd been sent there. His crime?

Arson.

CHAPTER EIGHT

"Somebody told me it was some silly mistake the cook made. Brought foxglove leaves into the house by mistake for spinach—or for lettuce, perhaps. No, I think that was someone else. Someone told me it was deadly nightshade but I don't believe that for a moment because, I mean, everybody knows about deadly nightshade, don't they, and anyway that's berries. Well, I think this was foxglove leaves brought in from the garden by mistake. Foxglove is Digoxo or some name like Digit-something that sounds like fingers. It's got something very deadly in it—the doctor came and he did what he could, but I think it was too late."

Agatha Christie
The Postern of Fate

Well. Now that I knew Dwight's criminal history, I didn't have to be a rocket scientist to figure out that he was St. T's resident arsonist. In fact, I didn't know how Deputy Walters had managed to overlook him—unless the deputy suspected that Dwight might be the Townsends' hired torch, in which case the idea might not bear too much scrutiny.

Dwight's motive? It was possible, of course, that he *had* been hired by the Townsends. But his bank account and low-rent lifestyle didn't suggest that he'd earned any extra pocket money lately. Much more likely was the motive suggested by the entries in Mother Hilaria's journal. It wouldn't be the first time an employee sabotaged something just so he could repair it. Dwight had been Johnny-on-the-spot at all three fires, proving himself an indispensable candidate for promotion to farm manager. "Don't hurt none fer a man to be rekkanized fer helpin' folks out," he'd said after he pulled Ruby's Honda back from the brink of disaster. Helping folks out? That was a laugh. I'd bet he spilled the logs there in the first place, just so he *could* "help out."

I agreed with Dwight about one thing. He should get the credit he deserved for what he had done. Unfortunately, that might not be so easy to arrange. The evidence I had turned up was entirely circumstantial. Without physical proof of his guilt, Dwight would never be charged with arson.

I did have the 303 cartridge and the cigarette pack from the cliff top, however. Tomorrow, I'd take them into town and leave them with Walters, along with my story about yesterday's shooting. With luck, one or both would yield his prints, which might persuade the county attorney to go for unlawful possession of a firearm by a convicted felon *and* aggravated assault with a deadly weapon. Both were third-degree felonies that could get Dwight two to ten years and five thousand dollars apiece—plus the unserved time from his original sentence.

But whether or not Dwight could be returned to jail, there would be no more fires. One of Mother Winifred's mysteries was solved. She could give Dwight his walking papers—and I could be forgiven a touch of pride at having wrapped up the investigation so quickly.

Unfortunately, I wasn't going to unravel the mystery of the poison-pen letters quite so quickly. What's more, there had been two deaths at St. T's in the last five months, and both victims—Mother Hilaria and Sister Perpetua—had been connected to the letters. It seemed to me an ominous connection.

I was beginning to feel uneasily urgent about talking to

Olivia and to John Roberta, if I could find her. The clouds had blown away and the afternoon sun was warm when I left Sophia and walked toward Hannah, a two-story building bisected by a green-tiled hallway that ran the length of the building. The only thing that kept Hannah from looking like a college dorm was the absence of screaming girls dashing down the corridor in various degrees of undress—and the doors. Every dorm I've ever visited was remarkable for the door decorations. These doors were blank. They wore nothing but a name and a number.

Feeling uncomfortable and distinctly out of place, I checked the roster I'd brought with me, located Olivia's door, and knocked. Then knocked again, harder. No answer. Olivia wasn't there.

According to the roster, John Roberta's room was on the second floor, at the far end. Ignoring her instructions I climbed the stairs, found her door, and knocked. Again, no response.

I was luckier with the housekeeper, who lived at the other end of the second floor. Sister Ruth was a soft, pillowy woman in her forties with a face as round as a full moon, a fractional smile that came and went nervously, and conscientious eyes magnified by thick glasses. She was dressed in a full, flowing habit with a rosary at her waist. She didn't invite me into her room, but through the door I could see that it had the bare simplicity of a monastic cell: a bed covered with a smooth gray blanket, a straight chair, a small chest of drawers, a desk, its surface immaculate. The walls were empty except for a picture of a woman bound to a cross on a heap of firewood, her eyes cast toward a dark and stormy heaven while a malicious-looking soldier lurked in the shadows with a flaming brand. Beneath the picture was a table with an open Bible.

Sister Ruth walked fast for a woman of her girth. I followed her to Sophia, where she opened the door of a storeroom and pulled a cord, lighting a pale bulb so high in the ceiling that its forty watts barely brightened the gloom.

"Mother said you needed assistance," she said. The words were carefully enunciated, the tone helpful. "What is it you're looking for?"

"A hot plate," I said. I glanced around. All manner of things were stored here for future use, arranged in fastidious order on shelves that ran the length of the room. Sheets and blankets, pillows, towels, soap, toilet paper, cleaning supplies, flower vases, an ancient typewriter, a couple of lamps, boxes of lightbulbs. The monastery's quartermaster depot, organized with a quartermaster's skill and attention to detail.

A distressed look appeared on Ruth's face. "Something's gone wrong with your hot plate? I'm *so* sorry. I inspected Jeremiah myself just before you moved in. I'm *sure* I checked to see that everything was in order." Her agitation seemed to be increasing, as if she were personally responsible for the failure of my hot plate. "I'm *very* sorry you've had a problem. If I had known, I—"

I stemmed her apology hastily. "Pardon me, Sister. There's no problem with Jeremiah's hot plate. I'm looking for the one that was in Mother Hilaria's cottage."

Sister Ruth blinked rapidly behind her thick glasses, seeming not to hear. "But if your hot plate is functioning, you shouldn't require another." She folded her hands at her waist. "Perhaps Mother Winifred did not explain our rule. Each cottage, you see, is provided with only *one* hot plate so that occupants cannot prepare meals in their cells. All of our residents are expected to dine communally, and the hot plates are meant only for the occasional cup of coffee or—"

"Excuse me, Sister," I said. "I don't want to cook on Mother Hilaria's hot plate. I simply want to *look* at it."

"Oh, dear." She gave me a nervous half-smile. "I fear I have misunderstood. And I very much fear that you and I have made an unnecessary trip. The item you are looking for is no longer in our inventory."

"Did the sheriff take it?"

"The sheriff?" She opened her eyes very wide. "Why should the sheriff want it?"

"Then it was discarded?"

She shook her head.

"I don't understand," I said. "What happened to it?"

Her hands twisted nervously. "I don't think . . . I wish you hadn't . . ." She stopped, clasped her hands as if to quiet them, and spoke with an effort. "It was taken. From this room."

I stared at her. "Someone stole it?"

"*Stole* it?" She looked horrified. "Of course not!" A corner of her mouth was trembling. "This room is never locked, so it couldn't have been stolen."

I couldn't argue with her logic. I spoke more gently. "When did this loss occur, Sister?"

"A few weeks ago. Before Christmas." Her words were stumbling, as if her tongue had gone numb. "I'm afraid I can't be precise. It was soon after Sister Rowena inquired—" She caught her lower lip between her teeth.

Sister Rowena, the infirmarian, who had been with Perpetua when she died. "Sister Rowena asked about the hot plate?"

She dropped her head so that all I could see was the veil covering her hair. "I know I should have confessed to Mother Winifred that I misplaced an object assigned to my care. But it was Christmas and I had so many other things to do. I felt the hot plate would surely turn up again. There are bare wires in the switch, and it isn't safe to use."

"Bare wires?"

She nodded. "Anyway, no one would wish to use it after . . ." Her voice trailed off. She was fumbling with her rosary.

"I see," I said.

"I will speak to Mother immediately and inform her of my carelessness."

"Thank you for your trouble," I said.

"I am very sorry that I couldn't be more helpful."

"You've been very helpful," I said.

She pulled the light cord. The room went dark.

When I got to Rebecca, the building that housed the St. T sisters, I had two matters to take up with Sister Dominica. I started with the one that was at the top of my mind.

"Foxglove?" Dominica repeated. Her normally expressive face was blank. "Did I? I really don't remember."

I pushed aside a pair of jeans and sat down on her bed. I felt much more at home here than I had in Hannah. The space was more like a college freshman's bedroom than a nun's cell. A battered Spanish-style guitar stood in one corner on a stack of sheet music, the pink flowered bedspread was rumpled, and books and papers were piled on the dresser and shelves. A coffeepot sat on a hot plate, beside an untidy tray of coffee makings and packaged snacks.

"Come on, Dominica," I said. "You can't have forgotten. Why did you ask?"

Dominica was wearing a flowing blue robe with gold moons and stars printed on it. Her loose hair was parted in the middle and rippled over her shoulders. She made a face. "It seems sort of silly."

I sighed. "It's not silly, Dominica. What made you ask the question?"

"It wasn't a what. It was a who."

Aha. Maybe we were getting someplace. "Who was it?"

"Agatha Christie."

"Agatha . . . Christie?"

"Yes. Have you read *Postern of Fate*?"

"I don't think so," I said, feeling distinctly let down. "Is that one of the Miss Marple books?"

She shook her head. "Tuppence and Tommy. Somebody accidentally confuses foxglove and spinach, and puts them into a salad. The whole family eats it and gets sick. But I didn't see how that could have happened. Spinach doesn't look anything like foxglove—or am I wrong?"

"No, you're right," I said. "The leaves of both plants are lance-shaped, true. But spinach is smooth and foxglove is hairy. Foxglove is a different shade of green too."

"Actually," Dominica said, "the victim doesn't die from the foxglove. The killer takes advantage of the accidental poisoning and deliberately puts digitalis in the coffee." She smiled. "Fiendishly clever, wouldn't you say?"

"Fiendishly," I muttered. Personally, I think it's unfortunate when a writer uses a plant to kill somebody. It gives plants a bad press. That's not to say that people don't die of herbal poisonings, of course. Before firearms were invented, plants were the weapon of choice. Tens of thousands of people must have died from ingesting hemlock or monkshood or foxglove, with no one the wiser. In fact, I read recently that in the last ten years, there have been something like five thousand digitalis fatalities. Not an insignificant number. Still, if you're inventing a fictional murder, there are plenty of other creative ways to bump somebody off.

"Here," Dominica said, taking a book off the nightstand. "You might enjoy reading this. You can decide for yourself whether Agatha Christie got it right or not."

"Thanks," I said, and took the book.

"Anyway," Dominica went on, "the same week I was reading *Postern of Fate*, it was my turn to weed the herb garden. I looked down and there it was, right under my nose. Foxglove, I mean. No flowers, just a bunch of hairy green leaves, wearing a name tag. I was curious about the poison and I thought maybe—" She shifted uncomfortably, as if she wanted to say something else.

"And?" I prompted.

She gnawed her lip. "We really do have problems here, you know, and Olivia is responsible for a lot of them. It crossed my mind that it would be easy to sneak some foxglove leaves into her salad and . . ." She made a nervous pleat in her blue robe. "It was only a stray thought, but it was very wicked. It isn't anything I'd really *do*," she added hastily. "When I made that silly remark about getting rid of her, I was just joking."

"It doesn't pay to joke about poisons," I said. "If somebody dies, people have a way of remembering—"

Her eyes flew open and her hands went to her mouth. "Sister Olivia hasn't died, has she?" she whispered in an anguished voice. "If she did, I'd feel terrible! It was so *wrong* of me to wish her ill!"

Dominica's response was a bit over the top, but I didn't think it was an act. Anyway, she was worrying about the wrong person. "Olivia's fine," I said. "As far as I know, that is. I haven't been able to find her. I need to ask her what she knows about the letters."

Dominica's eyes went dark. "From what Mother said at supper last night, I gather she's told you about the one I received. And Miriam too."

"Yes," I said. We had come to the second matter I had to take up with her. "You still don't have any idea who wrote it?"

She glanced at me, her cheeks reddening, and I thought how vulnerable she looked. "That's what makes it so awful," she said bleakly. "I keep wondering who has such a horrible, poisonous malice in her heart. What could I have done to make someone hate me enough to write that kind of lie?"

"Could the writer have seen something that led her to the wrong conclusion?"

"I suppose." She lowered her voice, as if someone might be listening outside the window. "Since Margaret Mary left, Miriam is my best friend. We go for walks together. We touch. Sometimes we hug—the normal kind of contact between friends. But we're not lovers." The blush rose higher. "I've been tempted, but not with Miriam."

"What did you make of the rue leaf in the letter?"

"I didn't know what to think. Was I supposed to feel

rueful? Repentant? But I didn't do anything wrong!''

"No one knows about the letters but Miriam and Mother Winifred?''

"And Margaret Mary. I wrote and told her." She looked down at the toes of her shoes—gold plastic slippers—peeping under her robe. "It might not seem like much to you, being accused of having a woman lover. But I was very hurt. I felt . . . violated, as if the letter-writer had stolen something from me.''

I felt her pain. It was her reputation that had been damaged, perhaps, but more than that. Her estimation of herself. Her peace of mind.

"I was glad I could tell Margaret Mary," Dominica said simply. "She knows my deepest heart.''

"Has one of the sisters given you a clue—a word; a look, even—that she knows about the letter?''

She gave her head a sad shake.

"Has anyone referred to you and Sister Miriam as particular friends?''

Another headshake, sadder.

"Have you been threatened, or has anything happened to your belongings?''

"You mean, like Sister Anne's swimsuit? No, thank God." Then she paused, pulling her brows together. "Except for . . .'' Her eyes went to the guitar in the corner.

"Except for what?''

"I really don't think it can have anything to do with—''

"Tell me, Dominica," I said firmly.

"That guitar belongs to my cousin. I borrowed it because mine got burned up in the fire.''

"The Thanksgiving fire?" No, that was a grease fire in the kitchen. "It must have been the Christmas Eve fire.''

She nodded. "I'd left it inside the sacristy, you see. Miriam and I—she plays the flute—were going to play Christmas carols for the congregation at the end of the service. We'd been practicing for a month, and we sounded pretty good. But then the fire happened, and my guitar burned, and we never got to perform."

"How about Miriam's flute?" I asked. "Was it destroyed as well?"

"No, she'd kept it with her. It was just my guitar. I didn't really think much about it at the time. We were all so frightened by the fire, you see. But afterward I began to wonder about it. How my guitar got burned."

"What do you mean?"

There was a crease between her eyes and her voice was troubled. "I'm almost a hundred percent positive that I left it just inside the door of the sacristy, where it would be handy when I needed it. But when the fire was out, there it was at the back of the room—what was left of it. It had been leaning against the curtains. The only thing I could think of was that somebody had moved it."

"Did you ask?"

"No. I mean, I wasn't absolutely sure where I left it, and it didn't seem all that important—in comparison to the fire itself, I mean." Her voice faltered. "Do you think that the person who wrote the letter also set the fire?"

"No," I said. Dwight was many things, but he wasn't literate enough to be the poison pen. Dominica might have forgotten where she put the guitar. Or someone else might have thought it was in the way and moved it to the back of the room. Or the letter-writer, chancing on the fire, had seized an opportunity to exact a penance—a fitting penance, she might have reasoned, since Dominica was about to perform with Miriam.

"How about Miriam?" I asked. "Has she experienced anything of the sort since the two of you received the letters?"

"You mean, like what happened to my guitar? I don't think so, but you could ask." Dominica frowned. "You're thinking that my guitar was burned because I wouldn't do what the letter-writer told me to do?"

"Maybe," I said. The whole thing was getting much

more complicated. "Back to the fire—where were you when it occurred?"

"In the choir with the other sisters. Father Steven had started saying Mass. I smelled smoke, and then John Roberta—she was sitting at the end of the choir next to the sacristy—got up and slipped into the sacristy to see what was happening. Then she ran out and whispered something to Father Steven. He told us all to leave."

John Roberta had been in the sacristy, alone, with the fire and the guitar? "Did the sisters leave the choir area immediately?"

"We couldn't. Father Steven got fuddled—he really doesn't think very clearly sometimes—and told everybody to go out the main doors at the back of the church. Which meant that the congregation had to leave first. There was a lot of confusion. Dwight ran up with the big fire extinguisher from the front of the church, and he and Father went into the sacristy. And Gabriella and Rosaline went to get the hose. And of course the men of the congregation were milling around, trying to be helpful. Carl Townsend was telling them to carry the statues out and a couple were trying to lift the stone font, and John Roberta was having one of her asthma attacks, which she does whenever she gets anxious."

John Roberta again. "Do you know her well?"

"Not really." Dominica hesitated. "She's an odd sort of person, very shy and anxious about everything—afraid of her shadow, really. I feel sorry for her. She wants to go to a sister house out in Arizona, where the climate would be better for her. But she can't."

"Why not?"

"Oh, the usual." She made a disgusted noise. "Mother Winifred told her she could go, but Reverend Mother General hasn't approved her request because Olivia thinks she should stay here."

"Why?"

"Because without her, the score would be nineteen to

twenty in St. T's favor, that's why. Poor John Roberta is so paranoid that she sees a devil behind every tree, but this time she's got it right. She's a prisoner here until Olivia is safely installed as abbess.'' Dominica made a face. "I'm sure John Roberta wasn't glad to hear that Perpetua had died, but if she was, I for one wouldn't blame her. Maybe now she can get to Arizona."

"I see," I said. As I said good-bye, I couldn't help wondering just how badly John Roberta wanted to leave St. T's. And how much she knew about foxglove.

Sister Anne's bedroom was at the other end of Rebecca. Unlike Dominica's cluttered room, it was immaculate and tidy, although it had none of the starkness of Ruth's. The bed was covered by a blue plaid spread and a heap of blue-flowered pillows. Under the window stood a low, cloth-covered table on which were arranged a statue of Mary, another of Kwan-yin, the Japanese goddess of mercy, and an enigmatic jade buddha. Sister Anne did a lot of reading, I noticed. Neatly stacked on her desk was a book on running, one or two on yoga, and several about women and spirituality, including one I had read, Rosemary Reuther's book, *Womanchurch*. My eyebrows went up. When it came out, Reuther's feminist book had raised plenty of controversy, because it suggested that women should establish their own alternative worship, rather than accommodating themselves to the traditional male-dominated worship service.

Anne was dressed in black ankle-length tights and a loose white cotton shirt with the sleeves rolled up, which made her look like a teenager. She was barefoot and her long dark hair was fastened at the nape of her neck with a leather thong. I didn't have to introduce myself, and she waved away my use of "Sister." She directed me to sit in an upholstered chair by the window, which looked out onto a sloping lawn bordered by a dense, shrubby mass of mesquite and cedar.

"I've been expecting you." She sat down on the bed. "I thought you might want to talk about the letter. And the swimsuit too, of course."

"The whole thing must have been unnerving," I said.

Anne gave a small shrug. Her olive skin was smooth, her small, triangular face closed and private. She looked as if she wouldn't be easily unnerved.

"Do you mind telling me about it?"

She folded her legs into a lotus position and spoke with a quick, active intelligence. "The spot where we swim is secluded. My suit was an ordinary swimsuit, not at all revealing. Actually, the letter struck me as being kind of crazy. Nobody in her right mind would write stuff like that. And there was that little bit of rue." Her chuckle was ironic. "Herb of Grace, Mother Hilaria called it. She said the priests used to use it to sprinkle holy water and drive the devil out of the church. So maybe the rue was supposed to purify me." Her eyes glinted. "Or drive me out, like the devil."

"Your swimsuit was stolen from your room?"

She nodded toward a dresser. "From the second drawer."

Something about Anne's response puzzled me. I had expected her to be offended, even outraged by the theft, but she seemed almost to brush it off. "Was your door locked?" I asked.

"We don't lock doors around here," she said. "There's no need."

Obviously there was a need, considering that Mother Hilaria's hot plate had also been taken. I persisted. "How did you feel when it happened? Did it bother you that somebody would steal a piece of your clothing and trash it?"

She shrugged. "Sure. But it bothered the others a lot more."

"The others?"

"Some of the older sisters went to pieces when they saw it hanging on the cross in the chapel." The corner of her mouth quirked. "I guess it was the ketchup on the crotch that set them off."

"On the *crotch*?"

She laughed deep in her throat. "Mother didn't tell you?" She pulled her thick rope of hair over her shoulder and twisted it around her hand. "They thought it was blood, you see. It reminded them that even though we are nuns, we're real women, with real bodies. Women's bodies. Every month, we shed real blood." A smile flickered briefly and disappeared. "I wanted to leave the bloody thing up there to give us something to think about. But Olivia said it was obscene. Mother Winifred said it was blasphemous. So I took it down."

"You can't blame them," I said.

She tossed her hair back and leaned forward, her eyes bright. "Exactly! They're not to blame. For hundreds of years, the church fathers have taught us that women's blood is obscene—that *women* are obscene. The Church is afraid of our bodies, afraid of sex. That's why all this insistence on celibacy. The Church is afraid of *women*!"

Anne's face had come passionately alive as she spoke. I studied her for a moment. Her political agenda might be irrelevant to what had happened. On the other hand . . .

"So the bloody swimsuit didn't bother you," I said quietly. "I suppose you were even glad to see it hanging where everybody had to look at it."

She unfolded her legs and slid off the bed. "Mother Hilaria was wrong when she told me not to talk about the letter. Every woman here should have been talking about the attitudes that spawn that kind of poison." She walked to the window. "But that bloody swimsuit—it was right there where people *had* to see it. Mother Hilaria couldn't tell people not to talk about it."

"Did they? Talk about it, I mean."

"Not as much as I would have liked." She sighed. "It's hard for women who have grown up in the Church to confront its attitude toward women. But they've got to see how it can poison everyone. The letter-writer, for instance. Her poison comes from the Church itself.''

"But surely someone who writes such letters—''

"Don't you understand?'' Anne's dark eyes were flashing, her body tense with the vitality of her argument. "It's not her fault! She's as much a victim as somebody who gets one of her letters. It's the *Church* that's poisoning people's hearts!''

Anne would have made a great trial attorney. She had just delivered the criminal-as-victim defense as passionately as I'd ever heard it. I paused for a moment, letting the energy of her words ring in the quiet room.

"If someone else hadn't hung the bloody swimsuit on the cross,'' I said at last, "would you have done it?''

She turned toward the window again. Half of her face was in shadow. "Perhaps.''

"Perhaps you did,'' I said.

There was a long silence as she stood, not looking at me. "You're right,'' she said after a minute. "I hung it there. I wanted it to be part of our liturgy.'' She paused. "I don't know. Maybe the symbolism was too subtle. People didn't react the way I hoped.''

"I take it, though, that the letter was genuine—that you didn't write it yourself?''

She was offended. "Of course the letter was genuine! Other people have gotten letters, too, haven't they?''

They had, and Anne might have written them, as easily as writing one to herself. But somehow I didn't think so. I answered with another question. "Since you received the letter, have any of your possessions been tampered with? I'm not talking about the swimsuit, of course.''

She answered immediately. "Yes, actually. Somebody cut the strings on my tennis racket.''

"When was this?''

"A few days after I got the letter—three or four, maybe.''

"Where do you keep your racket?''

"There." She pointed to a racket hanging on the back of her door. "I thought at the time there might be a connection."

Dominica's guitar, Anne's racket. I wondered whether any of Perpetua's belongings had suffered a similar fate. Probably not. She had done her penance.

Anne went back to the bed and sat down. "I suppose you know that my letter wasn't the first. But maybe you don't know that Mother had found out who wrote them. She was planning to put a stop to it."

"She knew?" I stared at her. "Did she tell you who it was?"

She shook her head. "She didn't say how she was planning to stop it, either. But it had to be something pretty drastic. Removal to another house, maybe, or even expulsion. Whatever it was, she said she had to talk it over with Reverend Mother General. She wouldn't do that unless it was really serious."

"And then she died," I said quietly.

She looked at me for a moment, started to speak and stopped, started again. "I wonder . . ."

"Wonder what?"

The words came slowly, almost reluctantly. "Do you suppose that the letter-writer . . . had something to do with Mother Hilaria's death?"

I watched her face. "What makes you ask?"

She moved her hand over the plaid spread, smoothing it. "When it happened, I believed what Mother Winifred told us. About the hot plate and the puddle of milk and Mother Hilaria's bad heart. But now . . ." She paused and looked up at me. "The thing is, Mother Hilaria *did* know who was writing those letters, and she intended to do something about it. Then she died. Was it a coincidence, do you think, or something else?"

"I don't know," I said. "I'd like to find out." I pushed myself out of the chair. "Thanks for your help," I added, and hesitated, thinking of another question. "Feeling the way you do about the Church, Anne, how can you go on being a part of it?''

Anne raised her chin. "I don't intend to."

"What are you going to do?"

"A friend of mine has established an order in Chicago— a group of women who live together and work in a hospice. They have no connection with the Catholic Church. It's a big move for me, but I'm ready to make it. In fact, I'm anxious to leave. There's a limited amount of room in the Chicago house, and if I don't go soon, they'll give my space to someone else."

"Why are you staying?"

"Because I don't want to tip the balance. Actually, I think change would be good for St. T's. We're too insular, and there's a tendency to be fixed in our ideas. In my opinion, Reverend Mother General has the right idea, and I personally don't think she's the Wicked Witch of the West, the way some people do. But she's chosen the wrong person to make changes. Olivia is a despot."

I smiled a little. "No redeeming qualities?"

Anne considered. "She's determined, you've got to give her that. But she's made too many enemies. If you ask me, she'd better watch out. Somebody might slip something into her salad."

CHAPTER NINE

Rue in Thyme should be a Maiden's Posie.
                    Scottish proverb

Rue has a reputation as an anaphrodisiac (reducing sexual excitement) and an abortifacient. . . . Unfortunately, the active dose of various extracts of the plant . . . is at the same level as a toxic dose.

                              Steven Foster
                              Herbal Renaissance

I was still thinking about what I had learned from both Anne and Dominica as I walked up the path to Jeremiah. The thoughts were driven out of my head by a deep voice.

"Hello, China."

Tom Rowan was lounging on the front step, blue-jeaned legs and boots stretched out in front of him, a brown Stetson tipped forward over his eyes. There was a blue nylon zip bag on the porch beside him. He sat up and thumbed his hat back.

"You look surprised. Didn't Mother Winifred tell you I'd be stopping by?"

"Yes, she did. I guess I lost track of time."

"Nothing new about that. Remember?" He gave me a slow grin. "We'd have a lunch date and you'd work right through it. Dinner, too." He scooted over so I could sit down next to him. The narrow wooden step made for a cozy fit.

"I wasn't the only one," I said. "Remember the Saturday afternoon we were supposed to go out on Alex's boat? You got involved at the bank and forgot all about it. And the evening my mother was taking us to the Opera Guild dinner and you stood us *both* up?"

He held up his hands, laughing. "I confess, Counselor. I'm guilty, you're guilty, we're both guilty." He dropped his hands. "I guess we both could have done a lot of things differently."

We sat quietly for a moment. I don't know what Tom was thinking, but I was wishing I could go back and do at least some of it differently—not for him, but for me. If I'd been willing to give a little more, maybe I could have learned something. Of course, there might not have been much to learn: Tom had been as arrogant as I, and we'd pushed one another around rather badly. But I might have learned something that could have smoothed those rough early days with McQuaid.

Tom looked up at the cliff on the other side of the Yucca. "You've got a lovely spot for a retreat," he said. The sky was blue now, no clouds. The sun, dropping toward the western horizon, spilled a golden light over the cliff. "Nothing ever happens here."

I grunted. Nothing much ever happens? How about a little arson, a few poison-pen letters, two questionable deaths, a power struggle between monastic factions, and a feminist revolt against the masculine authority of the Church? But unless Tom spent a lot of time here or cultivated an inside informant, those were things he probably wouldn't hear about. "Do you come out here often?" I asked.

"Not often enough." He rested his crossed arms on bent knees. "Maybe I'll ask Mother Winifred if I can stay for a couple of weeks this spring. I'm glad I've had this time with my father, but I need to get away. Sometimes the old man . . ." He let the sentence slide away.

"Rough, huh?" I asked. I remembered Tom Senior as a

man who liked to pull the strings, call the shots. When somebody like that is confronted by the Big C, the fallout can be tough on everybody.

The corner of Tom's mouth turned down. "He's got a list as long as your arm of things that have to be finished in the next few months—some of which strike me as pretty damn ridiculous. The trouble is, I get roped into his agenda whether I want to or not."

"How long has he been ill?"

"The cancer was diagnosed a year ago." He shook his head. "You'd think he'd take a vacation, travel, do things he's been putting off. But it's only made him work harder. He always was strong as an ox, you know, and he's still in pretty good physical shape. Oh, before I forget, he sends his regards—and he wants you to have dinner with us. How about tomorrow night?"

"Okay," I said, shoving down a little gremlin of eagerness.

"There's not much to choose from in Carr, but the Tex-Mex at the Lone Star dance hall is more Mex than Tex. Not half-bad."

I nodded. "But as I recall, you were into up-scale food. A different cuisine every night." Back in Houston, we had a regular restaurant routine: Malaysian on Monday, Thai on Tuesday, Indian on Wednesday, and so on. We could eat out every night and not hit the same restaurant more than once a month. "Did you get tired of gourmet glitz?"

"More or less. But that's another story. Anyway, Dad was chompin' at the bit, wanting me to come back and take over for him." He laughed shortly. "But by the time I cleaned things up in Houston and got ready to leave, he'd decided he wasn't quite ready to cash in. So we've tailored one job to fit two people. It hasn't been easy."

The bank's situation couldn't be all that secure, either. "I read that the FDIC's taken control of nearly a thousand Texas banks in the last ten years," I said. The small banks were the most vulnerable, of course. If the oil crash hadn't brought them down, the real estate nosedive had.

Tom picked a grass stem and stuck it between his teeth. "True enough. But Dad's always been conservative, and the bank is in good shape. Assets are up, loans, Fed funds sold, et cetera, et cetera." He slanted an amused glance at me. "If you want to see a balance sheet, China, I can get you one."

"I'm not here to look at your balance sheet," I said. I was suddenly, uneasily aware of the warm solidity of his hip next to mine on the narrow step. I wanted to move away but I couldn't, unless I stood up and broke contact altogether. And I found myself not quite wanting to do that. The familiar electric charge was still there between us. It felt good.

He sat there for a minute, arms crossed on his bent knees. I had forgotten how hefty his wrists were, how strong and capable his hands. "Cowboy hands," I used to call them, hardly the hands of a banker. I pulled my eyes away from the curl of blond hair at his shirt cuff. I wanted to say something to break the silence, but I couldn't think of anything.

"So tell me about your life," he said. "What are you doing now that you're not practicing law?"

That was safe enough. I told him about moving to Pecan Springs, and about the shop.

"I guess I'm not surprised," he said. "You always liked plants. Is that why you're here? To check out the garlic?"

I shifted my position, pushing one leg out in front of me, putting an inch of daylight between us. "I'm on retreat. I came to get away for a while."

"Stu Walters doesn't tell it that way."

"Stu Walters sucks eggs," I remarked mildly.

He chuckled. "You'll get no argument from me on that—or from half the town, either. Thing is, though, Stu usually knows which eggs to suck and which to leave in the nest. That's how he and the sheriff keep their jobs. This county is *muy* political." He was looking away, across the river, his mouth amused. "So how's the big investigation coming, Detective Bayles? Caught your little firebug yet? Which nun is it?"

I hate to be patronized, even by Tom Rowan. "Matter of fact, I have," I said deliberately. "I wouldn't call him a 'little' firebug, though. He's already done four years at Huntsville on two counts of arson."

Tom's head swiveled around.

"Unfortunately," I went on, "the evidence is circumstantial and the county attorney probably won't prosecute. But we may still nail his tail. He took a shot at me yesterday afternoon. Three shots, as a matter of fact."

Tom was staring, his gray eyes open wide, the grass stem hanging from his lower lip. "Somebody *shot* at you?"

I pointed to the top of the cliff. "From up there. Townsend territory."

"He missed you?"

"Do I look dead? He wasn't trying to hit me. He was trying to scare me."

He tossed the grass stem away. "You've been saying 'he,' so I assume it wasn't one of the sisters. It wouldn't be Father Steven, either. Which leaves the maintenance man. Dwight somebody-or-other."

I eyed him. It was interesting that he hadn't mentioned the Townsends as a possibility. "If you ask me," I said idly, "the only mystery is why Stu Walters didn't finger Dwight in the first place."

"He told me he thought it was one of the sisters."

"That's what he told me, too. But he might at least have run a background check, or talked to Dwight's parole officer. She could have clued him in on the prior which is the clincher." I paused. "Only thing I can figure is that Walters assumed that the real arsonist was on the Townsend payroll. Doing a little dirty work for the neighbors, so to speak. So he didn't look all that close."

Tom's eyes narrowed. "My, my, you *are* a suspicious

lady. Quick, too. Takes some folks months to ferret out the politics in this county.''

''I've had a little experience with crooked cops and smooth politicians. In my former life, that is.''

''Yeah.'' He grinned. ''Makes you kind of dangerous, doesn't it?''

I met his eyes and read the intention in them as clearly as if he had spoken. It was like a jolt of electricity, stopping my breath, tightening my stomach muscles. Me, dangerous? Tom was the one who was dangerous. Between my shop and my relationship with McQuaid, I had more than enough to occupy me. I didn't need any complications—especially one with so many powerful memories hooked to it.

Tom looked away too, and the corners of his mouth quirked. ''Dangerous from . . . well, Dwight's point of view. How'd you get onto him?''

''Superior detective work. A cartridge casing and an empty cigarette pack.''

He shook his head. ''You never cease to amaze me.'' He sat for a moment, then added, more seriously: ''That was one of my problems when we were together, you know.''

''What was a problem? That I amazed you?''

''That you were so blasted resourceful. You didn't need anybody but yourself.'' There was a bitterness in his tone that surprised me, but it was gone when he added, ''So what's going to happen to Dwight?''

''The least that can happen is that he's out of a job; the most, that he goes back to Huntsville. It all depends on whether he left prints, and whether the county attorney and Pardons and Paroles decide to take any action.'' Where the county attorney is concerned, it depends on what kind of caseload he's carrying and whether he wants to put the effort into the case. Where Pardons and Paroles is concerned, you never can tell. It sometimes depends on who's lurking in the background.

Tom took off his hat and put it on the porch beside him.

"So what do you think? Was Dwight acting on his own hook, or was he in it with somebody else?"

The question sounded casual enough, but I'd have bet there was something beneath it. I wouldn't have been a bit surprised if the bank was *muy* political too. In a small town like Carr, the county commissioners did plenty of deals with the local lending institution. For instance, somebody— Tom's bank, no doubt—held a pretty healthy mortgage on that Southern plantation ranch house I'd seen yesterday.

Was Dwight working for somebody else? I spoke warily. "Anything's possible, I guess. The guy's checking account was pretty anemic, but he could have stashed the cash somewhere else—in another bank account, maybe, or in a tin can behind a loose board."

"What do you think?" Tom insisted.

I pushed myself to my feet. "I think that once Dwight is out of here, the sisters can put away their firefighting gear." If the Townsends were behind the arson, they'd lost their inside man. And if Tom had anything more than a passing acquaintance with the Townsends, he could pass that message along.

Tom leaned back on his elbows, squinting up at me. "You haven't changed a bit, you know. You still play your cards close."

"Do I?" I countered.

"Hey, come on, China. Give a guy a break." He got to his feet and picked up his hat. "I didn't drive all the way out here to arm-wrestle with you."

"I thought you came to talk business with Mother Winifred."

His sudden, teasing grin lightened his whole face. "Oh, yeah? Then how come I brought this?" He reached for the blue nylon bag.

"What's that?"

"You'll see." He slung the bag over his shoulder. "Come on. Let's go for a hike."

I eyed him. "Where?"

"I don't know. Anywhere." He gestured toward the cliff. "How about up there? The view is pretty spectacular."

"Up *there*?" I groaned. "Do you know what that trail's like?"

"Yeah. A nice stroll for mountain goats." He grinned. "I'll bring the goodies. All you have to do is get your butt up there. Now stop fussin' and come on."

The climb was easier in the daylight, and the landscape—which had been serene and lovely in the moonlight—was even more impressive under the late afternoon sun. The exercise of climbing seemed to ease the tension between us, too. I was grateful.

When we reached the top, we found a flat limestone ledge and sat on it, watching the sun glinting off the Yucca's silver ripples, feeling its warmth on our backs. I heard the raspy *chit-chit-chit* of a titmouse in a thicket of juniper and the chiding murmur of the river, chattering to itself at the foot of the cliff. A great blue heron, gliding from a tree to the river's edge, was a moving shadow across the rock. The falling sun cast a red glow over the serenity of St. Theresa's.

"So," Tom said. "Now that you've caught your crook, you can get some peace and quiet."

"I wish," I said regretfully.

He picked up a stone and tossed it over the cliff. It fell free all the way to the bottom, where it splashed into a dark pool. "Oh, yeah? What's up?"

There wasn't any reason not to tell him. It took only a couple of minutes to sketch the situation: the accusing letters, Mother Hilaria's cryptic diary, John Roberta's whispered hint that she knew something. And the two deaths.

By the time I finished, Tom was frowning at me. "Diary? Mother Hilaria kept a diary?"

I was a little surprised that Tom had focused on the diary, out of all the things I'd told him, but I only nodded.

"That's where I got the information that puts the finger on Dwight as the arsonist."

"Anything else?" he asked casually.

"Not enough," I said. "You've got to read between the lines." I looked at him. His question was almost too casual. "Why are you asking?"

He looked away. "Just that . . . it's hard to believe that all this has been going on in this calm, peaceful place. You think somebody actually *murdered* those two nuns?"

What did I think? To tell the truth, sitting here with Tom in the bright light of late afternoon, with a postcard-pretty view of St. T across the river, the idea seemed pretty far-fetched. "The JP—Royce Townsend—ruled that Mother Hilaria died of a heart attack," I said. "And there won't be an autopsy report on Sister Perpetua until later in the week. As to murder—there's certainly no evidence."

"Well, I can't buy it," Tom said. "Nuns don't do those kinds of things."

"That just shows how much you know," I snapped. "You only have to be here a couple of hours to realize that there are all kinds of emotional currents and cross-currents eddying around this place, some of them pretty turbulent."

Tom pulled the nylon bag onto the ledge between us and unzipped it. "Well, there's certainly been plenty of turbulence since the merger," he said in a conciliatory tone. "The two groups don't have much in common."

"About as much as Austin and Dallas," I said. "Or San Francisco and L.A." I peered into the bag. "What's all this stuff?"

"Happy hour." He handed me two long-stemmed plastic wineglasses and went back to the bag. "I suppose you've heard that the Mother General wants to build a retreat center here. She thinks it would make money for the order."

"She's probably right." I set the glasses on a rocky out-cropping and took the paper napkins he handed me. "I never knew that the Church was obliged to show a profit to its principle stockholder, though. By the way, I met Sadie Marsh this morning.''

''Sadie's something else.'' He pulled out a cold bottle of zinfandel and a corkscrew. With a deft motion, he extracted the cork and handed me the bottle. ''You pour,'' he said, diving into the bag again. ''There's cheese and crackers here somewhere, and some other stuff.''

There was indeed cheese, a creamy Brie and a tangy blue, along with smoked salmon, chunks of raw celery, broccoli, crab-stuffed mushrooms, and buttery crackers—none of which came from the Carr corner grocery. I poured the wine and we touched rim to rim, our glances meeting and sliding away again.

''To old times,'' I said.

''To good friends,'' he amended. We ate and drank in companionable silence as the sun slipped lower behind us. I was feeling relaxed now, warmer, looser, happier. It could have been the wine, or the sun on my shoulders, or Tom's company. Whatever it was, it felt good.

Tom put what was left of our happy hour—a few crackers, some leftover dip, the empty zinfandel bottle—into the bag. ''I'm curious,'' he said. ''How did you and Sadie Marsh happen to get together?''

I chuckled. ''She came over to size up Mother Winifred's hired gun.''

''I wonder what she thought of you. More to the point, what did you think of her?''

''As you said: She's something else. If she gets her way, St. T's will grow garlic till kingdom come.''

Tom shrugged. ''That's what she wants, all right, but she doesn't have any leverage.''

''Maybe more than you give her credit for,'' I said unguardedly, thinking about the deed restrictions.

''Oh, yeah?'' Tom's look sharpened. ''What kind of leverage could she have?''

I shouldn't have opened my big mouth. The old deed was Sadie's trump card, not mine, and she ought to decide when to play it. Also, I was beginning to wonder about Tom's curiosity. But of course, where property and money are concerned, banks are always curious. And never neutral, I reminded myself. Tom would side with the player who controlled the dollars. He wouldn't have any choice.

I changed the subject. "Tell me about the Townsends," I said.

"Carl and Rena?"

"And the boys."

He shrugged. "You probably know the type—high rollers in a closed game. Carl's a loan shark who trades in favors. He'll do one for you and charge you three. Rena is a political power broker in county politics. The oldest boy, Royce, is a doctor—not the best in the world, actually. There have been several complaints at the local hospital, and I hear another doctor is opening a new practice next month. But Royce has also gotten himself elected justice of the peace, so he's in on almost everything that happens in his precinct, which includes the town of Carr. There's another son, Byron. He used to practice law. Now he's a county judge."

"That's a lot of power to be tied up in one family."

"It's not unusual in a rural area. It would probably be a good idea for you to stay clear of them." Before I could respond, his tone lightened and he circled my shoulders with his arm, pulling me against him. I knew I should pull away, but it felt familiar, comfortable. "So, old friend. What's your personal life like?"

"The shop keeps me pretty busy."

"Any boyfriends?"

Boyfriend? Not the word I'd used to describe my relationship with McQuaid. "One."

"Just one?" He looked down at me, his face inches away. "It's serious, then?"

"We've been dating for several years." Why was I so reluctant to talk about McQuaid? Maybe it was because he was part of my life back there, and I was here—*here* to get away from *there*. "We've been living together since last May."

"Why aren't you married?" he asked bluntly.

Why? It's a question McQuaid asks from time to time, more often now that we're living together. Maybe it's because personal independence is a high priority with me, higher than family values. Maybe it's because I'm still learning who I am and what I want out of life. How many reasons do you need for not being married?

Tom dropped his arm and got to his feet. "Maybe you haven't found the right guy," he said. He grinned and held out a hand to help me up. "Or maybe you found him and let him get away, say, eight or nine years ago."

I couldn't help laughing. "Modest, aren't we? You haven't changed, either, you know. Still the same arrogant SOB."

He slung the bag over his left shoulder and hooked his right arm through mine. He glanced down at me, his eyes reminding me of past intimacies. "Are you happy, China?"

I thought of the long hours at the shop and the pressures of living with McQuaid and Brian. And of the quiet pleasure of being alone in Jeremiah with no demands to meet, no obligations to fulfill—once I had settled the business of the letters. "I don't know," I said. "That's part of why I'm here, I guess. To figure it out." We were walking slowly in the direction of the path and the downhill climb. "What about you?"

"What about me?"

"Are you happy?"

He laughed shortly. "Happy? Hell, no. There's too much up in the air. Dad's cancer, personal finances, things at the bank that need to be changed but can't as long as he's in the picture. My life has been on hold for the last couple of years."

Personal finances. I wondered what that was about. "Any girlfriends?"

"Since you?" He chuckled. "Come on, China. Who could possibly replace you?"

"Be serious," I said. "You haven't been twiddling your thumbs and hoping you and I would stumble across one another and fall wildly in love again."

He dropped my arm and took my hand instead. "I was married for a couple of years. A woman named Janie."

"Past tense?"

He nodded.

"What happened?"

"It didn't work."

"Why not?"

"Like us, sort of." He shrugged. "There was a lot of competition from our careers. Janie was—still is—a TV anchor woman for Channel 6, very sexy, very beautiful, very busy. After the flame died down, we didn't have a lot in common. Unfortunately, the divorce was messy."

Messy? I wondered if it was the "messy business" Mother had mentioned. He fell silent for a minute, while I debated whether to ask him if the failure of his marriage was one of the things that had brought him back to Carr.

"That bit about our falling wildly in love again," he said, interrupting my thoughts. "It's not outside the realm of possibility."

"Yes, it is," I said. "I'm committed."

He grinned. "You are?" The question just missed being a challenge.

I tried to pull my hand away, but he was holding it tightly. He drew me against him. "We'll just see about that," he murmured, and kissed me hard, long.

The kiss fanned a spark of body-memory I had thought was long extinguished. I pushed him away. "I need to go," I said. "I have to talk to Mother Winifred before supper."

"You haven't changed a bit, have you," he said, and grinned.

●　　●　　●

I caught Mother Winifred in her herb garden at twilight, a half hour before the supper bell. She was trimming the lower branches from a young chaste tree, its trunk still pale gray, unfurrowed.

"Did you know that the seeds of this tree used to be used to fend off temptation?" she asked, holding out a bundle of reddish brown twigs. "People called it the Tree of Chastity."

I thought of Tom's kiss. "Maybe we could use a little of it these days." I told her what I had learned from J. R. Nutall, and what I had concluded about Dwight's guilt. "The case is entirely circumstantial," I added, "which means that the county attorney probably won't prosecute."

"Well, then, what do you suggest?" she asked.

"I think we should let things ride for tonight," I said. "Tomorrow morning, I'll drive into town and talk with Deputy Walters. Is there a car I can borrow?"

Mother pulled down one of the slender branches and clipped it. "We have two cars, but I'm afraid that both are in use. Sister Rowena has one, and Sister Olivia the other. Dwight drives our GMC, of course—he's taken it to town this evening. But there is another truck you can use. It may be past its prime, but it works fine."

"Thanks," I said. I could drive over to Sadie Marsh's ranch as well, and tomorrow evening, drive into town for dinner with Tom and his dad. "Since Dwight's an ex-felon, his prints are on file. If they match any prints on the cigarette pack or the cartridge case, the deputy and the county attorney will decide whether there's enough to make an assault charge stick. They may decide not to arrest him at all."

Mother piled the clipped branches together. "In which case I'll simply discharge him." She smiled. "It will be an enormous relief to stop worrying about the place burning down around our ears." She picked up her pruning shears. "If you can only resolve the other matter as handily, all my prayers will have been answered."

"I'm afraid it's not going to be quite so simple, Mother." We turned to walk toward the cottage. "I'll know more after I've talked to Olivia and John Roberta, though."

Mother glanced up at me. "That may take a while, my dear."

"Why?"

She paused to replace a rock that had been jostled out of the border and onto the path. "Because neither of them are here. John Roberta suffers from asthma, you see, and she had an attack after Mass this morning. Her inhalator couldn't be found, and she was getting worse, so Rowena drove her to the Carr County Hospital for treatment. She'll be there at least another day, perhaps more. Dr. Townsend apparently wants to do some tests."

I frowned. "Did you talk to Townsend yourself?"

"No. Rowena handles that sort of thing." She glanced at me. "Why are you asking?"

I was asking because early this morning, John Roberta had sought me out, anxious to tell me something that Sister Rowena might consider "disloyal." A few hours later, Sister Rowena had spirited her away. Those two events seemed entirely too coincidental to suit me. And what was this business about the inhalator being misplaced?

But that was beside the point, at least for the moment. If John Roberta was in the hospital, it shouldn't be all that difficult to talk to her. I could do it tomorrow morning, after I talked to Stu Walters. In the meantime . . .

Mother put her basket beside the cottage door. "What about Olivia?" I asked, following her into the cottage. "She isn't here either?"

Mother went to the small bathroom to wash her hands in the basin. "She's been summoned to the motherhouse at El Paso," she said through the open door, "to confer with Reverend Mother General. She drove into Austin this morning and caught a plane. She'll be back Tuesday morning."

"Isn't that rather unusual—for a sister to see the Mother General?"

"Before the merger, Olivia was St. Agatha's abbess," Mother reminded me. She sighed as she dried her hands. "I imagine they're planning strategy."

"Strategy?"

"For the election. Reverend Mother will probably telephone tomorrow with word that we should vote as soon as possible."

"But I thought Maggie's return—"

Mother Winifred came back into the room, pursing her lips. "Reverend Mother has approved Margaret Mary's petition to resume her vocation, on the condition that her voting privileges be suspended for a year. Until she's sure she wants to stay, that is." She sighed again. "A perfectly reasonable suggestion."

On the face of it, yes. But given Reverend Mother General's motives . . . "I suppose that means that Sister Olivia will be elected?"

"I suppose." Mother dropped into a chair. I noticed how pale she looked, her skin the color of old ivory. "I'm sorry to see the changes coming."

"But you're not willing to oppose them?"

Mother shook her head tiredly. "Hilaria would have, I'm sure." Her shoulders slumped; her voice was muffled. "But opposing Reverend Mother's authority goes against everything I've been taught. And I'm seventy years old. I'm ready to step aside and let someone else do this work."

I frowned. "I still think—"

"Don't you understand?" Mother Winifred raised her head. "After Olivia has taken over, my time will be my own. See that clump of lemongrass?" She pointed. "I forgot to dig it up and the frost killed it. Next year, when Olivia is doing this job—and doing it quite well, I'm confident—that won't happen. She and Reverend Mother General have assured me that the herb garden—especially the apothecary's garden—will be one of the conference center's major assets.''

I was beginning to sense some of the pressure that had been brought to bear on Mother Winifred. But there was another side to the argument, and I pressed it. ''Don't you feel you have an obligation, if not to St. Theresa's, then to Mrs. Laney and Mother Hilaria? If it's possible to preserve their dream for this place, shouldn't you try?''

Mother Winifred gave me a small smile. ''Sadie is perfectly capable of preserving Helen Laney's dream. And to tell the truth, there's very little I can do.''

I thought of what Tom had said. ''But without your help, Sadie will be in the minority. She *needs* you.''

Mother's voice firmed. ''If God wants St. Theresa's to be a contemplative house, my dear, that's what it will be, no matter what Reverend Mother and Olivia have in mind. If He prefers us to operate a retreat center here, that's what we will have, regardless of what Sadie Marsh and Sister Gabriella want.'' Her eyes softened. ''I feel He prefers me to look after the lemongrass.''

I could hardly argue with God. There was a space of silence, then she said, ''Before we go to supper, please tell me: Have you learned anything about the letters?''

''Two things,'' I said. ''The letter-writer had nothing to do with the sacrifice of Anne's swimsuit.''

Her brows went up. ''No? Then who—?''

''I'm afraid you'll have to take my word for it.''

An answering smile glimmered on her mouth, as if I had confirmed something she'd already guessed. ''Very well, then. The other thing?''

''Mother Hilaria's hot plate is missing from the storage room. Ruth says it disappeared sometime last month, right after Rowena inquired about it.''

''Oh, dear.'' Mother looked deeply troubled. ''Oh, dear. But if you're thinking that Rowena took it, I must say that I can't agree. She's an extraordinarily conscientious woman.'' She thought for a moment. ''But for that matter, so is Ruth. She treats every item, even the toilet paper, as if God had assigned it to her custody. Oh, *dear.*''

I sat down across the table. "If it won't make us late to supper," I said, "I'd like to hear about Mother Hilaria's death."

It wasn't hard to re-create the scene in my mind as Mother Winifred spoke. The day, a Saturday, had been quite cool for September, and the afternoon and evening were rainy. Mother Hilaria ate supper as usual, stepped into the office to do a half hour's worth of paperwork, then went back to her cottage on the other side of Rebecca, stopping in the garden to pick some tansy and a few stalks of late-blooming golden yarrow.

When she went into the cottage, she put the blossoms into a vase, placed it on her desk, and settled down to work. "She was always busy with one project or another," Mother Winifred added. "This time, it was Hildegard of Bingham. She was working on Hildegard's *Book of Healing Herbs*. I'm hoping to continue her work, when I get some free time."

Mother Hilaria had taken out a tablet of handwritten notes on Hildegard, the abbess of a Benedictine convent during the twelfth century, and began to work. At some point, she apparently decided to make a cup of chocolate. The hot plate was on a wide shelf in the back corner of the living-sitting area, next to the small sink.

"Her shelf looked very much like mine," Mother Winifred said, nodding toward it.

I turned to look. There was the shelf, with a hot plate on it, and beside that, a small sink. Under the shelf was an apartment-size refrigerator. The rest of the story was tragically simple. Mother Hilaria had filled her kettle from the water tap, put it on the hot plate, and got out a tin of cocoa mix. As she took a quart carton of milk from the refrigerator, she dropped it on the floor. It broke open and spilled where she was standing. Without thinking, she reached for the knob to turn off the hot plate. It gave her a severe shock, which jolted her heart into arrhythmic spasms that quickly led to full cardiac arrest. John Roberta found her body an hour later, when she came for a late-evening talk they had scheduled.

"Did anyone examine the hot plate?" I asked. "Ruth said something about bare wires in the switch. That suggests the wires were somehow stripped."

Mother frowned. "I don't know anything about that. I thought the thing was just old, and somehow malfunctioned."

It was possible that the old insulation became brittle and simply disintegrated. But it was also possible that the process had been accelerated.

"I wonder—" I said. Just at that moment, however, the supper bell began to ring, and we stood to go. But Mother had one more thing to tell me.

"This is on a much more pleasant subject," she said as we went to the door together. "I expect you'll be glad to know that one of our prayers was answered this afternoon, rather dramatically. Sister Gabriella was quite pleased. In fact, she jumped up and down a time or two. I don't think I've seen her that excited in years."

"Really?" I paused with my hand on the knob. What kind of prayer deserved that sort of response?

Her blue eyes twinkled. "Yes, really. The Cowboys beat the Packers, 21–14, in the very last second. The announcer had quite a catchy name for the winning play."

"Oh?"

"Yes. He called it a Hail Mary pass." She was beaming. "Football is like life, my dear. God likes to keep people on their toes until the very last play."

CHAPTER TEN

If a man be anointed with the juice of Rue, the
poison of Wolf's-bane, Mushrooms, or Tode
stooles, the biting of Serpents, stinging of Scor-
pions, spiders, bees, hornets and wasps will not
hurt him, and the Serpent is driven away at the
smell thereof.

John Gerard
The Herbal or General History of Plants, 1633

I had hoped to talk to Rowena after Sunday night supper,
but she didn't appear. Maybe she'd stayed at the hospital
with John Roberta. Dwight didn't show up—probably still
in town. And Maggie wasn't there, either. Mother had said
she'd decided to extend her personal retreat and was taking
her meals alone. I was glad for her. Coming back to the
inner life from the outer world was a major move. It was
good that she could settle into it at her own pace.

But Maggie knew the monastery's history, and I knew I
could trust her. I wanted to get her opinion on some of the
questions I was turning over in my mind. I needed to talk
to her as soon as she surfaced again.

I ate quickly—the meal was tomato soup with basil,
grilled cheese sandwiches, cabbage slaw seasoned with car-
away, and a beautifully ripe apple—and went back to Jeremiah. After the day I'd had, I was ready to pamper myself.
I lit a vanilla-scented candle, added lavender oil to a tubful
of warm water, and climbed in. I leaned back and closed
my eyes, letting the thoughts go, letting my body soak in

the lavender-scented silence. After a long while I scrubbed with rosemary soap and a loofah, relishing the gentle raspiness. When I toweled off, I pulled on a pair of silky pink pajamas—how long had it been since I'd worn anything but a ratty old tee shirt to sleep in?—and climbed into bed with the Agatha Christie mystery Dominica had given me. The sheets were smooth, the light fell on the pages exactly the way I like it, and the cottage was so quiet I could hear the rippling murmur of the river not far from my door.

But my mind kept returning to the real-life mysteries at St. Theresa's, the plots of which had gotten considerably more tangled in the last twenty-four hours. With luck, I had managed to solve the simplest puzzle, the business of the fires. By tomorrow, the affair would be in the hands of the Carr County authorities and Dwight's plot would be closed out.

The other plot, though, was as mazelike as one of Agatha Christie's mysteries. I found a piece of scrap paper and jotted down its basic elements—the ones I knew about so far, anyway. The poisonous letters to Perpetua, to Anne, to Dominica and Miriam, and the letter to Mother Hilaria, missing and presumed destroyed. Mother Hilaria's diary, with its cryptic references to talks with Sister Olivia and Sister R. The bloody swimsuit had proved to be a red herring, but Anne's mutilated tennis racket and Dominica's burned guitar had yet to be accounted for. And Mother Hilaria's hot plate, missing since Rowena had inquired about it. I frowned. That hot plate bothered me. I kept thinking about Ruth's remark about the bare wires.

I reached into the drawer of the bedside table for the roster and wrote down the nine R names. I had already met three of them: Rachel, the sister who had deplored Perpetua's autopsy; the housekeeper, Ruth; and the elusive John Roberta. There were six others I hadn't yet encountered: Rowena the infirmarian, Rosabel, Rose, Rosaline, Ramona, and Regina. I felt as if I were snared in a sticky cobweb of Rs.

Muttering a curse, I stared at the list. Wasn't there a way to narrow it, or at least focus my efforts? I found the room roster and checked to see which ones lived in Hannah. Of the nuns I hadn't yet talked with, four were St. Agatha sisters: Rowena, Ramona, Rose, and Regina. I'd speak with them tomorrow.

And of course, there was the ubiquitous Sister O. I wrote the name *Olivia* and drew curlicues around it. I'd be waiting for her the minute she got back from her visit to the motherhouse.

And then, as an afterthought, I added Father Steven's name to the list. In his role as confessor, he would have talked to all of these women. The relationship between priest and penitent is as sacred as that between attorney and client, but he might have picked up something he would be willing to share. Anyway, I knew nothing about the man. Maybe he was a more significant player than I had imagined. Maybe—

I woke up with a start when my book slid onto the floor. I looked at the clock. It was only nine, but suddenly I was too tired to read. I had a right to be tired, though, and satisfied to boot. I hadn't learned as much about the letters as I would have liked, but I'd figured out the identity of the arsonist. By this time tomorrow, Dwight would be in Stu Walters's hands, and the deputy and the county attorney could figure out what they wanted to do with him. I slid under the sheets, turned off the light, and stretched out, feeling quite pleased with myself.

I didn't get to sleep long. I was awakened just before 10 P.M. by the frantic clanging of St. Theresa's bell—four hard clangs, a missed beat, then another four clangs. I jumped out of bed, pulled on my jeans and a sweatshirt, and grabbed my flashlight.

Halfway up the path to Sophia, sprinting, I caught up with Maggie. Her jacket was on inside out over her flannel pajamas, and she was carrying a small fire extinguisher.

"What's happened?" I gasped, tugging at her jacket. "Why is the bell ringing?"

"It's the fire bell!" she cried. She flung up her arm, pointing. "It's Sophia! It's on fire! Oh, God," she wailed. "We can't lose *Sophia*!"

But when we got to the scene, along with a half-dozen other sisters, we could see that there wasn't much danger of that. The fire was small and confined to the porch. Someone had piled some rags—oily rags, probably—on an upholstered rocking chair. Lit, they had blazed up immediately. The upholstered seat had been harder to ignite, but when it did, it produced a pall of black smoke. It was the smell of something burning that had awakened Mother Winifred, sleeping with her window open—and it was Mother, still dressed in her long-sleeved, high-necked nightgown, a coat thrown over her shoulders, who had reached the bell first and sounded the alarm.

Gabriella ran into the refectory and grabbed a fire extinguisher. That, together with the one Maggie had brought, proved to be enough to smother the flames. By that time, all of the sisters had arrived on the scene and were milling around in nightwear, slippers, and coats. They were shivering with cold and apprehension, and their white faces were pinched and frightened. With them, surprisingly, was a man in his late sixties. He helped me drag the smoldering chair off the porch and into the yard while Gabriella emptied the extinguisher onto it. The man's skull was totally bald and the left side of his face was scarred so badly that his mouth had a permanently cynical twist. He was wearing a dark woolen sweater and a clerical collar.

"Father Steven!" Mother exclaimed. "What are you doing here?"

He surveyed the ruined chair with distaste. "I left a book in the sacristy this morning. It belongs to someone else, and I promised to return it. So I came back to get it—and saw this." His face twisted. "How can this be happening again? Someone must be . . . quite mad!"

There was a commotion among the sisters, and Sister Miriam pushed her way to the front of the group. "Look!" she cried in an anguished voice. "It's my portrait!"

Then I realized that among the charred debris were fragments of an artist's canvas. "Your portrait?" I asked.

"Of Mother Hilaria," Miriam said. Her voice was full of despair. "I worked on it for months. It was finished just yesterday. We intended to hang it first thing tomorrow in the chapel entry."

"Where was it?" I asked.

"In the hallway, inside Sophia," Miriam said. "That's where the rags came from, too—they're my paint rags. I put a box of them beside the door so they could be taken out tomorrow for disposal."

I'd been wondering why the arsonist had added Miriam's portrait to the kindling, but that answered my question. It made good fuel.

Mother put her arm around Miriam's shoulders. "I'm so sorry, my dear," she said softly. "But there's nothing you can do about it tonight." She raised her voice and spoke to the group. "We must all go back to bed, Sisters. The fire is completely out, and there is no more danger."

"There is always danger where there is a disregard for the holy will." The thin, high voice belonged to Ruth. She was huddled under a heavy shawl, her glasses reflecting the last flickers of the dying flames. "No one among us is safe when—"

"That's enough, Sister." A large, heavyset woman with a determined face interrupted her. She put an arm around Ruth's plump shoulders. "We can't answer any questions tonight. We must all go back to bed—and pray for forgiveness for our sins."

But there was one question I had to answer. I looked around.

Where was Dwight?

•   •   •

The morning dawned bleak and chilly, with a strong wind blowing out of the north. I dressed in gray cords, a thick blue sweater, and a fleece-lined jacket, and headed for the parking lot to look for Dwight's truck. But the big GMC was still missing, as it had been the night before. My knock on Dwight's door went unanswered, again. When I pushed it open and went in, the cottage was empty.

"I have no idea where he is," Mother Winifred said when I caught up with her on the way to breakfast. Her forehead was deeply furrowed. "I know he left yesterday afternoon, because he waved as he drove past. Maybe he found out that you suspected him of setting the fires and ran away."

"If that's true," I asked grimly, "who set last night's fire?"

It was a crucial question. In each of the other three instances, Dwight had been first at the scene, eager to prove how handy he was by putting the fire out—but not last night. Last night, he was conspicuous by his absence. He hadn't been there.

Or had he? Had he discovered I was onto him, and changed his MO to confuse things? That was probably what had happened. He had merely gathered up an armload of the nearest fuel—Sister Miriam's painting and the box of rags that had fortuitously been left in the hall—dropped it into the chair, and touched a match to the pile. Then he stayed back in the shadows, watching us while we put out the blaze.

That was how I had settled it in my mind by the time breakfast was over and I found the truck Mother Hilaria had promised me, a rusty green Dodge four-on-the-floor that steered like a World War II tank and roared like a 727 under full throttle. I wasn't too happy with the explanation, but it fit the facts, more or less.

I drove into town and parked the truck in front of the sheriff's office, which was located in the basement of the Carr County courthouse. The office, painted institutional gray and lit by flickering fluorescents, was manned by a frizzy-haired, bubble-gum-chewing dispatcher whose fuchsia lipstick was an off-key jangle against her fire-engine-red blouse.

"Depitty Walters?" She fished a pink Dubble Bubble out of her pocket and added it to the wad in her mouth. "He ain't bin in yit. Try Bernice's. That's where he us'ally hangs out this time o' mornin'."

Sure enough, I found Stu Walters at Bernice's, his boots propped on a chair. He was swapping cop stories with a couple of good old boys over coffee and the remains of a short stack, egg, and bacon. Grudgingly, he followed me to a table at the back, where the cigarette smoke wasn't quite so thick and we could talk privately. I grinned at Bernice, chic in a maroon *I'm an Aggie Mom!* tee shirt and tight white jeans, and accepted a cup of coffee. It was hot and black and bitter and I shuddered as it went down.

Stu Walters gave me a condescending look. "Put hair on your chest," he said.

"Not on *my* chest," I said firmly. To the tune of Buddy Holly's "Peggy Sue," I reviewed the situation, described Dwight's run-in with Mother Hilaria, and offered my take on his motive for the torchings—four of them, now. When I was finished, I handed over the evidence in two neatly labeled plastic bags.

"I'll be glad to swear out a statement on the aggravated assault charge, if you decide to go for it."

"Dwight?" he asked disbelievingly. He poked the bag with his finger, staring at the contents. "You're sayin' it was *Dwight* who set those fires?"

I nodded. "The probation officer said for you to call her if you've got any questions about his prior. It appears that he fell out with an auto mechanic in Fredericksburg and fired his garage—and just happened to burn down the senior citizens center next door."

"Sure coulda fooled me," he muttered.

"The only trouble is that I didn't see him around during

last night's fire,'' I said. ''I figure he was probably back in the cedar brake, watching.''

''Did ya see him this morning?''

I shook my head. ''Could you track him down? And would you let me know when you and the county attorney have decided what to do about that assault charge?''

I was about to push my chair back when we were joined by a gray-haired, deeply tanned man in a dark sport jacket and string tie. He might have been in his sixties, but he was tall and lean and handsomely distinguished.

''Mornin', Stu,'' the man said.

Walters gave the man an uneasy grin. ''Mornin', Mr. Townsend.''

Ah. Carl Townsend, I presumed. I held out my hand. ''Good morning, Mr. Townsend,'' I said pleasantly. ''My name is China Bayles. I'm visiting out your way and drove past your ranch yesterday. Beautiful—a real showplace.''

I was watching for a flicker of recognition when he heard my name, but I didn't see it. If he'd paid Dwight to take a shot at me, you'd never guess it from his smile. He took my hand, holding it a second longer than necessary.

''You like the place, huh?'' He took off his hat, pulled out a chair, and sat down. His smile showed a lot of teeth. ''We've put plenty of work into it.''

The deputy was about to interject something—probably a remark about who I was—when Bernice yelled that he had a phone call. With a narrow-eyed glance at me, Walters left the table. Another piece of luck, I thought. I'd better take advantage of his absence.

''Yes, a great spot out there,'' I said. I leaned toward Townsend. ''Perfect country for tourists. In fact, I hear there's some interest in developing the area. A retreat center, conference center, something like that?''

Townsend hesitated, as if he were debating how to handle my question. But I was friendly and he was by nature a boastful man. He was also a man who enjoyed women. He moved his leg an inch toward mine. ''So you've heard what they're plannin' to do with the monastery on the other side of the river?''

I nodded. ''The garlic farm, you mean?''

''That's what the nuns are doin' right now,'' he said. ''But the head honcho of the order—she's out in El Paso—has talked to me about the possibility of turnin' it into a resort. Golf, tennis, swimming, conference facilities, even a heliport.'' He settled back comfortably and his leg came another inch closer. ''Of course, she's thinkin' mainly about invitin' the Pope for a vacation, but I'm thinkin' about all those bankers and business types in Houston and Dallas.'' The smile showed more teeth. ''Folks are tolerant these days. No reason we can't mix and mingle.''

''Well, sure,'' I said. ''And any kind of development out that way is going to enhance the value of the neighboring ranches. And I understand that vacation ranches are big tourist attractions these days. More money in that kind of thing than there is in cows.''

''You bet.'' He was emphatic. ''I tell you, the best is yet to come. This little town, it's gonna see some real changes. We're all gonna get rich.'' He waved at Bernice. ''Hey, darlin', how about some of that black tar you're pourin'?'' Bernice bore down on us with the coffeepot.

''And you're on the County Commissioners Court, aren't you?'' I said admiringly. ''With you behind the idea, the development will be a lot easier. You can push the highway improvements and handle the environmental stuff that usually gives developers fits. I'm sure there won't be any delays with you at the wheel, so to speak.''

''You got it,'' Townsend said sunnily. ''Fixin' to jump on it like a frog on a pond lily. Soon as we get word from the big chief nun that she's goin' to dump some dollars into the project.'' He circled Bernice's waist with his arm as she poured his coffee. ''Hullo there, Bernice. Been missin' me, darlin'?''

''Not too much, t' tell th' truth.'' Bernice wriggled out of his grasp and took a safe step away. ''Say,'' she said to me, "how you doin' out at the monastery? Got that bucket by your bed the way I told you?"

Townsend frowned. "Monastery?"

"You get tired of that nun-type food, you just come on in here and I'll feed you," Bernice said cheerfully. "Y'hear now?"

Townsend's warmth had cooled faster than a blue norther. "You're one of that bunch out there?" he demanded. "Why didn't you let on? You pumping me for information or something?"

I pushed my chair back and stood up. "It was really nice meeting you, Mr. Townsend. Sorry I can't stay to chat." I was just leaving when Stu Walters finished his phone call and strode back to the table.

But I didn't quite make my getaway.

"Hey," Walters said. He was grinning, not pleasantly. "You know whut, Miz Bayles? Turns out yer wrong 'bout Dwight. He didn't do it. He's cleaner'n a whistle. Like I tole you, it's gotta be one o' them nuns."

I stopped. "He didn't do it?"

"Didn't do what?" Townsend asked.

"What do you mean he's clean?" I demanded.

"What the *hail* didn't he do?" Townsend roared.

Walters gave his belt an uneasy hitch. "Set them fires at the monastery. Miz Bayles was hired to find out who done it. She fingered Dwight."

Townsend fixed his eyes on me, all geniality gone, a scorpion about to strike. "Who hired her?" he growled.

"The nuns," the deputy said.

Townsend's face was getting red. "Sheriff know about this?"

"Yessir, he does," Walters said uneasily. "He an' me, we figgered it couldn't hurt none, though. She wadn't likely to come up with anythin'." His grin showed a gold tooth. "We was right too. There was 'nother fire last night. An' Dwight, he was somewhere else."

"How do you know?" I asked.

" 'Cause that was Joe Bob on the phone jes' now." His voice was filled with triumph. "Joe Bob is the night-shift deppity. He picked Dwight up 'bout nine last night in Bimbo's parkin' lot. Ol' Dwight was drunk as a skunk, an' Joe Bob pitched him in jail to sleep it off. He's bin there all night. Fact is, he's there right now."

It was one of the more humiliating moments of my recent life. I had been so dead-set on proving that Walters was wrong and the arsonist wasn't one of the sisters, that I had violated a rule I had learned a long time ago: God will forgive you for fooling the judge and the jury. God won't forgive you for fooling yourself.

I got out of there as fast as I could. But when I reached the door I could hear Walters and Townsend guffawing. The sound was still ringing in my ears when I got to the Carr County Hospital, on the east side of town.

The hospital was a small, one-story building on the corner across from the elementary school. There were a half-dozen cars and pickups in the front lot, but no other sign of life. Inside, the small lobby was empty except for a fax machine, a phone, and a computer, angled so I could see the monitor. A yellow happy face was bouncing around the blue screen, urging me to "Have a Heart-Healthy Day."

I checked my watch. It was nearly nine, and there were several more items on my list of errands. I didn't have time to waste. I went to the double doors at one side of the lobby, pushed them open, and walked down the empty hall to the nurses' station. I was greeted by a starched nurse in wire-rimmed glasses with the scowl of someone annoyed with the world in general and her corner of it in particular.

"I'm looking for a patient by the name of Sister John Roberta," I said. "She checked in yesterday afternoon. Can you tell me what room she's in?"

The nurse gave me a waspish look. "Patient location information is available at the lobby desk."

"I would have got it there if I could have," I said. "The

problem is, there's nobody at the lobby desk. Just a phone and a fax and a computer.'' Somehow, I'd thought that a small-town hospital would be more friendly than hospitals in the big city. I guess institutions are institutions, wherever you find them.

''Go back to the lobby and wait,'' the nurse commanded. ''I'll get somebody to help you.''

A few minutes later, a dark-haired young woman in a plaid shirt and denim wraparound skirt appeared, ''Cherie Lee'' printed on her happy-face name badge.

''Sorry,'' she said brightly, and set down a steaming mug of coffee. ''We don't get a whole lotta traffic on Monday mornings. My cousin Alma stopped in—my mama's brother's oldest girl, who I haven't seen for months an' months—and I took a break. Who was it you was askin' for? We'll just have a look right here in the computer and—'' She made an exasperated noise. The happy face had been swallowed by a blank screen. ''Well, *darn* it. Wouldn't you just know? We're down again. Can I get you some coffee while we're waiting?''

The coffee—three ounces of a pale brown liquid that tasted like the water they'd used to wash out the pot—came in a white plastic cup. While I sipped it, I thought about what had transpired in the cafe a little while ago.

If it was true that Dwight had spent the night in jail, I had to eliminate him as an arson suspect. Of course, he still might have taken a couple of shots at me, but why? I was back to square one, with two big questions staring me in the face.

If Dwight hadn't set the fires, who had?

If Dwight hadn't shot at me, who had?

They weren't questions I was going to answer sitting around in the waiting room. I went to the desk and persuaded Cherie Lee to ask the starchy nurse to check the charge sheet. It showed that *Roberta, Sister John* had already been released—at 8:45 A.M., while I was talking to Carl Townsend at the cafe. When I spoke to yet another nurse, the one who had actually overseen the discharge, I learned that the patient had left with a woman in street clothes. A nun? The nurse didn't know.

"I was worried about her," the nurse said. "She was crying. It's not good for asthmatics to be upset, you know. Emotional events are likely to trigger an attack. I wondered whether it was a good idea to release her, but Dr. Townsend had already approved it." She looked up as a man approached. "Oh, hello, Dr. Townsend."

Royce Townsend had none of his father's affability and good looks. He was round and short—shorter than I, and I'm only five-six—with brown hair and dark eyes, closely spaced. His upper lip was fringed with a sparse mustache and his chin receded behind a small, nattily trimmed beard. He wore a white lab coat, a stethoscope, and a pair of five-hundred-dollar eelskin cowboy boots.

"This is Ms. Bayles, doctor," the nurse said deferentially. "From St. Theresa's. She's asking about Sister John Roberta."

Royce Townsend, MD and JP, looked me up and down, and a furrow appeared between his eyes. "From the monastery?" His voice was surprisingly deep for such a small man.

"Yes," I said. "I particularly wanted to talk with Sister John Roberta—"

"You've missed her," he said brusquely, still frowning. "You aren't by any chance staying in the cottage by the river?"

"As a matter of fact, I am. Why do you ask?"

"Because I recognize you. You were messing around down at the river Saturday afternoon. I was having some target practice up on the cliff and—"

I sucked in my breath. "*You're* the one who shot at me!"

"I did not shoot *at* you," he said with some dignity. He balanced on the balls of his feet. "I was sighting in my new rifle and heard you screaming—your hysteria was quite unnecessary, I might add—and glanced down and saw you.'' His voice became petulant. ''I must say, Ms. Bayles, you were never in any danger.''

''How was I supposed to know that?'' I retorted.

He smiled thinly. ''My brother and father and I use that cliff quite frequently for target practice. I suggest that you stay clear of our range, particularly on weekends. I don't enjoy treating gunshot wounds, especially on my day off.'' He turned on his heel and walked away.

I was angry enough to go after him, but the nurse put a restraining hand on my arm. ''It won't help,'' she said in a half-whisper. ''He'll never admit he's wrong. Whatever you say to him is like water off a duck's back. Better just forget it.''

Forget it? I wished I could. But it wasn't just anger that made my face burn. I knew now that I had been wrong on two counts. Dwight hadn't shot at me, and he hadn't set the fires. I had accused an innocent man.

Some detective I was.

Of course, Dwight wasn't innocent of the theft of Mother Hilaria's journal, I reminded myself as I parked the truck in front of Our Lady of Sorrows Catholic Church. But that recollection didn't do much to redeem my self-esteem. When I got back to the monastery, I'd have to let Mother Winifred know that I'd been wrong. Worse yet, I'd have to tell her that the arsonist was still at large. That was the worrisome part, of course. So far, the fires had been small ones, but what if a little fire got out of control?

And now that I knew Dwight wasn't involved, there was something else I had to consider—a possible connection between the fires and the letters. The fire in the chapel had burned Dominica's guitar. Last night's fire had destroyed Miriam's painting. There was a link here, and it was on my mind as I went to look for Father Steven.

The church, which stood on one corner of the square, was a narrow, white-painted frame building with stained-glass windows down both long sides, four steps up to a pair of double doors in front, and a steeple on top. I followed the path around the building to a gray stucco cottage behind a privet hedge. A ceramic goose planter filled with frost-killed marigolds sat by the front door, and on the grimy stucco wall beside the door hung a cross made out of cholla cactus. Under it was a handprinted sign with sloping letters that announced that Father Steven Shaw lived there. Father Steven, who had been present at last night's fire.

The priest still had traces of sleep on his eyelids when he answered the door. The ugly, wrinkled scar on his face extended up the side of his neck and across the left side and top of his head. His hair grew patchily, I guessed, and he had shaved his head bald. He was quite tall and very thin, almost emaciated. He was wearing a striped pajama top, drawstring cotton pants, and corduroy house slippers. Over his pajamas he had drawn the sweater he'd worn last night, which still bore the acrid odor of burning rags.

"China Bayles?" he repeated, when I introduced myself. He had a thin, high voice that sounded curiously off-key. He rubbed one eye with the back of his hand. "Oh, yes. China Bayles. You're the one Mother Winifred asked to look into the fires." His eyes narrowed. "Do you know what happened last night?"

He obviously didn't recognize the woman he had helped to pull the chair off the porch. "I was there," I said. And so were you, I reminded myself silently. You were present at all the other fires too.

"The whole thing is horrible." His nostrils flared. "I hope you'll be able to stop . . . whoever it is."

"I wonder if I might talk to you, Father. About the fires, and another matter."

He stepped back, reluctantly, I thought. "I suppose you'd better come in, then."

I followed him to the kitchen, where he motioned me to a chair at the kitchen table while he hunted for a clean coffee cup. He found one in the dish drainer, then ransacked the cupboard for instant coffee, which he finally discovered in the refrigerator freezer. After another search, he located the kettle on top of the refrigerator and the matches behind an open loaf of bread on the cluttered counter. I was glad I'd already had coffee. It might be a little while before this cup was ready.

"Things are rather a mess," he said, striking a match under the kettle. "My housekeeper had her seventh baby on Saturday, and I'm eating my meals at Bernice's." He glanced at the full sink, and I could read the distaste on his face.

I was tempted to suggest that there were several surefire ways to ensure that the housekeeper was always around to cook and wash up, but my recommendations would almost certainly reveal that I was on the devil's side of the birth control question. I made a noncommittal noise.

Father Steven began searching in the refrigerator and emerged with a pint of half-and-half. He sniffed it, made a face, and threw it in the garbage. "I doubt you'll discover anything about the fires. The arsonist is clever." He returned to the cupboard once more.

"I was surprised to see you there," I remarked. "Wasn't it a little late to look for a book?"

He shrugged. "Not really. I frequently suffer from insomnia, and when I do, I go for a drive. In fact, I was only a few miles from St. T's when I realized that I had left the book in the sacristy. I was just leaving when I heard the bell." He put a jar of powdered creamer on the table and sat in the opposite chair.

I was watching him closely. His eyes were hooded, and the twist of his scarred mouth seemed bitterly sardonic. But that aside, there was nothing in his face that revealed whether he was telling the truth or not.

I changed the subject abruptly. "Mother Winifred has also asked me to look into the five poison-pen letters."

He pulled his brows together. "Five? Perpetua, Anne, Dominica, Miriam—" He glanced at me. "You know something I don't."

"Mother Hilaria received one as well."

"Hilaria?" The priest's surprise seemed totally genuine. If he were the letter-writer and this was an act, it was a good one. "What was *she* accused of?"

"I can't tell you, because I haven't seen the letter. I can't tell you what her penance was, either."

"Her . . . penance?"

"The letter-writer demanded a public penance of each of the sisters. Perpetua complied. The other three refused. Soon after, each of them lost something important to them."

His eyes were watching me, unreadable. "You're suggesting that the letter-writer . . . that she is exacting a penance?"

I nodded. "The only way to stop her is to reveal her identity." I gave him a direct look. "Do you know who she is?"

"No, although I . . ." He shook his head. "What is said during confession is between the penitent and God."

Client-counselor privilege. I knew all about it. I took the roster out of my purse and unfolded it. "I'm not asking for privileged information, Father. This is a list of the forty sisters at St. Theresa's. Can you point to any who might be able to help me?"

He tightened his lips, and his mouth took on a grotesque twist. "I don't think so." The words came out almost in a squeak.

I leaned forward, pressing the point. "I don't need to tell you how serious this is, Father. Someone who takes it on herself to write accusing letters and exact involuntary penance—she's playing God."

The kettle began to whistle, and Father Steven got up and went to the stove. He came back with the kettle and splashed hot water over the coffee granules in my cup. He poured himself hot water, too, returned the kettle to the stove, and sat down again.

"I suppose there are several who might help," he said

with obvious reluctance. He took a pair of glasses out of his pajama pocket, put them on, and picked up the paper. "You should talk to Olivia. Rowena, Ruth, perhaps Rose. Yes, Rose—" He tapped the list. "Certainly John Roberta. And Perpetua."

"Perpetua is dead."

He blinked behind his glasses. "Yes, of course. Dead. That's too bad. She would have been willing to help you."

"Did she know who wrote the letters?"

He sighed. "She . . . made an accusation."

"And you can't tell me whom she accused?"

He took off his glasses and put them back into his pajama pocket. "What good would that do? She might have been mistaken. She was quite old. She was also a little crazy."

But she might not have been mistaken. And now she was dead.

"Who else has made an accusation?" I asked with greater urgency. Did John Roberta know what Perpetua knew? Was that what she had been so eager to tell me— and why she'd been so afraid?

"No one." He stirred his coffee so furiously that it slopped out onto the already soiled tablecloth.

And that was all I was going to get out of him. When I left a little later, he was standing in the kitchen, rubbing his wrinkled white toadstool of a head and scowling at the sinkful of dirty dishes.

CHAPTER ELEVEN

Woe unto you, scribes and Pharisees, hypocrites!
for ye pay thithe of mint and anise and cummin,
and have omitted the weightier matters of the law.
Matthew 23:23

Mother Winifred had given me a hand-drawn map that led
me to the M Bar M, Sadie Marsh's ranch, a couple of miles
north of St. Theresa's. I pushed the Dodge, but it was
twenty to eleven when I pulled into the ranch yard and
parked next to Sadie's blue Toyota.

If I'd been expecting something like the Townsend plantation house, or even the more modest Texas-style ranch
house at St. Theresa's, Sadie's would have disappointed
me. The small frame house was weathered a silver gray
that almost matched the gray of the metal roof. It sat in the
middle of a square of unkempt, winter-browned grass. The
yard had once been graced by a large tree, but there was
nothing left of it but a sawed-off stump that served as the
pedestal for a five-foot red windmill that turned creakily.
Obviously, Sadie didn't care much for making things
pretty.

What *did* she care about? The answer lay to the right
and behind the house: a large, new-looking barn with an
attached paddock surrounded by a white-painted fence. The
exercise and training area for the horses Sadie raised, I
supposed. And beyond that, a much larger field, looped by
more wooden fence. Expensive fence.

The wind was blowing cold out of gray clouds, bringing

with it needles of chilly rain. I pulled up the collar of my jacket and stuck my hands into the pockets. If it rained tomorrow, Tom might not want to go riding. At the thought, I felt a prickle of disappointment that caught me by surprise. Was I looking forward to it that much?

Sadie opened the door at my first knock. She was wearing jeans and a red sweater and boots, and her steel gray hair was snugged back from her strong face with a red bandanna. "Glad you could make it." She motioned with her head. "This place is a bitch to heat when the wind's in the north. Come on—it's warmer in the kitchen."

The kitchen floor was covered with scuffed gray vinyl, the wall over the sink was lined with open pine shelves stacked with crockery and canned goods, and the curtains at the windows were plain muslin. Pans and utensils hung on the wall over the gas stove. The only decorative touch was a red geranium blooming on the windowsill and a large Sierra Club calendar on the wall over the scarred pine table. It pictured two paint ponies running across a snowy meadow with mountains in the background. Through an open door I could see into a bedroom, the neatly made bed covered with a striped blanket, a dresser decorated with a lamp and a row of well-worn books between carved wooden bookends. Flannel pajamas and a purple bathrobe hung from wooden pegs on the wall. The house belonged to a ranch woman who didn't care whether her possessions were pretty as long as they did their job.

Sadie had been working at the table. A sheaf of stapled pages was laid out there, next to a stack of posters advertising an organizational meeting for a local environmental group. "What would you like to drink? Coffee? Tea? There's peppermint, if you'd rather."

"Peppermint," I said gratefully. I'd had enough caffeine to wire me for the whole day.

She turned up the fire under the kettle. "I hear that you and Tom Rowan are old friends," she said.

I glanced at her. It was a strange opening. "We knew

one another in Houston," I said guardedly. "Eight or nine years ago." Who had told her? And why was it important?

"Maybe you'll strike up the friendship again," she remarked.

"I doubt it," I said. "I've got plenty else on my plate. And there's somebody else in my life."

Did I imagine it, or was she relieved? "I'll get that deed," she said, and left the room. A minute later, she was back with a legal-size manilla envelope.

The deed was dated twenty-five years ago, and began with the familiar KNOW ALL MEN BY THESE PRESENTS. It affirmed that, in consideration of the sum of one dollar, Helen J. Laney herewith granted, sold, and conveyed to the Sisters of the Holy Heart all that certain eight hundred acres of land more particularly described by metes and bounds as shown on the addendum attached, with the restrictions and upon the covenants, dedications, agreements, easements, stipulations, and conditions specified on the attached pages, et cetera, et cetera.

I turned the page, found the addendum with the surveyor's report, and turned that page too. And there they were, rigged to go off like dynamite in the faces of Sister Olivia and the Reverend Mother General. The first restriction placed a moratorium on all construction except that required by the monastery's agricultural enterprises for a thirty-year period beginning five years from the date of the deed. The second restriction required that after the moratorium had ended, two-thirds of the sisters in residence at St. Theresa's must approve any and all construction, *and* such construction must be consistent with the monastery's original mission. A final emphatic sentence drove the point home. "These restrictions are intended to ensure the property's continued dedication to the contemplative purposes for which it is herein conveyed."

Two-thirds of the sisters? That meant a simple majority couldn't control the monastery's destiny.

Sadie put a cup in front of me, dropped in a tea bag, and

poured boiling water over it. The fragrant peppermint scent wafted upward, restoring me. She sat down at the end of the table with her own cup.

"Well?" she demanded. "What do you think?"

"Where were the order's lawyers when this deed was executed?" I asked. "I can't imagine why they would accept these restrictions."

Sadie chuckled. "What could they do? Helen and Hilaria weren't the kind of women who could be pushed around. Helen knew exactly what she wanted and she wasn't going to let a passel of lawyers get in her way. Anyway, they didn't want to look a gift horse in the mouth, especially when the horse was known to bite. Helen made it clear that the order wouldn't get an acre if they didn't take it on her terms. At one point, she even threatened to give the land outright to Hilaria, screw the order."

"But Hilaria couldn't accept it," I objected. "She had taken a vow of poverty."

Sadie's smile was sly. "You didn't know Hilaria. Independent as a hog on ice. By the time this thing was signed"—she tapped the deed with her knuckle—"she'd had a bellyful of church politics. She was ready to pull out and establish her own community. Mother General either agreed to the deed restrictions or the order would lose the whole ball of wax. And all this was happenin' on the heels of Vatican Two, you know. Things were changing everywhere. Orders were breaking up. Communities were going their own way. Mother General decided to take what she could get, restrictions and all."

"And now," I said, dipping my tea bag up and down, "nobody remembers."

This situation happens more often than you might think. There are plenty of old deeds whose odd restrictions and covenants lie buried and forgotten in a courthouses and safety-deposit box willing. This kind of thing is the stuff of litigation, of course. It makes real estate lawyers skip all the way to the bank, rejoicing.

"Amen," Sadie said comfortably. "That particular Mother General has gone to her reward, and the order's changed law firms. And now that Hilaria is dead, and Perpetua, nobody remembers." She sipped her tea, her eyes bright over the rim of her cup. "Nobody but me. I've got a memory like an elephant."

I put my cup down and folded the sheets of stiff paper. "Your position is a bit precarious, wouldn't you say?"

"You're thinkin' that somebody in the hierarchy might offer to slip me a little payola to forget what I know?" Sadie snorted through her nose. "I didn't just fall off the watermelon truck." She slapped the stack of environmental posters. "I've had my share of battles. I know how bidness is done. I wouldn't take a nickel of their money."

That wasn't what I meant, of course. Hilaria and Perpetua had both known about the deed restrictions. Both were dead, and the local JP had questioned both deaths. Sadie's knowledge might make her vulnerable in a different way. But the Church wasn't the medieval Cosa Nostra it had once been, riddled with conspiracy and skullduggery. It had become more civilized since the days it had sponsored the witch burnings—hadn't it? Still, if I were Sadie, I'd watch my back.

"The current Mother General didn't get where she is by being anybody's fool," I said. "Before she commits St. Theresa's capital to a building program, she's going to take a look at that deed." I could imagine what she'd say when she actually read it. "One glance will tell her she can't turn the monastery into a vacation resort without risking a lawsuit."

Which made me stop and think. In this case, who would have standing to sue? Members of the Laney Foundation Board, collectively and individually, of course. Members of the St. Theresa community. Even the Townsends, who might claim that the order's violation of the deed restrictions constituted fraud and that they should get the land back, as Mrs. Laney's heirs. Not that they would do anything of the sort, judging from Carl Townsend's boasts. It sounded as if he and the Mother General were anticipating a long and lucrative partnership. Still, I could picture dozens of lawyers gleefully contemplating the thousands of billable hours it would take to shepherd the potentially large flock of unruly litigants through the courts.

"You're right about the Big Mama in El Paso," Sadie said. "That's what Hilaria always called her—Big Mama. But just 'cause a chicken has wings don't mean it c'n fly." Her hawk-nosed face wore a look of smug satisfaction. "That's what I told her on Saturday. Big Mama, I mean."

"You did?"

Sadie thumped the table with her cup. "I sure as shootin' *did*. I called her up and told her I'm tired of all this skulkin' in the bushes, riggin' elections, playin' the numbers. St. T's won't settle down as long as she keeps siccin' one side against the other, and that's just what I told her." *Thump* went the cup again. "I don't have any say about what goes on inside the order. But Helen put me on the foundation board so I'd speak my piece about spendin' her money and managin' her land. She never intended it to be used for golf courses and tennis courts. She meant for the deer and the armadillos and the wild things to have it." *Thump thump*. "That's why I told Big Mama that I mean to bring the matter up at the board meeting tomorrow." *Thump thump thump*.

I blinked. "How did Big—how did she respond?"

Sadie's mouth was wry. "Said she'd take it under advisement." She pushed her cup away. "Next thing I heard, Olivia was flyin' off to El Paso faster'n a prairie fire with a tailwind."

Of course. A roadblock of this size would require extended discussion, not just with legal counsel, but with the person who was expected to head St. Theresa's. I wondered whether Olivia had learned about the deed before she left, or whether it had been stuck under her nose when she got to El Paso.

Sadie pulled out another chair and propped her feet up on it. "You ask me, we're talkin' war. Trouble is, though, Winnie isn't keen on a fight. She says she's too old, but it's not age that's holdin' her back. She's a sweet old gal, and I love her, but she does toe that line." She sat back and clasped her hands behind her head. "I figger that's why the Mother General put her in Hilaria's job. Winnie will do what she's told and when it comes time, she'll step down and keep her mouth shut."

The description fit Mother Winifred pretty well. "Given that attitude," I said, "I'm surprised that she'd ask me to look into the fires."

"My idea," Sadie said. "She does sometimes listen to reason." Her grin got wider. "Tell the truth, it wasn't a half-bad idea. You turned out better'n I hoped."

"How do you think the board will react to the news about the deed?" I asked.

She made a shrug with her mouth. "We'll see. But that's not the only bidness I mean to bring up." She pulled her strong brows together, her expression darkening. "That's why I want you there, Counselor."

"Me? At the board meeting?"

"That's what I said." She swung her boots off the chair and planted them on the floor. "All hell's gonna break loose, China. I want somebody there as an independent observer. Somebody who knows the law and can come up with an opinion, fast."

"There must be other lawyers in this county you could call," I said. "Anyway, you want somebody in civil law. I was a criminal lawyer."

"I don't care what kind of law you know or don't know. A quick, sharp mind is what I'm after, one that ain't muddied by local politics. I want somebody who can see the issues."

"What kind of business do you expect to bring up?" I asked warily.

Sadie hesitated, studying me, as if she were deciding how

far I could be trusted. Finally she stood, walked to one of the cabinets, and opened a drawer. She took out a fat white envelope, sealed, and dropped it on the table in front of me. "It's got to do with the trust assets," she said. "The information is in this envelope."

"You're talking about the foundation's seven million?" I corrected myself. "No, that was only what went into the kitty. The total must be up to fourteen or fifteen million now."

Her lips thinned. "You know as well as I do, China. What goes in don't necessarily come out."

"You're suggesting that something's wrong with the investments?"

Her grin had a knowing edge. "Be there tomorrow, ten o'clock sharp. That's when I'm openin' this envelope. I guarantee you, it's goin' to cause one hell of a ruckus. That board's goin' to be dizzier'n a rat terrier pup at a prairie dog picnic."

"Are you going to let me look at it?"

"There's nothin' you could do about it today," she said. She put the envelope back in the drawer and closed it. "Now, how about another cup of that tea?"

I shook my head. "I have to talk to Mother Winifred." I stood up too. "I'll see you at the board meeting tomorrow, then."

"Right," she said. Her look became fierce. "And you keep this under your hat, d'ya hear? I don't want you givin' away any secrets. There's a few people would give plenty to know what I've got planned for tomorrow so they could figure up a way to stop me."

"Who?" The Reverend Mother General, Sister Olivia? And Carl Townsend, of course. Who else?

"I'm not going to say." She looked straight at me. "It's like my daddy used to tell me. What you don't know can't hurt you none."

I've had plenty of clients tell me that, and when they did,

I tended to agree with them. But there was something else I wanted to know.

"I wonder," I said, "what you can tell me about Father Steven."

She sighed. "You know, sometimes you've just got to ask yourself why the Church tolerates these guys."

"What do you mean?"

Her tone was sour. "Go listen to him preach. Hellfire-and-damnation stuff. Confess your sins or burn."

"I didn't think Catholics were big on that sort of thing."

"This one is." She laughed raspily. "He glowers over that pulpit like the congregation is nothing but toads and vipers, and then he lets 'em have it with both barrels. Fire and brimstone."

"Has he been in the parish long?"

"Three or four years. He came here from Houston."

From Houston. "From the congregation at St. Agatha's?"

She nodded. "But he didn't come here directly. He was out of the priest business for a year or so, while they patched him up."

"Patched him up? Oh, you must mean the scar on his face. What happened?"

She cocked her head. "You didn't know? He was in a fire."

I stared at her, making the connection. "What kind of a fire?"

"Don't think I ever heard," she said. "But whatever it was, it seems to've twisted his mind worse than his face. The sisters won't confess to him unless they just have to."

"I'm not sure I understand."

"He puts real teeth in his penances. Tell somebody a lie? Forget the Hail Marys—he makes you go back and tell them the truth. Borrow somethin' that doesn't belong to you? He has you put it back *and* ask the person you took it from for forgiveness. It's enough to keep most people away from confession indefinitely, particularly somebody who cheats on his taxes.'' She chuckled mirthlessly. ''Or diddles the company books.''

As I said good-bye, I was thinking about Father Steven's fire-scarred face and his insistence on penance, and wondering just why he had appeared at the fire the night before.

By the time I got back to St. Theresa's, the noon meal was over and the refectory was empty, except for a sister sweeping the floor and another wiping off the tables.

''I know I'm late, but do you suppose I could get some lunch?'' I asked the sister wielding the broom. She smiled in the direction of the kitchen and went on with her work.

The kitchen was clean and roomy, with a light green tile floor, open pantry shelves along one wall, two large gas cookstoves along another, and a couple of sinks along a third. The middle of the room was taken up by a long stainless-steel worktop with shelves under it, neatly filled with nested bowls and pots.

''Well, hi, China. I was hoping you'd get back before I finished.''

I turned around. It was Maggie, straightening up from a large commercial dishwasher. She was clad in khaki pants, a gray sweatshirt with the sleeves pushed up, and a large white apron that enveloped her from knees to shoulders. She looked happier than I'd ever seen her and less subdued, as if she had tapped into a new source of energy, as if she had started to come to life again.

''I thought you were on retreat,'' I said.

''I'm back.'' She pushed in the rack, shut the door, and turned a knob. The dishwasher began to make a gargling hum. She was smiling. ''*Laborare est orare*. To work is to pray. To bake lasagna is to say, 'Hey, God, thanks for good things.' '' She picked up a sponge and rinsed it out under the faucet. ''Missed you at lunch.''

I leaned a hip against the work counter. ''I've been out making inquiries, as we say in the detective business.''

''Mother told me.'' She gave me a wide grin. ''So I

understand that congratulations are in order, Sherlock. When are they going to arrest Dwight?''

''They're not,'' I said shortly. ''I screwed up. Big time.''

''You mean, you couldn't make them believe he really did it?''

''No. I mean he really *didn't* do it.''

Her mouth fell open. ''Then who did?''

I ran cold water into a glass and took a couple of gulps. ''Royce Townsend says that he's the one who was doing the shooting. He wasn't shooting at *me*, though. He was sighting in a new rifle.'' That's what he said, and I couldn't think of a reason that he'd volunteer a lie.

Maggie's face was sober. ''What about the fires? Dwight didn't do that, either?''

''Nope. He was sleeping off a drunk in the county hoosegow when the rocking chair was torched last night.''

She stared at me, sobered. ''You mean, whoever did it is still—''

''—out there somewhere,'' I finished.

Her eyes glinted. ''Well, if it wasn't Dwight, it could have been the Townsends. They—''

''I met Carl Townsend this morning,'' I said. ''He didn't show a hint of recognition when he heard my name.'' It was true. Thinking back over the conversation with Townsend, there wasn't a single clue that he was involved with the fires. Anyway, he had no motive. He was hoping to make some sort of cooperative development deal with the Mother General. What's more, lighting little nuisance fires didn't strike me as Carl Townsend's style. If he was going to put a match to something, he was the type who'd burn it down and brag about it afterward.

''Who says it has to be *Carl* Townsend?'' Maggie retorted. ''He's got two boys. One of them could be responsible.'' She pushed up her sleeves. ''It was Royce who shot at you?''

''That's right.'' I shook my head. ''But I don't think he had anything to do with the fires.'' Royce was too much like his father. He wouldn't condescend to something as trivial as a small fire.

Still, it made me think. Yesterday, Dominica had asked whether the person who wrote the letters had also set the chapel fire that burned her guitar. I'd said no, because I was so sure that Dwight was the arsonist. But I'd been wrong about Dwight. Maybe I was also wrong about the connection between the fires and the letters.

And then I suddenly thought of something else—Sister Miriam's portrait of Mother Hilaria, burned the night before.

"Of course!" I exclaimed.

"What is it?" Maggie asked.

"I've just revised one of my basic assumptions," I said. "I think our arsonist *is* the same person who's writing the letters." I looked hungrily around the empty counters. There wasn't even any peanut butter and jelly in sight. "Are there any leftovers hiding in the fridge?" I asked. "I'll never make it until dinner without refueling." And dinner would be late that night, because I was eating with Tom.

"I saved you a little something," Maggie said. She opened the refrigerator and took out a plate. "Lasagna, raw veggies, and applesauce. Will that do it?"

"Sounds great." While Maggie was heating a large serving of lasagna in the microwave, I added, "John Roberta checked out of the hospital this morning. I need to talk to her. Did she show up for lunch?"

"Nope." Maggie poured milk into a glass. "She's gone."

"Gone!" I was suddenly apprehensive. "Where did she go?"

"Home." Maggie handed me the glass. "Her mother died last night. Her sister picked her up at the hospital and the two of them are driving back together. She'll be back, but Mother isn't sure when."

Her sister. Maybe I could stop worrying. Maybe. "Where's home?"

"St. Louis, I think. Somewhere in the Midwest."

I sat down at the table, not quite satisfied. "Mother Winifred is *sure* the woman was John Roberta's sister? It couldn't have been someone else, pretending to be—"

"What? What are you talking about, China?"

I sighed. I was probably grasping at straws, trying to make a mystery where none existed. "Oh, nothing," I said. It was too bad that John Roberta's mother had died, and too bad that I couldn't ask her who she was afraid of. But if I couldn't reach her, neither could anyone else. And if she were truly afraid for her life at St. Theresa's, she'd probably feel a whole lot safer in St. Louis.

Still, I couldn't help feeling I'd run up against a stone wall. I couldn't talk to my two most promising informants, John Roberta and Olivia. I was down to the three Rs— Ramona, Rose, and Regina—and Sister Rowena, the infirmarian, all of whom Father Steven had mentioned.

Maggie took the plate out of the microwave and put it in front of me. "Don't burn yourself," she said.

The lasagna was bubbling and fragrant with basil and thyme. I picked up my fork. "Father Steven," I said. "What do you know about him?"

Maggie leaned against the counter. "I don't really *know* anything," she said. "I've heard a few things, that's all."

"What have you heard?"

"Just gossip." She shifted uncomfortably. "You know how it is in a place like this. Sometimes I think you can never really get to the truth of anything. Everyone's got opinions, and no facts."

"So what's the gossip?"

Maggie hiked herself up on the counter. "That he's on probation with the diocese."

"But he's been here three or four years."

"Four."

"That's a long time to be on probation."

She gave me a straight look. "What I hear is that he's on probation for life. The bishop is supposed to be watching him. If he screws up again, he's—" She made a slitting motion across her throat.

"No kidding?" I thought of Father Steven's bitter, sardonic face, his fire-and-brimstone sermons. "What did he do that was so bad?"

"Choirboys," she said, and let me think about that while she swept the floor and wiped the stove.

I finished the lasagna, ate my applesauce, and took my plate to the sink to rinse it, still considering whether someone who messed around with choirboys might turn to writing accusatory letters and setting fires. "Are you busy this afternoon?" I asked, putting the plate in the drainer.

"It depends," Maggie said. She hung up her apron, took a jacket from a hook, and shrugged into it. She glanced around the kitchen to make sure that everything was in order. "I need to be back here by three o'clock. I'm making apple strudel for dessert tonight. But I've got time to help you, if that's what you're asking."

I gave her a grateful look. Maggie had lived in this place for a long time, and people trusted her. "How about going to the infirmary with me to talk to Rowena?"

"You think *she* might be involved?" Maggie asked, startled.

"She's certainly a possibility," I said, and on the way to the infirmary, I filled Maggie in on what I'd discovered the day before. She listened soberly, until I got to the part about Anne hanging the ketchup-stained swimsuit from the cross.

She smiled. "Anne would love to radicalize St. T's."

I wanted to tell her that Anne was planning to leave, but I wasn't sure whether I should. "Do you think that could happen?"

"It could. Reformers aren't isolated any longer. There's a network, and moral support. When you're under the gun, support counts for a lot. Anne could make a change."

"What about you?" I asked. "Do you want to make changes?"

She gave a little shrug. "Right now I just want to find my way again, be quiet and listen for a little guidance. Of course, if Reverend Mother General insists on building a retreat center here, I suppose I'll have to take a stand." She lifted her chin. "Somehow I feel that God's rooting for the garlic."

And God had Sadie's help. But Maggie would hear all about that tomorrow, after the board meeting was over and the news leaked out. "What can you tell me about Rowena?" I asked.

"Not much, actually. She managed St. Agatha's infirmary for the last ten years or so. Somebody told me she used to be a registered nurse."

"I wouldn't think there's much need for an infirmary in a place like this—not anymore, anyway."

She nodded. "In some ways, it's a relic from the days when monastic communities were more closed off. Still, sisters need a place where they can be looked after when they have the flu or a bad cold. A lot of them aren't exactly young anymore. And then there are the little things—cuts, bruises, poison ivy, things like that." She gave me an oblique look. "It happens less often now, but nuns—especially novices—used to have quite a few psychosomatic ailments. The infirmarian was supposed to be able to tell whether a sister was really sick or suffering some sort of nervous complaint."

I didn't ask what happened to the sisters with the nervous complaints. "Does Rowena have enough patients to keep her busy full-time?"

"I doubt it. Word has it that if Olivia becomes abbess, Rowena will be her administrative assistant. The infirmary will be phased out."

"That's interesting," I said. I remembered John Roberta's flurried, frightened whisper, and the panic on her pale face. *Sister Olivia says we have to stick together. And Sister Rowena says if I tell, I'm being disloyal. They might—*

"Yes," Maggie said. "From what I hear, Rowena and Olivia make a good team. They think alike."

CHAPTER TWELVE

Wilde Rue is much more vehement both in smell
and operation, and therefore the more virulent or
pernitious; for sometimes it fumeth out a vapor
or aire so hurtfull that it scorcheth the face of him
that looketh upon it, raising up blisters, weales
[welts], and other accidents. . . .

John Gerard
The Herbal, 1633

The infirmary was housed in two small connecting rooms
at one end of Hannah's first floor. I thought the place was
empty until I heard the thump of a metal pail in the other
room.

Maggie went through the connecting door and almost
bumped into a heavyset, powerful-looking woman on her
hands and knees, energetically scrubbing the floor with a
soapy brush. The single bed had been stripped to the bare
mattress and pushed against the wall, and the window was
flung open. The smell of pine oil disinfectant was heavy
on the chilly air.

"Sister Rowena?" Maggie asked. "I'm Margaret Mary,
and this is China Bayles. I hope we're not interrupting."

Still on her knees, Sister Rowena straightened. Her face
was flushed with exertion, her veil was askew, and the hem
of her navy skirt was pinned up with a large safety pin,
showing thick calves and navy stockings pulled up past her
knees. Her pale thighs bulged out over the tight elastic tops
of the stockings.

"Interrupting?" she snapped. "Of course you're inter-rupting. Thank God. I am *sick* of scrubbing this floor." She dropped her scrub brush into the bucket with a splash. "Give me a hand, will you? These knees aren't as young as they used to be."

Stepping forward to help her up, I recognized her. Sister Rowena was the woman who had taken charge of Sister Ruth the night before. She was a woman of sixty, perhaps, although it's hard to judge someone's age when you can't see her hair. Hers must have been dark, though. Her intim-idating brows, almost a man's brows, were nearly black, and I could see faint traces of dark hair on her upper lip. The hard, square hands she held out, one to Maggie and one to me, were reddened by the hot water and detergent.

We tugged and Rowena clambered heavily to her feet. She unpinned her skirt and adjusted her veil, muttering.

"The next time we have a clothing vote, I'm voting no on the habit, regardless of what Olivia says. Really, in this day and age, we ought to be able to—"

She broke off and looked at me with a scowl. There was a large dark mole to the right of her mouth and another beside her nose. Her shoulders were broad, her arms stout. Standing, she was the shape of a fireplug, with just about as much grace.

"China Bayles, eh?" Her voice was rough, no-nonsense, and she barked her words like a cadet commander. "You're the one Mother Winifred brought in to get to the bottom of the fires."

"That's right," I said. No wonder John Roberta had been in such a tizzy. Rowena's scowl alone was enough to send a nervous person into an immediate fright.

She took a towel from the doorknob. "Well, I can tell you right off that I don't know anything about any fires. Haven't seen anything suspicious, haven't heard anything." She wiped her hands and slapped the towel back on the doorknob with a And-that's-all-there-is-to-it gesture.

"You were at last night's fire."

"I was there at *every* fire. I *live* here, like it or not." She glanced down her nose at Maggie. "I understand you're coming back."

Maggie nodded.

"I hope your vocation's stronger than it was last time," she said firmly, as if she were speaking to a young girl. "And I hope you don't expect things to be the way they were before you left."

I cleared my throat. "I'd also like to ask you about Perpetua and John Roberta."

Rowena gave me a dark look. "John Roberta has nothing to do with either the fires or the letters," she snapped. "She doesn't have the imagination to do anything sinful." She glanced at Maggie, then back at me. "Excuse me. I'm going to sit down." She walked heavily through the door, limping, one hand on her hip. "Next time these floors need scrubbing, one of the younger sisters can do it."

There was one bed in this room, two chairs, and a small desk. Above the desk was a built-in cabinet with a lock on the door, and above that, a shelf filled with medical reference books. Maggie sat on the bed, I took one of the chairs, and Sister Rowena sat at the desk, painfully stretching her leg out. She began to massage her right knee through the fabric of her navy serge skirt. After a moment, she looked up at me.

"Maybe I can save us some time if I tell you exactly what I know," she said brusquely. "Number one, I've never received a poison-pen letter. Number two, I've never written one. So you can scratch me off your list." She snapped her mouth shut as if she had said the last word on the subject.

"I'm not suggesting that you have a direct knowledge of the letters, Sister," I said quietly. "I thought perhaps someone else might have spoken about them to you, or in your hearing. John Roberta, for instance. She stopped me yesterday morning, shortly before she fell ill. She was urgent about wanting to see me. We agreed to a time later in the day, but she didn't come.''

"She didn't come because she was in the hospital." She began to knead the other leg, working her powerful fingers into the muscle. "John Roberta doesn't have any more idea about those letters than I do." Her fingers stopped moving for an instant. "Of course, she may have convinced herself that she does." She began kneading again. "In my opinion, John Roberta is a very sick woman."

"I'm told she suffers from asthma," I said.

"Her asthma is real enough. But it's her emotional excitability that's making her sick. She's paranoid, to put it bluntly." She straightened. "She's hysterical."

"I see," I said. An alarm was buzzing in my head. It would be very easy for this woman, a registered nurse and the monastery's resident expert on nervous complaints, to brand a sister hysterical. Once that happened, the hysterical sister would be completely discredited. Nobody would believe a thing she said. It was a pernicious strategy.

Sister Rowena folded her heavy arms. "So what was John Roberta's story *this* time?"

"I don't know," I said. "We didn't get that far."

A look of relief ghosted across Rowena's face, and she turned away. "Well, don't bank on her to solve your mysteries for you. You can't trust a thing she says. She's totally unreliable."

Maggie spoke up. "I heard she might be moving. Is it true?"

Rowena made a clucking noise with her tongue. "Why sisters waste energy gossiping about other sisters, I'll never know."

"Is it true?" I asked, more sharply.

Rowena straightened. "Sister Olivia and I have located a house where John Roberta can get counseling, in a desert climate that will relieve her asthma. If Reverend Mother General would give her permission—" She paused. "But that's another story."

The buzzing was louder. Render the troublemaker untrustworthy, her story unbelievable, and send her away. It was an ancient trick, much used to silence difficult women. Was that what was going on here? Or was John Roberta *really* a paranoid hysteric suffering delusions of persecution?

Rowena was continuing. "At the moment, John Roberta is on her way to St. Louis to attend her mother's funeral. By the time she returns, I hope Reverend Mother General will have agreed to reassign her." She paused, putting an emphatic period to this part of the conversation. "Now, what else would you like to know?"

I took a deep breath. Talking to this woman was like questioning a hostile witness. I was out of practice, and not doing a very good job. "I understand that you were with Sister Perpetua when she died. She received one of the letters, perhaps the very first one. Did she say anything that—"

Rowena smoothed her skirt over her knees. "Perpetua said a lot of things, Ms. Bayles, none of them very sensible. Even when she had her wits about her, she was a babbler. Toward the end, she babbled a good deal. Quite senile."

"Did she babble about anyone in particular?"

Rowena pulled her dark brows together. "I don't think I could report, in good conscience, what Perpetua said. She wasn't in control of her faculties."

Same song, second verse. John Roberta was paranoid, Perpetua was senile. There was nothing I could do to force this woman to give me information, just as I could not force Father Steven to tell me what I suspected he knew. I changed my tack. "Do you know why Dr. Townsend has ordered an autopsy?"

"Of course I know." She was scornful. "He wants people to think that Perpetua did not die a natural death. He'd like to discover that somebody brewed up some of Mother Winifred's foxglove and dosed her with it."

"Is that what happened?"

She gave me an acid smile. "I have told Mother Wini- fred repeatedly that it is dangerous to maintain that still- room. It is entirely possible that one of the younger sisters—they're not at all supervised, you know, no matter what Mother Winifred says—made some sort of terrible mistake."

"Did anyone other than you administer medications to Perpetua?"

Her chin snapped up. "No, of course not. And all my medicines are in that cabinet right there, locked up."

I let her think about the implications of that for a mo- ment. "I see," I said.

She regarded me narrowly. "Well," she said, with rather less truculence, "the autopsy report will settle all this non- sense. Perpetua was an old woman. She died of natural causes."

Rowena might be lying. And even if she were telling the truth as she saw it, she might be wrong. Somebody else might have helped the old woman along without Rowena knowing anything about it.

I stood up. "Who visited Sister Perpetua toward the end?"

"Several of her friends. Mother Winifred. Olivia, Ruth, Ramona. Father Steven, of course. He was here when she died. There may have been others." She shifted on her chair. "Now, if that's all you have to ask—"

"Where is the hot plate?"

The question caught her utterly off guard. Her eyes wid- ened as she looked up at me. "The . . . hot plate?"

"Sister Ruth says that the hot plate from Mother Hi- laria's cottage has disappeared from the storage room. Did you take it?"

She squared her shoulders and managed a scoffing smile. "Did I take it? What in the world would I want with it? It's . . . it's dangerous."

"You haven't answered my question, Sister."

Her expression was half-defiant, half-apprehensive. "Does Ruth say I took it?"

"She says it was in the storage room from the time Mother Hilaria died until you spoke to her about it. When she went to look for it, it was gone." I stood over her, keeping my eyes fixed on hers. "Did you take the hot plate, Sister?"

Her lips thinned and pressed together. She seemed to be wrestling with something inside herself—the truth, perhaps. Her glance slid to Maggie, who was sitting very still. The silence stretched out. Finally, in a low, resigned voice, she said, "Very well, then. Yes, I took the hot plate."

"Why?"

She didn't look up. "Because . . . I was asked to take it."

"Asked? By whom?"

Her chin was trembling and her voice was scratchy. "Mother Winifred directed us to talk to you about the letters." She brought her chin under control with an effort. "She didn't say we had to talk to you about anything else. I don't want to answer any more—"

I leaned down. "Who asked you to take that hot plate, Sister?"

She pressed herself back in her chair. "What you're thinking is wrong, you know." She swallowed. "You really don't have any idea what you're—"

"I need to see that hot plate, Sister Rowena. This is a very serious matter, you know. If the sheriff's office gets involved . . ."

"The sheriff? But why should—" She blinked rapidly. "Well, you can't see it. Not just now, anyway. Not this minute. Maybe later."

"When?"

Her head drooped. There was a long silence. "When Olivia gets back," she said at last.

"Lord deliver us!" Maggie said as we left Hannah.

"Amen," I said. "What do you think? Was she telling the truth?"

She hesitated. ''I wasn't sure, in the beginning, anyway. That business about John Roberta being paranoid and Perpetua babbling and so on—it's all very convenient, isn't it? But she did tell, after all. About the hot plate, I mean.''

Yes. It had taken an effort for Rowena to tell us who had the deadly hot plate, but she *had* told us. Which suggested that what she had said about John Roberta and Perpetua had also been the truth, at least in the narrow way she had framed her reply. People usually don't lie about small things and then tell the incriminating truth about something much more significant.

Maggie turned to me. ''Who's next? Who else are we going to interrogate and intimidate?''

''If that's what you think we did to Rowena,'' I replied tartly, ''you're dead wrong. *I* was the one who was intimidated.''

''Oh, yeah? Didn't sound like it to me,'' Maggie said in a wry voice.

I consulted my list. ''Sister Rose is next, and after that, Ramona.''

Maggie's head tilted. ''Rowena, Rose, Ramona—do I see a pattern?'' She frowned thoughtfully. ''And John Roberta too. What's going on?''

''It's a long story. Let's find Rose and Ramona first. If there's time after we've talked to them, I'll tell you.''

There was plenty of time, because our conversations with Rose and Ramona were fairly short. We found Rose in Mother Winifred's herb garden, bundled up in a red wool jacket, pruning back an unruly horehound. She was a shy, fragile, fortyish woman who spoke in a feathery voice and kept her eyes cast modestly downward.

''I'm afraid I'm not a very good source of information,'' she murmured apologetically. ''I stay to myself, mostly. I work in the laundry for four hours every morning. Whenever I can, I come here.'' She glanced around. ''This is much nicer than our little garden at St. Agatha's. Whatever changes Sister Olivia and Reverend Mother General are planning, I hope they'll keep the herb garden. Although, of course," she added hastily, "it *is* up to them."

"You know that Mother has asked me to see what I can learn about the fires that have occurred in the last few months. And the letters several people have received."

"I don't know anything about the fires," she said quickly. "Like everyone else, I find them very frightening. Last night was awful. If Mother hadn't smelled the smoke, Sophia might have burned down."

"And the letters?" I asked quietly. "Do you know anything about them?"

She bit her lip. "No, I really don't. I mean—"

"Father Steven suggested that I talk to you about them. He seemed to think you might have a special concern."

She glanced up quickly, then away. She seemed to have trouble meeting my eyes, but that might be a normal behavior for her. "Did he? Well, I suppose—I mean, I did speak to him."

"Do you have a special reason for being concerned?"

She looked down again, and pulled a dead leaf off the plant. "You're asking whether I've received one of the letters?"

"Yes," I said, hoping for an answer. "Have you, Sister?"

She shook her head fervently. Too fervently? Her pale hand seemed to be trembling.

"Do you know someone who has?" Maggie asked.

Another headshake.

I frowned. "Then why did Father Steven think you might—"

Her face was suddenly fierce. "Because I told him what happened to me!" She sank down onto the stone bench beside the path, as if her knees wouldn't support her.

"Can you tell *us* about it?" I asked gently.

She was fighting back tears. After a moment, she swallowed and choked out, "When I was a novice, someone in our class wrote . . . notes." Her voice grew stronger. "She slipped them into our books or left them for us to find under our pillows or in the bathroom. I guess it started out as a prank, because the first ones were rather silly. Amusing, even. But then they began to say accusing things, hurtful, *virulent* things. And then—'' She pulled in her breath.

''Go on,'' I said.

She shook her head. ''I know this is hard for you to understand. Little notes, pranks, jokes—you must be thinking it's all very trivial. A tempest in a teapot.''

To tell the truth, that's exactly what I was thinking. But trivial incidents can loom large and threatening in a community that's closed off from the outside. If you live in the teapot, the tempest fills your entire world.

''Please,'' I said. ''I want to hear.''

She firmed her mouth and went on, haltingly. ''One of the other novices—my cousin Marie, and dearer to me than a sister—got several of the letters. She began to question her vocation, and a few months later, she asked to leave. Once she got out in the world, she . . .'' She stopped, swallowed, tried again. ''She lost her bearings. She got involved with drugs. Three years later, she was dead.''

Maggie dropped down beside Rose and put an arm around her shaking shoulders. ''I'm so sorry,'' she murmured sympathetically. She fished in her jacket pocket and pulled out a wad of tissues. ''Did you know at the time who was writing the letters?''

Rose took a tissue and blew her nose. ''At the time, I preferred *not* to know, and I've been glad ever since. If I knew who she was, I don't think I could . . . I might have done something that . . .'' Her eyes were swimming with tears. ''Those poisonous letters *killed* Marie! If it hadn't been for them, she would have remained in the order. She'd be happy and content now, safe in the service of God. That's what I told Father Steven. Whoever is writing these letters is breathing out the same poisonous air. It can infect all of us!''

I wanted to say that Marie's vocation must have been

pretty shaky to start with, but it would have sounded heartless. And Rose was living with the truth as she believed it. There was no point in questioning her version of the story.

"I suppose someone spoke to the novice mistress about the letters," Maggie said.

"I believe so. I didn't feel it was my place, of course. All I could do was pray. I pray now, for Marie's soul and for the soul of this hateful person."

I studied her: a shy, quiet woman who spent time by herself, who worked in the herb garden where she could pluck a rue leaf or two to tuck into her letters. But Sister Rose's guileless distress hid nothing darker than her own sorrow. There was nothing to connect her to either the fires or the letters. Maggie hugged her, I thanked her, and we left.

Sister Ramona seemed a more promising informant, not only because Father Steven had mentioned her, but because she was one of the few people who had visited Perpetua before her death. After a short search, Maggie and I found her with several sisters in the craft room, working on the wreaths, swags, and braids that had helped to support St. T through the lean years. While they worked, they were listening to a Gregorian chant on a cassette player. I looked around at the quietly industrious group, surrounded by beautiful materials and intent on their crafting, and wondered how long they'd be doing this. At least some of them, I was certain, would prefer it to running a conference center or cleaning up after church bigwigs. I know I would.

Sister Ramona was a tall, elegant sister with flawlessly beautiful skin and long graceful fingers, the nails carefully shaped and nicely manicured. She might have been in her forties. She wore a denim apron over her habit, and she was standing in front of a heavy wooden easel that held a large straw wreath base in the shape of a heart. She had covered the heart—pretty skimpily, I thought—with dried artemisia and clumps of small heads of garlic. Beside her were boxes of red strawflowers, pink and red globe amaranth, and bright red celosia, and a spool of red twist ribbon.

Sister Ramona stepped away from her work, studying it unhappily. "I tell Sister Miriam that I'm not very good at making these things, but she says I have to keep trying." She spoke petulantly, in a carefully modulated voice that sounded as if she might have had dramatic training. "It's crooked, isn't it? Maybe I should stick some more of those red things on the left. Would that help?"

I thought she should take it apart and start over again, but I didn't want to say so.

Maggie lowered her voice so she wouldn't be heard by the others. "This is China Bayles, Sister. Mother has asked us to help her answer some questions."

"Oh, yes, the investigator." She gave up on the wreath and began folding the twist ribbon into uneven loops. "Well, all I can tell you about the fires is that they frighten me to my very bones. The thought of somebody burning the place down around our ears is enough to keep me awake all night." She shook her head, sighing dramatically. "And how anybody could write those horrible letters—"

"What can you tell me about them?" I asked.

"Me?" Her eyes widened. "Well, I've never gotten one myself, if that's what you're asking. And of course I have absolutely *no* idea who's writing them. Not a clue, as Jessica Fletcher would say. But I have a theory about the bigger picture."

"The bigger picture?"

She looked down at the bow she had made and clucked crossly. "There, do you see? I've got it crooked *again*. I am so wretchedly clumsy at making these hateful things. I'd almost rather work in the kitchen than—"

"What bigger picture?"

She pulled the bow apart and began to loop the ribbon again. I wanted to take it out of her hands and show her how, but she probably wouldn't have thanked me. "Well, there's something awfully odd going on here, wouldn't you say? I mean, there was Sister Anne's swimsuit hanging on the cross, just dripping with blood. They tried to tell us afterward that it was ketchup, but I know better.'' She held up the bow, examining it critically. ''And of course nothing like that ever happened at St. Agatha's. Life was much different there, much more varied. We had access to the theater and music and—Oh, *blast!*'' She glared at the bow. ''But it's the best I can do. Really, I'd rather work in the laundry than try to please Sister Miriam.''

I tried again. ''What about the bigger picture, Sister?''

She picked up the glue gun. ''The blood was a sign, wouldn't you say? A portent, like all these terrible fires. And Mother Hilaria, dying in such a cruel way, and Sister Perpetua being taken. Who knows where it's going to end? I go to bed every night wondering if Hannah will burn to the ground before dawn.'' She dropped a large dollop of melted glue onto the bow.

''I understand you visited Sister Perpetua before she died.''

''That's right.'' She thrust the bow onto a bare spot in the wreath and held it for a moment. ''She was my novice mistress at the motherhouse in El Paso. I thought I should say something encouraging in her last illness.''

Maggie tilted her head. ''Excuse me for interrupting, Sister. Were you in the same novice class as Sister Rose?''

Sister Ramona straightened the bow and stepped back, cocking her head. ''There. I hope Sister Miriam is satisfied. Of course, she'll tell me there's not enough artemisia and that the loops aren't even, but—'' She paused, frowning. ''What did you ask?''

''About the novice class,'' I prompted.

''Oh, yes, Sister Rose. Yes, we were in the same class.''

''Then maybe you recall the letters,'' Maggie said. ''Poison-pen letters, Sister Rose said they were.''

''Poison-pen letters?'' Ramona began picking glue off her fingers with a distasteful look. ''Yes, of course I remember. It was a sad affair. One of the novices left because of it, and others got their feelings hurt. But I never saw any of the letters myself, and it was a very long time ago. Years and years. You might ask Sister Regina. She's bound to remember. She was always in the thick of things."

"Sister Regina was in your class?" I asked.

"Oh, yes," Ramona said promptly. "She's older, of course, because she was a nurse before she took her vows. Sister Olivia was in the same class. She and Sister Regina were friends. We called them the Bobbsey Twins because they were always bobbing up here and there, wherever you least expected them. They seemed to know things the rest of us didn't." She stepped back and wiped her hands on her apron. "Well, it's done, for better or worse."

"How about the other sisters here at St. T's—were any of them in your class?" Maggie asked.

"Oh yes, several. Sister Allegra and Sister Ruth and Sister Rachel. Oh, and Sister John Roberta, too." She pursed her lips. "Of course, we were all quite devoted to Sister Perpetua, God rest her soul."

Olivia and Regina, the Bobbsey Twins. *Questioned Sr. O about Sr. P's letter,* Mother Hilaria had written. And later, she had questioned Sr. O and Sr. R about the letter to Sister Anne.

"You said something about a bigger picture," I said. "What did you mean by that?"

Ramona shook her head. "It's just a theory. You probably don't want to hear it." She picked up a whisk broom and began brushing bits of dried flowers into a little pile.

I frowned. "If you have information—"

"Well, it's not exactly information. It's more like an explanation." She swept the flowers onto a piece of paper and dumped them into the trash can beside the table. "It's about the children of Israel, you see."

"The children of Israel?"

"God punished them by making them wander in the desert for forty years."

"I'm afraid I still don't—"

She gave me a pointed look. "*This* is the desert. And we're the children of Israel. We're being punished, although for what I don't know."

"I gather you don't like it here," Maggie said dryly.

"Like it here?" Sister Ramona gave a short laugh. "*Like* it here? Let me put it this way, Sister. I do not enjoy sweating in the sun in the fields in July. I detest the smell of garlic. I have no talent for making wreaths. I am *not* cut out for desert living."

"Why not ask for a transfer?" I asked.

"I already have," she said. "As soon as Reverend Mother General approves my request, I'm to go to our sister house in San Francisco." Her eyes took on a faraway look. "San Francisco. Can you imagine? It will be heavenly. Simply heavenly."

I didn't need to ask when she expected her request to be approved. Mother General might not know a thing about garlic, but she obviously understood a great deal about carrots and sticks.

"*Now,*" Maggie said as we left the barn. "I want to hear everything."

I told her what I had learned from the journal, including the fact that Mother Hilaria herself had received a letter.

"So," Maggie said when I finished, "all roads lead to Sister O and Sister R."

"The Bobbsey Twins." An odd nickname. I wondered how much animosity—and perhaps fear—might be behind it.

Maggie paused, frowning. "You don't suppose this poison-pen thing goes all the way back to the novitiate, do you?"

"I'm beginning to think it might." I looked at my watch. "I need to talk to Mother Winifred and let her know about Dwight. And I really have to talk to Olivia before I go any further—but I can't do that until tomorrow. That's when Mother expects her back from El Paso." I wondered what kind of mood Olivia would be in when she returned. Not good, I guessed.

Maggie thrust her hands into her jacket pocket. "A few of us are getting together this evening to talk about the way things are going here. Would you like to come? We're meeting in Miriam's room. There'll be wine and munchies."

"The way things are going here—the changes, you mean?"

"Yes. There doesn't seem to be much we can do as long as the Reverend Mother General has her mind made up. But we're going to brainstorm anyway."

"Sorry," I said. "I'm having dinner in Carr tonight."

Maggie eyed me. "With Tom Rowan, I'll bet."

"And his father," I said quickly. Too quickly, maybe.

A smile quirked at the corner of Maggie's mouth. "Want me to say a prayer for you?"

"Why? Do you think I need one?"

"Why not?" she countered briskly. "A little prayer never hurt anybody."

CHAPTER THIRTEEN

The antidote which Mercury gave to Ulysses
against the beverage of the Enchantress Circe has
always been supposed to be rue.

Eleanour Sinclair Rohde
A Garden of Herbs

The Weasell when she is to encounter the serpent
arms herselfe with eating of Rue.

W. Coles
The Art of Simpling, 1656

The Lone Star Dance Barn was a couple of miles south of
town on the Fredericksburg Road, just past Marvell's Meat
Locker (Deer Processed Here—Try Our Venison Sausage!)
and the livestock auction barn. It was fully dark by the time
I parked the Dodge in the gravel parking lot and headed
toward the building, pulling my denim jacket tighter around
me. I was wearing a plaid flannel shirt under the jacket, as
well as Levi's and boots and a wool cap, but the wind was
cutting right through me. When it gets cold in Texas, you
feel it.

The Lone Star Dance Barn was a giant metal building
the size of an airplane hangar, splashed with red and blue
neon. I opened a side door and found myself in an old-
fashioned Texas dance hall, with a scuffed wooden floor
bigger than a basketball court and a bare, uncurtained stage
at one end. Scarred pine picnic tables were arranged a couple of rows deep around three sides, and beer signs and

banners—the tawdry graffiti of the country dancing crowd—covered the walls. It was 7 P.M. on a Monday night and the place was cold and empty and down-at-the-heels, like an old tart at midweek. But I knew what it would be like come Saturday midnight: the air hazy blue with tobacco smoke and loud with the wail of amplified fiddle and six-string guitar, the wooden floor packed with blue-jeaned, Western-shirted guys and gals wearing polished boots and silver belt buckles big as pie plates, arms linked, hip-to-hip, stomping and yeeha-ing happily through the Cotton-Eyed Joe.

There was no yeeha tonight, only the muted revelry of the barbecue joint at the front of the dance hall. This room was smaller and cozier, paneled with splintery barn siding and decorated with Texas memorabilia: rusty license plates that went back to the twenties, a *Don't Mess with Texas* sign over a Texas A&M trash barrel, Texas flags (all six of them), paintings of old barns and privies afloat on improbable oceans of bluebonnets, the stuffed head and shoulders of an enigmatic longhorn with red marbles for eyes. George Strait crooned a ballad on the jukebox, a cowgirl waitress in skintight jeans and Dolly Parton boobs shouldered a tray of beer pitchers through the crowded tables, and diners were hunched earnestly over plates of Tex-Mex, which is traditionally served in portions designed to satisfy the appetites of the entire Dallas defensive line. There was enough food on the tables to feed a third-world country for a week.

I did a quick scan of the room. Tom wasn't there, so I took a table against the far wall, putting as much distance as possible between me and the jukebox. I accepted a menu from the top-heavy waitress and ordered a Dos Equis. While I was waiting, I sat back to think about my conversation with Mother Winifred, which had taken place at the foot of the garden in a fenced-in corner that was the home of a black and white potbellied pig named Delilah.

"Gabriella thought up her name," Mother had said as

she opened the gate. "She built that clever little house over there, too." The house, which was about five feet tall at the peak of its pitched roof, looked like a Hansel and Gretel cottage, with casement windows, a chimney pot, and a window box full of colorful plastic flowers. There was a miniature wooden ramp Delilah could walk up, and a pig-size swinging door, with her name painted on it in Old English letters. Mother dumped a panful of apple peels into a small trough and Delilah began happily to sort them out, deciding which to eat now and which to hide in her mound of hay and save for a midnight snack.

I knelt down and scratched Delilah's back while I made a full confession.

"You mean, Dwight *didn't* do it?" Mother exclaimed when I'd finished. "But I thought you said—"

"I jumped to the wrong conclusion," I said. There'd been plenty of justification, of course, but when it came down to it, that wasn't an excuse. I stood up. "I'm sorry, Mother."

"It's not your fault," Mother said.

"Yes it is," I said unhappily. "Of all people, I should know better." Some of my clients had been falsely accused, and I'd had to work hard to get them acquitted. And here I'd gone and done it myself. "It was a terrible mistake."

"Perhaps," Mother said. "But I do see the Lord's hand in it."

Mother must have better eyes than I have. "Where?"

She smiled. "Well, if Dwight hadn't gotten drunk and spent the night in jail—"

"You think the Lord put him there?"

"He works in mysterious ways, my child." She went to a faucet and refilled Delilah's water pan. "Of course, I'm glad to know that Dwight is innocent," she added. "Except for stealing Mother's journal, of course." She put the pan on the ground and Delilah, still chortling happily about her treasure trove of apple peels, trotted over for a drink. "But now we're back where we started. If Dwight didn't set the fires, someone else did.'' She looked up at me, distressed. ''I'm sorry to tell you, but the sisters are very upset over the fire on Sophia's porch last night, especially in view of the fact that you are here to stop such things.''

I wasn't surprised. Some probably thought that last night's fire might have been provoked by my presence, as perhaps it had.

''I've been wondering about Father Steven,'' I said. ''Sadie told me that his face was scarred in a fire. Is that true?''

''So I've been told,'' Mother said. She bent over to stroke Delilah's happy pink ears. ''It happened at St. Agatha's, some years ago. I don't know any of the details, but I'm sure Sister Olivia does.'' She straightened up, and Delilah, courting more attention, rubbed against her ankles like a cat.

I already had quite a few questions for Sister Olivia. I added that one to the list.

''I also heard that Father Steven is 'on probation,' '' I said, ''for something that happened in the past—at St. Agatha's, I assume. What does that mean?''

Mother gave an exasperated sigh. ''Don't the sisters have anything better to do than gossip? But it's true, I'm afraid. There were several incidents involving . . . well—''

''Boys, I was told.''

She shook her head. ''So sad, really. The poor children. But the bishop is to be commended. He's taken quite a firm stand on the matter. Father Steven has the strictest orders not to—'' Her jaw tightened. ''But that has nothing to do with your investigations, I'm sure. Unless you think he could somehow be involved with—''

''With what? The fires?''

She looked at me. ''Oh, surely not.''

''He was here when each of the fires occurred, even last night. Did you believe him when he said he'd come after a book?''

''I took what he said at face value, I'm afraid.'' She

shook her head helplessly. "What possible motive could he have?"

"I don't know, Mother," I said. "But perhaps I'll have more answers after Sister Olivia tells me about the fire at St. Agatha's, and how Father Steven was injured."

I was still thinking about my conversation with Mother Winifred when Tom and his father walked in.

"How come you're not sitting under the longhorn?" Tom asked, jerking his thumb toward the table in the corner. "That's where Lyndon Johnson always used to sit when he stopped here."

"I didn't wear a hat," I said.

Tom Senior's blue eyes glinted. "Woman's got a right good sense of humor," he said to his son. "Makes up some for that outlandish name of hers." He spoke in an exaggerated Texas drawl that, to out-of-state ears, would probably sound like a parody. It wasn't. People in Texas—especially in rural Texas—really do talk that way.

"Hello, Mr. Rowan," I said.

He pulled out a chair and sat down. "What I wanta know," he said abruptly, "is how come you broke it up with my boy." His lopsided grin showed that he was only teasing. "Not good-lookin' enough for you?"

Tom's father was a tall, slightly stooped man in his mid-seventies with a weather-beaten face and thick, silvery hair. Except for a look of weariness and a few more lines, he didn't look much different from the man I'd met in Houston eight or nine years before. He was wearing a tweed sport jacket with an array of pins on the lapel—Chamber of Commerce, Knights of Columbus, Lions Club—and a bolo tie.

I grinned back. "How do you know Tom wasn't the one who broke it up with me? Maybe I wasn't pretty enough for him."

He chuckled shortly. "If I thought the boy was that stupid, I'da drowned him when he was a kid. How the hell are you, China?"

"I'm fine," I said, and glanced at Tom, suddenly (and in spite of myself) feeling finer. He was relaxed and handsomely blond in a suede vest, open-collared blue shirt, and city-blue denims. He smiled, and I remembered yesterday's kiss. The electric tension was suddenly there again, crackling in the air, lightning before a storm. I smiled back, tipping my head nonchalantly, but I'm not sure I brought it off.

To my relief, my Dos Equis arrived, Tom and his father ordered longnecks, and we fell into a discussion of the menu, which featured several rather adventurous items for a rural Tex-Mex joint. Tom and his dad decided on a large plate of nachos and the house salsa, reputed to be hotter than hades, to occupy us until the rest of the food arrived. Figuring that my mostly veggie monastery meals gave me a little leeway, I went for the steak *tampiqueño,* which was billed as an eight-inch pancake of mesquite-grilled beef enfolding onions and hot peppers, topped with cheese and ranchero sauce, plus *chicharrónes*—Mexican-style chitterlings. Tom Senior and Junior ordered the usual medley of enchiladas and *chalupas* and *chiles rellenos* and refried beans. (Ordinary beans are fat-free and good for you. Why does lard have to taste so great?)

The ordering accomplished and the nachos and salsa duly delivered and given pride of place in the middle of the table, we moved to the munching stage of the meal, trading (as Texans invariably do) tall tales of the hottest salsas we have ever eaten. Finishing our repertory of salsa stories, we moved to recent history, and Tom asked me about the progress of my investigations. Figuring I might as well get it over with, I repeated my story of this morning's events—making it as amusing as possible—and admitted to having been wrong about Dwight on two counts. Then Tom asked the question I was getting tired of hearing.

"If Dwight didn't set those fires, who the hell did?"

"I'm working on it," I said. "Ask me tomorrow." After I talked to Sister Olivia, and found out the truth about the fire that had so profoundly scarred Father Steven.

"So ol' Royce has taken up target-shootin', huh?" Tom Senior asked with a grin. "Gotta keep your eye on them Townsends. Devious sons of bitches. Rena too. Among the four of 'em, they've got the county trussed up like a bull calf in a ropin' contest."

I pressed him for information about the Townsends, but he wasn't forthcoming. My guess was that they were big customers at the bank and it didn't do for him to bad-mouth them any more than he had to. But I did manage to learn some Rowan family history that I'd either never known or had forgotten.

Tom Senior had come back to Carr from the war in the Pacific with a Silver Star he'd earned on Iwo Jima for taking out a Japanese pillbox when his squad was pinned down by machine-gun fire. He married his high school sweetheart, Harriet, and had a son, Tom Junior. A few years later, he succeeded his father, Old Tom, as president of the Carr State Bank, which had managed to survive the Depression, but not by much.

When Tom Senior took over, business began to look up. He moved the bank out of the small brick building it shared with the feed store and into the two-story modern facility I'd seen on the square. Over the next three-plus decades, he tripled its staff and quadrupled its assets. Then Harriet died and illness struck him, and a couple of years ago Tom Junior—newly divorced from the woman he'd told me about yesterday—came home to move into Tom Senior's spot at the bank. He had also moved into the family home.

"Two guys bachin' it," Tom said wryly. "You can guess what that's like." He grinned at his father. "Although I've got to admit the old man can cook up a mean pot of spaghetti. His apple pie isn't half-bad, either."

"After Harriet died, it was either learn to feed myself or starve," Tom Senior said. "Hell, there's a limit to the number of bologna sandwiches a man can eat and live to tell it. Although I won't be tellin' it long," he added, without a trace of resentment or self-pity. "Doc Townsend says I can forget about makin' it to the half-century mark at the bank."

"What do those doctors know?" Tom grunted. "You've fooled 'em before. You'll fool 'em again."

Tom Senior went on as if his son hadn't spoken. "The boy here is carryin' on the fam'ly tradition." He glanced at Tom fondly. "Third-generation banker. Can't beat that with a stick. Course, it's in the blood. The Rowans are the best bankers in Texas, bar none."

"Watch it, Dad," Tom cautioned. "You'll break your arm patting yourself on the back."

The old man scowled. "Yeah, well, one thing I ain't so proud of, let me tell you." He picked up his beer. " 'Less you get off your can and start workin' on it, there ain't gonna be a fourth generation."

Tom colored. "Come on, Dad," he muttered. "You agreed—"

"He tell you about that woman he married on the bounce, after you and him split the sheets?" Tom Senior pointed his beer bottle at me, his pale eyes narrowing. "TV star, she was, name of Janie."

On the bounce? Tom wasn't looking at me.

"Real beauty. Family with money, too. Father's got a big spread down in Bexar County." The old man scowled at Tom, shaking his head. "Shoulda hung on to Janie when you had your rope on her, boy. Shoulda had a kid or two so there'd be somebody to take over the bank after you."

"Maybe I'll sell the damn thing," Tom muttered.

Tom Senior's mouth tightened. "You do that, and I'll come back to haunt you, sure as little green apples. I'll bring your mama with me, too."

Tom snorted. "That a promise, you old buzzard?"

His father saluted him with his beer bottle. "You can bet your best bull on it, boy."

The banter was light and practiced, but Tom seemed uneasy and the old man's voice had a ragged edge. I wondered what kind of conflict was hidden under the camaraderie. How often did the father worry that the son would let the family bank fall into the hands of the massive multinational financial corporations that have already grabbed up so many small-town banks? How often did the son threaten to sell out and move back to the city after the father was dead?

The meal arrived, we dug into our food (mine was more than passable), and the subject of the conversation shifted.

"Tom tells me you've got a place of your own over in Pecan Springs," Tom Senior said. "You like bein' in bidness for yourself?"

"Most of the time." I thought of the recent Christmas rush and my feelings of being swamped under a tide of too much to do. "Sometimes it's a lot to handle." In a burst of ill-advised candor, I added, "Pecan Springs is getting too big and touristy. Sometimes I feel like finding a quieter place. Like Carr. You've got a pretty town here."

"Glad to hear you say that." Tom Senior beamed. "Yep, real glad. You own your shop?"

I nodded, and went on saying things I shouldn't have. "The building as well. Right now, I rent out half of it, but I've got to figure out what I'm going to do with—" I was about to say that I had to make a decision about the tearoom when Tom Senior interrupted.

"Well, it's easy enough to relocate. Let your tenant take over the building. Or sell. Price of property in your part of Texas has gone up like a hot-air balloon in the last few years. You'll make out like a bandit, moneywise. Movin' won't cost you much, either."

"It's a nice idea," I said, "but I really don't think—"

"Why the hell not?" the old man demanded. "You said it yourself, Carr's a real purty town."

"It certainly is, but I'm not—"

"*Sure* you are, girl. We need women like you here. Anytime you're ready to make your move, I'll see you get what you're lookin' for."

Tom leaned forward and put his hand on his father's arm. "Hold your fire, Dad," he said. "You promised you wouldn't—"

"Caroline!" The old man raised a hand to the cowgirl waitress. "How about a cup of coffee?" He turned to me, disregarding his son. "Carr's a *fine* little town, China. Sure, it's underdeveloped compared to where you are now, but that's a plus. Anybody who can tell a widget from a whangdoodle can see the potential here. You sign on with our outfit, girl. The best is yet to come."

Tom shook his head disgustedly. "You sorry old son of a gun," he muttered. "Can't tell you a damn thing."

The best is yet to come. Hadn't I heard that assertion just this morning? "Sounds like you and Carl Townsend are singing the same song," I said. "He told me this morning that when the monastery is turned into a resort, everybody in the county is going to get rich."

"Carl told you that?" The muscles around the old man's eyes tightened perceptibly. "His mouth flaps at both corners. There ain't no deal yet."

"What do you think about the chances for change at St. T's?" I persisted. Tom Senior was the Laney Foundation Board's banker. He knew how much money there was, and what the Reverend Mother General intended to do with it. Of course, he didn't know about the deed restrictions. And he didn't know what was in that white envelope Sadie had shown me.

Or did he? The old man seemed suddenly uncomfortable. He glanced over his shoulder, shoved his chair back, and stood up. "Listen, there's Lou over there in the corner. I need to see him about the Knights of Columbus barbecue comin' up next Saturday."

Tom glanced toward the corner. "Tell Lou I'd like to work my shift early in the day, will you?"

His father nodded. "Send Caroline over to the corner with my coffee." He clapped one hand on Tom's shoulder, the other on mine. "I got a real estate broker who'll help you find the right location for your shop, China. When you got it picked out, Tom here will see you get money to fix it up.'' He leaned down between us and whispered loudly. ''And when you're settled in, you give Tom-boy a holler. All he needs is a good wife, and he'd be just about perfect.'' He squeezed my shoulder and was gone.

I stared after him wordlessly, shaking my head.

''Sorry about that, China,'' Tom said. He shoved his plate away. ''The old man is . . . Well, he's got high hopes for this town.''

Not just for the town. I narrowed my eyes. ''Come clean. Did you give him reason to hope that we might—''

''You know better than that.'' He cleared his throat. ''But the old man's no fool. He'd like to see me settle down, and he's always liked you—a lot more than Janie, to tell the truth. And he thinks his age gives him the right to say whatever jumps into his mind.''

''Obviously,'' I said dryly. ''But I hardly think it gives him the right to go around propositioning potential daughters-in-law.''

''Look, China.'' Tom leaned forward and put his hand on my arm. His voice was taut, his eyes intent. ''You know I'm attracted to you. As much as before. No, more.'' His hand tightened. ''Before, I was a young stud with a dozen deals in his pocket. I was easily distracted, and it was hard for me to know what I wanted. Now I know. I want you. I want us to go back where we were and start over again. Is that possible?''

I could feel the warmth of his grip through the sleeve of my flannel shirt. My heart bounced and my stomach tightened involuntarily. I pulled in my breath.

''Yes,'' he said quietly. ''I see it is.''

I took my arm back. ''I don't think so,'' I said.

''What's holding you? Is it the guy you live with?''

McQuaid's face rose in front of me, curious and lively. What would he say if he could overhear this conversation, could feel the chaos inside me? The pause lengthened.

"Do you love him?"

Even if I'd been absolutely clear about my feelings for McQuaid, I'd feel awkward sharing them with Tom. "I'm living with him," I replied evasively. "We've lived together since last May." Only eight months—was that all? It felt like eight years.

"Well, hell, China," he said, exasperated. "People live together for all kinds of reasons. Because they enjoy sex, because two is cheaper than one, because they like the security. What kind of thing do you two have going? What does it mean to you?"

What does it mean to me? What *does* it mean? What are McQuaid and I to one another? Housemates who share a bed as well as board? Or something more? It's a question I've mostly managed to duck. McQuaid and I live together comfortably and companionably and with a minimum of fuss. We enjoy one another in the important ways. Maybe it isn't the stuff of romantic novels, but it works. It's been enough. Then again, confronted with the possibility of something more, was it still enough?

I looked down at my plate. I was talking more to myself than to Tom. "It's a good relationship," I said.

He made a scornful noise. "That's it? Just 'good'? You're kidding! 'Good' isn't good *enough,* and you know it, China." His voice softened. "We were a hell of a lot more than just 'good.' We were super, incredible, tremendous, fantastic. . . ." He ran out of superlatives. "Remember how it was for us in the beginning?"

I remembered, and even after all the years, the memory was warm enough to melt stone. I remembered lying in each other's arms at 3 A.M., bodies joined, hearts hammering, breath like sweet fire. I remembered champagne dinners at romantic restaurants, an hour or two stolen from the evening's work at the office, dawn breakfasts and lingering kisses, with roses on the table.

That was the first six weeks. After that . . .

After that, there wasn't as much time for dinners at romantic restaurants, and the dawn breakfasts had been replaced by a 7 A.M. cup of coffee and a wave as we headed for our cars and the day's work. He accused me of being too busy, I accused him of being preoccupied.

He lifted his hand and touched my face. "We can go back and do it again, China. Only this time, we won't let our careers kill the romance. It'll be like before, only better. Super, fantastic, out of this world. Never just plain 'good.' "

And I knew it was possible. I felt the physical attraction tugging at me, the flame of remembered passion turning my insides soft. I heard the old laughter, tasted the old wine, and knew I could hear it, taste it again, and it would be even sweeter. Tom and I had been swept by desire once, and nearly swept away. It could happen again.

But between then and now, I had met McQuaid. I had lived with him and learned that sustainable love doesn't grow out of superheated physical passion, but out of simply holding hands and holding on, day in and day out. I'd learned that "good" really *is* enough, not because you're settling for something less, but because "fantastic" and "incredible" burn you out emotionally, just as life in the fast lane burns you out physically. And I thought now of McQuaid and Brian and Howard Cosell and Khat and was suddenly swept by a wave of affection for our ordinary, unromantic life, with its heaps of wet towels and clutter of dirty socks, its lizards in the closet and dead toads in the refrigerator. Our undeniably ordinary, utterly unromantic, inexplicably *good* life.

Tom put his hand over mine. "You can't deny that you're physically attracted to me."

We were into truth tonight. "You're right," I said. "I am attracted to you, Tom. Very much."

"Aha!" He was triumphant. "Well, now that we've established *that*, the rest is—"

He was interrupted by the cowgirl with the coffee, and then by another cowgirl who took away the plates, and then by a couple of his customers, who'd just unloaded a truck of Beefmaster steers at the sale barn down the road and wanted to brag to their banker about the good deal they'd wangled. By the time they'd moved on, Tom Senior was back at the table. We talked for a few minutes, then I glanced at my watch and drained my coffee cup.

"It's getting late," I said. I looked at Tom. "I'll see you at the board meeting tomorrow."

Tom Senior frowned. "The foundation board? Those meetings are closed, except on the invitation of a—"

"Sadie asked me to come," I said.

The old man's face grew red and he half-rose. "Sadie Marsh? What the hell does she want you there for?"

Tom put a hand on his father's arm. "Take it easy," he said.

"I want to know what Sadie's got up her sleeve," the old man said, his voice rising. "What's that woman up to, anyway?" He glared at Tom, his breath coming harder. "You find out, boy. It's your bidness to know what's comin' down. You can't afford to be blindsided by nobody, not even Sadie. *Especially* not Sadie."

"Whatever it is," Tom said firmly, "I'll take care of it." He put his hand on the old man's shoulder. "Simmer down, Pop. You know what Doc Townsend said about getting excited."

"Screw Doc Townsend," the old man spat out. He sank back in his chair. "Son of a bitch can't pour piss out of a boot with the heel up."

Tom's laugh was unconvincing. "Anyway, I think I know what Sadie's got up her sleeve. I'll handle it."

I glanced at him. Was that the truth? Did he know about the deed restrictions? Maybe he knew about the envelope too. Or was he telling a lie designed to quiet his father?

"Well, you're gonna have your hands full," the old man muttered, subsiding. He seemed to have forgotten me. "Sadie's got ten-pound brass balls and a mouth like an Arkansas hog caller. I'll come to that meeting tomorrow and settle her hash. If I don't, she'll—''

"I said I'll take care of Sadie, Dad," Tom said sharply.

"And I said I'll be there." His father's mouth was set into a stubborn line. "I'm gettin' out of your way fast as I can, boy. Don't push."

I shrugged into my coat, embarrassed by the exchange. I gave the old man my hand and a smile. "Perhaps I'll see you again before I go back to Pecan Springs, Mr. Rowan."

With an effort, Tom Senior remembered his manners. "You comin' over to our place for a nightcap?"

I shook my head. "I don't want to keep Mother Winifred's truck out too late. She might worry about it."

Tom stood up. "I'd worry, too, if I were her. That old truck is practically an antique—worth as much dead as alive. I'll walk you out to the lot and make sure it starts."

As I said good night to Tom Senior, he pressed my hand between his dry, cool ones. "You mind what I say now, China. We'll be lookin' for you back here soon as you get things wound up in Pecan Springs."

I murmured something and pulled my hand away.

"You've got to give it to Dad," Tom said, holding the door open for me. "He just won't give up. Doc Townsend has told him to turn the business over to me. If he's got any energy, he's supposed to concentrate it on stuff like the Knights of Columbus—and stay out of the bank."

I bent into the cold, clean wind, letting it wash through me. "It's tough," I said. "For both of you."

He put his arm around my shoulders. "Let's not talk about that. As I recall, when we were interrupted you were in the middle of telling me that you lust for my body."

We reached the old green Dodge. "Something like that," I said. I opened my purse, found the truck key, and put it into the door.

"Wait," he commanded. He pulled me close against him and kissed me, gently at first, then with a mounting passion that reverberated in my bones and blood. I felt myself responding, the warmth pulsing through me.

"You make me feel like a kid in love for the first time, China," he whispered huskily, touching my face, my hair. He tipped my head back, his eyes fastened on mine. "Come home with me. Let me make love to you."

Somebody opened the door of the barbecue joint and an old Elvis song—"Love Me Tender"—floated out. Somebody else was laughing, light and high. A car door slammed, a dog barked. Above us, far away, the stars looked down, amused.

I started to speak, but he laid his finger on my mouth, silencing me. "I know. You're living with the guy, you've got commitments. But he's there and you're here. You're a free woman, China. You can do what you choose. Come home with me."

A free woman. Freedom. That was what I'd wanted, wasn't it? That was why I'd taken time off, come out here. I wanted to make new choices, open my life to new directions. The passion was pulling me to Tom. All I had to do was say yes.

"No," I said. I pulled away.

He frowned. "Don't tell me you don't want me. I just kissed you, remember? Your body said yes. So don't lie. Don't make it hard on yourself. Okay?"

I wasn't lying, to myself or to him. I *did* want him. Standing in the parking lot under the flashing neon sign, Elvis's voice like liquid passion, it was easy to want this man, easy to say yes. It was a great deal harder to want what I already had. McQuaid and Brian, the house, the shop. Yes, even the shop, damn it.

"Let's call it a night, shall we?" I opened the door and climbed into the truck.

He stood up straight. "Just say no, huh?" His laugh was light, but it had a bitter undertone. "Too risky? Big moral dilemma?"

"Morality doesn't have anything to do with it," I said.

"I'm just figuring out what I want." I stuck the key in the ignition.

"What you want is me," he said firmly. "Listen, China, there's no reason we can't. We're not strangers. We're both free." He spaced the words for emphasis. "You're your own woman, totally independent. You don't owe anybody anything."

He was right. I didn't owe anything to anybody. Except myself.

I had my hand on the key. "That's why it's no."

His sigh was raw, heavy. He put a hand on the open door handle. "Don't run away, China. I've never really stopped loving you. Who's to know if we please ourselves tonight?"

Are all protestations of love and lust, however heartfelt, doomed to sound like dialogue from an old movie? "I really have to go now," I said. I pulled the door shut and turned the key.

The engine turned over, coughed regretfully, and died. I pumped the gas pedal a couple of times and cranked it again.

Another cough, almost a hiccup.

The third time, it didn't even burp.

"I am *not* believing this," I muttered. Tom had stepped back and was watching me, hands in his coat pockets, an unreadable expression on his face. After a long, embarrassing moment, I rolled down the window. "You don't happen to have a pair of jumper cables, do you?" I asked in a small voice.

He eyed me for a moment, calculating, not in any hurry to answer. "What's it worth to you?" he asked finally.

I stared at him. Damn it, he was *serious*! I picked up my purse. "I'll call the garage."

He looked at me a moment longer. And then said, explosively, "Oh, shit."

It took ten minutes to dig the cables out of his car, hook them up, and start the truck—neither of us saying more than the necessary *put this here* and *turn it over when I tell you*. When we were finished and the truck was running again, he came around to the door.

"Listen, China, I'm sorry. I wasn't trying to bargain. I was just—"

"Thanks for the jump," I said. "I've got to go now."

His mouth quirked. "Yeah, well, at least we had Paris." He shoved his hands into his pockets. "That's something."

I raised my hand, fighting the almost irresistible temptation to say, "Here's lookin' at you, kid." I shifted into first gear and drove off.

I stopped at the first phone booth, left the truck running and hopped out, and called McQuaid. I was eager to hear his voice, feel connected again. But it was Brian who answered the phone.

"Dad's playing poker with Sheriff Blackwell," he said. "Hey, China, you done good." He sounded excited. "Real good."

I frowned. "I did good?" I asked cautiously. "What did I do?"

"You know. You guys really know how to pray. Maybe it's because everybody out there is so holy."

"I'm not so sure about that," I said. Arson, poison-pen letters, questionable deaths, a political takeover . . . "Excuse me, Brian, but I think I missed something. What are we talking about?"

He giggled, elated. "You mean, you didn't hear yet? The Cowboys beat the Packers yesterday. Coach said on TV it was the answer to a prayer. I figure it had to be yours."

"Credit where credit is due," I said. "Listen, tell your dad I called, okay? Tell him I'm having a great time and I wish he was here." And at that moment, it was true, definitely true. I wished McQuaid were here, wrapping me in his arms, holding me tight, nuzzling me.

"Yeah," Brian said, "you wish he was there. Anything else?"

I hesitated. "Tell him I love him. Lots and lots. Tons."

"Mush," he said with eleven-year-old disgust.

"And I love you too," I said, feeling generous. "And Howard Cosell and Khat and—" I stopped. Not Einstein. I had to draw the line somewhere.

"Thanks," he said, grudgingly grateful. "Me too. Say, China, will you ask those nuns to keep praying? Next week it's the 'Niners."

CHAPTER FOURTEEN

Conscience, anticipating time,
Already rues the enacted crime.

Sir Walter Scott
Rokeby

It was my alarm clock, not the fire bell, that jarred me out of a sound sleep at first light the next morning. I got up, pulled on my sweats, and took a brisk walk along the river. I surprised a white-tailed doe drinking at the water's edge and startled a great blue heron, statuesque in a quiet pool, waiting for a silver minnow to dart out from under a rock. He lifted heavily into flight, flapped across the river, and dropped into another pool, where he fixed a suspicious eye on me. The wind had swung back around to the southwest again, and it was warming up. It was going to be a cool, crisp day, one of Texas's January jewels.

Back at Jeremiah, I grabbed a quick shower, brushed my teeth, and combed my hair, feeling virtuous for having fended off temptation the night before. I pulled on cords and a sweater and set off for breakfast, ready for whatever fireworks Sadie Marsh might launch at the board meeting.

As I passed the green Dodge truck in the parking lot on the way to the refectory, I patted it affectionately. Given its performance in the Lone Star parking lot last night, I'd been a little worried about the twelve-mile drive from Carr to the monastery. I hadn't relished the idea of getting stranded and having to hitch a ride to St. T's from some colorful local character on his way home after a hard night's drinking.

But the truck behaved and the only person I met was hardly colorful. At the turnoff to the monastery, I encountered a Honda. It came from the opposite direction, made a sharp left in front of me, and stopped at the gate. Somebody—it was too dark to see who—got out hurriedly, retrieved the key and opened the gate, then drove through, leaving it open. I drove through, closed it, then drove fast to catch up, curious to know which of the nuns was out at this late hour. I pulled into the lot behind Sophia just as the driver, dressed in dark slacks and a dark jacket, got out.

"Sister Olivia!" I said, surprised. "I thought you weren't coming back until tomorrow."

She recognized me and stiffened. "My plans changed," she said, taking a small suitcase from the backseat.

I thought of my list of questions—Mother Hilaria's hot plate, Father Steven's scar, the letters. "Now that you're back, I'd like to make a time to talk. It really is important that I ask you about—"

She slammed the car door and locked it. "No," she said. She came around the car and the light fell on her. Her face was a white mask, her eyes two dark smudges.

"I don't mean that we have to talk right now," I persisted. "How about after breakfast tomorrow?"

"No," she said again. Her voice was rising, frantic, half-hysterical. "I have nothing to say to you. Nothing at all, do you hear?" She pushed past me into the dark. I could hear the staccato tattoo of her heels on the cement sidewalk.

"Good morning," Maggie said cheerfully, interrupting my thoughts as I came around the truck. "It's a pretty day, isn't it?" She gave me a quick glance. "How'd it go last night?"

"How'd it go?" I repeated, still wondering why Sister Olivia had been so anxious to escape from me. She had been almost running.

The corners of her mouth twitched. "You know. Your date. With Tom."

"Oh, that." I grinned. "It was okay."

She held the door open as we went inside Sophia. "What? No champagne and roses?" Her mouth twitched. "No propositions?"

"There was a proposition," I said offhandedly. "I just said no."

The twitch became a smile. "You see? Never underestimate the power of prayer."

"Oh, so that was it," I said. We went into the refectory, and I sniffed appreciatively. Fresh cinnamon rolls this morning. Ah, yes.

There was ample time between breakfast and the board meeting to talk to Olivia and get straight on what she knew about the letters and the fires. But even though I waited until the last sister had come through the refectory door, Olivia didn't show up. She wasn't in the office in Sophia, either, or in the chapel, in her room, or with Regina in the infirmary. And Mother Winifred, who was doing some paperwork at the desk in her cottage, couldn't suggest where else I might look.

"I didn't even know she'd returned from the motherhouse," she said, sounding slightly miffed. "In the old days, nobody went anywhere or came back from anywhere without asking Mother's permission." She straightened a sheaf of papers and stuck them into a file folder. "But Olivia is a law unto herself, and I'm a very lame duck. Reverend Mother General will probably call today and tell me when to schedule the election." She put the papers into a drawer and looked at the clock on the wall. "It's almost time for me to be off to the board meeting."

"I'll be there too," I said. "I saw Sadie yesterday and she asked me to come. She wants legal counsel, I gather."

From the look on her face, Mother was not pleased. "I love Sadie dearly," she said with irritation, "but she has the capacity to do the order a great harm. We've got enough difficulty on our hands without her stirring up trouble.''

There wasn't anything I could say to that, but I did have a question. ''Before we go to the meeting, there's something else I want to ask you about,'' I said. ''I gather that a number of the sisters here did their novitiate together under Perpetua. Ramona mentioned that Olivia and Regina knew one another even then.''

''And Ruth, as well,'' Mother said. She took a navy sweater off a peg on the wall and pulled it on. ''I was at the motherhouse when that class came through, and I remember the three of them. Regina and Ruth were good friends, always getting into some sort of mischief. Olivia felt she had to stand up for them. She showed quite a bit of leadership capability, even in the novitiate.''

''She stood up for them?''

''Oh, yes. You wouldn't know it to look at either of them now, because they've both settled down and become quite serious. But Ruth and Regina were once quite fun-loving. Mischievous, really. They enjoyed little pranks.'' She smiled. ''One or two of their practical jokes got them into trouble with Perpetua, as I recall.''

''I see,'' I said, thinking that I was beginning to see a great deal. ''Do you think Olivia would talk to me about some of those pranks?''

''I don't see why not,'' Mother said. She stepped in front of a mirror on the wall and ran a comb through her white hair. ''Or you could ask Ruth or Regina directly. But why do you want to know about all that old business?''

I wanted to know because I was beginning to make some connections between what had happened at the novitiate twenty years before and what was happening here now. But I wasn't comfortable sharing my thoughts with Mother Winifred until I had talked with Olivia and sorted it out some more—especially after having been so wrong only yesterday.

I glanced at my watch. ''If we're not going to be late to

that meeting, we'd better go. Shall we walk to Sophia together?''

The board meeting was held in a long, narrow room adjacent to the monastery office. It was high-ceilinged, wood-paneled, and bare of decoration, except for a painted statue of Mary in one corner, a heavy dictionary on a wooden stand in another, and a pendulum clock on the wall. Its hands showed nine fifty-five.

Three of the board members were already in the room when we got there. Tom got up from the head of the table, where he was sorting through a stack of papers, and came to greet us. He was wearing a suit and tie, and he looked tired, as if he hadn't slept very much. He shook Mother's hand and gave me a quick nod. His eyes slid away. I thought I understood. He was embarrassed about last night.

"Is your dad here?" I asked.

He shook his head. "Something came up at the last minute and he couldn't make it."

Mother Winifred tugged at his sleeve. "May I have a word with you, Tom?"

I went around the table and sat down beside Sister Gabriella, who was talking to a plump, brown-haired woman in a too-tight lipstick-red suit with a fussy blouse and pearls. She turned out to be Cleva Mason, the one who had missed the last four board meetings. She slanted a glance around the table, licking her lips with a nervous tongue.

There was a stack of papers in the middle of the table, probably the board's agenda. Tom finished talking to Mother Winifred, looked at his watch, then at the clock. He seemed unusually jittery. He glanced around the table and cleared his throat.

"If everyone's ready . . ." he said.

"Sadie's not here," Sister Gabriella said.

"Oh, okay," Tom said, and I had the impression that he'd been hoping to start without her. He looked at his watch again. "I guess we'll have to wait, then."

"There's plenty of coffee," Mother Winifred said, gesturing to a table at the end of the room where coffee and cups had been set out. "She'll probably be here in a few minutes."

But at ten-fifteen, we were on our second cup of coffee, we'd almost run out of small talk, and Sadie still hadn't arrived. Tom was more tense and withdrawn than I had seen him, with a wary, nervous look. I wondered once again whether he knew what Sadie was going to bring up this morning. From the look of him, I'd have said yes. But how had he learned it? Sadie had kept her intentions to herself.

Gabriella touched my arm. "It's not like Sadie to be late," she said quietly. "She had a lot riding on this meeting."

"Maybe we'd better call her," I said. "She might have slept through the alarm."

Gabriella left the room. A few minutes later, she was back. To Tom's questioning glance, she said, "Nobody answers the phone."

"She's on her way over, then," Tom said. He shuffled the papers, obviously anxious to begin. "There are several information items on the agenda. We could handle those first. She'll be here by the time we're ready to get to the substantive issues."

But the information items—mainly having to do with paying the legal bills in the aftermath of the lawsuit—were read and discussed by ten forty-five, and Sadie still hadn't arrived. Tom looked up at the clock again. He seemed to be debating what to do. "I think we should go ahead without her," he said finally.

I pushed back my chair. "Sadie has some vital information to present. She'd be here unless something happened. It is okay if I borrow the truck again, Mother Winifred? I'll drive over and see what's keeping her."

Tom licked his lips nervously. "It's not a good idea to drive that old truck over there," he said. "If it didn't start, you'd be stranded. We'll take a break, and I'll drive you."

I frowned. At best, being alone with Tom would be uncomfortable.

Gabriella leaned toward me. "Go, please," she urged in a low voice. "Sadie wouldn't be late if she could help it. I'm afraid something's wrong over there."

Tom's cream-colored Chevy Suburban made the trip in something under ten minutes. We didn't encounter Sadie along the way. We didn't say much to one another, either. Tom's face was set and his jaw was working, and I couldn't think of anything to say that wouldn't lead us back to the subject we had closed last night. Anyway, I shared Gabriella's apprehension about Sadie. She had planned carefully for the board meeting, and she'd been looking forward to it. She wouldn't have missed it unless—Unless what? What was wrong?

The M Bar M was deserted when we drove in. Sadie's blue Toyota was parked on the gravel apron in front of the house, so she was still around, somewhere. Without a word, Tom and I got out, went up to the front door, and knocked, then knocked again.

Nothing.

Tom tried the knob, but the door was locked. We went around to the back door, which stood partly ajar. I stepped inside and called, but there was no answer. A couple of minutes' searching was enough to convince us that Sadie wasn't inside. We started for the outbuildings, calling as we went. Tom strode ahead, moving fast. I had to run to keep up with him.

The metal-roofed barn was a long, narrow building, lined up on a north-south axis, with double doors at both ends. The floor was hard-packed earth. The west side of the barn was stacked to the roof with baled hay and feed sacks. The east side was lined with a row of wide stalls that opened at the back into the fenced paddock. Three of the stalls were occupied, two by decorous paint ponies that thrust out their noses inquisitively, looking for carrots. The third contained a brown horse with a silky dark mane, wearing a leather bridle. The horse was skittish, prancing, his eyes rolling.

"Goliath," Tom said over his shoulder. "Sadie's horse."

We found her in Goliath's stall. Her jeans-clad, denim-jacketed body was sprawled facedown on bloody straw, head twisted unnaturally to one side, steel gray hair matted with blood. One arm was pinned under her, the other flung out. Goliath tossed his head with a shrill whinny and shied away from us against the fence.

"Jesus," Tom breathed out.

He shoved the gate open, rushed in, and grabbed the horse's bridle. As Goliath reared, he yanked. "Out of the way," he gritted. "I've got to get this killer out of here."

While Tom was locking the horse into the next stall, I ran in, knelt in the straw beside Sadie, and felt at her neck. A moment later, Tom joined me.

"Is . . . is she alive?" he asked.

"Yes," I said. "There's a pulse. Not much of one, but a pulse."

He rocked back on his heels, his face blanched. "She's alive," he whispered, as if he were dazed. "What'll we do?"

"We've got to get help." I yanked off my jacket and spread it over Sadie. "Give me your coat. There's got to be a phone in the house. How quick can the EMS get out here?"

Tom didn't answer. He seemed dazed. He dropped his head into his hands. "She's alive," he whispered again. "Dear God, she's—"

"Tom!" I shook him. "Get the EMS! Tell them we've got a head injury here, possible brain trauma. Tell them she was kicked in the head by a horse."

His head came up swiftly, and his staring eyes connected with mine. "Yeah," he said. He swallowed. "Yeah, right." He scrambled to his feet, energized, peeling off his suit coat. "There's a phone by the barn door. I saw it when we came in." He tossed me the coat.

I turned Sadie on her side, rolled Tom's coat into a pillow, and propped up her head, touching her wound. She had sustained two crushing blows to the head, one above her ear and slightly forward, the other lower, behind the ear. The blood was dark and crusty; the edges of the wound were dried. Her face was drained of color, the leathery skin slack and gray and very cold. She'd been lying there for some time—how long, it was hard to tell. I stared down at her, feeling a sharp, poignant sadness. All her schemes and dreams, all her passion, all come to nothing. All come to this.

Tom was back. "They're on their way," he said. He glared at Goliath, who was standing, head hanging, in the nearby stall. "I ought to shoot that animal. He's always been vicious. Don't know why Sadie keeps him around."

Sadie moaned and stirred and I bent over her. "Sadie," I said into her ear. "Just be still. Help is on the way. You're going to be all right."

Her eyelids flickered. She tried to speak but the words wouldn't form. Her eyes closed.

Tom dropped to his knees and took her hand. "How is she?" he asked.

"She came around for a minute, but she's out again."

His face tensed, jaw muscles working. "Did she say anything?"

I shook my head and stood up. "She's in shock. We need blankets."

"You go," he said. "I'll stay with her." Holding her hand, he bent over her. "Sadie," he whispered urgently. "Sadie, can you hear me? You're safe now. The horse can't get you."

I sprinted. In the bedroom, I tossed aside a purple bathrobe and grabbed two blankets off the unmade bed. I was on my way back through the kitchen when I saw the white envelope on the table. I grabbed it and jammed it into the pocket of my slacks. Then, just outside the door, I saw something lying on the ground and picked it up. It was a white and blue rectangle, immediately recognizable. It was an airline boarding pass with Olivia's name on it.

I stared at it. When I'd first seen Olivia driving the Honda last night, turning into St. Theresa's lane a little after ten, she had been coming from the direction of the M Bar M. In the parking lot, she had been frantic, half-hysterical. She'd practically run away from me. And now I knew why.

I knew that Olivia had been here last night, with Sadie. She had come here straight from the airport and fresh from her discussion with the Reverend Mother General. And I knew what the two women had said to one another. I could see them sitting at the kitchen table talking, could imagine Olivia's pleas for time, her desperate efforts to persuade Sadie not to reveal the deed restrictions. I could hear her begging Sadie to give her a chance to work out some sort of deal.

And I could imagine Sadie's response. She'd have been impassive and poker-faced at first. She'd have hidden her enjoyment of Olivia's frantic pleas. But in the end she wouldn't have been able to conceal her triumph at having Olivia and the order exactly where she wanted them. I could see, as clearly as if I'd been here, Olivia's fear, her tightfisted anger, and finally her fierce, uncontrollable outrage. I could hear Sadie's chuckle, spiraling into a derisory laugh, and picture Olivia's face, wrenched with passion—

But could I imagine Olivia following Sadie out to the barn? Could I picture her smashing her victim in the head, then dragging her into the stall? Could I see her, ignited by a compelling sense of purpose and inflamed by a vision of—

Yes, I could. Bloody hands have administered the sacraments and bloody hearts have ruled the Church. Bloody murders in the name of all that's holy are woven into the history of Christianity. It didn't take much imagination to see Olivia transfigured, in a moment of raging impotence, into an instrument of vengeance.

But neither this boarding pass nor my testimony about Olivia's behavior in the parking lot would be enough to convince a jury that a woman who had spent her life serving God had suddenly gone berserk and attempted to murder her neighbor. Evidence that she had been in her victim's kitchen wasn't enough. Evidence that she had been in the barn with Sadie—that was what I needed.

Back in the stall, I spread the blankets over Sadie's motionless body. "Any change?" I asked breathlessly.

Tom shook his head, his face strained, eyes shadowed. "Her pulse is erratic. Her breathing's shallow. She'll be lucky to pull through. Damn horse—I'll see that he's shot!"

I pulled the blanket up and turned her head slightly. "Tom, look," I said. "Sadie is taller than I am, and Goliath isn't all that big. Could he have inflicted these wounds?"

"He could have if she was down." He nodded toward a bucket of half-spilled oats in the corner. "See? She came in here to feed him and bent over with the bucket. Something spooked him and he reared up. Sure, he could kill her. Those forelegs are like sledgehammers."

"But if he'd got her down, would he have stopped at that?" I asked. "She was helpless, bleeding. He'd surely have trampled her. But there's not another mark on her body. And when we came in, the horse was as far away from her as he could get, at the back of the stall."

Tom's face was grim. "Are you suggesting it wasn't the horse?"

I got to my feet, opened the gate, and went into the paddock. Goliath was calmer now, standing beside the fence, his head hanging. As I approached he nickered, an anxious, questioning sound. I don't know much about horses, but this one didn't look like a killer. Frightened, yes, sides heaving, eyes rolled back. But not savage, not vicious. Not like a horse who had tried to kill his owner.

Tom scrambled up. "Stay away from that animal," he cried. "He's dangerous!"

"I don't think so," I said. I made a soft noise in my throat and reached up to stroke Goliath's neck under the long, rough hair of his mane. "That's a good boy. Steady now." I stood for a moment rubbing his shoulder, then slid my hand down his leg until I was kneeling and looking closely at his left foreleg, his hoof. I ducked in front and examined his right foreleg, his hoof. Then the hind legs, the hind hooves.

What I saw confirmed my suspicions. There was no blood on the horse, no physical evidence that he had touched Sadie. It wasn't proof that Olivia had struck her down, but the knowledge moved me one step closer to that conclusion.

"Damn it, China!" Tom had opened the gate and was coming at me. "Do you want the horse to kick you too?" At the sound of the loud voice, Goliath snorted and shied. I backed away, and Tom grabbed my arm.

"Damn bullheaded woman," he muttered. "That's all I need, to have you trampled by a killer horse."

I pulled free. "He's not a killer, Tom. If the horse did it, there'd be evidence embedded in the wound—dirt particles, straw, stuff like that. But it's clean, as clean as those hooves. The horse didn't do this. Somebody tried to kill her."

Tom gave a harsh, strangled laugh. "That's crazy, China."

I heard the wail of a siren. The ambulance was coming up the lane.

CHAPTER FIFTEEN

I wear my rue with a difference.
                    William Shakespeare
                    Hamlet

I ran out of the barn, waving at the orange and white EMS ambulance. A few minutes later, two uniformed attendants, their faces grave and intent, were working swiftly and competently, taking Sadie's vital signs, starting an IV, conferring by cell phone with the hospital. In another couple of minutes, they were easing her onto a gurney. While I watched, I saw something small and silvery fall from her clothing onto the straw. I bent over to reach for it at the same moment that Tom did. I clasped his hand.

"Don't touch it," I commanded.

He froze, immobile, his eyes locked on mine. I let go of his hand and stood up. The attendants were watching us curiously. "Do you have a piece of paper?" I asked.

One of them fished in his shirt pocket and pulled out a card with CARR COUNTY HOSPITAL printed across it. As they began to maneuver the gurney out of the stall, I knelt and slid the card under the object. It was a small silver cross— not a pendant, but a lapel pin—with some sort of emblem in the center. It was what I needed. The evidence that proved that Olivia had been in the barn with Sadie.

Tom glanced at it and looked away again. "It's just . . ." The words stopped. His mouth was drawn tight and I couldn't read his eyes. He cleared his throat as I folded the card into a square packet and put it carefully into the pocket of my slacks. "It's just Sadie's cross. Why . . . are you going to all that trouble?"

"Because it might not be Sadie's cross. And the owner might have left prints on it." Confronted with the cross and the boarding pass I had found in the kitchen, maybe Olivia would confess.

One hand steadying the IV, the chief attendant turned. "We're ready to roll. Are you two riding with us?"

Tom scrambled to his feet. "We'll follow in my car."

I shook my head. "You follow. I'm going to notify the sheriff's office. I'll stay until Walters gets here."

Tom opened the gate and stood back so I could step out of the stall. His jaw was tight. "You're making more out of this than it is, China. Accidents happen all the time in ranch country. Walters isn't going to drive out here just to look at the place where Sadie got kicked in the head by a horse."

I stayed firm. "This is a crime scene, and that's how I'm going to report it. Walters needs to get his butt out here and do a search. There may be other evidence that could identify Sadie's attacker."

We reached the ambulance just as one of the attendants was climbing into the rear with Sadie. As the other closed the doors, I heard a cell phone buzz. The attendant spoke into it, listened, then turned to Tom. "If the dispatcher got the name right when you called in, you must be Tom Rowan?"

"Yeah. I'm Rowan."

"That was the hospital calling. You need to come with us, sir. Your father's just been admitted."

Tom looked as if he had been struck by lightning. "Dad? But how . . . why . . . ?"

"Sorry, sir. I don't have any details. We'll be running the lights and the siren. Stay with us."

Impulsively, I reached out to Tom. "Oh, Tom, I'm sorry. Your father's a fine man. He—"

"Yeah, sure." He pushed me away.

The attendants were already in the ambulance, revving the motor. Tom sprinted for his car and was gone.

When I got through to Stu Walters, he answered with gruff irritation. Being wrong about Dwight had obviously earned me no brownie points.

"What is it this time?" he growled.

"I'm at the M Bar M. Sadie Marsh has been attacked."

That got his attention. "Attacked?" I heard the scrape of a chair being shoved back. "Who attacked her?"

"Hard to say. Tom Rowan and I found her a little while ago, in a horse stall in the barn. Head wounds, serious. Tom says her horse kicked her. I think she was bludgeoned. EMS is taking her to the hospital now. The crime scene needs to be secured. And it would be best to have a forensic physician examine the wound before it's cleaned up and—"

"This ain't Houston, lady," he said, with barely disguised sarcasm. "We ain't got no forensic—"

I cut in. "Then tell the doctor who treats her to inspect the wounds carefully, save samples of any debris he removes, and be prepared to testify in court to the nature of the instrument used in the attack."

He was heated. "Now just a goldurned minute here! Who do you think you are to—"

"Excuse me, Deputy Walters," I said crisply. "I don't have time to argue this matter. I've found evidence that suggests that one of the sisters at St. Theresa's may be involved. I'd like your permission to talk to her informally and see if I can determine the extent of her involvement."

When he spoke at last, Walters was incredulous. "You're sayin' that one of them nuns bashed Sadie Marsh over the—"

"That's what I intend to find out," I said. "Unless, of course, you want to handle the questioning yourself. In that event, I'll be glad to arrange it." I paused, giving him time to catch up. "I'll stay with you while you interrogate her.

Of course, Mother Winifred will also want to be there, so she can report your questions to the Reverend Mother General. And perhaps we should tape the interview, just in case the bishop has any concerns." I paused again. "Although, come to think of it, the bishop will probably want to send one of his lawyers."

"His lawyers?"

"Of course. You don't think the bishop will allow a nun to be questioned by the police without—"

He interrupted. "Sounds to me like this mighta been an accident. 'Round here, folks is allus gettin' kicked. An' don't forgit that you screwed up that Dwight bidness, and you was real positive 'bout him."

I shifted uncomfortably. "Yes, but I have physical evidence that a certain nun was here last night."

"Well, it's yer hide."

"You're saying that I have your permission to question the woman?"

"Yeah, that's what I'm sayin'. But hey, I don't want you thinkin' that you're—"

"I know." I sighed. "I'm not officially on the team, untrained and a woman and all that. If I got hurt, I might sue the county."

"Took the words right outta my mouth," he said.

When I got back to St. Theresa's it was almost noon and the board—what was left of it—had adjourned to the refectory for lunch. I took Mother Winifred out into the corridor and gave her Tom's version of what had happened to Sadie.

"Why, that's impossible!" she whispered, distraught. "Sadie trained Goliath herself. He'd never hurt her, or anyone else."

"I said it was Tom's theory," I reminded her. "When I examined the horse, I couldn't see any evidence that he had kicked her. And there's nothing about her wound that suggests an accident with the animal."

There was a silence. Mother's eyes were enormous with shock and bewilderment. "But if not the horse, then—" She shivered with a sudden chill. "Who did this awful thing, China?"

"I need to talk to Olivia, Mother."

Her hand went to her mouth as if to stifle a gasp. "But you can't believe that *she*—"

"I think it's better if I don't try to explain it just now," I said gently. "But I have two pieces of physical evidence that prove she was with Sadie last night. I would like you to be present when we talk. And I must tell you that I have Deputy Walters's permission to question her."

"To . . . question her? Olivia, of all people! She can't be involved in—She couldn't have—"

"I'm sorry, Mother Winifred. We need to talk to Olivia, and quickly. Where do you think we might locate her?"

Dominica was the one who finally found her, a half hour later, in the chapel. Olivia had apparently been there for several hours, for when she came out of the dim light, her veil was askew, her habit was wrinkled, and she was blinking behind her gold-rimmed glasses. She seemed confused and disoriented. I had expected her to refuse to talk to me, or at least to put up some resistance. But the middle-aged nun who stood before me, head bowed, shoulders sagging, was nothing like the iron-willed administrator I had met my first day at St. T's. When I told her we needed to talk, she agreed submissively and almost, I thought, with relief.

A few moments later, Olivia, Mother Winifred, and I were in Mother's cottage with the door closed and the kettle heating on the hot plate. Olivia sat at the table, knees and feet together, hands tightly clasped in her lap. The skin under her eyes was pouchy, her nose red, her cheeks blotched. She had been crying.

I spoke quietly. "There are a great many secrets at St. T's, Sister, and you seem to be at the heart of all of them. But we can't afford secrets any longer. There is too much at stake, too many people being hurt."

She didn't answer.

"On your way back from the airport last night, did you stop to see Sadie Marsh?"

A tic appeared at the corner of her compressed lips. She bowed her head, staring down at her locked hands, folded as if in prayer. Her knuckles were white.

I tried again. "When you went to the motherhouse this weekend, did the Reverend Mother General tell you about the deed restrictions that Sadie had brought to her attention?"

Mother Winifred put the tea things on the table and sat down beside me. "Deed restrictions?" she asked, perplexed.

I spoke to Olivia. "Knowing that Sadie was the main obstruction in your plan, you stopped by her place last night to change her mind. Isn't that true?"

Olivia looked up as if she were about to speak, but she continued to cling to her silence.

I took the boarding pass out of my pocket and laid it on the table in front of her. She glanced at it. A moan escaped her lips and her face went white.

"I found this at Sadie's," I said. "Just outside the kitchen door."

"Yes, I was there," she said, almost inaudibly. I could hear Mother's sharp intake of breath.

"Thank you," I said gently. "Now, tell us what happened."

Olivia was chewing on her lower lip. The silence thickened. Outside the window, a chickadee piped his penetrating four-note whistle. On the hot plate, the kettle was beginning to hum.

Mother Winifred spoke, her voice calm and unexpectedly firm. "You must tell us what happened, Olivia, and what you know. Answer the question, please."

Olivia glanced at Mother with faint surprise. She hesitated, then lifted her head. "It wasn't quite the way you say." Her voice was taut with the effort required to keep it from trembling. "I know Sadie Marsh. I know that when she says something, no matter how stupid, she sticks by it."

"So you weren't trying to change her mind," I said.

"I told Reverend Mother General that seeing Sadie wasn't going to do any good, but she instructed me to try to talk reason into her. I obeyed. But Sadie had already made up her mind. She wouldn't listen."

Mother Winifred had sat forward on the chair. Both of us were totally captured by Olivia's thin, reedy voice. "What time did you arrive?" I asked.

"I flew into Austin about seven-thirty and telephoned to make sure she would be there. I drove straight from the airport. I got there about nine-thirty. She was ready for bed."

Beside me, Mother stirred. The kettle was beginning to whistle faintly, but I don't think she heard it. "What time did you leave?" I asked.

She moistened her lips with her tongue. "About a quarter to ten. It didn't take long for her to make her position clear. I could see that nothing I could say would change her mind." The blotches grew brighter, and color suffused her neck. "But I had promised Reverend Mother General to give it my best effort, so I did."

"What did you say?"

Her voice seemed to strengthen. "I tried to get her to see that she was making a mistake. I told her that the retreat center would bring a new life to St. Theresa's, that it would contribute jobs and revenue to the local economy." She stopped, cleared her throat. "I told her to think carefully before she closed off those possibilities, because once closed, they couldn't be opened again."

"How did she respond?"

"How do you think?" she asked bitterly.

"Just tell us, Sister," Mother said.

"She laughed." Olivia looked down at her clasped fingers and loosened them until they began to shake, then pressed them tight again. Her voice had thinned to a thread, each word pulled out of herself with an obvious effort. "She said that after the board meeting there'd be no hope of developing a retreat center here. She said that . . . the only way to stop her was to . . . kill her."

Olivia's last sentence paralyzed Mother Winifred and me in absolute, horrified attention. Into that frozen silence, the kettle poured its shriek like the cry of the dead. Blindly, Mother Winifred got up and.groped toward it.

I spoke, not so much from a desire to hear the truth as to get the awful, bloody business done with. "What happened then?"

"Then?" Olivia looked at me, her eyes opaque, staring, behind her glasses. "It was over. I left."

"You . . . left?"   .

"Yes, I left. What else could I do?" She raised her clasped hands to her breast, speaking with weary despair. "I drove back here."

"That's when I saw you?"

"Yes. I went to my room and tried to sleep, but I couldn't. When everyone went to breakfast, I went to the chapel to pray."

"For forgiveness, I trust." Mother Winifred's voice was ragged. Her hand shook as she poured hot water from the kettle into the teapot.

"For forgiveness?" Olivia cried wretchedly. Half-imploring, half-rebellious, she lifted her eyes toward heaven. "I was praying for guidance! What in the name of Christ am I to *do* with my life? Does He mean me to dig in the dirt for the rest of my days?" Her voice shattered and she wrapped her arms around herself, bending forward, rocking back and forth. "If anyone should pray for forgiveness, it's Sadie Marsh. She thwarted God's plan for this place!"

"Olivia, Olivia," Mother remonstrated softly. "Only human plans can be thwarted. *His,* never."

Olivia raised her head. Her eyes were filled with tears

and her chin was trembling. If I had not seen that bloody body lying in the straw, had not seen how ruthlessly Sadie had been struck down, I would have felt pity for her. She seemed so utterly destroyed, less a criminal than a victim of her own high expectations, her hopes for a dream that would never be real.

And now that her defense against the truth had been breached, we had come almost to the end. There was only the admission left, only her final confession. For that—

I took the card out of my pocket, unfolded it, and held it out. "What is this, Olivia?"

She glanced at it, then away. "It's a cross," she said helplessly. Her voice cracked.

"It's your cross, isn't it?"

"Mine?" She wiped her eyes with her sleeve. "No, of course not. Why would I have a cross like that?"

"Why—?" I looked down. I'd been in a hurry when I picked up the cross, and I'd put it in my pocket without examining it closely. Now I did, and saw what I hadn't seen before.

In the center of the cross was an emblem. On the emblem were two letters, a K and a C, elaborately intertwined. K and C. The Knights of Columbus.

F. Lee Bailey once said that you should never ask a witness a question you didn't already know the answer to. "If you do," he said, "you deserve whatever the hell you get."

I *had* known the answer to my question. I had been absolutely confident that Olivia would say, "Yes, that's my cross." But I had been wrong, disastrously wrong, wrong *again*. I looked down at the cross. There were two people who might have worn it, and neither of them were in this room.

I cleared my throat. "So you . . . you had nothing to do with the assault on Sadie Marsh?" It was less a question than a bewildered statement of the unthinkable truth that was just beginning to dawn on me.

"The assault?" Olivia's gasping perplexity was even greater than mine.

"Tom Rowan and I found her this morning in the barn at the M Bar M. She had been hit on the head and left for dead."

"Dead!" Olivia half-rose. Her face registered both profound distress and a fierce, undisguised hope. "Sadie Marsh is *dead*?"

"No," I said. "At least, she wasn't when the ambulance took her to the hospital. But she has severe head wounds. She may not live."

She sank back weakly. "Did she—? Did the board—?"

"Look at the old deed?" I shook my head. "She didn't make it to the meeting. Somebody tried to kill her to keep her from talking."

Her voice was thick, her eyes staring. "Somebody—But who—? Why—?"

I shook my head, swallowing hard, painfully. "I don't know. Not yet." I could guess who, but I didn't want to. I'd been wrong so many times in the last few days. I could only pray I was wrong this time too.

"You thought it was me!" Olivia was breathing through her mouth, short, panting breaths, like a dog. "You really believed I could have killed Sadie!" She threw back her head and began to laugh, a grating sound that ended in a crazy, gasping cackle. "You thought I—"

"Olivia!" Mother Winifred put a hand on her shoulder. "Get hold of yourself!"

Olivia stopped as suddenly as if she'd been gagged. She collapsed against the chair, her eyes closed. "I hated her for being so smug," she whispered. "I despised her for keeping me from doing what God wants me to do. But I didn't kill her."

There was one last thing. "What was she wearing?" I asked.

"I told you. She was ready for bed. She was wearing a purple bathrobe and flannel pajamas." She opened her eyes and held out trembling hands. "You have to believe me. I'm innocent!"

A purple bathrobe and flannel pajamas. The recollection of the unmade bed I'd seen this morning came back to me, and I realized its significance. Sadie had slept there last night, after Olivia had left. She had been attacked early this morning, after she dressed but *before* she had time to make the bed, by the owner of the cross I held in my hand.

I folded the small silver object back into its cardboard packet and put it into my shirt pocket. Olivia couldn't help me determine what had happened to Sadie, but there were three other mysteries to be solved, and she had the answers to both.

"You may be innocent of this morning's assault," I said, "but you are guilty on other counts. You know who murdered Mother Hilaria. You know who wrote the letters, and you know who set the fires. I want you to name that person."

Mother gasped. "Murdered? Mother Hilaria was *murdered*?"

Olivia's face was waxen. Her hands clutched the arms of her chair; her eyes were fixed on me. "You . . . know?" she whispered.

I nodded. "But I can't prove it, and I can't obtain her confession. You are the only one who can make her tell what she has done."

The silence crouched between us, waiting and wary. At last she shook her head.

I held her eyes. "You want to become the spiritual mother of these women. How can you expect them to turn to you for guidance and comfort and at the same time protect a sick individual who threatens their safety?"

Mother put her hand over Olivia's. "If you know who she is, you must lead her to confession, my child, and quickly. There has been another letter, delivered in the same manner, with the same enclosure—a leaf of rue."

Olivia closed her eyes. Her voice was thin and thready. "Who received it?"

"Gabriella. The accusation was . . . ridiculous, or worse." Mother's voice was profoundly sad. "Confession is the only way the writer can be redeemed, Olivia. And if you have been concealing her identity, it is *your* way to redemption, as well."

Olivia clutched Mother's hand in both her own and began to sob.

I stood. "I'm going to the hospital, Mother. But I should be back this evening. After supper, please gather the sisters—all of them—in the chapel."

Mother slipped her free arm around Olivia's shoulders and looked up at me. "The chapel? Yes, of course. But why?"

I looked at Olivia, still sobbing. "Because," I said quietly, "it's time you assembled a Chapter of Faults. Sister Olivia is ready to accuse a sister who has sinned."

I left the cottage and hurried down the path to the parking lot and the truck. I had lied to Olivia when I said I knew who killed Mother Hilaria. I didn't know—not exactly, that is. I had narrowed it down to two people.

And then down to one. As I walked across the parking lot, I met two nuns coming toward me. I stopped to speak briefly, and held out my hand to each to thank her for her help. When I left them a moment later, I knew which of the sisters Olivia would accuse.

But I shouldn't be so confident. I had made too many mistakes in the last few days. Maybe I should confess *my* errors to the Chapter of Faults.

CHAPTER SIXTEEN

His Physicke must be Rue (ev'n Rue for Sinne).
George Wither, 1628

Why, what a ruthlesse thing is this, to take away
life. . . .

William Shakespeare
Measure for Measure

Every minute of the drive to the Carr County Hospital, I
could feel that cross burning in my pocket like a hot coal
straight from hell. Based on the information I had now, it
belonged either to Tom or his father, both of whom were
members of the Knights of Columbus.

Tom or his father. One or the other had attempted to
murder Sadie Marsh, but I didn't know which. And I
couldn't imagine why either one would have done it—until
I remembered the short bit of conversation at the Lone Star
the night before. The old man had been deeply upset at the
idea that Sadie had invited me to the board meeting. *What's
that woman up to, anyway?* he had demanded. Tom had
answered, sharply, *I'll take care of Sadie, Dad.*

And then, when I pulled up in front of the hospital just
before three o'clock, I remembered something else: the envelope I had retrieved from Sadie's kitchen table this morning. The fat, sealed envelope Sadie had shown me the day
before. She had implied that the contents had to do with
the foundation's trust accounts, which were under the control of the bank—under the control of Tom Rowan, Senior

and Junior. The trust accounts that by now should amount to fourteen or fifteen million dollars.

But maybe not. *You know as well as I do,* Sadie had said, *what goes in don't necessarily come out.*

I took the envelope out of the back pocket of my cords and unfolded it. It wasn't sealed. And it wasn't fat. It contained just one sheet of paper.

I'll never know what else Sadie had stashed in the envelope—records of the actual transactions, probably, with account numbers and balances, obtained from Mother Hilaria. What was left was only one sheet of paper, filled with single-spaced typing, dated yesterday and signed "Sadie Marsh." It was the text of a statement she must have planned to read at the board meeting—and, from the look of it, to release to the county attorney. Whoever had taken the other pages probably meant to take this one as well.

What goes in don't necessarily come out. The first paragraph told me why Sadie had made that bitter remark. The accounts that had been opened with something close to seven million dollars now amounted to two hundred ninety-some thousand and change.

I stared at the page, incredulous. St. Theresa's legacy had been stolen! Who had done it? *How* had it been done?

When I finished Sadie's report, I knew how, more or less, although the financial transactions were complicated and the details confusing. But I still didn't know who, or rather, which. I sat for a long time studying the paper, trying to see in it the face of the man who feared so deeply for his reputation—his, and his family's, and the bank's—that he was willing to murder to protect it.

Was it Tom? The Tom Rowan I'd known in Houston, the wheeler-dealer, the boy banking wonder, would certainly have been slick enough to pull off a complicated fraud like this one. According to Sadie's statement, the first transaction hadn't taken place until after he'd returned to Carr and gone to work at the bank. Yes, Tom certainly had the ability—the means—to pull something like this off, and the opportunity. And the potential millions were a strong motive.

Or was it his father? The old man had both opportunity and motive, yes. But did he have the means? He'd been a small-town banker all his life. Was he capable of the complex financial maneuvering required for an embezzlement of this size? And the attack on Sadie had certainly required some strength—was he capable of using the weapon, whatever it was, that had injured her?

Or maybe it was both of them. Maybe they had worked together to carry off the fraud, one calling the shots, the other providing the expertise. Perhaps both of them had gone to see Sadie early this morning, to plead with her not to expose them, maybe even offer her some sort of enticement. When she'd refused, they had bludgeoned her. Tom had seemed shocked enough when we discovered her lying in the stall, and even more shocked when he found that she was still alive. But he was certainly capable of faking it. He'd tried pretty hard to convince me that the horse had done it, too. And Sunday afternoon, when I'd told him about Mother Hilaria's diary and mentioned the leverage Sadie might have, he'd been very curious and even apprehensive. His reaction had seemed suspicious then. Now, in the light of the attack on Sadie, it seemed even more suspicious.

The report had nothing more to tell me. I folded it into the envelope and put the envelope in my purse, feeling infinitely sad. It was time to talk with the Rowans, father and son.

The yellow happy face was still bouncing across the computer monitor on the reception desk in the Carr County Hospital, and the desk was once again deserted. I pushed through the doors and walked rapidly to the nurses' station. A different nurse was there, wearing different glasses—plastic-rimmed, with sharp cat's-eye points at the outer corners—but the same stiff white uniform and the same starchy annoyance with the world. Her badge identified her as Vera Williams, RN.

"I'm looking for Sadie Marsh's room," I said.

She glanced up to see if she recognized me, discovered that she didn't, and went back to the form she was filling out. "Patient information is available from the receptionist in the lobby. Back through those double doors, please."

I leaned on the counter and assumed a cheerful drawl. "I checked there first, Vera, but Cherie Lee's on her break, wouldn't you just know? She's my cousin—my daddy's sister's second girl. O' course, you'd never know it from lookin' at us. She got all the purty in the fam'ly." I chuckled. "I c'n see you're real busy, but I wonder—could we take just one eentsy peek in your computer?"

Thus propitiated, Vera became almost human. "Who are you looking for?"

"Sadie Marsh."

"Oh, yes. Intensive Care. Down the hall, to the left."

There was another nurses' station in Intensive Care, this one staffed by a redhead with freckles and a cheery expression.

"I've come about Sadie Marsh," I said. "She was admitted earlier today."

The cheeriness vanished as if it had been wiped off her face. "Are you a member of the family?"

"No," I said. This time, I opted for something closer to the truth. "I'm her attorney. I found her."

She shook her head. "I'm very sorry."

"Excuse me?"

"We did everything we could."

"Oh," I said. In my pocket, the cross blazed brighter and hotter.

She leaned over and began to shuffle pieces of paper. "Maybe you can help us fill in the deceased's personal info. Do you know the name of her next of kin? Husband? Children?"

"No," I said bleakly. "She lived alone. I don't know

that she was ever married." I leaned forward. "What was the cause of death?"

She kept on rummaging among the papers. "Let's see, what am I looking for? Lord, sometimes I'd forget my head if it wasn't—Oh, yes, here it is." She found a piece of paper. "We need a social security number. And insurance information." She fixed her gaze on me, inquiring. "Did she have coverage?"

"I don't know. How did she die?"

She frowned. "I thought you said you found her."

"I did. But—"

"She was kicked in the head by a horse, wasn't she? That's what the EMS guys said."

"That's what it *looked* like. But there was reason to believe that someone—" I stopped. "Was the cause of death confirmed by the doctor who examined the wounds?"

"Of course," she said. "Doctor Townsend went ahead and put it on the death certificate."

I was startled. "He's already signed the death certificate?"

"Well, yes." She shuffled a few other papers. "He was on the floor when she died so he just went ahead and wrote it up. He's the JP, too, you know, which makes it convenient. He likes to be prompt. He never leaves paperwork lying around for later." She thrust a form at me. "Here it is. See?" She pointed with an inch-long pearly pink nail. "Accidental death due to head trauma. Kicked by a horse. Now, about that insurance coverage—"

"Did Doctor Townsend look closely at the wound?"

She raised her chin and compressed her lips, a clear signal that my questions were trying her patience. "I really don't know. Now, if I can just get you to give me the insurance information so we can get the billing wrapped up—"

"I'm sorry. I can't tell you anything about Sadie Marsh's insurance. Did Deputy Walters come over from the sheriff's office?"

She was almost amused. "The *sheriff's* office? You've got to be kidding. They don't bother about people who get kicked by horses or run over by bulls or bit by rattlesnakes. Or stung by bees. You'd be surprised how many people nearly die from bee stings. Why would the sheriff bother about a horse?"

Why indeed? And who knows what happened between the time I called Stu Walters and the time Sadie Marsh died? Maybe the deputy had a political reason for not investigating. Maybe he talked to the EMS techs or Tom, and they convinced him it was an accident. Or maybe he just hadn't gotten his investigation in gear before Royce Townsend, MD and JP, made the accidental-death theory official.

Whatever the reasons behind it, the result was an accomplished fact. Now that Townsend had recorded the cause of death, it would be damned difficult, if not impossible, to get it changed. A doctor—especially Townsend—would be reluctant to admit that he'd failed to examine a fatal injury closely enough to determine what had caused it. And a JP would hate to confess that he'd closed a possible murder case before the sheriff's office had started to look into it. I could talk to Townsend, but I wouldn't get very far. As far as Carr County was concerned, Sadie had been kicked to death by a horse, and that was that.

I took a different tack. "Let me ask you about Mr. Rowan. Mr. Tom Rowan, Senior. He was admitted this morning as well."

"I'm afraid that—"

"Don't tell me *he's* dead, too!"

"He's in guarded condition. His son is with him now, and I really can't permit another—"

"What's the room number?"

"I'm sorry. I can't—"

I assumed my sternest courtroom demeanor. "I am an attorney, Nurse. Mr. Rowan, Junior, would not be pleased if I were not permitted to see his father in order to discuss certain urgent legal matters."

She hesitated. "Well, since he's your client—"

"What room?"

"One-ten."

"Thank you."

"You're welcome. When you have a chance, will you have your secretary call us with Miss Marsh's insurance information and social security number?"

"Oh, absolutely." I turned and walked away.

The blinds had been adjusted to block the sun streaming in through the west window. Tom Senior was lying motionless under a white sheet on a narrow, railed bed. His nose and mouth were covered by a plastic respirator mask, and his skin was a lifeless gray. He was hooked up to some sort of humming apparatus on a cart beside him—life support, I supposed. A respirator. Tom Junior was standing at the end of the bed, shoulders slumped, hands in his pockets. His face was bleak.

"How is he?" I asked quietly.

"Hanging in there."

"What happened?"

"Coronary. The last thing he needs with his lungs in the shape they're in." He gestured at the machine. "Doc's got him on a respirator."

The old man raised his hand, feebly gesturing at the mask.

"Take it easy, Pop," Tom said. He stepped forward, bent over his father, and gently eased off the mask. "Doc says you can't leave this off too long, or you'll be in trouble."

The old man turned his head toward me. He looked like a cadaver, his eyes, dark-rimmed, sunk into his skull, his cheeks fallen in. His voice was faint and raspy. "That your girl, boy? The one we ate with last night?"

Last night? Was it only last night that I'd had dinner with Tom and his father? And only yesterday that Sadie had been ready to blow the whistle? Twenty-four hours had changed everything.

"Yeah, Dad." Tom took my hand and pulled me forward. "It's China."

"Good." The old man stretched thin lips in a ghastly smile. "Glad you've got somebody, now that I'm checkin' out. You're not too old for kids, either of you. Get to it."

Tom dropped my hand and shook his father's shoulder lightly. "Hey, you old coot. I don't want to hear that kind of talk. You're not in any danger of—"

"Don't give me that, boy. Now's no time to screw with the truth." With an effort, the old man picked up the mask and put it over his face, breathing heavily. He pulled it aside enough to ask, "Where's Father Steven? Thought you called him."

"I left a message." Tom forced a grin. "What do you want the priest for, anyway? You're not in that bad a shape."

"You can't lie for shit, boy."

"It's true, Dad," Tom protested. "You'll be up and around—"

The old man's sigh was slow and heavy. "Yeah, sure. Up and around, and then what? Back down again in a month or two. And in the end—" He turned his head to look at the respirator. "More of this, and nurses messin' with you every ten minutes, and a helluva lot of pain." He closed his eyes. His eyelids were thin parchment. "Forget the priest. He can't absolve me, anyway."

Tom's eyes slid to me. "You're not thinking straight, Pop. Wait until you can—"

"Listen to me, boy. You've got to handle this so the bank doesn't get hurt. I killed—"

"Shut up, Dad," Tom said fiercely.

The old man closed his eyes. "You keep a civil tongue in your head, Tom-boy. I killed that meddlin' woman, and I'm not goin' to be around to suffer the consequences. But you are, and so's the bank." His breathing was more and more labored. "It's up to you, Tom. You got your work cut out for you. Damage control, that's what they call it."

"I don't know what you're talking about." Tom sounded desperate. "Sadie got kicked in the head. Anyway, she's not dead. She's right down the hall in Intensive—"

I touched his arm. He started, as if he'd forgotten I was there, and looked at me. I shook my head slightly.

His eyes went dark. "She's dead?"

I nodded, and he seemed to slump. He turned aside as I went to the bed and leaned over it. The old man had pulled the mask back over his face and was breathing raspily.

"What happened in the barn, Mr. Rowan?" I asked.

I thought he might object to my being the one to ask the question, but he seemed to welcome it. He slipped the mask aside. "My kinda woman," he said. "You get that boy to handle this right, or it'll ruin his name. He's got to fix it, before it brings down the bank." With great effort, punctuated by periods of silence imposed by the mask—longer and longer, as the story went on—he told the whole story.

Tom Senior had called Sadie the night before to ask her what she had up her sleeve, and she'd told him that she intended to blow the whistle on the bank fraud. If she did that, he knew it was all over. It might take a while, but the bank would go under, like the Singapore bank that was sunk by a junior official speculating in Japanese investments. Or like the one in Orange County, California, which filed for bankruptcy after an investment officer lost a billion or two in derivatives—risky stock ventures that lure investors out of the safe shallows into the treacherous deeps.

And it was derivatives, of course, that had been the devil in the old man's woodpile. He had begun his term as trust official by investing conservatively, as he always had. But Carr County had been struck by a three-year drought that forced a couple of big ranchers to go under, leaving their loans unpaid. To cover those losses, he had borrowed from the Laney Trust, using its assets as leverage in increasingly speculative markets. Occasionally he did well, and once or twice had brought the trust account almost back to where it should have been. But one spectacular loss forced him to double up on his stock purchases in order to make the money back before anybody found out. When that attempt failed, the Laney Trust was left holding the bag—an empty bag.

He stopped at last, exhausted. I pulled the mask over his face again. He lay there, eyes closed, pulling in each breath as if there wouldn't be another. Tom sat in a chair on the other side of the bed, his face buried in his hands.

I turned to Tom. "Why didn't he just let Sadie tell and be done with it?" I asked. "A lot of people—experienced investors, big-time brokers—have lost their shirts in derivatives. Your father was the foundation's legally designated fiduciary officer. Unless it could be proved that he intended fraud, neither the board nor the order had any recourse against him, or against the bank. Even if he'd been brought to trial, he probably wouldn't have been convicted."

Not in this county, anyway, where the bank, like the company store, had a hand in the pocket of every prospective juror. A good defense lawyer would have convinced everybody that Mr. Rowan had done what he did to save the bank, the town, and the county from financial disaster. Anyway, the junior official in Singapore only got six years. Even if the county attorney had managed to wring a conviction out of the jury, Mr. Rowan's sentence would have been probated on account of age and physical condition.

Tom didn't answer, and I couldn't tell whether he had heard me. A nurse came in to check the respirator and the electrical apparatus, and left again. After a moment, the old man's eyes opened. He signaled me to remove the mask.

"Why didn't I let Sadie spill it?" he asked hoarsely. "Because all I needed was time. Just a few weeks, a couple of months at the most. I could've turned the situation around."

Tom's head came up swiftly. "I told you, Dad. There's nothing left to leverage."

"When did you find out about all this?" I asked Tom Junior.

"Last night, after Sadie told him what she planned to do. We were up half the night talking about it. I told him I'd take care of it, although I wasn't sure what that meant." He closed his eyes, numb and defeated. "Honest to God, China. I never figured he'd go out there to see her."

The old man's face seemed even grayer as he gasped out the words. "It was worth a shot, wasn't it? Sadie has . . . had a lot of respect for you, Tom. I figgered she'd hold off if she knew you were takin' over. I told her you'd make sure the foundation got its money."

"That's a lie, Pop." Tom shook his head sadly. "You've got to face it: Jesus Christ himself couldn't bring that money back."

The old man ignored him. "I told her to just sit tight. I told her you'd fix it so nobody'd know diddly. But she wouldn't listen." His frail voice soured. "Truth is, she was happy as a hog in mud that the money was gone. She didn't want it back. Can you b'lieve it? She was *glad* it was gone." He was shaken by a fit of coughing, and when it was over, he pulled at the mask like a drowning diver.

"Glad?" Tom asked dryly. "That's hard to believe."

I believed it. Sure, the deed restrictions tied up the land. But for all Sadie knew, an aggressive, hard-nosed church lawyer might get those restrictions set aside. With the trust fund depleted, however, there wouldn't be a nickel to build a retreat center or a golf course or a tennis court. St. Theresa's eight hundred acres would stay exactly as Helen Laney had wished, and the nuns would go on as they were, contemplatively growing garlic.

"So it wasn't you she was after," I said to Mr. Rowan, "or even the bank. It was the order all along."

"Yeah, but it wouldn't have stopped there. Once she started talking, it'd have been like a tornado through a tomato patch. The bank would've gone, and once the bank went, the town would have dried up too."

His voice trailed off. He was running out of steam. "So what happened?" I prompted gently.

"The more she held out, the madder I got," he said. "She went out to the barn to feed her horse, and I followed her, still arguin'. I finally just . . . lost it. There was a mattock leanin' against the wall. I grabbed it and swung. She went down like a sack of corn and I hit her again."

Across the bed, Tom groaned.

The old man turned his face away. "Go look under the hay bales at the north end of the barn. That's where I hid the mattock."

Tom looked at me, his face a mask of desperation. "What are we going to do?"

The old man roused himself. "I'll tell you what we're goin' to do," he said with unexpected clarity.

Tom looked down. "Oh, yeah? You got some more bright ideas, Pop?"

His father snorted. "You bet. See that switch?" He gestured with his eyes at the humming electrical equipment. "I can't reach it. You're goin' to flip it for me."

"You're crazy," Tom said. "I can't do that!"

"Sure you can," his father replied. "You can turn it back on again when I'm gone. Who do you think is goin' to know? Doc Townsend?" He grunted. "That turkey is dumb as a dodo bird. Dumb as a box of rocks."

Tom's mouth hardened. "If you think I'm going to help you kill yourself, you've got another think coming."

The old man lifted a trembling hand, his voice wispy, failing. "You want me to beg, son? Well, I'm beggin'."

"Forget it," Tom said. "There's no way—"

"Look at me, boy," the old man whispered desperately. "I can't go on livin' like this, tied to a bed. I'm *beggin*', damn it!"

This was between father and son. I went out into the hall.

A half-hour later, Tom came out of the room, red-eyed. "It's over," he said. He sagged against the wall.

"People have the right to choose how they want to die."

"Sadie didn't."

There was a silence. After a minute, I said, "Did you think your dad might still be there when we drove over to the ranch this morning?"

He shook his head. "I left home before seven. I thought I'd talked him out of going to see her. But when she didn't show up, I knew the old man had out-foxed me." He pushed himself away from the wall. "I guess I'd better go over to the sheriff's office. This isn't the kind of thing I can tell Stu Walters over the phone."

"Why tell him anything?"

He looked at me. "Because Sadie's dead. My father killed her. And then he committed suicide, with my help. Or I killed him, if that's how the county attorney wants to look at it."

I shook my head. "Sadie was kicked in the head by a horse. Her death certificate says so."

His eyes were large and staring. "You're kidding."

"It's Doctor Townsend's expert opinion," I said, "ratified by the local JP." I shook my head. The old man was right. Dumb as a box of rocks.

"You knew that, and you let Dad commit—"

"People have the right to choose how they want to die," I said again. "What would you have chosen for him? That he drag out his dying for another month? Maybe even two or three?"

"Oh, Jesus, China," he whispered, agonized, and reached for me. He pulled me against him, burying his face blindly in my shoulder, weeping for his father. I wept, too, but my tears were for Sadie.

After a moment I pushed Tom away and stepped back. "What do you know about your father's will?" I asked.

"His will?" He wiped his eyes with the back of his hand. "I'm his sole heir, I suppose. Why?"

I reached into my pocket and pulled out the cross, the only evidence that Tom Rowan, Senior, had been with Sadie Marsh that morning. "This belongs to you now," I said, and put it in his hand. Sadie's death would be mourned, but not avenged.

But perhaps it had been. Her killer lay dead beyond the door. I figured she'd call it even.

CHAPTER SEVENTEEN

At one time the holy water was sprinkled from
brushes made of Rue . . . , for which reason it is
supposed it was named the Herb of Repentance
and the Herb of Grace.

> Mrs. M. Grieve
> *A Modern Herbal*

Here in this place
I'll set a bank of rue, sour herb of grace;
Rue, even for ruth, shall shortly here
be seen. . . .

> Shakespeare,
> *Richard III*

By the time I got back to St. T's that evening, I was ready
to give Mother Winifred and Olivia a hand with the Chapter
of Faults, if they needed it.

They didn't.

The sisters were already in the chapel when I arrived and
I took a seat in the shadows at the back of the room. The
chapel was lighted by flickering candles set into the wall
sconces, and I could smell the sweet muskiness of incense.
The chairs had been moved into a large circle, and for the
first time I saw all of the sisters of both groups sitting together, heads bowed as Mother finished a simple prayer.

"Forgive us our transgressions," she said quietly, "and
give us the grace to forgive those who have transgressed
against us. In Christ's name, amen."

While Mother stood silently, I scanned the circle. Yes, Olivia was there, seated next to Gabriella. Across from her, on the far side of the circle, sat the women with whom I had spoken over the past few days: Ramona, who was longing to escape to San Francisco; Ruth, her hands folded quietly over her pillowy bosom; Regina, square-shouldered and firm; Rose, who said she'd never wanted to know who had driven her cousin Marie from the novitiate. I didn't see John Roberta, whom I presumed was still in St. Louis. But Anne was there, and Dominica, and Miriam, and Maggie, and all the others. The room was tense with waiting silence, taut with anticipation.

Mother stood for a moment more, her hands folded at her waist. Then she raised her head.

"We are here this evening as a community," she said, "to celebrate a Chapter of Faults, an ancient tradition of religious life. We will ask for mercy for our own sins and the sins of others, and we will pray for the redemption that brings us new life through the mystery of grace and compassion." She looked around. "These are not empty words, but healing words. It is God's grace that allows us to be touched with the consciousness of our shortcomings. It is His grace that leads us to repentance, and His compassion that redeems even the most unspeakable sin. These are the true mysteries of the divine life that lives in each one of us, the mysteries that will allow us to knit the unraveled ties of our community." She turned to Olivia. "Sister, you will lead us, please."

As Mother Winifred took her place in the circle, Olivia stood. "Our Chapter tonight has one purpose," she said. Her voice trembled, and I saw one or two St. Agatha sisters glance up sharply, questioning.

Olivia stopped, cleared her throat, and went on. As she spoke, she seemed to regain some of her former authority. "We are here to confront the sister who has caused our community so much pain and anguish in the last few months, whose groundless accusations have made our hearts heavy, and whose heedless disrespect of life and property has robbed us of peace and calm.'' She paused. The room was so quiet I could almost hear the sound of our beating hearts. Then she spoke.

''Sister Ruth, I accuse you.''

There was no outcry, no loud gasp, not even the rush of expelled breath. No one stirred. But there was an unmistakable heightening of the tension, a subtle, focused energy sweeping around the circle, gathering force. All eyes turned to Ruth, who sat with her head still bowed, her hands still folded over her breast, as if she had heard nothing.

Then Regina, next to her, bent over. She spoke softly, but we could all hear what she said. ''It's time, Ruth. Your sisters are waiting to hear your confession.''

Obediently, Ruth stood, her conscientious eyes hidden behind the flickering reflections of the candle flame on her thick glasses. She fumbled for the rosary at her plump waist and cast her eyes upward, as if to heaven. I remembered the picture on the wall of her cell, the painting of the bound saint about to be burned to death on a pile of branches. Was that how Ruth imagined herself?

''Sister,'' Olivia said again, more softly now, ''you cannot be forgiven unless you confess your transgressions. Tell us, please, what you have done.''

Ruth lowered her gaze and looked around the circle, wonderingly, as if she were not entirely sure why so many eyes rested on her. Then, in a flat, uninflected voice so low I had to strain to hear it, she spoke. As I listened, it seemed to me that her recitation of sins was just that—a recounting of what she had done, a summing-up. I heard no consciousness of guilt in it, no awareness that others felt she had done wrong.

Yes, she had written several accusing letters—five, she thought. She had written them, after much prayer, because it was her duty, because there was no Chapter of Faults at St. Theresa's. She had enclosed the leaves of rue in her letters to symbolize regret and repentance, and had suggested a penance, such as had always been required at the Chapter of Faults. If the sinner failed to perform it, she had imposed a penance herself. And yes, she had set the fires at St. Theresa's—small fires, in the craft room, the kitchen, the chapel, on the porch. They symbolized purification, she added simply. They had not been meant to harm or to destroy.

It was a stunning confession, and her listeners sat as still as if they were carved of stone, scarcely even breathing. When she finished, she looked questioningly at Olivia, her round cheeks placid and calm, her eyes unblinking. "Is this all you require, Sister?"

If Ruth showed no sadness, no consciousness of her trespass, Olivia did. Her face was twisted with a jagged pain and she was holding her arms tightly against her side, as if she were clutching Ruth's guilt to herself.

"Mother Hilaria?" she whispered. "Did you cause her death?"

Ruth seemed to consider. "I suppose I caused it," she said thoughtfully, as if she were making an important distinction, "but I didn't *intend* it. I pulled the insulation off the wires to give her a shock. It was her penance for allowing such moral laxity among the sisters here. I didn't know it would make her heart stop."

The room, which had seemed warm to me when I came in, now seemed bitter cold, and I shivered. Regina and Gabriella were weeping silently, the tears running down their faces.

Olivia seemed to have shrunk. "And Sister Perpetua?"

"I did nothing to harm Sister Perpetua," Ruth said firmly. "She was my novice mistress. You know that, Sister Olivia, since you and I were novices together. She corrected us sternly when we trespassed. She was a model of rectitude. I am sorry she is gone."

"Thank you, Sister." Olivia bowed her head, her face veiled in shadow, and sat down. Rose was now sobbing softly.

Mother Winifred stood, her shoulders bowed as if she bore a heavy weight. "We have heard your confession, my daughter," she said. "Now you must ask the forgiveness of those you have wronged or endangered."

"Wronged or endangered?" Ruth asked slowly, as if she were weighing the meanings of the words.

Mother lifted her chin. "Surely you see that it was wicked of you to write the letters, Sister." She might have been speaking to a very small child. "It was wrong to set the fires. Your actions endangered the life of every sister here."

Ruth's face didn't alter, but she gave the impression that she was agreeing only under duress. "Well, then," she said reluctantly. "Since that is the case, I suppose . . ." She resigned herself to the task with a sigh. "I ask your forgiveness for my sins and wrongdoings, Sisters. I am heartily sorry for having offended."

How many times had I heard a defendant plead, "Not guilty," and know in my heart that the words were a lie? Ruth's plea for forgiveness was a lie, too, or perhaps a kind of plea bargain. She didn't sound heartily sorry, or even sorry at all. She sounded as if she were doing what she'd been told to do, no more, no less. There could be no redemption in such a confession, I thought.

But although Ruth's words fell sadly short of what Mother Winifred might have wanted, the sisters' response did not. They stood, joined hands, and followed Mother in their reply, which was a little ragged, but rich with heartfelt love and healing compassion.

"We forgive you, Sister, for we too have sinned. Go in the mercy and grace of God, and be blessed."

I stood, too, in my corner, and emotion rose in my throat. The love and compassion I felt in this room might be as close as I'd ever feel to God, but it was enough. It was certainly enough to heal the rift, however broad and jagged, in this small community, to bless its future. And to bless me, too.

Ruth stood for a moment, as if she wasn't sure it was all over. Finally, she turned to Mother Winifred. "My penance?" she asked. There was something almost like eagerness in the tilt of her head. "If I've sinned, I must do penance."

Mother's voice was sad. "Tomorrow I will ask our Reverend Mother General to consult with me on the matter of your penance. You will be informed, Sister."

"Thank you," Ruth said, and sat down.

And that's all there was to it. Another prayer, a moment of silence, and everyone filed out of the chapel.

No one said a word. There was nothing left to say.

"Who was the other sister you thought Olivia might accuse?" Mother Winifred asked. It was the next afternoon, warm, sunshiny, the temperature in the low seventies—the kind of crisp, cool day you remember when the Texas sun has charred the August grass and even the sage has wilted. Mother and I were sitting on the wooden bench in the corner of her garden. Tom was leaning against the stone wall beside us, his face held up to the sun.

"I thought it might be Regina," I said. "She had been in the novitiate at the time the first letters were written, and at St. Agatha's when the fire occurred there. And she confessed to taking Mother Hilaria's hot plate from the storeroom. But when I met her and Ruth in the parking lot and saw the rash on Ruth's hand and arm—"

Mother frowned. "The rash?"

Tom shook his head disbelievingly. "You could tell she was guilty from a rash?"

"I could guess," I said. "Mother had told me that Gabriella had just received a letter containing a leaf of rue, and I know that some people are sensitive to the plant. The juice causes a rather unpleasant dermatitis that looks like a bad sunburn or a severe case of poison ivy. I thought it was entirely possible that Ruth was the one who had picked the rue to put in her poison-pen letter."

"Just out of curiosity," Tom said wryly, "would you have entered the rue—and Sister Ruth's rash—as evidence in court?"

"Maybe," I said. I laughed. "I suppose I'd also have had to call a couple of botanists as expert witnesses to describe the effects of the plant. Then again, we have Olivia's accusation and Ruth's confession. And Regina told me this morning that Ruth had experienced dermatitis before—apparently on the occasions when she picked the leaves to put into the letters."

"It's ironic," Mother said softly, "that the plant she employed as a symbol of regret and repentance was a witness to her guilt."

I nodded. "By the way, Regina also told me that the fire that scarred Father Steven was entirely accidental. He fell asleep with a cigarette and caught the mattress on fire—which clears up that mystery."

Mother turned to Tom. "Let me say again how sorry I am about your father, Tom." Her voice was filled with sympathy. "He made some foolish mistakes where the foundation's investments are concerned, but he was not motivated by personal greed. He was a fine man in spite of his failings. We will all remember him fondly."

Mercy and compassion, I thought. Would Mother Winifred be so forgiving if she knew that the old man had killed her friend Sadie? But perhaps she would.

Tom glanced at me. In the twenty-four hours since his father and Sadie Marsh had died, the *Carr Bulletin* had carried the stories of the two deaths, Sadie's in the left-hand column, Tom Senior's in the right, each column headed by a black-bordered photograph. The banner headline over the stories read "Prominent Local Citizens Die." The newspaper had not made any link between the deaths. More to the point, a call from the sheriff's office (from the dispatcher, actually—Stu Walters didn't take the time to call me himself) had informed me that a thorough investigation of Sadie Marsh's death had revealed that it was accidental.

It was over. Mostly, anyway. There were a few loose ends to be tied up—a last confession and a pledge.

"I want you to know, Mother," Tom said, "that I will do my level best to restore the foundation's assets. It's going to take a while, but you have my personal assurance that—"

Mother Winifred shook her head gently. "I understand what you're saying, Tom, and I'm pleased that you want to assume the responsibility." She smiled. "But we take our vow of poverty and simplicity quite seriously, even joyfully. It doesn't confine us or keep us from doing what we want. On the contrary, it frees us to pay attention to our spiritual life. The three hundred thousand dollars in the account now will yield enough each year—in addition to what we earn from our garlic—to make the necessary repairs to our buildings. That's all we care about. We're better off without the rest."

Tom raised his eyebrows. "That may be. But I doubt that the Reverend Mother General is going to be quite so philosophical. Have you notified her yet?"

Mother's smile became slightly strained. "I talked with her by telephone this morning. She was perturbed by the news, of course—both Sadie's death and the loss of the funds. But she agrees that there is nothing to be gained from making any of it public. The lawyers will be consulted, but Reverend Mother General was quite definite about not wanting any negative publicity."

Tom could read between those lines, just as I could. "Perturbed" probably didn't do justice to Reverend Mother General's reaction. But she wouldn't have been anxious to reveal that a major embezzlement had occurred on her watch. She would hush up the whole thing, leaving Tom to quietly recoup his father's losses as he could. And allowing St. Theresa's the freedom—the *precious* freedom— of going about its ordinary work.

And that was the essential paradox in this whole business, it seemed to me. Mrs. Laney's gift, which she had hoped would free the monastery to pursue its contemplative ends, had almost destroyed it. In the Church as in the rest of the world, the prospect of money fosters greed and covetousness. Like a capital-rich corporation ripe for takeover or a bride with an enticing dowry, a wealthy St. Theresa's was a prime target. Poor, it was safe, a prize nobody wanted. With neither money nor land at stake, the sisters who wished to live quietly and contemplatively could go on growing garlic. The others would be free to go to one of the order's sister houses, where they might find a different way to serve. Olivia and Regina, I was sure, would be the first to leave. And with their going, the terrible chasm that had divided the community could be bridged, and it could become whole once more.

Dominica stepped through the gate. "Mother, this phone message just came for you." She handed Mother a folded piece of paper. "If you have any questions, I'm supposed to phone the office and tell the secretary—"

Mother Winifred scanned the note. "No," she said, "no questions. Thank you, Sister."

When Dominica had gone, Tom extended his hand to Mother Winifred. "I'll be in touch in a couple of days to set up the agenda for the next board meeting." He turned to me. "Will I be seeing you again before you leave, China?"

The question hung in the air between us, real, challenging. The moments we'd shared in the hospital and our secret knowledge about what had happened between Tom's father and Sadie Marsh had created a new and special kind of intimacy, had forged a bond that was even stronger than the very real physical attraction I still felt for him. It would be easy to say yes and discover what deeper intimacies might grow between us.

But if I had learned anything in the last few days, it was

the importance of being true to the one true thing that centers my life.

So I said, "No thanks, Tom. I want to spend the rest of my time here getting some rest. And doing some thinking." I'd already done a little bit of both, enough to realize that the only thing wrong with my life was an overabundance of *good* things. All I needed to do was search out the center—the thing I wanted most to be, wanted most to have and do—and use it as a compass.

He nodded, bent over, and kissed my cheek. "I'm in your debt, China. If you ever need a loan—"

"Thanks," I said, and grinned. "There's nothing like having your own personal banker."

When Tom had gone, Mother Winifred looked down at the paper folded between her fingers. "It seems that today is a day for coming to conclusions. The message that Sister Dominica brought—it's the result of Sister Perpetua's autopsy. There was no trace of digitalis in her system. She died of simple cardiac arrest." She lifted her eyes heavenward. "Praise God," she said fervently.

And damn the doctor, I thought. Dumb as a box of rocks. But I was glad for St. T's and glad for Perpetua. She had lived to the end of her time and left when she was ready. I was even glad for Ruth, who had told all of the truth in her confession the night before.

We sat for a moment in silence. "I suppose I must face the problem of Sister Ruth," Mother said at last. "The decision is mine to make, you see. Reverend Mother has asked me to stay on as abbess."

I wasn't surprised. Considering everything that had happened, not even Reverend Mother General would want to make a change in St. Theresa's leadership now. "I hope you're not too unhappy," I said. "I know you wanted to get back to your garden."

Mother looked out across the neatly kept enclosure, her gaze lingering with love on the subtle winter textures and colors. Her sigh was very light. "I suppose the sisters are my garden," she said. "They are the growing things I am meant to cultivate and serve." A twinkle came and went and her voice grew determined. "I will simply have to be firm about my own priorities, that's all."

I smiled, wondering if she knew that she was speaking for me as well as herself. I was already starting to make a list of my priorities, and I wasn't surprised to find McQuaid's name at the very top, with Brian's beside it. The shop came next, but I would be making some changes there. When I got home—

But that could wait. I still had a question or two for Mother Winifred. "What about Ruth?" I asked. "What will happen to her?"

Mother turned back to me. "Last night, I saw that she is a desperately sick woman. She needs a great deal of counseling and strict supervision, which can't possibly be provided here. But the problem is more complicated than that. Olivia and Regina knew that she was responsible for Mother Hilaria's death and that she was setting the fires. What is it you call them—accessories after the fact? Before I can make any decisions, I must ask your legal opinion." She took a deep breath, as if she were steeling herself for my answer. "Tell me what will happen after the authorities charge Ruth with Hilaria's death."

"Sister Ruth isn't going to be charged, Mother," I said. "A murder charge would never stick, and the county attorney won't try for voluntary manslaughter. If Ruth were not a nun, she might be charged with injury to an elderly person—that's a Class A misdemeanor, for which she could get a year in jail or a two-thousand-dollar fine. But the county attorney would probably settle for reckless conduct, which is only six months and a thousand dollars tops, hardly worth the expense of a trial. He wouldn't even consider an accessory charge against Olivia or Regina."

Mother shook her head. "You sound so sure."

"I've made plenty of mistakes since I got here," I said

rucfully, "but I'm sure about this. Not even Stu Walters would be dumb enough to charge a nun."

Mother's face was bleak. "Then she'll get away with Hilaria's murder."

I reached for her hand. "People get away with murder all the time, Mother. Sometimes the police do a lousy job. Sometimes it's the prosecution that screws up. And sometimes the defense outmaneuvers everybody else, or hires better experts, or gets a lucky break." I made myself stop. This was one of my hot-button topics. "If you're looking for justice," I said more gently, "you'll have to make your own. The penance you assign will be the only justice Ruth will face—until Judgment Day, anyway."

Mother seemed to relax a little. "Well," she said, "I'm glad you got this whole unhappy business wrapped up. Oh, by the way, I should tell you that Dwight gave me his notice this morning. He's going to work for the Townsends."

"I'm not surprised," I said. I paused. "Now that everything's out in the open, Mother, what's going to happen to the community?"

"Reverend Mother and I haven't talked about it yet, but in view of the way things have turned out—I'm thinking of the trust fund, of course—I'm confident that St. Theresa's will be allowed to pursue its mission without any more interference."

"And the sisters who want to leave?"

"They're free to go as soon as they can make arrangements. Olivia, too, of course." She smiled. "She isn't so different from Hilaria, you know. She has the same determination, the same drive. With maturity and experience, I expect she'll do quite well—somewhere else." She looked at me. "Like Tom, we're in your debt, China. Is there something we can offer you, something we can do, to repay you?"

I thought about that. "You might ask Sister Gabriella and her crew for a special prayer for next Sunday," I said. "I understand that the Cowboys are up against the 'Niners."

RESOURCES

For readers who are interested in herbs, the following may be helpful.

1. If you're intrigued by St. Theresa's garlic farm and would like to start your own, read *Growing Great Garlic,* by Ron Engeland (Filaree Productions, Rt. 1, Box 162, Okanogan, WA 98840). If you're hungry for St. T's simple, earthy way of life, *A Garlic Testament: Seasons on a Small New Mexico Farm,* by Stanley Crawford, HarperCollins, 1992, is delightful soul food. Or if you're simply hungry, try *Glorious Garlic: A Cookbook,* by Charlene A. Braida.

2. You'll find a discussion of foxglove (definitely not an herb to experiment with!), in Mrs. M. Grieve's *A Modern Herbal,* which actually isn't all that modern. Dover Publications, 31 E. 2nd St., Mineola, NY 11501, has re-published the original 1931 edition, unabridged. See pages 323–326. Steven Foster includes more up-to-date information on the plant's phytomedicinal qualities in *Herbal Renaissance* (1984, Peregrine Smith Books, Layton, UT 84041).

3. The biblical plants Mother Winifred has placed in her garden are only a few of those she might have included. Two books on the subject are *Gardening with Biblical Plants,* by W. James (Nelson-Hall, 1983), and *Bible Plants for American Gardens,* by Eleanor Anthony King (1942, republished by Dover). While I was planning *Rueful Death, The Herb Quarterly* published a fascinating article (Fall, 1994, pp. 26–31) about the construction of the Rodef Sha-

lom Biblical Garden in Pittsburgh, revealing some of the hidden mysteries of garden plotting.

4. My thanks go to Madalene Hill, Texas herbalist and past president of the Herb Society of America, for the reminder that rue is a powerful rubefacient—that it has the ability to redden skin and even to blister. In *Southern Herb Growing* (Shearer Publishing, 1987, p. 113), Madalene and her daughter Gwen Barclay relate this interesting anecdote, contributed by Mary Jo Modica, from the University of Alabama Arboretum:

> Several volunteers and I were working in the herb garden in shorts on a very sunny day. . . . We were weeding near a large rue that was in flower and fruit. Two days later we all had second-degree burns on our legs and arms. . . . After a great deal of research, we discovered the rube-facient power of rue is not to be taken lightly. Evidently, everywhere the glandular flowers and fruits touched us, the oils they released magnified the rays of the sun, resulting in very painful burns.

5. Another older book, *Plants of the Bible*, by Harold N. and Alma L. Moldenke (1952, republished by Dover), gave me much rue lore, including the fascinating reference to the superstition about guns. From Mrs. Grieve's *A Modern Herbal* I also learned that rue-water sprinkled here and there repels fleas, along with other fascinating oddities. (For instance, in Pliny's day, rue was thought to be good for the eyes, so painters ate quantities of it.) I also drew from Eleanour Sinclair Rohde's *A Garden of Herbs* (1936, republished by Dover). She offers this puckery, "rue-full" recipe, from *The Good Housewife's Jewell*, 1585.

Preventive Against the Plague
A handful each of rue, sage, sweet-briar and el-
der. Bruise and strain with a quart of white wine,
and put thereto a little ginger and a spoonful of
the best treacle, and drink thereof morning and
evening.

6. Rue is said to derive its name from the Greek word *reuo*,
to set free, which may be a guarded reference to its virtue
as an abortifacient. Etymologically speaking, the word has
nothing to do with the English verb "to rue" (to regret, to
wish one had acted otherwise), which comes from the An-
glo-Saxon noun *hreow*, regret. But these two homonyms
were inevitably associated, linking the plant rue with the
idea of ruing or regretting, making it a "sour herb of
grace." The archaic English noun "ruth," meaning compassion and mercy, along with the modern English adjec-
tive "ruthless" also derive from *hreow*. Thus, Shakespeare
finds "ruth" and "rue" synonymous: "rue, even for ruth,
shall shortly here be seen. . . ." These mysterious inter-
weavings of symbol and meaning are too tempting for the
novelist to ignore.

7. Susan and Bill Albert publish an occasional newsletter
called *Partners in Crime*, containing information about
their books. If you would like to be on the mailing list,
send a one-time subscription fee of $3 to *Partners
in Crime*, PO Box 1616, Bertram TX 78605-1616. You
may also visit the *Partners in Crime* Web site at
http://www.mysterypartners.com.

If you enjoy the
China Bayles mystery series,
you will also want to read
DEATH AT DAISY'S FOLLY
by Robin Paige.

Robin Paige is the pseudonym of
husband-and-wife team
Susan Wittig Albert and Bill Albert
who together write a
Victorian mystery series
featuring Sir Charles Sheridan and
Kate Ardleigh
as the detective team.

A cock was crowing in the coop at the foot of the dark orchard when Harry Gordon, groom to His Highness the Prince of Wales, entered the stable. Inside, the air was warm after the early morning chill, scented with the earthy fragrance of horse and hay, and in the gloom Harry could hear the delicate music of pigeons cooing and the gentle *whuffle* of a horse. In all of his fifteen years, Harry had found no better place on a frosty morning than the inside of a grand stable.

The stables here at Easton Lodge were not as large or as modern as those at Sandringham, where His Highness's three great sires stood to stud, servicing something like a hundred mares a year in addition to the Prince's own brood stock. But the Easton Lodge stables were not inconsiderable. The Countess of Warwick, whose family home this was, kept her own horses here, together with the tall chestnut hunter left by the Prince for his frequent visits. This morning, the stable was full of horses brought in for any of the weekend guests who might choose to ride.

Harry walked down the aisle between the shoulder-high wooden stalls, admiring the handsome horses and still marveling at the amazing fortune that had brought him here, so far from home. Until a month ago, he had been one of the dozen or so Sandringham stableboys, assigned to curry and feed His Royal Highness's horses and muck out the stalls. He had never been farther from the estate than the village school two miles away, and that for only the few obligatory years required to spell his tedious way through the *Royal Reader*. Having emerged from his education nearly unlettered, he had gone to service in the Sandringham stables, and had yet to earn sufficient holiday to make the half-day walk to the nearby market town.

But all that was changed, and now the whole world lay at Harry's feet. A few weeks ago, he had saved the Princess of Wales from a nasty fall by grasping at the reins of her rearing horse, frightened by a stable cat. The Prince and Princess, known for their loyalty toward those who served them well, had thanked Harry graciously. The next day, Princess Alexandra had sent his mother, an undercook in the Sandringham kitchens, a basket of jellies and sweets, with a handwritten note of praise for her son's courage. The day after that, the chief steward of the stables had summoned the fifteen-year-old boy, bestowed on him a smart new livery, and instructed him to make himself ready to join the Royal entourage. Harry was to travel with the Prince and attend His Highness's horses, wherever they might be stabled.

Harry's remarkable elevation in rank had been the proudest moment of his young life, and that of his mother, as well. Her son's unexpected distinction gave her something to boast of over tea in the servants' hall.

"So 'andsome in 'is livery, my 'Arry is," she was heard to tell her gossips in the kitchen, "that 'e's bound to catch th' eye o' th' Queen when th' Prince goes next t' Balmoral. Then 'e'll be raised to 'is proper station as a Royal footman, 'e will, and 'e'll powder 'is 'air an' wear pink poplin knee breeches an' shiny silver 'paulettes th' size o' pot lids."

With or without epaulettes, Harry was proud to be numbered among the Prince's traveling household. At Sandringham, the stableboys were at the bottom of the servants' hierarchy, "grubbin' i' the muck an' mire," as his mother said, far below the elevation of the senior staff—the Upper Ten, or the Uppers, as they were called. Life on the lowest rung of this social ladder often entailed cold food, scanty victuals, and meager holidays. But on tour with the Prince, Harry had discovered to his delight, his life was quite different. Here at Easton, for instance, where distinctions of rank were observed belowstairs as carefully as they were above, Harry, a mere groom, outranked not only the Countess's stableboys and grooms, but her ladyship's chief groom as well—or so it seemed to Harry.

At meals and between, he was awarded all the honors befitting his status, such as slices of grouse and pheasant left from the table abovestairs, and magnificent sweets, and even a glass of the estate's best homebrewed beer, served by a solicitous kitchen maid with a seductive smile. For Harry, life had suddenly become very sweet.

The Royal stall which housed Paradox, the Prince's hunter, was marked with the Prince's insignia. Harry stopped before it, set down the wooden bucket filled with oats, and cocked his head, frowning slightly. In the dimness, Paradox was moving about, stamping a nervous forefoot, flicking an anxious tail. Something had disturbed him. It was none of the Easton grooms or stableboys, Harry knew. They were a lazy lot and had arrived at the servants' breakfast late, accepting their reprimand with sleepy-eyed equanimity. It was none of the gentlemen, either, for although one or another might rise for a dawn canter across the Essex hills, last night's entertainment—parlor games, Harry had understood from the footmen's sly comments at breakfast—had been late and boisterous. Breakfast was already laid upstairs for the earliest risers, but Harry would have wagered a tanner that none were yet out and about.

He'd have lost his money. While the young groom was still pondering the horse's nervousness, a nearby door opened with a creak. A man—a gentleman wearing Norfolk tweeds and a shooting cap, a stick under his arm—was briefly silhouetted against the light, then slipped inside and closed the door. He moved furtively, and Harry's frown became a knowing grin. Surreptitious assignations were commonplace at country house parties, according to the footmen who had reported on last night's frolic. While Harry personally felt that such a rendezvous was more appropriate to a lady's chamber, behind a discreetly closed door and between scented sheets, he could also imagine that a more daring lady, or one whose husband had a jealous turn, might prefer to carry on her amorous intrigues somewhere else—in the straw, even. Harry grew warm, recalling the brazen allure of the kitchen maid who had placed her hand on his—

But now was not the moment for such thoughts, pleasant as they were. Silently, he raised the wooden bar and slipped into the Royal stall, ducking under Paradox's warm belly. If a lady were expected, she would no doubt soon appear, and it would not be prudent of Harry to make his presence known. Best wait in the stall until the business were over. But Harry had as much curiosity as the next man, and he wanted to see which of the ladies had consented to a tryst in the stable. Was it the red-haired one he'd glimpsed sweeping across the croquet lawn yesterday afternoon, her hair like flaming embers? He had heard that red-haired women were looser in their morals than other women, and she was said to be an American. Perhaps—

The door creaked again, and Harry stood up to peer over the side of the stall. He saw a cloaked woman enter, close the door, and stand still for a moment, as if getting her bearings.

"Over here," came the husky voice of the waiting man, and the cloaked woman turned swiftly. The light was poor, but Harry did not think it was the red-haired lady. It might even have been a slender man. Unfortunately, the answering voice offered no clue. It was low and husky and had a certain sweetness, but it could have been that of either a woman or a man.

"Where is your colleague?" the cloaked figure asked. "I assumed that he would be here as well."

"Momentarily," the other replied. His voice was eager. "Then you have decided to join us?"

"Quite the contrary. I wish no part of this sordid business, and I've come to tell you so. I am a loyal subject of the Crown. Some of the things you have proposed would be deeply embarrassing, and might even tend toward treason."

Treason! Harry thought, all idea of a tryst flying out of his head. A plot against the Prince! What were they scheming? An accident to the Royal person? A plan to blow up the Royal train? He had better listen closely, so that he could report the conversation to the proper authorities—to the Prince himself! His reward would certainly be that pair of silver epaulettes his mother was so anxious for him to win.

"Oh, but I say!" the first man protested. "You have it wrong. All we mean to do is—"

Beside Harry, Paradox moved restlessly, pawing the straw with a shod hoof. Harry tensed, catching out of the corner of his eye a fleeting movement in the shadows behind him. He turned and saw a pale face looming over the side of the stall, a hand upraised, wielding a heavy object, about to strike.

It was the last thing Harry saw.

And watch for
Death at Devil's Bridge
the fourth Victorian mystery
by Robin Paige.

365 days of recipes, crafts, and tips from

Susan Wittig Albert

SUSAN WITTIG ALBERT

China Bayles'
BOOK of DAYS

365 CELEBRATIONS OF THE MYSTERY
MYTH, AND MAGIC OF HERBS FROM
THE WORLD OF PECAN SPRINGS

Now Available
978-0-425-20653-9
Berkley Prime Crime Trade Paperback

SUSAN WITTIG ALBERT

The New York Times *bestselling*
China Bayles series

THYME OF DEATH   0-425-14098-9

China Bayles left her law practice to open an herb shop in
Pecan Springs, Texas. But tensions run high in small towns,
too—and the results can be murder.

WITCHES' BANE   0-425-14406-2

When a series of Halloween pranks turns deadly, China must
investigate to unmask a killer.

HANGMAN'S ROOT   0-425-14898-X

When a prominent animal researcher is murdered, China
discovers a fervent animal rights activist isn't the only person
who wanted him dead.

ROSEMARY REMEMBERED   0-425-15405-X

When a woman who looks just like China is found murdered
in a pickup truck, China looks for a killer close to home.

ALSO AVAILABLE:

LOVE LIES BLEEDING	0-425-16611-2
CHILE DEATH	0-425-17147-7
LAVENDER LIES	0-425-17700-9
MISTLETOE MAN	0-425-18201-0
BLOODROOT	0-425-18814-0
INDIGO DYING	0-425-18828-0
A DILLY OF A DEATH	0-425-19399-3

AVAILABLE WHEREVER BOOKS ARE SOLD OR AT
PENGUIN.COM

(Ad # B126)

GET COZY IN THE WORLD OF
BEATRIX POTTER
FROM AUTHOR

SUSAN WITTIG ALBERT

In 1905 in the beautiful English Lake District,
Beatrix Potter is dealing with the loss of her
fiancé and the challenges of becoming a farmer.
Meanwhile, her animal friends—Tabitha Twitchit,
the senior village cat; Rascal, the courageous
terrier; and the wise and cunning cat Crumpet—are
quietly solving mysteries and making sure that life
in the village stays on an even keel.

The Tale of Hill Top Farm
978-0-425-20101-5

The Tale of Holly How
978-0-425-20613-3

The Tale of Cuckoo Brow Wood
978-0-425-21506-7

penguin.com

GET CLUED IN

berkleyprimecrime.com

Ever wonder how to find out about all the
latest Berkley Prime Crime mysteries?

berkleyprimecrime.com

- See what's new
- Find author appearences
- Win fantastic prizes
- Get reading recommendations
- Sign up for the mystery newsletter
- Chat with authors and other fans
- Read interviews with authors you love

Mystery Solved.

berkleyprimecrime.com